GIANTS ON THE HILL

GIANTS ON THE HILL

LEE RODDY

WORD PUBLISHING
Dallas • London • Vancouver • Melbourne

PUBLISHED BY WORD PUBLISHING

DALLAS, TEXAS.

Published in association with the literary agency of Alive Communications, P.O. Box 49068 Colorado Springs, Colorado 80949

Book design by Mark McGarry
Set in Garamond

LIBRARY OF CONGRESS CATALOGING-IN-PUBLICATION DATA

Roddy, Lee, 1921–
Giants on the hill / Lee Roddy.
p. cm.
ISBN 0–8499–3492–3
1. California—Gold Discoveries—Fiction. I. Title.
PS3568.O344G53 1994 94–21915
813'.54—dc20 CIP

PRINTED IN THE UNITED STATES OF AMERICA

4 5 6 7 8 9 0 1 LB 9 8 7 6 5 4 3 2 1

To Cicely

No words can tell
how wonderful she is.

PROLOGUE

FROM HIS hiding place under the wharf, The Watcher furtively leaned forward and squinted across Yerba Buena Cove. His hard, dark eyes strained to penetrate the damp, chilling morning fog that shrouded the harbor.

He could barely make out the storm-battered *Terrapin* slowly emerging from the fog. The brig's two masts were shredded, and the entire ship listed badly to starboard. She had obviously been a cargo carrier hastily converted for passengers.

There was no proper docking area. Short wharfs jutted from the ends of streets into the bay, so the ship dropped anchor into the choppy waters. At once, dozens of small boats with untidy rowers shoved off from the shore. The crews, acting as runners for eager owners of San Francisco's many canvas hotels, bent to their task. Each sought to be the first to reach the vessel and bring passengers ashore.

The Watcher cautiously peered from behind a barnacle-encrusted piling to better see the men lining the ship's rails. He pulled his dirty jacket closer about his thin body, shivering in the late May sun.

As always, he was careful to keep a low profile. This discretion had earned him a reputation which brought sizeable pokes of gold dust for quick, silent jobs well done.

For two weeks, he had constantly watched the semaphore on Signal Hill which announced the arrival of a vessel. Each time he was disappointed. His bitterness grew as the modest down payment in gold ebbed away. The final large payment would not be paid until the intended victim arrived and the task was finished.

He was so intent on spotting his quarry that he ignored the stench of the mud flats. He didn't even hear the salty water swirling around the pilings. He focused on finding his lone victim whom he desperately hoped would be on this ship.

Suddenly, he tensed, aware that something was happening among the passengers about to disembark.

Usually, the men vied with each other to be the first off a vessel. Now, however, the passengers held back, providing a path to the ship's superstructure. Their heads swiveled that direction and they swept off their hats.

The Watcher frowned, not understanding such totally unexpected behavior. He craned his thin neck forward for a better look through the human path on deck. Then he made a snorting noise of satisfaction.

That's him!

Aldar Laird perfectly fit the description given the waiting man. He automatically reached his right hand to the back of his neck. He felt the reassuring presence of the eight-inch knife sheathed between his shoulder blades.

Satisfied, he absently moved his fingers to touch the birthmark on the right side of his face. It began as a two-inch wide splash of unsightly reddish-purple slanting down from under his slouch black hat. The mark spread across the cheek to narrow again and disappear at the corner of thin lips.

He would wait until the victim came ashore and was away from the crowds. The moment he was alone so there would be no witnesses, it would be done, quickly and silently.

Suddenly, The Watcher sucked in his breath. *He's got a woman with him! Two of them!*

He unconsciously shifted his cramped position. The movement startled a nearby wharf rat on a support beam. The man's eyes followed the rat's dash for safety into the dark recesses of planks under the wharf.

The Watcher turned his eyes back to the *Terrapin.* He stared hard, trying to understand the totally unexpected presence of the women.

While the waiting killer silently cursed the abrupt change in the situation, he watched the tall, blond young man reach the railing. He started down the swaying ladder, then looked up as the hatless white woman behind him discreetly held her ankle-length black skirt tightly about her with her left hand. With her right, she held onto the bouncing ladder.

Even from this distance, the waiting man could see that she was slender and no older than twenty. She was also very pretty with reddish-gold hair parted in the middle and tied in back with a dark ribbon. Her face was pale and gaunt, suggesting that she had been very ill on the three-month trip from New York.

The second woman following on the ladder was about the same age, but she was more than pretty. She was a beautiful Negress with pale tan skin and shiny black hair worn shoulder length and loose.

The Watcher subconsciously licked his lips and stared appreciatively at both women. His breathing became a little ragged. Nothing like either of them in San Francisco, he told himself, probably not in all of California.

A small trickle of saliva started forming in the right corner of The Watcher's thin mouth. He swallowed hard, the adam's apple in his skinny neck bobbing convulsively.

He hesitated, then took a slow, thoughtful breath. He struggled with a sudden, risky thought.

The temptation was too great, so for the first time since he had used his knife for profit, he broke his own rule to never be seen anywhere near an intended victim. Before he had taken a dozen steps, he was breathing hard. He stealthily made his way toward where his victim and the two beautiful women would come ashore.

GIANTS ON THE HILL

CHAPTER I

THE FIRST small boat's crew shipped oars, and Shiloh glanced apprehensively at her new husband. "The boat's scraping bottom, so how do we get to the shore?"

Aldar Laird stepped into the shallow water that came up to his hips. "I'll carry you from here."

Secure in Aldar's arms, Shiloh turned to her female companion. "Mara, if you wait here, Aldar will come back for you."

"I can take care of myself," the mulatto replied. There was no trace of an accent in her cryptic words.

Mara gripped her bone-handled umbrella and a small carpet bag in preparation for leaving the bouncing boat. One of the bearded Caucasian crewmen reached out to help her, but she gave him a smart crack across the knuckles with the umbrella handle.

"That's Mara," Shiloh told Aldar, then turned her gray-green eyes toward shore.

About a dozen men, mostly hotel runners waiting with carriages, silently stared at the newcomers. San Francisco was largely an all-male land in late May 1849.

Two black men emerged from behind the others and started rapidly wading through the surf toward Mara.

Shiloh smiled. "No need to get your feet wet, Mara. Just sit tight a minute."

"I don't need any help from the likes of them. More'n likely, they're fugitives from the slave catchers, or else they're off that smelly whaler anchored over there." She used the umbrella to point toward an abandoned whale ship swinging at anchor with a hundred other dead vessels.

Nevertheless, Mara managed to delay momentarily by fussing with her carpet bag until the two black men splashed alongside. Both were close to six feet tall, but one was more broad-shouldered than the other.

The thinner man reached out to help, but Mara ignored him. Instead, she let herself be lifted by the larger man. He grinned broadly at his companion, then triumphantly carried Mara through the surf, following Aldar with Shiloh in his arms.

Aldar was breathing hard from carrying his wife's hundred and two pound body through the surf, but he spoke enthusiastically. "Isn't this everything I told you, Shiloh?"

She let her gaze sweep over the community that was to be her new home, confirming what she had seen from the ship's deck. A wave of doubt swept over her. San Francisco was *not* what she had expected! Not at all! Still, she managed to smile at Aldar.

Shiloh forced herself not to shiver from the cold, damp fog that played hide-and-seek with the sun.

"I've never seen anything like it," she replied honestly.

"I've missed this place," he said enthusiastically. His blue eyes swept to the right and the majestic entrance that John C. Fremont had christened the Golden Gate. "See how the sunlight peeks out from the fog and glistens on the water? Smell those breezes blowing in from the Pacific! And look at that fog! It's different from any I've seen anywhere else. I love it!"

To Shiloh, this was a wild and primitive place thousands of miles from her family home. But the bay was truly magnificent, and she was with Aldar, so she wanted to share his enthusiasm. "It really is beautiful," she answered.

"This is going to be a real city someday," he continued, wading onto the sandy shore. He lowered Shiloh to her feet on a wooden walk made of barrel staves. It took her a moment to adjust to the strangeness of not having a ship move under her feet. She took a couple of uncertain steps and satisfied herself that she could again walk on something solid.

"This is your new home," Aldar said, sweeping his hands over the land. "Our home, I mean."

The ocean and the entrance to the harbor were gorgeous, but Shiloh was keenly disappointed at the ugly, dark clot of civilization spread over the sand dunes. She closed her eyes as fine blowing sand stung her face. She silently groaned with inner doubt.

On the trip from New York down the Atlantic, across the Isthmus of Panama and up the Pacific coast, Aldar's sweeping descriptions of San Francisco had conjured up a mental vision of a beautiful city. Instead, Shiloh saw an open sewer of a bay and a scabrous mass of uncontrolled human habitation on land. In the foreground, a series of sand dunes were covered with the most disorganized clusters of canvas tents, wooden shacks, and other makeshift shelters.

Shiloh was dismayed at the looks of this stark place, where the only redeeming features were some steep hills rising in the background. One hill in particular soared grandly into the sky. The rest of the community wasn't at all what she had anticipated from Aldar's descriptions.

He had not told her about the lack of regulations that permitted dumping anything anywhere on land or cove, and the building of shelters haphazardly, ignoring common sense. This had allowed the occupants to spread in wild abandon across the giant natural amphitheater of sand hills of the community recently renamed from Yerba Buena to San Francisco.

To hide her disappointment, Shiloh turned her head as though to check on Mara being carried a few steps behind. But Shiloh's gaze swept beyond Mara. To their right and left, great smelly masses of garbage drifted in and out on the waves. Beyond the surf, abandoned ships rested at anchor, their rotting masts scratching idly like skeletal fingers against the fog and the sky.

Up and down the shoreline on both sides, Shiloh glimpsed discarded remnants of tents, empty boxes, old trunks, pieces of clothing, parts of wagons, a giant black metal cook stove, and other debris.

Shiloh glanced at Mara for her reaction to their new home. She didn't seem too interested in the community as the big black man put her down. He smiled down at her. "I'se Samuel," he said. "He's Joseph."

Mara nodded at both men but turned and walked away without even thanking them.

Shiloh flinched at Mara's behavior, then turned her attention to Aldar.

Aldar pointed out objects of interest as he told Shiloh more about her new home. "Straight ahead, this is Montgomery Street which you can see runs along the shore. That's the principal street. There's been talk of filling in this cove, so that Montgomery Street may someday be inland."

"There certainly are a lot of peaks," Shiloh commented, trying to sound positive.

"That nearest one is called Signal Hill. See how the semaphore is turned? That signals our ship's arrival. But there's another big hill that's going to be special for us. And that's just the beginning of sights I'm going to show you."

"I'm anxious to see them with you," she replied.

For the first time in her life, she was to have a home of her own, so she wanted it to have a sense of peace, of belonging. Yet she silently fought back a wave of disappointment in San Francisco's appearance.

"As soon as I see Philander and tell him the good news from Washington, we'll tour the whole peninsula," Aldar assured her. "We'll walk on the beach, watch the fog come in at dusk, and enjoy the finest seafood."

"Sounds wonderful." In spite of herself, Shiloh shivered at the cold penetrating wind that raised gooseflesh along her arms. She forced a smile to mask the sick feeling inside. She hadn't thought she would be homesick, but she suddenly longed for the sturdy old Pennsylvania farm house with its acres of pleasant green fields and endless stands of trees. Here there were only barren, hilly sand dunes, cold fog, and a harsh wind.

Aldar laughed and gently tipped her face up so he could look into her eyes. "It's wonderful because I found you, and you're here with me."

"I always want to be with you."

She looked away at the sound of running feet. She observed a large crowd of men approaching in blue and red shirts, alerted by the semaphore. Most were on foot. A few drove an assortment of hacks, coaches, or mud wagons pulled by horses or mules. They slowed at sight of the two women.

She commented, "I've never seen so many nationalities or such strange clothing. It looks as if everyone in town's coming down to meet our ship."

"Actually, most of the those are runners hired by the hotels, restaurants, and other commercial ventures to get all of us to go with them. But Philander might send a wagon for us. I'll go look, but first I'd better make sure the ship's crew understands what to do with our trunks and the pickax heads."

Aldar guided Shiloh and Mara behind a stack of wooden barrels and crates by the plank sidewalk. Shiloh started to reach out to restrain him, not wanting to be left for even a moment in this faraway land that had recently been won in the war with Mexico.

Aldar didn't notice her motion, but strode off, long legs swinging, his water-soaked boots making sloshing sounds. He had brought boxes of pick heads without handles, reasoning that wood was plentiful in the Mother Lode foothills. Miners would pay much more for the metal heads alone than pick and handle would bring back east.

Shiloh stared apprehensively after him.

"Don't let it bother you, Shiloh." Mara readjusted her clothing, still ignoring the two black men who had seen her safely through the surf. They stood uncertainly, looking at each other, then back to Mara, obviously unwilling to leave such a beautiful woman even though she seemed to disdain them.

"Is it that obvious how I feel?" Shiloh asked.

"To me, yes; but I don't think your husband will notice. He's so excited about being back, he's like a little boy."

Shiloh followed him with her eyes as he purposefully strode along the plank sidewalk toward the bearded master of the *Terrapin* supervising cargo unloading.

With an effort, Shiloh tore her gaze away to where runners were streaming toward the other passengers now ashore from the ship. The runners started shouting their employers' services.

"This way to the Harper House, finest hotel west of New Orleans. Comfortable ride in our light hotel coach."

"Right this way to the best restaurant outside of Boston."

"Follow me to the fastest vessel going upriver to the gold fields."

A brown-skinned man in ragged clothes boldly approached Shiloh and Mara. Shiloh involuntarily drew back as he flashed a broken-toothed grin, swept off his tattered sombrero, and bowed slightly.

"Ah, Señoritas! Welcome to San Francisco!" He reached out to take the small carpetbag Mara carried. "I weel carry your bag for only two dollars!"

Shiloh's eyes opened wide at such an outlandish price. "Two dol—?" Her words were broken off as Mara brought her bone handled umbrella smartly across the man's knuckles.

The startled runner jerked his hand back and glanced up in surprise at the mulatto woman. "Touch anything before you're told," she said quietly, "and you'll have so many broken fingers, you won't even be able to dress yourself."

Shaking his fingers, the man retreated, muttering in Spanish. Shiloh shifted her gaze to the two black men. They obviously wanted to get acquainted with Mara, but they held back, unsure of what reception they would get. Shiloh smiled to herself, grateful for Mara, who had been closer than a sister from the day they'd met as little girls.

Shiloh heard her husband's familiar step coming toward her on the echoing plank walk. She eagerly turned toward him as he approached.

"Our baggage and my picks won't be unloaded from the ship until later." He took her arm. "Let's get away from here and see if Philander has sent a driver for us."

"He doesn't know we're coming," Shiloh reminded him.

"He knows I'm due back about now, so maybe he's having a carriage sent around with each ship's arrival."

Aldar's boots clumped loudly on the wooden planks as he led his wife toward shore. Shiloh fell into step beside him, trying hard to keep an open mind about this new community stretching before her.

Mara walked a few paces behind, silent as usual, except for the sound of her high-topped shoes on the wooden wharf. The two black men followed at a discreet distance, but Mara didn't look back at them. Shiloh felt sorry for them, but she was used to Mara using men, then ignoring them.

When they stepped onto the plank walk at the street, Aldar stopped. "See that hill over there?" he asked.

She followed his pointing finger to the farthest south of the three major peaks. It was incredibly steep, the top isolated under the sky.

"Nothing like that in Pennsylvania," she replied, unsure of what significance the hill had for her husband.

"Nor anywhere else in the world," he agreed. "That's the one I mentioned. It's called Fern Hill. It's such a poor name for such a noble place. From up there, I'll bet you can see the most fantastic scenery anywhere."

Growing more enthusiastic, he added, "After I check with Philander and see how business is going, I'll try to find a way to the top of that hill."

Shiloh shaded her eyes to better see the hill that towered grandly above everything. "Not even a mountain goat could climb that! So how could you?"

"Not just me, us! Someday, I'll build you a fine house up there!"

She shook her head and smiled at the absurdity of the idea. "How are you going to do that?"

"Haven't figured that out yet." He started walking again. "But that's part of the dream."

Aldar Laird the dreamer! Her adoptive father's taunting words leaped from memory.

She shivered slightly, unsure if it was from the cold, cutting wind or remembering the way her adoptive parents had greeted her announcement that she was going to marry Aldar Laird. The promised warmth of Aldar's love was worth the risk of disapproval by her adoptive parents, Martha and Eldon Edgeworth.

Martha Edgeworth, always aloof and cool to Shiloh, had tried vainly to change Shiloh's mind. "You've only known him a month," she stormed. "He came here a stranger, telling tall tales about some express business in California, and you believe him! You don't know a thing about him! He'll get you away out there, thousands of miles from home, and abandon you! You'll end up penniless and alone in a strange land. Mark my words, Shiloh!"

Eldon Edgeworth's practical farmer attitude had been more direct. He conceded, "Aldar's a mighty fine looking man, I'll grant you that. I guess there wasn't a female in Parks Pond, girl or full-grown woman, didn't covet him when you took him to church last Sunday. But looks ain't everything. You'd be better off to marry Seth Collins. He's a fine neighbor and solid farmer. Best kind of stock for raising a family."

All her life, Shiloh had smiled and obeyed, but not this

time. She eloped with the golden-haired man with a world of golden dreams. He had painted glowing word pictures of how well he and his partner, Philander MacAdams, were doing with their new business venture. MacAdams and Laird Express Company was already taking in a thousand dollars a day with no end in sight, not even with the countless competitive lines popping up like mushrooms after a spring rain.

The dreamer in Aldar most appealed to Shiloh, for she wanted more out of life than the farm boys offered at home. She liked Aldar's vision and innovative ideas about someday owning stagecoach lines, drayage businesses, and perhaps steamboats or even a railroad line.

Now, nearly ninety days out of New York, the parental warnings echoed mockingly in Shiloh's ears. She tried to shake off the eerie feeling that she should have listened to them.

Aldar's voice interrupted her thoughts. "I don't see any sign of Philander, but we'll give him a few more minutes."

Shiloh nodded. She wasn't concerned. Aldar would make all the decisions and take care of her, as her adoptive father had done. She looked around at the great building activity more closely. The sound of saws and hammers drew Shiloh's attention.

Everywhere, a building boom was going on. She saw it in the abandoned ships that had been hauled up on shore and hastily converted into hotels or other uses. She saw it in the crude wooden buildings and more substantial structures becoming visible farther up the street and beginning to run up the hills of San Francisco.

Suddenly, a man shouted from the roof of a nearby frame house. He pointed with his hammer, then shouted again. Other men yelled, and more hammering stopped. Distant male voices took up the cry, and the saws fell silent. Each yell was taken up farther away, continuing on and on, like an echo.

Shiloh frowned, glancing up at Aldar. "What are they saying?"

"They're shouting, 'Women!' They got a look at you and Mara."

"They're all staring!" she said under her breath.

"And why not?" he answered with a grin. "When I left San Francisco, there weren't many women of any kind here except . . . uh . . . well, not the kind of women you'll meet socially." He paused, then added, "You'll get used to it, Shiloh. You, too, Mara."

No, I won't! Shiloh's stubborn but silent denial came automatically.

Aldar said, "They're coming to get a better look."

The nearest men swarmed out onto the sand dunes, staring in obvious amazement at the new arrivals. Shiloh squirmed uncomfortably, waiting for Aldar to do something.

Aldar squeezed her hand reassuringly. "They won't hurt you. They're just curious."

Shiloh wanted to run from the swelling mass of men streaming out of beached ships, commercial buildings, makeshift dwellings, or ragged canvas tents. At the same time, she was fascinated by the sight of them. There were at least fifty men already running, slipping on the sandy dunes, or clumping noisily on the plank walk. In the distance, at least another hundred men streamed into view, heading downhill toward the wharf. Shiloh had never even imagined such a possibility.

All the gawking men removed their hats and ducked their shaggy, uncombed heads in polite greeting while continuing to gaze in frank admiration at the two women.

Aldar pointed out the various nationalities. The Chinese wore loose-fitting blue clothing, their black hair hanging down their backs in long queues from under their wide brimmed hats. Barrel-chested, brown-skinned Kanakas from the Sandwich Islands grinned broadly and waved in friendly greeting.

Sonorans from Mexico sported wide sombreros and ragged clothes. The men with serapes over their shoulders were Chileans. The white-skinned, unshaven men in red or blue shirts, suspenders, and muddy boots were miners on their way to or from the mines.

"Most of these men are Americans," Aldar explained, "but many are from other countries, mostly Italy, England, France, and Ireland. There are a few Germans which we call Dutchmen, and some Australians. Almost all of them are under forty, and most are less than thirty, like me. There are some thieves and worse among them," Aldar concluded, "but nobody's going to harm you."

Shiloh wasn't so sure. She fought a feeling of panic that made her want to run. She glanced at Mara, wondering if she felt the same way. It was instantly apparent that she did not. Mara studied the men with dark, thoughtful eyes. A hint of a smile tugged at the corner of her lips.

Shiloh thought, *She's enjoying this! How could she, after all that's happened to her?*

"We can't stand here!" she whispered to Aldar, indicating the watching crowds. "I feel like a prize horse on display."

"You're the most beautiful creature I've ever seen," he replied, suddenly sweeping her into his arms. "I want everyone to see you."

"Aldar!" she said fiercely under her breath. "Put me down! Everyone's watching! What'll they think?"

"Who cares what they think?" He spun around, making her heavy dark skirt flutter above her high-topped shoes. "Shiloh, I'm so proud of being your husband I could bust! And I'm going to make you happy! You hear me? I'm going to make you the happiest woman in the world because you've made me feel as if my life is just beginning!"

Shiloh's strict Victorian upbringing had allowed her to exchange one chaste kiss when she became engaged. In spite of Aldar's protests, there had been no other until the wedding.

But that had been in another world, Shiloh decided with a gentle sigh.

The men watching didn't really matter; being loved did. After nineteen years of deprivation of that emotion, she wanted most to love and be loved. Aldar loved her; she had no doubt of that. She didn't like dreary San Francisco, but if that's where her husband was, Shiloh decided she must learn to accept this place and even find beauty in it. If Aldar loved this place, then she would learn to love it too.

As Aldar gently lowered her to the ground, a grimy youth with only a hint of beard separated from the first wave of oncoming men and hurried up. He swept off his hat with his left hand and produced a small buckskin pouch with the right. "Beggin' yore pardon, Mister," he said to Aldar without taking his eyes off Shiloh, "But this here's got six ounces of gold dust. I'd be obliged to give it to you if'n I kin jist touch the hand of yore lady."

Shiloh pressed close to Aldar, instinctively seeking protection from something beyond her understanding.

The bold youth reacted to her movement with a quick apology. "I don't mean no harm, Missus. I got me a mother back home, an' a passel o' sisters, an' I'm so blamed lonesome to see the likes o' ye that I'd give every blessed cent I own jist to feel the touch of a woman's hand, and maybe hear a kind word."

Shiloh was stirred by the youth's obvious sincerity. She looked questioningly at Aldar.

He nodded slightly and cleared his throat. "I'm Aldar Laird of MacAdams and Laird Express Company. This is my wife, Shiloh, and her companion, Mara."

"Howdy do, Missus. I'm Rufus Sanders, late of ol' Kaintuk." The youth looked at the mulatto and nodded slightly. He extended his right hand with the poke toward

Shiloh. "Take it, Ma'am. And I'd be obliged if ye could see yore way clear to lemme jist touch yore hand."

Shiloh hesitated until she felt her husband's gentle push. "Go ahead," he urged quietly.

She cautiously extended her right hand. "I'm pleased to meet you, but I don't want your gold," she told him firmly.

"I do," Mara said. She reached out and took the pouch with one quick motion.

The young miner nodded his approval to Mara and immediately turned his empty palm to grasp Shiloh's. He held on firmly but gently, looking down at their hands. "I'll be dad-blasted! I don't reckon I kin remember the las' time I felt anything so downright wonnerful!"

Shiloh gently removed her hand. "Thank you, Mr. Sanders."

The other men had fallen silent at Sanders' brashness, but now they surged forward, offering gold coins, nuggets, leather pouches, or other items for the same privilege Sanders had been granted.

Shiloh drew back involuntarily as her husband raised his voice. "Gentlemen, I'm sure you understand that my bride and her companion are tired from our voyage. If you'll excuse us, we'll be on our way."

He turned and led the women away. The men followed, some calling out a final offer, but most fell into a respectful silence.

Shiloh whispered, "They're still behind us!"

"I can't blame them, Honey. They'll likely try to follow us all the way . . . hey! There's Clay Patton!"

A tall, slender man with a huge crop of curly black whiskers turned the corner from Washington Street onto Montgomery. He drove a pair of brown mules hitched to a two-seat delivery wagon. The driver, sitting on the high seat directly behind the mules, hauled back on the reins, stopping beside the plank walk while the crowd of curious men circled the scene in curious silence.

"Clay!" Aldar boomed, reaching up to shake the driver's hand. "I'm mighty glad to see you!"

"Same here, Aldar," the driver said. When his hand was released, he quickly tied the reins around the brake handle and stepped down.

He and Aldar thumped each other on the back in obvious great affection, inquiring about each other's health and smiling broadly. Then they turned back to the women.

Aldar said, "Shiloh, this is the man I told you about. Clay Patton. Handles a team better than anyone I've ever met. He's also a mighty fine drummer, but I can't get him to go on the road to get business as I do."

"Ma'am," Clay spoke the single word while lifting his sweat-stained hat by the wide brim. He had dark wavy hair and tanned features.

"How do you do, Mr. Patton?" Shiloh replied formally, her eyes taking in his rugged good looks. He was at least two inches taller than Aldar, with broad shoulders, narrow hips, and deep brown eyes.

Shiloh added, "This is my companion, Mara."

Clay's eyebrows lifted slightly as he took a closer look at the second woman. He tipped his hat and nodded politely without speaking.

Mara did not acknowledge the introduction.

Aldar's boyish enthusiasm bubbled up. "Clay, isn't she the prettiest little thing you've ever seen?"

Shiloh flinched, surprised that he would speak of her so boldly with any man, especially an employee.

"Congratulations, Aldar." Clay had just a hint of a drawl, but there was a coolness that had not been there a moment ago when the men exchanged hearty greetings.

Shiloh glanced sharply at the driver, sensing silent disapproval of her.

Aldar explained with a good natured grin, "I believe Clay thinks I should not have brought you out here."

Shiloh felt a flash of resentment. Part of it was directed toward her husband for his indiscretion in discussing her with this stranger. She couldn't direct her annoyance at Aldar, so she inquired politely of Clay.

"Oh? Why is that, Mr. Patton?"

He shrugged, releasing the lines from the brake handle. "Seems to me that's a question for your husband to answer if he wants."

She settled back onto her seat in silence, but she had a sudden uncomfortable feeling about Clay.

That feeling wasn't shared by her husband. He clapped the driver warmly on his shoulder. "I'm sure glad Philander sent you to meet us! Shiloh was getting upset about all the fuss those men were making."

"He didn't send me. I figured it was about time you got back, so I've been watching the semaphore and coming here to check each time a ship comes in."

Shiloh saw a slight frown cross her husband's brow. "Didn't Philander know I was due in about now?"

Clay shrugged. "Can't rightly say." It was a noncommittal answer that somehow made Shiloh slightly uneasy. Apparently that was also true of her husband.

Aldar asked sharply, "Something wrong at work, Clay?"

He hesitated slightly before answering. "Let's just say I'm mighty glad you're back, Aldar." He quickly changed the subject. "If you'll help the women aboard, I'll stow that carpet bag. Where's the rest of your stuff?"

"Not unloaded yet. We'll have to come back for it later."

Shiloh silently settled into the front seat. Aldar swung up beside her while Mara took the back seat.

Aldar asked, "Clay, is there something going on at the business that I should know about?"

He turned to mount his high seat, saying over his shoulder, "You didn't get back a bit too soon, Aldar."

Shiloh glanced in frustrated concern at her husband, who

was still frowning but silent. Clay clucked to the mules. They rapidly pulled away, leaving the disappointed crowd of men behind and Shiloh with a rising sense of apprehension.

Near the waterfront, The Watcher mounted his jackass and began following at a discreet distance.

CHAPTER II

SHILOH LEANED toward her husband and spoke softly above the soft rhythmic crunch of the mules' hooves in the sand. "Do you think Mr. Patton meant something's seriously wrong?"

"I doubt it." Aldar patted her hand reassuringly. "Philander is always fighting with somebody, but whatever it is, I'll fix it tomorrow. Meanwhile, there's nothing for you to worry your pretty head about."

Shiloh felt reassured. Everybody except her adoptive parents liked Aldar, who was always friendly, confident, and assured. Yet a tiny knot of doubt made Shiloh fret silently as the mules plodded along Montgomery Street, following the shoreline.

She felt awkward about the men who stopped to stare, but she was pleasantly surprised to see some substantial brick buildings scattered among frame ones. This showed a tendency toward permanency in San Francisco which Aldar had explained had grown from a hundred or so in population a few years ago to about 10,000 last summer.

"I don't see any churches," Shiloh commented ruefully.

"There are a few," Aldar replied as they turned onto Washington Street, heading inland. "We'll find one next Sunday." He leaned forward slightly and raised his voice. "Clay, what's the latest news from Congress?"

"I thought you'd have later information than anything we know here, seeing as how yours is the last ship to arrive."

"The last I heard, Congress still couldn't agree about California."

"That's still true, according to some men who arrived on another ship a week or so ago. They brought news that Congress hadn't acted one way or another. Now there's a rumor that Governor Riley—"

"Riley?" Aldar interrupted. "What happened to Richard Mason?"

"Brigadier General Bennet Riley relieved Colonel Mason last month. That's six governors California has had in about a year. Civil and military governors: Sloat, Stockton, Fremont, Kearny, Mason, and now Riley."

Clay shook his head. "They're a strange lot. Kearny was replaced by Mason, and Fremont was taken back to Washington under arrest, facing a court martial."

"John C. Fremont?" Aldar's voice held surprise.

Clay nodded. "California politics is a mess."

"Sure is. I wonder what Riley will do?"

"They say he's going to call for a civil convention, even though he's a military commander. That's so the people can make up their own minds about whether they want a territorial government for California, or what."

"What about statehood?"

"Last word we had was that Congress is still split over admitting any more states because of the fight over slavery." Clay shifted his eyes to Mara. "Begging your pardon," he said softly. "I wasn't thinking."

"Mara has her freedom papers," Shiloh explained. "Has had since she was a little girl."

"Reckon she might want to keep them handy then," Clay replied solemnly. "There are only a few buck Negroes around, and they have to be careful."

"Oh?" Shiloh said, "Why is that, Mr. Patton?"

"Call me Clay, Ma'am. Anyway, around here, there's no real

law or anybody to enforce it. The *Alta California,* that's our local newspaper, ran a story saying that San Francisco doesn't have proper executive offices, and warning of danger from what the paper called 'the assassin's knife and fire.'"

Aldar asked good naturedly, "Clay, are you trying to scare these women?"

"Don't mean to, but I was just pointing out that freedom papers don't mean much around here. Some men figure the few Negroes in California really escaped from their owners back east. Some don't stay long."

Shiloh inquired, "What happens to them?"

"They just disappear."

Shiloh was genuinely concerned. "How?"

"Two possibilities, Ma'am. Either they got shanghaied by some ship's master needing a crew real bad . . ."

"Shanghaied?" Aldar interrupted.

"New thing since you left. As you must have figured from all those abandoned vessels in the bay, crews almost always jump ship and head for the gold country. Masters, real desperate to get a crew, have been paying certain saloon keepers or crimps to drug the drinks of able-bodied men. They wake up on their way to Shanghai, China, or some other far off place."

"That's barbaric!" Shiloh exclaimed.

"I think of it more as slavery," Clay replied.

"And there's no way to stop it?"

"Nobody's found a way yet. Anyway, even if there was a law and someone to enforce it, how's a shanghaied man going to complain when he's far out at sea?"

Shiloh shuddered, then remembered the black men who had helped Mara. "What's the other possibility you mentioned?"

"Well, slave catchers grab Negro men for the reward, and ship them back east under the Fugitive Slave Law."

"Even if they're free?"

"Yes, Ma'am. Slave catchers figure all Negroes are escaped slaves."

Shiloh thought, *He's warning me that the same thing could happen to Mara.* Shiloh avoided looking back to see Mara's reaction to this unexpected threat.

Clay added with a touch of drawl, "I watch where I go. So does Aldar. You and Mara might do the same."

Shiloh clutched Aldar's arm in sudden fright. He smiled reassuringly at her. "Don't worry! Nothing's going to happen."

Shiloh fervently hoped that was true, but remembered that Aldar always said everything would be all right.

He held her hand but looked up at the driver's back. "Clay, did the president and Senator Benton ever settle their dispute about California?"

"Nope." There was a hint of disgust in the word.

Aldar explained to Shiloh. "Last year, President Polk and his cabinet claimed that after the war with Mexico ended, the government already in existence in California should continue until Congress provides a better one."

"Sounds logical," Shiloh commented more in the way of conversation than interest. Women couldn't vote, so Shiloh had never paid much attention to politics except regarding slavery. She added, "But Zachary Taylor is now president."

"Yes, since three months ago. But that doesn't matter. Senator Benton is so powerful that last year he sent a letter to the people of California saying that the civil and military government brought on by the war with Mexico was now null and void. Benton claims military governors like Riley can't change the laws."

"Sure is a mess," Aldar commented.

Clay slapped the reins along the mules' rumps. "Old Senator Benton defies the president and wants Californians to meet in convention and come up with a government of our own until Congress finally acts."

Aldar asked thoughtfully, "Do most men here agree?"

"From what I hear, they do. So I guess that's why Bennet Riley's calling for a convention."

"It'll be interesting to see what happens," Aldar remarked.

Shiloh glanced around at the sand hills dotted with occasional clumps of oaks. "Where are we going?"

"To our house. Clay's been taking care of it while I was gone."

Early in their relationship, Aldar had explained how he bought the property from a native *Californio.* He was of a noble old family until the war with Mexico ended and the *gringos* came. They treated him with such indignities that he had moved to remote Napa Valley.

A few minutes later, Clay rounded another corner onto a quiet street. There was only one house, a one-story adobe structure with a wide veranda and a neatly tended garden.

"Oh!" she exclaimed with delight. "After seeing all those tents and shacks, I didn't dream there was anything this lovely in all of San Francisco!"

Shiloh studied the solid house with its red tile roof and stout wooden beams protruding from the ends of the eaves. Brightly colored flowers spilled from clay pots suspended from the eaves on leather thongs. A small garden graced both sides of the path leading to the front door.

When the team stopped, Aldar stepped down and turned to help Shiloh out of the wagon. She wondered if the Southern-born driver would do the same for her companion.

Mara saved any possible embarrassment. She stepped effortlessly from the back seat before Clay had climbed down over the front wheel. She shook the fine sand from her umbrella and carpet bag and scrutinized the house.

Clay handed Aldar two large metal keys. "I kept the keys you gave me when you left to go east. This key's to the main house. The other's for the cookhouse."

Aldar offered the smaller key to Mara. "There's a bed, dining area, and kitchen in your quarters. It's separate from the house because of fire danger from the stove."

Wordlessly, Mara took that key and hurried off down the path with her small carpetbag.

"Well," Clay said, turning back to face Aldar. "I'd better get back to the ship and pick up your trunks."

Aldar nodded, mentioning the boxes with the pickax heads. "Thanks, Clay," he said quietly. "Would you mind keeping them safe until morning?"

"I figured on doing that." He reached up to the box and retrieved an 1848 pocket Colt. "Better take this."

"Why?"

Clay shrugged. "Lots of trouble around town lately. Some folks are even talking of forming a committee of vigilance." He laid the pistol in Aldar's hand, then quickly climbed to the high box on the wagon. "Be careful," he said, picking up the lines.

"I will," Aldar promised, shoving the weapon into his waistband.

Shiloh frowned. She had grown up around shotguns and rifles, but she'd never known Pennsylvania farmers to carry handguns. A revolver was for use against people, she felt, and that was wrong.

From his seat, Clay asked, "You want me to bring you back some supper?"

Shiloh didn't like the idea of being out at night in a strange town where a pistol was needed. "That would be nice, don't you think so, Aldar?"

"We'd appreciate that, Clay."

He nodded. "Be back shortly." He politely touched the brim of his hat. "Ma'am," he said to Shiloh, then slapped the lines across the mules' rumps. The animals swung around and headed downhill with a rattle of chains and a creak of harness leather.

Shiloh asked, "Aldar, is he married?"

"Widower." He started walking toward the gate.

Shiloh fell into step beside him. "What happened?"

"He never said, but I gathered that it was something terrible."

"What else do you know about him?"

Aldar let Shiloh pass before him through the gate before replying. "Not much. He never talks about personal things. I just know that he came from Texas, and he sure knows how to drive a team."

"He made me nervous with his hint of trouble at work, and giving you that gun."

"I think he was just being careful because you're here. I've always heard those Texas men were gallant around women, especially pretty ones."

Shiloh stopped on the gravel patch as the sun suddenly disappeared. She glanced up to see fog starting to form at the bottom of the hills. There was something ominous about the silent, fast-moving mist.

"Turning cold," Aldar said, taking Shiloh's hand. "Let's get inside."

He continued leading her along the path toward the house. "Mara's a strange woman," he commented. "I get the feeling she doesn't like me."

"She'll learn to like you, although she doesn't trust men much."

Aldar glanced at Shiloh, but she seemed to have said all she wanted. "I wish you hadn't let her come west with us."

"We both wanted to come together. She's the only person I ever knew who showed any warmth or caring for me, except you."

Aldar nodded, compassion welling up inside him as he recalled Shiloh telling him how she had been a newborn foundling who was first taken into the home of a small slave-holding family in Virginia. Later, she was adopted by Eldon and Martha Edgeworth of Pennsylvania.

Shiloh never knew who her birth parents were. The only clue was a small white leather-bound New Testament and Psalms that had been folded into the blankets with the infant girl. Tucked inside the testament were two locks of hair. One was short, dark, and curly, the other was long and red-gold. There was no writing in the testament except a single word inside the front cover: *Shiloh.*

She was wet nursed by Mara's attractive slave mother, but Shiloh spent most of her time with Mara, whose father was the handsome teenage son of a neighboring plantation owner.

Mara's mother died when Shiloh was about a year old and Mara was two. The Edgeworths, an older couple visiting from the North, saw the two girls playing together shortly after the funeral. More out of what Shiloh had often heard called "Christian duty" than love, the childless couple arranged to adopt Shiloh. She confided to Aldar that she suspected that her adoptive parents had another motive: to enhance their status in their farming community and home church. This was especially important as the Edgeworths became more active in the abolitionist movement.

The Edgeworths had not planned on taking Mara north with them although both little girls cried hard at parting. Hours later, with Shiloh still sobbing, the Edgeworths returned, bought Mara, took her home, and freed her from slavery.

Mara's name remained unchanged, but the little white girl was christened Rachel Ann Edgeworth. However, she preferred to be known by the name Mara had called her from earliest memory: *Shiloh.*

As the couple came to the steps leading onto the veranda, Shiloh looked up at her tall husband. "You do understand about Mara and me, don't you?"

"I've heard about a Negro and white child playing together

while they were growing up. But I never heard of them staying close once they were grown."

"Maybe Mara and I were different," Shiloh said, "because all our lives, we needed each other."

Aldar frowned thoughtfully. "I can understand that. But now you've got me."

"And I'm very glad." She laid a small hand on his forearm. "I also hope Mara will someday meet a special man and go off to establish her own home. But as I told you before we left Pennsylvania—"

"I know!" Aldar held up a restraining hand. "But now that we're here, I want us to be—us, just you and me."

"That's the way it's going to be, darling. But until we get settled, please be patient about Mara."

Aldar mounted the wooden steps onto the veranda. "I'll try."

"Thank you." Shiloh looked wistfully up at him. "Except for finding my birth parents, I've never had many dreams of my own, but now I have yours . . . "

"Ours," he interrupted with a smile.

"Ours," she agreed. "Together we'll make them come true."

Aldar opened the door. For a moment, Shiloh couldn't see anything in the dark interior, but she felt a rush of cool air touch her cheeks. At the same time, Aldar swept her up into his arms so suddenly she gasped.

"What're you doing?" she cried, looking into his smiling face.

"Carrying my bride over the threshold, of course." He pushed through the door, the gun butt banging against the solid wooden frame. "That first time at your folks' place didn't count." He kissed her, then set her on her feet in the parlor. A fine quality carpet cushioned her landing.

"Brrr!" she said, "It's cold in here."

"I'll build a fire." Aldar glanced at the fireplace. "No wood in here. I'll look outside." He removed the pistol from his waistband and laid it on top of a carved walnut highboy. He went out, closing the door behind him.

As her eyes adjusted to the darkness of the room, Shiloh nodded approvingly, admiring the tasteful furnishings, fine imported carpet, and graceful accents. She hurriedly toured all the rooms, letting her fingers lightly touch the fine French furniture. Both bedrooms had a layer of dust on the highboys and two chairs. In the larger room, she nodded appreciatively at the sight of two large mirrors in heavy gilded frames. One was behind a marble-topped washstand where a flowered ceramic water pitcher with graceful basin rested. The second mirror was on a closed door which Shiloh assumed was a closet. Under the high bed, she glimpsed a chamber pot which matched the pitcher and basin.

She passed a window and pulled the draperies back, waving the dust away when it tickled her nose. She looked out onto the patio with its glistening red tiles and hanging clay pots brimming with bright flowers.

Nice! she told herself, moving toward the mirrored door. She opened it and wrinkled her nose at the faint musty odor. Shiloh closed the door and quickly searched the parlor for a candle to light against the coming darkness.

She interrupted her search as she heard her husband's step outside the door. She hurried to open it for him. He entered with an armload of oak logs and some pieces of broken wooden boxes for kindling. The cold, foggy air followed him in. He dropped the wood beside the fireplace.

While Aldar got flames started, Shiloh found two tallow candles. She lit them in the fireplace, settled them firmly into holders that had been carved of ivory, and set them on the mantle.

Aldar stood up as the fire started crackling through the dry kindling. Wordlessly, he pulled her to him and kissed her lightly on the lips. "Happy?" he asked.

She tried to forget her disappointment in the smelly bay,

wet fog, and cold wind that had blown fine particles of sand into her face all afternoon. "I'll remember this time forever," she said wistfully.

"Even when we're rich and live up on Fern Hill?"

She returned his teasing smile. "Up there where the goats can't climb?"

"Maybe they can't, but *we* can."

Her smile slowly faded. She said seriously, "Being with you is what makes me happy, so anywhere you go, I'll go."

Aldar's blazing eyes captivated her as he eased her to the floor in front of the fireplace. He held her tenderly, not saying anything for a few moments. Then he lightly stroked her hair and began to speak softly. "It won't be easy."

"Climbing that hill?"

"No, I mean, building up the business the way I dream it should be." He sat up beside her. His voice lost its soft, tender tone. "You see, everything in California depends on two things: water and transportation. Water's too hard to control because it's going to be political. But transportation is mostly a business proposition, with some politics mixed in, of course. I understand business, and I've learned a little about politics."

"I'm sure you have, and I know you'll succeed." She paused, then added, "I'm concerned about Clay."

"You are? Why?"

"What did Clay mean about your not getting back any too soon? And why wouldn't he answer you when you asked if something was wrong at work?"

"I told you not to worry! Whatever it is, I can handle it tomorrow when I see Philander."

She pushed herself out of his arms. "I didn't mean to interfere."

"You're not, really. But business is a man's world, and a wife shouldn't concern herself about such things."

Shiloh felt a surge of annoyance, but she took a deep breath and pushed it down. Then, after a thoughtful moment, she added, "I was surprised that you said anything personal to him about me." Shiloh was disturbed at the thought of men talking to one another about any woman, especially their wives.

"Clay's more than an employee," Aldar explained. "He's a friend."

"As long as I've got you to take care of me," she said, turning to bring her face close to him, "I won't concern myself about anything but making you happy."

"That suits me fine." He bent to kiss her.

The newlyweds were too caught up in the magic of their first night together in their new home to hear Clay's footsteps on the veranda.

A couple of hundred yards away, out of sight behind a sand hill, The Watcher turned his mule around and left the house behind, satisfied.

CHAPTER III

THE SKIES were clear and free of fog the next morning when Clay arrived with the delivery wagon. Shiloh greeted him warmly, hoping to break through the coolness she had sensed yesterday.

As she settled on the seat beside Aldar who was dressed for work, Shiloh looked up at the driver. "Mr. Patton, yesterday you . . ."

"I'd like you to call me Clay."

She nodded. "Clay, you seemed surprised that Aldar had brought back a wife."

"It's none of my business, Mrs. Laird." He turned away, released the brake, and started driving.

Shiloh felt her cheeks warm. *He means it's also none of my business to ask what he thinks.*

Aldar, sensing her discomfort, began discussing politics with Clay. The men talked freely, but Shiloh sat in silence.

They entered the business district where every man they met or passed turned to stare. Shiloh kept her eyes averted until she was distracted at an intersection by the squeal of frightened horses and a man's angry shouts. Shiloh glanced up the steep hill to her left. A team was down, with both horses threshing wildly in their harnesses. Their driver loudly cursed them from his seat on a low dray wagon with its load of barrels and crates.

"Oh, those poor animals!" Shiloh exclaimed. "That hill's too steep for them!"

"San Francisco is full of hills, so this happens all the time," Aldar assured her. "It's worse in the winter when the streets turn to mud."

Clay swiveled in the front seat. "Aldar, mind if I give that fellow a hand?"

Aldar started to rise. "Good idea. I'll help."

"You might get dirty," Clay warned, nimbly stepping to the sandy street. "No need for you to arrive at work all messed up." Clay walked toward the downed team.

As Aldar again sank into his seat beside her, Shiloh commented, "No team should have to climb such steep hills hauling heavy loads."

"I agree, but there's no other way."

"There should be. I feel so sorry for those horses." She turned to watch Clay.

At first, she thought the angry dray wagon driver wasn't going to accept Clay's offer to help. But after another glance at the frightened, downed team, the teamster handed the lines to Clay.

He walked with them to the horses' heads, knelt and began speaking softly while stroking the sweaty necks. Slowly, Clay worked the tangled harness off the near animal. Clay and the drayman helped get the horse to his feet. He stood, the whites of his eyes showing from fright. His foam-flecked sides still heaved as Clay began the same process with the other animal.

From a lifetime of living on a farm, Shiloh recognized the special rapport Clay had with animals.

"He's very good with that team," she commented.

"He's good at lots of things," Aldar replied.

Like knowing things he won't talk about, Shiloh thought. She remembered the rather ominous words Clay had spoken to Aldar yesterday. Without taking her eyes off the downed team, Shiloh asked, "Aldar, are you sure there's nothing seriously wrong at work?"

"Nothing I can't handle."

Shiloh sighed softly, but the sense of uneasiness didn't go away.

When both horses were up and harnessed again, Clay mounted the wagon with the reins in his hands. He braced himself, lightly flipping the lines with a soft command.

The team threw their weight into the harness. Clay released the brake. The wagon's wheels slowly lifted free of the shifting sand and moved steadily up the incline.

When the horses reached the next cross street where the hill momentarily leveled out, Clay let them stop and blow. He jumped down from the wagon, accepted a hearty handshake from the grateful teamster, then headed back toward Shiloh and her husband.

"Didn't I tell you?" Aldar asked Shiloh with obvious pride. "Clay's the best driver I ever met."

Aldar heartily complimented Clay as he took his seat again. He bobbed his head in acknowledgment and drove on without comment.

In a few minutes, Clay pulled over by a new, two-story wooden building. He looked over his shoulder. "Philander's moved the office since you left, Aldar."

"Nicer than the old one, all right." Aldar jumped down, then assisted Shiloh. "Clay, would you mind waiting? After Shiloh meets Philander and I see what his schedule is, I'll bring her back down."

Climbing the wooden stairs, Shiloh was ushered into a small, cramped room. A wide board set over two barrels formed a counter and a barrier to the rest of the room. Philander MacAdams looked up from his desk.

At thirty-three, he carried more than two hundred pounds on a big frame. His nose had been broken and not healed right. His jaw was square; his mouth was firm. He was handsome in a hard, rugged way.

Before Aldar could speak, his partner said gruffly, "It's about time you got back!"

"Good morning to you, too, and I'm glad to be back; thanks for asking," Aldar replied good naturedly without showing any offense at his partner's bluntness. Aldar added, "I got delayed, and here's why. Meet my wife, Shiloh Laird."

"Wife?" Philander shoved his chair back and stood up. "You got married?" His rumbling voice changed from gruffness to surprise, but he didn't sound pleased.

"Sure did!" Aldar beamed. "I was so proud to show her off that we took the Panama crossing because that's the fastest way."

Shiloh had started to acknowledge the introduction, but was cut off by Philander's quick question. "You walked across Panama, Missus?"

"Yes, but some other women did it too."

"You must be some woman!"

Shiloh lowered her eyes but didn't reply.

"She is!" Aldar said heartily. "She is."

Shiloh was aware that the partner was eyeing her thoughtfully. "I sure hadn't expected this," he said. "Aldar, we've got to talk now."

"This is our first full day back, so I'd like to show my wife around the town. Can't our talk wait?"

"No, it can't!"

Shiloh flinched at Philander's harsh reply.

Aldar turned to Shiloh. "Clay will drive you around for a while. Come back for me in about half an hour."

Philander's tone changed back to a growling gruffness. "It's going to take us all day to . . . "

"I know," Aldar interrupted. "But I'd feel better if she checked back. I'll walk down with her, then come right back."

Shiloh protested gently, "You have lots to talk about. I can go down by myself."

She smiled at Philander. "It was nice meeting you."

Shiloh saw Philander's eyes narrow, but he only nodded and said, "Missus."

She started to say, *Call me Shiloh,* then changed her mind. She walked down the stairs, disturbed by what had just happened, and wondering how it related to Clay's warning.

Shiloh stepped outside where Clay was currying the horses, his back toward her. She started to speak to him but stopped when she heard Philander's voice rise and float downward to the street.

"Now don't start that again, Aldar!"

Startled, Shiloh glanced up and saw that the second story office window was open.

"Why not?" her husband's voice was calm, but still carried well. "I thought you'd be pleased that I got all that help promised when I was in Washington."

"You know why!" Philander's voice was sharp. "I've been busting my backside to build up this business during the six months you were playing around with that woman!"

"She is not 'that woman!'" Shiloh heard her husband's voice take on a hard edge although he kept it quiet and level.

Embarrassed, Shiloh coughed softly so that Clay straightened up. He immediately lowered his eyes, and she knew he had also overheard. He looked directly at her and spoke in his soft voice.

"Don't mind him, Mrs. Laird."

Shiloh deliberately tried to avoid hearing any more of the men's quarrel from upstairs. She said, "Philander sounds so angry."

"It's just his way." Clay paused, then added, "Reckon they'll be awhile. Would you like to take a drive and see more of the city?"

Relieved, Shiloh nodded. "I'd appreciate that."

Clay offered his hand. She took it to step into the wagon, aware of the palm's roughness compared to Aldar's.

Clay clucked to the mules, and they moved into the sandy street.

Inside the office, Philander made an impatient movement to stop Aldar's quiet, even words. "All right! All right! I shouldn't have called her 'that woman.' But don't get off the subject. I'm running a business here, and anything that distracts from it is out of place! That includes your fancy ideas."

"You thought they were good ones when I left for Washington," Aldar said patiently, keeping his voice even. "What made you change your mind?"

"I've had time to think, that's what."

"But those are good, practical ideas."

"No, they're not! They've already pushed this company toward financial ruin."

"We were making over a thousand dollars a day when I left. That's strong growth."

"You think so, huh? Well, while you were away, I've tried to undo some of the problems your earlier wild ideas caused. I want you to stop talking foolishness and listen to me. Your ideas will ruin us, like expanding in too many directions. We're an express company, so let's keep it that way."

"We can't afford to be short-sighted, Philander! Our business is changing fast, just like everything else in California.

We're too limited, so I've got to make you see that the future includes all kinds of transportation, like stagecoach lines for passengers and mail, then move into steamers and possibly railroads. Just listen to me . . . "

"No, you listen to me! I let you go to Washington to see about . . . "

"You *let* me go?" Aldar broke in. "We're partners, Philander! Equal partners. Remember?"

"I know, but having you go east to try getting mail subsidies was a mistake. While you were gone, several other express companies started up. Some of them are growing very fast because their owners are attending to business, while you're off chasing some crazy dream!"

"It's not a dream! It's reality! We won't be in business long if we don't look ahead and . . . "

Philander interrupted. "We're wasting time talking about this! You're never going to change. Even if it ruins me, you're going to keep on . . . "

"We'll both be ruined if you don't listen!"

"I've got work to do, Aldar." Philander turned abruptly and began poring over papers on his desk.

Aldar started to stand, then settled back down in his chair. "Look," he said, keeping his voice low. "We can't go on like this. So let's not be so emotional and try to talk about this sensibly."

Philander swiveled away from his desk. "I'll try. But we need to make some changes around here."

Shiloh and Clay rode awhile in silence. It was the first time she had been alone with any man except Aldar since Seth Collins used to court her back home. Shiloh felt awkward about Clay's having overheard Philander's harsh remarks. Clay seemed deep in his own thoughts, not even offering to point out the sights. To ease the tension, Shiloh leaned forward and raised her voice.

"Mr. Patton, I heard your wife died."

She thought he flinched, but he didn't answer.

"I'm sorry," she apologized, "I shouldn't have made so personal a remark." He didn't answer, so to cover her embarrassment, she switched to a safer subject.

"I grew up on a farm," she commented, "but I've never seen anyone handle a team as well as you did awhile ago. How'd you learn to drive so well?"

"Had some experience, that's all."

"In Texas, I believe Aldar said."

"Born there, but left a few years back."

His brief reply held a hint of coolness warning her that he didn't want to talk about personal things.

"Aldar told me he met Philander when he was driving an ox team with freight into Nevada. At the time, Aldar was delivering express on muleback through the foothills. They got to talking, and Philander suggested the partnership."

"That's what I heard."

"When did you and Aldar meet?"

"Didn't your husband tell you?"

Shiloh realized Clay's parrying her question meant that he wasn't going to volunteer much. That thought embarrassed and yet angered her. She wondered, *What's he so secretive about?*

A chill settled over them, but it wasn't caused by the huge mass of fast-moving fog sliding silently across the azure sky, blotting it out and darkening the city.

Shiloh pulled her cloak tighter about her shoulders and silently fretted about things she didn't understand. Everything seemed to contribute to her sense of uneasiness and dislike for this faraway land, increasing her homesickness.

Shiloh glanced around at the all-male population that stopped to stare at her as the wagon moved along. "You'd think by the way those men look that there isn't another woman in all of San Francisco."

"There are a number of women, mostly Spanish speaking,

but there are almost no ladies, if you know what I mean. Well, except for some Mormon womenfolks who came in earlier with their menfolks. I never met any of their women. Lots of Mormons here, you know."

"I didn't know that."

"Oh, yes. Happened after their leader, Joseph Smith, and his brother were murdered five years ago."

Her attention shifted to the sound of children. She looked ahead to where three brown-skinned pre-teen boys with shovels were digging under a plank walk. Their two mongrel dogs barked and leaped excitedly about.

"Clay, what are those boys doing?"

"Shoveling rats out so the dogs can get them."

Shiloh was a farm girl who wasn't afraid of rats, but she certainly didn't care for them either. "Those boys should be in school," she observed as the wagon plodded past.

"A Presbyterian minister, Albert Williams, started one last month."

"That's good, so then the children should get both a good education and have spiritual training."

"The way San Francisco's growing, there'll soon be more women and kids than the few churches can handle." Clay paused before asking, "You ever teach young ones?"

"Back home, I taught them in church, of course. But I've had enough of that for a while. When Aldar and I find a church, I plan to just sit and listen to the preacher."

Church had helped to fill a great void in Shiloh's life. She touched the small New Testament which she always carried with her in her purse, as if to remind her that this simple testament—her sole inheritance—was the one true key to her identity.

Growing up and leafing through the testament with its locks of hair and that single penned word, Shiloh often pondered the significance of its contents. But it all remained a mystery, as did the reason her birth parents had abandoned her. Secretly, Shiloh wondered if somehow it was her fault. She grew up clinging to the God she read about in the pages of that small testament, many nights crying herself to sleep and praying, "Please, God, don't ever let me be abandoned again!"

Her cold, aloof, adoptive parents reared her without demonstrations of affection. When they were particularly harsh, Shiloh dreamed of someday finding her birth parents. However, at nineteen, there were still no clues. Moving to California had probably ruined any chance of ever knowing, but marrying Aldar helped make up for that.

Clay did not attempt to act as guide, but drove her to where she could see the bay and the hills across on the other shore. From this distance, the bay's true condition was not evident.

As they circled back toward the express building, Shiloh grudgingly admitted to herself that the area had a certain wild, unique beauty. That was especially true of the bay with the forested and unsettled hills across to the east. Even that didn't dispel the homesickness that clung to her.

Her thoughts drifted away so far that she wasn't aware they were back at the express company office until the team stopped. Relieved that she couldn't hear any more voices from the upstairs window, Shiloh said she would go see if Aldar was ready. Clay again offered his hand for her to step down. She climbed the stairs, still fretting about overhearing Philander's reference to her as "that woman."

She started to knock at the door, but stopped abruptly when she heard Philander's voice boom: "You know better than to talk politics with our accounts!"

"Now, don't get upset again. And be reasonable. You can't show me a single man in California who isn't talking politics!" Aldar's voice was still quiet but strong. "Statehood, slavery—you name it, everybody's talking politics."

"But you cost us the Denby Gladwin account because he favors a separate nation, and you told him we should be a state."

"Yes, I did, but I'll get him back, so don't worry. Anyway, I've got a right to my opinion, Philander, just as you and he have. So keep your voice down, please."

"You aggravate me, Aldar! Even if you do get him back, that won't make up for his business we've lost these past months!"

"Be fair, Philander. I didn't say anything to you when you tangled with Jefferson Locke over whether California should be admitted as a free or slave state."

"That was different, and you know it! Besides, Locke is hotheaded."

"And you're not?" Aldar's voice sounded slightly amused.

"At least I haven't been challenged to a duel." Philander shot back. He paused, then added, "You should have killed Kroeber instead of humiliating him. Those Dutchmen don't forget."

Shiloh sucked in her breath in shocked alarm. She had never heard Kroeber's name, and certainly didn't know that Aldar had fought a duel.

The voices inside fell silent, and chairs scraped on the wooden floor. Aldar's boots clumped loudly and he opened the door. "Shiloh!" he exclaimed. "I thought I heard you."

"You said to return in about half an hour."

"So I did. Well, some things have come up that require my staying here. I'll ask Clay to drive you home. Be right back, Philander."

They walked out and Aldar closed the door behind them. Shiloh whispered, "You fought a duel?"

A shadow passed over Aldar's face. He took her elbow and steered her down the stairs. "It was nothing, and it's over, so let's forget it."

Usually, Shiloh would have accepted that, but she was confused, frightened, and concerned. "Are you in any danger from that man Kroeber?"

"Of course not." He smiled, the same self-assured, confident way he had when they'd faced the thousand dangers of the Panama jungles and rivers.

"Please, Aldar!" She stopped on the stairs, keeping her voice low but looking up imploringly at him. "I've got to know about that duel!"

"Tell you tonight." He continued down the stairs.

They stepped outside where he helped her into the wagon, then asked Clay to drive her home and come back for him after five o'clock.

Shiloh didn't remember the ride back to the house. She silently contemplated all she had heard that morning. Who was Kroeber? Why had Aldar fought a duel? Who were those other men, Gladwin and Locke?

Shiloh stared at Clay's poker-straight back, confident that he knew. But she had already recognized his taciturn personality and knew he wouldn't permit himself to answer the questions that bubbled and boiled inside her.

At the house, Shiloh stepped down from the wagon without waiting to see if Clay would offer to help her. She thanked him and hurried to share her anguished thoughts with her lifelong confidant.

Shiloh found Mara hanging clothes on a line in the backyard. She listened in silence until Shiloh had finished pouring out her concerns.

"Fritz Kroeber," Mara began. "I heard the name."

"How?" Shiloh was genuinely surprised. They'd only been in San Francisco for a day.

"Remember the two men who met our little boat?" Mara's dark eyes held a hint of pleasure. When Shiloh nodded, Mara continued. "Samuel, he's the one who carried me. Joseph, he's the other. They both work in hotels downtown. Like all colored folks, they hear things."

"They've been here?" Shiloh asked, her eyes widening in surprise. "After the way you treated them?"

"I knew they'd come around. They talked, I listened, and

that's how I learned that this man they call the Dutchman challenged your husband to a duel."

"Why?"

"Samuel and Joseph didn't know."

Shiloh shook her head. "I can't believe Aldar fought a duel!"

"He had no choice. Since your husband was challenged, he had his choice of weapons. He chose pistols. They met down the peninsula at dawn. Seems like Kroeber got a bit hasty. His shot missed, and that was the only one he had. Your husband then had plenty of time. He raised the pistol real slow, and sighted carefully. The Dutchman—he's really from Germany—just stood there, looking straight at your husband."

"What happened?"

"Samuel told me that folks say your husband turned the pistol to one side and fired into the ground. Then he walked away."

"Oh, thank God!"

"Samuel says the talk is this other man was mighty humiliated. Seems like some kind of code in his country made your husband's saving shot an insult."

Shiloh felt the blood drain from her face. "You mean, Aldar's still in danger?"

"Maybe that's why Mr. Patton gave your husband that pistol."

Shiloh wasn't sure how she got through the rest of the afternoon. Her thoughts thrashed wildly about as she waited for Aldar to return home.

She heard the mules just before dusk and ran out to meet her husband. While Clay turned the team around, Aldar smiled and greeted Shiloh in his usual cheerful manner, as though nothing had happened.

Shiloh's anxiety erupted. "I heard you arguing with Philander today," she began. "He mentioned a couple of names I don't remember, then someone named Kroeber. Who are they?"

Aldar paused in the doorway to their room and looked thoughtfully down at her. Evening shadows touched his handsome face, softening the wavy blond hair and clear blue eyes.

"It doesn't matter," he assured her. "I'll take care of things."

"You always say that, but it does matter!" She clutched his arm. "Can't you see I'm frightened for you—for us?"

"Look, Shiloh, any man's going to have a certain amount of problems involving his work. But I can handle them, just as I told you before, so stop worrying."

"You mean you're not going to tell me after you promised?" When he hesitated, she exclaimed, "I'm your wife! Please don't leave me out like this!"

His cheery countenance slowly dissolved into a somber, brooding look Shiloh had never seen before.

"I think I'll take a little walk," he said brusquely, and turned abruptly away.

"No, wait!" she called, but Aldar didn't stop. His long legs carried him into the settling fog. Shiloh stared after him, feeling hurt, shut out, alone, and afraid.

CHAPTER IV

MARA LISTENED in silence as Shiloh tried to sort out her jumbled feelings.

"Am I making too much of this, Mara? Papa never discussed business with Mama, and certainly never with us. But before we were married, Aldar told me about all his hopes and plans for the future, so I thought it would be different with us.

"I'm frightened. Everything here is so strange! At home I felt safe and protected. I thought I'd always feel that way with

Aldar, but when he shuts me out, I feel so alone! Except for you. And it really upsets me when you and Aldar don't get along."

Mara answered bluntly. "I don't care for your husband, and he obviously doesn't care for me. I suppose that's to be expected, because he wants you all to himself, and you and I have always been as close as sisters.

"But," Mara continued, "I think I understand him too. He feels that I'm coming between you two. I don't want that any more than he does."

"I'm sure he understands our friendship."

"I doubt it, but that doesn't matter. I have plans for myself here in California, and I'm going to make them happen. That means sooner or later, you'll go your way and I'll go mine."

"You can't!" Shiloh impulsively reached across the table and grasped Mara's hands. "I need you!"

"No, what you need is to quit being so naive. All your life you've let others tell you what to do, to make decisions for you. That includes your parents, your husband, even me."

"I don't like to cause trouble."

"I know, but sometimes trouble just happens. You're stronger than you think, Shiloh. You chose to marry Aldar in spite of what your folks said. When Aldar said he had to get back to California fast, you went with him on the Panama crossing because it's the fastest route."

Shiloh sighed. "It took courage I didn't know I had to leave home and come to San Francisco. It's like another world. But I felt so secure because Aldar would always be there for me. When he shuts me out, I guess I panic a little."

"What're you going to do about it?"

"What do you think I should do?"

Mara smiled ruefully. "Has anything I've said meant anything to you? If I make the decisions, when will you ever learn to make your own?"

Shiloh protested, "When I was little, Mama and Papa

whacked me if I spoke up, especially Papa. I learned it's better just to keep my thoughts to myself."

"They never laid a hand on me, you know."

Shiloh nodded. Shiloh secretly thought her adoptive parents were a little afraid of Mara.

"Don't get off the point," Mara said. "Are you going to make a decision about Aldar keeping things from you?"

Shiloh sat in thoughtful silence before nodding. "I'll talk to him right after he gets back."

When Aldar walked in out of the evening fog, he was his usual cheerful self. "About ready for dinner?" he asked as though nothing had happened.

Shiloh ignored the tightness in her chest and struggled to keep her resolve. "No," she said firmly. "I'm not hungry. But we need to talk; I expect you to keep your promises. Tell me about the duel and those other men I overheard you and Philander arguing about."

"It was just business, and I wanted to keep you from worrying unnecessarily."

"I worry anyway. Besides, I don't want us to start our married life by keeping things from each other."

"I'm not keeping things from you."

"Then how come you never mentioned a duel?"

"No need. I grew up believing that some things were a man's responsibilities. I don't want to put unnecessary burdens on you."

"You're putting a greater burden on me by keeping silent about something that affects us both!" Startled at her own blunt retort, she hesitated, almost ready to apologize, but she was frightened and a little desperate. "I must know," she added quietly.

"I tell you it's not important." He reached both arms toward her, but she drew back. She looked into his handsome face and wanted to run into his arms. Still, she held her ground. "Please don't touch me until you tell me what I must know."

He slowly nodded. "I love you, Shiloh," he answered softly. "And you're right; I did promise. Walk with me and I'll tell you."

They bundled up against the cold damp fog. He took her hand and led her through the pale moonlight toward the eastern shore.

"I sometimes walk this way to work," he said. "It takes me across the sand dunes to the shore close to the office. There's a big rock at the water's edge where I sometimes sit to think. I call it my Dream Rock."

Shiloh resisted an impulse to remind him of his promise. "It's pretty around here," she observed, "but sort of remote. There's not a tent or shack in sight."

"That's why I like it. I can think through things undisturbed."

They crossed the last sand dune and came to the water's edge. He released her hand and pointed to a huge wave-carved boulder with surf lapping around its base.

"There it is. I usually climb up on top, but it might be a little risky for you in this poor light."

He swept his arms in both directions, the left toward San Francisco's faint lights from thousands of candles and campfires, the right hand toward the dark open bay with a shimmery path splashed across its surface by the quarter moon.

"Sometimes I think it's even prettier at night than it is in the daylight," he commented.

She let her gaze follow his hands. The last faint reddish-gold glow of the western sky silhouetted San Francisco's hills. An immense fog bank, resembling a cloud, rolled in across the sand dunes, now hidden in the moonlit shadows. The fragrance of evening cooking fires drifted along with the silent fog.

It is beautiful, Shiloh silently conceded, *but that isn't why we came here.*

He took both her hands in his. "Want to know what I dreamed about the last time I was on that rock?"

Aldar, the dreamer. Her adoptive father's words came to mind. But she loved Aldar's dreams, as she loved him. "Yes, very much," she assured him. "But I've about used up my patience waiting to hear about the duel!"

"Ah, yes! The duel." Aldar pulled her gently into his arms. Looking down into her eyes, he began. "It was a stupid thing that shouldn't have happened, but it did. About eighteen months ago I was in a restaurant having dinner. Kroeber and a woman of doubtful character were a few tables away.

"He had been drinking heavily, so when the woman kept trying to get my attention, he lost his temper. She got up from their table and came over to talk to me. Kroeber grabbed her and jerked her around. I protested his treatment of her and he slapped me. He had such a heavy accent I could barely understand him, but he challenged me to a duel."

"You didn't have to accept!"

"I figured that when he was sober, he'd forget it, but he didn't. He sent his second to arrange matters. You see, around here, there's a code of honor among some men with whom I do business. If I hadn't met Kroeber, I would have been thought a coward, and my business would have suffered."

"So for this 'honor' you would have died!" Her voice carried disbelief and anger.

Aldar's tone took on a hard edge. "Since I had the choice of weapons, I chose pistols because I'd had a little experience with them in the war. But if it hadn't been for Clay, I might have been killed."

"Clay?"

"He taught me how to handle a pistol. He's very good with one. He acted as my second. Dueling pistols only have one shot, so Clay taught me to stay calm and take my time. That saved my life."

"Thank God for that." Shiloh raised herself on tiptoes and lightly kissed him. "I know about how Kroeber shot too soon, and you fired into the ground."

Surprised, Aldar asked, "How do you know that?"

"Mara heard about it. What if he comes after you?"

"Kroeber's a hotheaded Dutchman, but I don't think he'll risk another duel."

"What's to keep him from just shooting you in the back?"

"Honor, my dear. He'd be run out of town on a rail for cowardice if he did anything like that." Aldar gently pushed her back and held her at arm's length. "You wanted to know about the duel. I told you. It's over and done with, so forget it."

"I'll try. But who were those other men Philander mentioned?"

"Gladwin and Locke? They wanted me to join them in their ventures, but they're not what I want for my future—our future, I mean—so I turned them down. Oh, we'll still do business together, or will when I've had a chance to resell them on using MacAdams and Laird Express again."

Shiloh felt relief. Aldar had put her mind at ease. She prompted, "Let's talk about our dreams."

"Our dreams," he said, lowering his voice. He held her close and whispered huskily, "Right now I have a special dream of my own. You are the most exciting woman I've ever known. Let's go home."

His meaning warmed her. She said teasingly, "I thought you wanted to go have dinner."

He nuzzled her ear, his breath hot against her neck. "That can wait."

"You give me little shivers," she whispered.

He kissed her hard, hungrily. He took her hand again and they hurried across the sand dunes toward home.

Neither of them saw the shadow of a man and his jackass standing off to the side, watching as they passed.

In the afterglow of their lovemaking, Shiloh felt warm and secure. She snuggled against Aldar, her head on his shoulder, looking up at the ceiling where the single candle on the nightstand made a hole in the darkness.

He did not sleep, but lightly played with a strand of her red-gold hair. "You hungry?" he asked.

"Not now. Tell me again about when you came here."

He sat up in bed, making the straw ticking complain as he propped his head against the pillow and resettled her head on his shoulder. "When I first got out of the army after the war, I came to San Francisco because I'd heard so much about it. I immediately fell in love with it. I especially loved the hills, and one in particular."

"Fern Hill?"

"Uh-huh. Terrible name for a magnificent hill like that. Someday I hope they rename it something more noble. Anyway, right away, I wanted to build a great house and live there. But not alone. I figured that someday I'd meet the right woman, and she'd share that home with me."

He paused to kiss her forehead. "Now that I've done that, the next thing is to make the other part of my dream come true."

"The stagecoaches?" she guessed.

"Most of the express companies in California began as Philander and I did, a man on a mule delivering packages and goods from one place to another. Served everybody from the individual miner to the biggest merchants, with the most money being earned from them, of course. Then came the wagons because they could hold more than a man could carry on a mule.

"But stagecoaches are next. They'll not only carry passengers and mail and newspapers, but they'll become the banks.

They'll carry gold and other valuables. Stage lines will branch all over California—especially if it becomes a state—tying the most remote mountain, valley, or coastal community to Sacramento and San Francisco and even Los Angeles. Of course, that little pueblo isn't much of a place right now. Stagecoaches and roads, shipping, and even trains will change all that."

Shiloh had heard the dream before, but she snuggled closer to him, her hand resting on the few golden curls of chest hair as he told it again.

"When I finally talked Philander into letting me go east—at my own expense—to try getting some federal government subsidy for carrying the mail to and from San Francisco, I stopped in Massachusetts where I'd heard about some new coaches called Concords."

Shiloh closed her eyes to better visualize the vehicles Aldar described.

"I've never seen anything so beautiful. They're high and proud, painted in bright red with gold trim and fancy decorations. They're big! There's room enough for fourteen passengers. Six ride inside with a swinging seat in the middle, like a hammock. Eight more passengers can ride on top with the baggage."

"A man would have to be pretty desperate to ride up there in the rain and wind and dust," Shiloh commented.

"There would be so many people waiting to ride that they wouldn't care. But you know, the most remarkable part of the Concords is their suspension system. Leather straps called thorough-braces cradle the coach so it rocks instead of bouncing along like bone-jarring mud wagons do. In a Concord, travel is real comfortable."

"And the horses?" Shiloh prompted when her husband fell momentarily silent.

"Not eastern horses," he replied firmly. "They're not tough enough for California, which is so big and spread out. Instead, we'll have wild mustangs captured and trained, six to a team.

They're wiry and smaller than eastern horses, but they have the heart and the lungs to outlast other animals. That's from all those years living wild and free on the open ranges, you know. Oh, I tell you, Shiloh, those mustangs will go where most horses wouldn't dare, and they'll pull those glorious Concord stages so that even Queen Victoria herself would be envious!

"We'll have relay stations every ten miles or so, with hostlers to change teams fast. There'll be hay and water for the mustangs, and rest stops for the people. I tell you, Shiloh, it's going to be something people won't ever forget."

"I'm sure they won't," she murmured, content in his embrace.

"From stages," Aldar continued, "we'll expand into paddle wheelers for the big rivers, like the Sacramento and the San Joaquin. We could possibly have coastal freighters and even oceangoing steamers that'll round the Horn. We'll take California's gold back east and bring more people here to live. Eventually, we'll run trains between major California cities. Everywhere our MacAdams and Laird transportation systems go, people will go too. They'll fill in the valleys, the mountains, and the coast, connecting everything by transportation."

Shiloh sighed in response to the delightfully vast scope of her husband's ambitions.

"Someday," he added wistfully, "we might even think about a transcontinental railroad system."

Shiloh had heard that before, but she was still unable to imagine such a thing. There were some two thousand miles of wilderness stretching between the Mississippi and the Sacramento Rivers. Still, it was an exciting thought.

"It's a beautiful dream," she whispered, nuzzling his chin.

"Of course," Aldar said, squirming slightly, "I've still got to convince Philander that all of this is possible. He doesn't see much beyond the dollar earned today."

"You'll make it happen," Shiloh assured him.

"No, *we'll* make it happen," he corrected her. He turned

and kissed her lightly on the mouth. He raised up slightly and observed, "But that's not going to happen tonight." His voice dropped, becoming low and husky with renewed desire. "Tonight we can talk about our more personal dreams. Like which do we want first, a boy or a girl?"

He kissed her ardently, and she responded. *A boy,* she thought as his lips continued to claim hers. *A boy, all blond and golden like you. Then I'll have two to love. He'll grow up and we'll all three ride all over California on transportation his father built from his dreams.*

She awakened at dawn to the sounds of angry but hushed voices of her husband and Mara outside the bedroom door. Shiloh threw back the covers and slid off the high bed onto the floor. Barefooted, she hurried to the front door. She opened it in time to see Mara hurrying away and Aldar, fully dressed for work, glaring after her.

"What was that all about?" Shiloh asked, motioning for her husband.

"When I started to leave for work, I caught her standing outside, eavesdropping."

"There'd be no reason for her to do such a thing."

"I don't know why she did, but I'm sure that's what she was doing. She got angry when I challenged her, and went storming off."

"I think there's been a misunderstanding . . . "

"No, there hasn't!" His tone was unusually sharp. "I've told you before, I have an uneasy feeling about Mara. I wish she hadn't come with us."

"I'll talk to her, but I'm sure . . . "

"You defending her?" he interrupted.

She was startled. This man who stood before her was not the same one who had shared dreams with her last night. "No," she protested. "I'm just saying that . . . "

"Oh, forget it. If you can get ready before Clay gets here, I'll take you to breakfast at the hotel."

Not wanting Aldar to leave while there was a lingering sense of tension between them, Shiloh dressed hurriedly. She fretted silently over the strained relationship between Aldar and Mara. Shiloh was sure that was what had made him speak sharply to her.

It was crucial that the two most important people in Shiloh's life get along, but on the long trip to California, Shiloh had seen the situation slowly getting worse. This morning, the tension seemed to be building toward a breaking point.

I've got to head that off, she told herself just as she heard Clay's team stop outside.

Shiloh left the bedroom and hurried into the parlor. As she entered, she saw Aldar pick up the revolver Clay had given him.

"Why are you taking that?" she asked.

He shoved the weapon into his waistband and covered it with his coat. "There's no sense in leaving it here. You can't shoot."

"I'm a farm girl," she reminded him. "I *can* shoot!"

"Rifles and shotguns, yes," he agreed, opening the door. "But did you ever fire a pistol?"

"No, and I don't plan to," she said, heading toward the waiting wagon. "And I hope you never have to fire another one."

There was no opportunity to talk privately on the short ride downtown to where Clay tied the team in front of a board-and-canvas structure. It carried a rough, hand-painted sign intended to offset its uncertain function: *New York Hotel.*

Shiloh laughed, aware that the structure was nothing more than rough-cut framing timbers over which an ancient piece of canvas had been stretched. She guessed the canvas had once been used as sails from one of the abandoned ships in the harbor.

"Don't laugh," Aldar said with an understanding smile. "Clay tells me this is one of the few places in all of San Francisco where the flapjacks are almost fit to eat."

"They should hire Mara," Shiloh commented, picking her way across the plank walk where sand crunched under her shoes. She caught the sound of raucous men's voices, and braced herself for being stared at again. "She's the best cook I've ever known."

He started to reach for the door, then stopped. "Why didn't I think of that? I'll tell the owner."

"Clay," he continued, "do you know who owns this place?"

The black-bearded driver nodded and followed Shiloh and Aldar through the door. "Denby Gladwin does. His second one. Just built it."

Gladwin? Shiloh's interest rose upon recognizing one of the names she had overheard Philander MacAdams mention yesterday to her husband. Aldar had lost the Gladwin account because Gladwin favored a separate nation, and Aldar told him California should be a state.

Aldar told Clay, "If he's in, I may have a chance to win his account back. If I get tied up, please see that Shiloh gets home after breakfast."

They entered the crude structure. The dining area was full of men who immediately fell silent. Even though Shiloh had guessed what to expect, she was still extremely uncomfortable as everyone looked at her.

"Please, Aldar," she said under her breath, "isn't there a private room?"

He turned to Clay, who nodded and pushed his way through the crowd, leading the way toward the back. The men at the rough-hewn tables tried to be polite and look away, but Shiloh felt her face grow warm as the men stole glances at her as she passed.

Shiloh was sandwiched between Clay and Aldar as they neared the far wall. There really was no separate room, just a table where canvas-and-board frames met to form a corner. The strange, respectful, but disturbing silence followed the trio as they reached the table.

Shiloh glanced up to see a stout man with a dead stub of a cigar in his mouth push through a side door near the far corner table. "Aldar!" he cried, whipping the cigar out of his mouth with his left hand and extending his right. "Glad you're back!"

"Thanks." Aldar shook hands, then introduced Shiloh. "Denby, this is my wife—well, bride, actually. Shiloh Laird, lately of Pennsylvania."

Gladwin bowed grandly. "Lady, I haven't seen the likes of you in more months than I can tell, but you're sure welcome. I own this place, such as it is. Anything you want is on the house."

Flustered, Shiloh didn't answer. She shot an appealing glance at her husband, who promptly asked, "Denby, you remember Clay Patton, don't you?"

"Sure do." For the first time, the man with the bulging middle and bare hairy black forearms took his eyes off of Shiloh. His gray eyes swept over Clay. They shook hands briefly, then Gladwin turned back to Aldar. "Well, I'll be double blasted! Aldar, you sure got yourself a mighty pretty woman here."

Shiloh was embarrassed at being discussed like a prize animal. At the same time, she was intrigued by the sense of power that seemed to exude in a silent wave from Gladwin. He turned toward the gawking male patrons.

"Get back to your breakfasts," he yelled. They obeyed, and Gladwin seated the three late arrivals. Without invitation, he pulled up a fourth chair and made it groan as he lowered his considerable bulk into it.

"Missus," he asked, dominating the conservation without apparent concern, "how'd this yellow-haired dreamer ever find the likes of you?"

Gladwin didn't wait for a reply. "Great move, Aldar!" he cried jovially, slapping him heartily on the shoulder. "If there's one thing that will give a man an edge in California politics, it's having a wife! And a pretty one too!"

Shiloh cast a bewildered look at her husband.

"Look, Denby," Aldar explained, "Shiloh and I haven't talked about . . . "

"You've never told her?" he broke in.

"No need to." Aldar's voice was calm and self-assured again. "I've told you that I don't believe California should ever be a separate nation. I haven't changed my mind."

"Aldar, you're pig-headed!" Gladwin's voice had lost its friendliness. "You're . . . beggin' your pardon, Mrs. Laird. There hasn't been a decent woman in this town for so long all us men have forgot how to talk proper." Gladwin turned to Aldar. "I had no call to speak like that. I'm downright sorry. It's my temper, you know."

"I know," Aldar said with a smile that looked forced. "That's what cost me your account with our express company."

"You can have it back." Gladwin's hearty friendliness returned to his voice. "And I'll guarantee you some other big ones too." His chair scraped as he pushed it back and stood. "Come back later and we'll work things out, Aldar."

Gladwin reached out and took Shiloh's right hand. He bent and lightly kissed the back of her fingers. "You're going to see and do things you never dreamed about back in Pennsylvania, Mrs. Laird."

He turned to leave, then swung back to face Aldar. "Remember what I told you months ago? This world belongs to those who know what they want, and are willing to reach out and take it. Think about it."

They ate hurriedly, with Shiloh barely tasting the only breakfast item. "Flapjacks," Aldar explained, "are about all that California men can make. They're usually undercooked, like these."

When they were back outside on the street, Clay said something about checking on the team's harness. As he hurried away, Shiloh lowered her voice to Aldar.

"What were you and Mr. Gladwin talking about?" she asked with some agitation.

"He believes California should be an independent country, and he's going to do all he can to see that happen. He wants power. Well, money and power. That's what a lot of people in California want, and they're willing to do whatever is necessary to get it."

Such ambitions had never entered Shiloh's mind. She frowned as the sharp breeze sent fine particles of sand stinging against her cheeks. "But why?"

"Because California is one of the richest prizes imaginable, just waiting to be picked, like a golden apple. Some men want it to be a state, but nobody can decide if it should be free or slave. Only a few, like Gladwin, want it to be a separate nation."

"Is he really serious about that?"

"Very serious, and so are his followers," Aldar replied as Clay started the wagon moving. "He told me that if California becomes a separate country, with the power its gold will bring, everybody involved can be rich beyond imagination."

"But what's that got to do with you?"

"He's got some crazy notion that I could be the front man, with him controlling from behind the scenes."

Shiloh almost laughed, then she checked herself. "Are you serious?"

"He is. Says I've got what it takes to get the people behind the separate-nation idea. But I not only don't agree with him, I think it's crazy."

Aldar paused, then continued. "As you heard, he also has a temper." Aldar shook his head. "I don't like the man personally, but I need his business. So I'll listen to him rave about his ideas, although I want no part of them."

Clay and Mara seated themselves in the wagon and Clay clucked to the team. He turned from his seat in front. "Steamer's in."

Shiloh, glancing ahead, saw only another sandy hill. "How does he know that?" she asked her husband.

He pointed. "The semaphore on Signal Hill. The way the arms are placed shows when a ship's in the bay, and what kind it is. You ever see a steamship, Shiloh?"

"Just sailing vessels."

"Clay," Aldar instructed, "drive down so we can take a closer look."

As they drew close, Shiloh saw that the passengers were already ashore. A tidal surge of men headed that way, reminding Shiloh of when she and Mara had come ashore.

"Must be more women," Clay commented.

As they drew closer, a bearded young miner in high boots and blue shirt ran up the street, kicking up sand with his speed, waving his hat and shouting.

"What's he saying?" Shiloh asked.

Aldar cocked his head to listen, then shook his head. "Clay, can you make it out?"

He turned to look down from his high seat. "He says there's women ashore, and one of them is Jessie Fremont."

Shiloh's interest perked up. "Mrs. John C. Fremont?"

Clay nodded. "Yes ma'am."

"I wonder what brought her here?" Shiloh mused.

"I don't know, unless her husband's court-martial is over and he's back in California. I'll bet that's it, and she's probably planning to meet him. If he's here, that means more politics." Aldar raised his voice, "Clay, drive down there so we can introduce ourselves and give Shiloh and Mrs. Fremont a chance to get acquainted."

Shiloh peered ahead, anxious to see another woman, especially the wife of the famous explorer and soldier.

As Clay reined in the mules on shore, wisps of smoke still trailed from the steamer *Panama* now anchored in Yerba Buena Cove. Shiloh studied the small boats being rowed from the ship to the surf. Where she had been carried ashore a few days before, now only eager would-be miners splashed through the surf in their high boots. Shiloh saw no sign of Mrs. Fremont or any other women until Aldar nudged her arm.

"There," he said, indicating a cluster of hotel runners. "She's already ashore."

Shiloh saw her then. Jessie Benton Fremont stood on the barrel-stave sidewalk with her six-year-old daughter, two other women, and three men.

"She looks terribly thin!" Shiloh exclaimed.

"Probably been sick, as you were," Aldar replied.

Clay commented, "I heard the steamer picks up passengers at Panama, so Mrs. Fremont must have crossed from the Atlantic side, as you did."

Instantly, Shiloh knew what Mrs. Fremont and her daughter had been through. Shiloh remembered with a shudder how she, Aldar, and Mara had crossed the Isthmus of Panama by dugout canoe and muleback. The memories of the jungle, the mosquitoes, the fevers, and other dangers flooded through Shiloh.

Impulsively, Shiloh suggested, "Let's offer her a ride to her hotel."

"She probably already has somebody coming for her."

"It won't hurt to ask. She looks so weak that she shouldn't have to stand out here in this cold, damp air a moment longer. Please, Aldar?"

"I'll extend your invitation."

As Aldar strode purposefully away, Shiloh turned to Clay. "It's so good to see another woman my age! I do hope Mrs. Fremont and I can be friends." She paused, then added thoughtfully, "She must have come here to meet her husband. But he isn't in San Francisco, is he?"

"Not to my knowledge. But he must have received a presidential pardon on court-martial charges back east. Otherwise, he couldn't return to California, and the only logical reason his wife would be here is to meet him. There's a military garrison at Monterey, so that's probably where he'll be."

"And she'll join him there." Shiloh sighed, then added hopefully, "Maybe we'll get an opportunity to know each other before she has to leave."

From her elevated position in the wagon, Shiloh studied Jessie Fremont and remembered the stories about her. When she was seventeen, she had defied her father, the powerful Senator Thomas Hart Benton of Missouri, and eloped with the famous explorer, John Charles Fremont. Now, eight years later, with her young daughter, Jessie had arrived in California. Shiloh thought Jessie Fremont's life must be filled with excitement!

Aldar hurried back with a report. "Mrs. Fremont sends her thanks and regrets, but she already has a ride. However, she would like to meet you."

Flustered and flattered, Shiloh took her husband's arm. Clay ground-hitched the team and followed.

Up close, Shiloh was shocked to see how much Mrs. Fremont's oval face and tired brown eyes reflected the hardships and illness she had experienced on her trip from New York to San Francisco. Her dark hair parted in the middle and swept back over her ears so only the tip of the lobes showed. Her body was so frail that it seemed the morning breeze might blow her into the bay.

Aldar made the introduction. Shiloh said formally, "How do you do?"

Mrs. Fremont replied in kind, then presented the other women, Mrs. Robert Allen and Mrs. Alfred DeWitt. Shiloh had assumed they were married couples, but when Aldar introduced the men, she realized her error.

"Shiloh," he said, "this is Thomas Butler King, personal representative of our new president, Zachary Taylor."

As they acknowledged each other, Aldar presented William Gwin, a tall, silver-haired man whose age Shiloh guessed was in the middle forties.

The last man introduced was Joseph Hooker, who had a military bearing and looked to be about thirty-five.

Shiloh realized that in the moments Aldar had been gone, he had not only met Mrs. Fremont and the other two women, but all three men, and remembered them enough to make smooth introductions.

Shiloh said to the women, "I believe all of you crossed the Isthmus of Panama on this trip?"

When they nodded, Shiloh exclaimed, "So did we! I daresay we would have many experiences to share. Aldar and I would be honored if all of you would accept an invitation to tea at our home soon."

"Thank you," Mrs. Fremont replied. "Speaking for myself, I'm grateful, but I'm on my way to Monterey to meet my husband."

Shiloh was disappointed but understanding as each of the new arrivals made excuses. After further brief comments, Shiloh, Aldar, and Clay said their goodbyes and headed back to the wagon.

Aldar asked, "Clay, do you recognize those names?"

"Not the women, but King is a former Georgia congressman and friend of our new president. King's coming here probably means that he's going to push for California to become a state instead of a territory."

Shiloh was again surprised that Clay, who drove a team of mules, knew so much about politics.

"What about Hooker?" Aldar asked.

"I don't know, but I'd say he's military."

"And Gwin? What do you know about him?"

"He's from Missouri," Clay answered. "He made a lot of money in the war with Mexico."

"War profiteer," Aldar said with a touch of distaste. "I heard a lot about him when I was in Washington."

Shiloh commented, "He reminds me of Andrew Jackson."

Aldar replied, "Gwin used to be under Jackson's patronage. Gwin's background is both law and medicine. He never practiced medicine although I've heard he likes to be called 'Doctor.'" Aldar turned to Clay, "Why do you think he's come here?"

"Same as lots of other men, I suspect. To run for office, as he did back east."

"He wasn't very successful there," Aldar added. "Served only one term in the House of Representatives."

"Maybe he figures he'll have more chance out here," Clay replied laconically. "Especially since the Democrats got whipped last year."

Aldar replied, "When I was in Washington a few months ago, I heard that Gwin told Senator Stephen Douglas that because Congress had not set up a government for California, we should act on our own."

"Makes sense," Clay agreed. "Gwin will probably push for statehood and maybe get himself elected as senator. But I wouldn't be surprised if Fremont doesn't give him a race for his money."

Shiloh looked thoughtfully at her husband and Clay, wondering what they knew that she didn't.

CHAPTER V

SHILOH SPOKE freely to Aldar now that they were alone. "I'm surprised that you and Clay know so much about politics."

Aldar bent to build up the flames in the parlor fireplace. "Every thinking man in California knows that everything that happens to us here depends on politics."

"But you never mentioned the subject when we were courting, or on the trip out here."

"Men talk politics; women don't."

"I know." She watched as the flames began to blaze and crackle in the fireplace. "By the way, have you found a place were we can worship tomorrow?"

Aldar stood and turned to face Shiloh. "The closest one is a gambling tent and saloon which closes for an hour for church services. It's so different it might give you something to write about to the family back east."

Shiloh considered the uniqueness of the idea.

Aldar continued, "I don't know who the preacher is, but he must be some kind of powerful person to persuade a saloon keeper to lose money so his place can be used to preach the gospel for an hour on a busy Sunday morning."

The idea was too intriguing for Shiloh to pass up. The next morning, Shiloh selected a demure dress of royal blue plaid from the trunk containing the trousseau of gowns, dresses, and frilly undergarments she and Mara had made when the identity of her future husband was still a mystery. Mara's delicate handiwork was in demand by all who saw it, as was her sense of style. Shiloh watched the contents of the trunk grow until lace, bows, and colorful bits of fabric spilled from its drawers. Shiloh was certain the Edgeworths had invested in the trousseau's materials, believing they were preparing Shiloh to become the wife of sensible Seth Collins. Today it was Aldar that she accompanied across the sand dunes to attend Sunday services in a canvas make-do "church." Shiloh was secretly glad that Mara chose not to go. There was the possibility that Mara would not be welcome in a white church, and there had been a strained silence between Aldar and Mara ever since their argument.

Aldar pointed out a hand-painted sign, *The Nugget Saloon.* It had been temporarily removed from over the door and now leaned against the side of the canvas-over-frame structure. A smaller sign over the tent door proclaimed, *Lord's Day Services. All Welcome.*

The tent resembled the New York Hotel, but on a much smaller scale. Shiloh was gratified to see that perhaps fifty miners in clean shirts and with the sand knocked off their boots were flowing toward the "church," as she suspected they had done earlier to the saloon.

Wrinkling her nose at the stale smell of spirits and tobacco as they approached the open tent flaps, Shiloh began to wish she hadn't come.

"Aldar!" A man's voice calling her husband caused Shiloh to turn around. A well-built man in military uniform pushed through the crowd. "I heard you were back."

Aldar steered Shiloh aside to where he could shake hands with the man. He was just under six feet tall with riveting blue eyes and a strong chin. He stood very erect in a stiff, formal way. Shiloh guessed he was about thirty.

Aldar said, "Shiloh, may I present William Rawlins, commandant of the Presidio here? Will, my wife, Shiloh."

They exchanged formal greetings, then Shiloh quickly lowered her eyes. She thought, *He's got a bold gaze, looking at me that way, and right in front of my husband too.*

Aldar steered Rawlins' attention away from Shiloh, asking what had been going on since he was away. Rawlins replied politely, but Shiloh saw him stealing quick glances at her.

"Mr. Rawlins, do you know the pastor?" she asked to hide her discomfort.

"Name's John Sledger. Frankly, I came because I heard he's not your usual Sunday preacher. They say he used to be a wild man back east, drinking and fighting. Naturally, I'm curious about what such a man will preach about."

Shiloh nodded. "Me too," she murmured, but inwardly she

wished for someone more conservative, like the combination farmer and preacher back in Pennsylvania.

Aldar took her hand and entered the tent. Rawlins fell into step beside Shiloh, sandwiching her between the two men.

To Shiloh's dismay, there were no chairs on the dirt floor. Shuffling boots raised a fine, powdery dust that tickled Shiloh's nose and made her want to sneeze.

The altar consisted of a rough-hewn plank laid between two large whiskey barrels turned upside down. Behind this, a pulpit had been made of a brandy keg placed on what had been the liquor bar. All signs of spirits had been discreetly removed from sight, but the sickening smell was everywhere.

The only woman in a roomful of bearded men, mostly under thirty, Shiloh was acutely aware of the eyes that kept flickering to her. Yet each time she made momentary eye contact with anyone, that person nodded politely and with obvious respect.

John Sledger entered through a side tent flap. He was a great bear of a man with massive chest and powerful arms that threatened to burst through his too-small dress coat. He carried his three hundred pounds on a six-foot, six-inch frame. He strode quickly to stand behind the pulpit.

"In the name of our Lord," he began with a voice that reverberated like thunder, "you're welcome." He lifted great arms and swept them over the congregation. "May the Lord bless you all. I'm glad you came to worship together, 'though I got a feelin' most of you came because you wanted to know if it's true that I killed a man with these." He held out immense hands and waited for the dramatic affect.

Shiloh leaned a little closer to her husband, now firmly convinced that she should not have come to hear a preacher who was totally unlike any she had ever seen before.

"Well," the Reverend Sledger continued when the silence was complete, "it's true. So after you stand through the singing and reading of the Lord's Word, in my sermon I'll tell you how it happened, and why I'm here today. Now, since we have no hymnals, I hope all of you can recall the words to . . . "

His sentence trailed off when he caught sight of Shiloh.

She unconsciously tried to step behind Aldar, but it was useless.

"Glory be!" the giant thundered, staring in open-mouthed amazement. "Is that a blessed angel standing there or a real live woman?"

Shiloh squirmed in great embarrassment as every eye turned toward her. She had come to worship, not to be the center of attention.

Aldar cleared his throat and raised his voice. "She's wonderful as an angel, but she's a very live woman. She's my bride, Shiloh Laird."

"Welcome, Missus!" Sledger stepped from behind his makeshift pulpit and pushed through the crowd of men. They parted before his bulk until he stopped in front of Shiloh, Aldar, and Rawlins.

"Shiloh? Is that your name?" His voice had settled down to a deep bass that was not much louder than a cat's purr.

She finally managed to speak through her embarrassment. "My Christian name is Rachel Ann, but everybody calls me Shiloh."

"Shiloh! A prophetic name for this city!" Sledger's voice lifted again. He swept the crowd with his sharp blue eyes that seemed to penetrate more than linger.

"In the Bible, you know," the preacher explained, "Shiloh was the place where Joshua brought the tribes of Israel. There, in the presence of God, lots were cast for where the Israelites were to be located in their new land. Later, Shiloh became the Ark's resting place until the Philistines took it."

The power of Sledger's voice surged through the tent. "Shiloh was a sign of God's presence back in that pagan land. It wouldn't surprise me none if this young woman bearing that name isn't a sign that He is again going to come among us in this most wicked city on earth." He paused, then added, "'Til Shiloh come.' That's in the Bible too."

Sledger turned back, moving through the packed crowd of men to his crude pulpit. "'Til Shiloh come,'" he repeated. "In our midst today stands a symbol of what it will take to make San Francisco and all of California civilized. Women!

"Whether we become a state or a territory or something else, California—especially San Francisco—will remain the devil's spawn until there is a flood of women like this pretty young one gracing us with her presence today."

His gaze settled on Shiloh, who had tried to make herself as small as possible. "Shiloh Laird, you are the hope and the future of this far-off land. God bless you for being a sign to us this morning."

Shiloh was greatly relieved when the singing began, followed by a Scripture reading, and then the sermon.

Sledger talked about the temptations men faced in nearly womanless California, and how it would be a better place with more women and their gentle, civilizing influence.

Shiloh was getting tired of standing, but forgot about that when the preacher took a long pause.

Finally he spoke, his voice barely audible. "But there are some women like Jezebel of old. It was over such a woman that these hands took a man's life."

Sledger held his huge hands so that everyone could see. "Before that, in the backwoods country where I plowed as straight a furrow as ever a man could do, I had a saintly mother, like some of you. Like you, I scorned her prayers and did what I knew was wrong. I had a temper, and I was quick to pull a cork from a jug, so I had many a fight. Never lost one.

"Then a young woman moved into our valley. Pretty as a day in spring, she was. Barely seventeen, she had a smile that could melt a winter pond. Eyes the color of a June sky, and laughter like a brook's song. Well, agin' my Mama's wishes, I started going with this woman.

"I wanted her, but there was also this young buck who wanted her. I thought she was mine until one night I followed her out behind the church house. She met some feller in the woods beyond the buggies and the wagons. I watched them kissin' for a spell, but when they laid a blanket on the ground, I went out of my mind.

"I rushed upon them, wanting to kill them both. But I reached for the feller, there in the darkness."

Sledger paused for a long moment, and Shiloh thought she saw tears in his strange blue eyes.

"There I took his life, with these." Sledger again held up his hands.

Nobody coughed or even shuffled so that the silence was complete until the preacher spoke again.

"He was my own brother."

Tears scalded the back of Shiloh's eyes and she was aware that men around her were whipping out handkerchiefs and noisily blowing their noses.

"The sheriff came, but I saw him coming, and I ran. Didn't stop for years. Fought me many another man, and emptied many a jug until one night, stinking of whiskey and sweat, I stumbled into a little country church.

"Through my drunken haze, I heard the preacher's voice, but I heard another voice inside me, still as the fog over these sand dunes. I sobered up, got right with the Lord, and headed for this place.

"Oh, I still got some powerful weaknesses, so I ain't never going to be no saint down here. But I'm here to help, and if there's a brother in this place that wants to get right with the Lord, I'll rassle the devil hisself to he'p git you free. Now, while we sing the invitational hymn, who wants to come to this mourner's bench so we can git started?"

After the service, Shiloh walked out between her husband and William Rawlins. Everyone seemed strangely moved in spite of the unorthodox preaching.

Shiloh glanced back to see some miners push their way through the crowd to fall on their knees with others. They knelt before the makeshift altar. *Strange how the Spirit works,* Shiloh mused.

John Sledger was outside the front tent flap to shake hands as others left. Shiloh wanted to speak to the preacher, but a short, balding man in a black suit started pushing through the crowd toward her.

Rawlins said under his breath, "Here comes Jefferson Locke."

The way he said that gave Shiloh a feeling that the two men were not good friends. When Rawlins added, "Excuse me, I see somebody I must speak to," Shiloh knew she was right.

Rawlins had moved away before Locke reached Shiloh and her husband. "Aldar Laird!" Locke exclaimed, showing crooked teeth in a broad smile. "I saw you in there with your lovely wife, and I had to meet her."

Aldar shook hands and presented Shiloh, adding, "He's strong on having California admitted to the Union."

"Mr. Locke," Shiloh said with a smile.

He turned to Aldar. "Have you changed your mind?"

Shiloh saw a flicker of annoyance pass across her husband's handsome face. Then he smiled and asked with forced cheerfulness, "Why don't I come by your place tomorrow and we'll talk? Now, if you'll excuse us, my wife would like to speak to the preacher."

Aldar took Shiloh's hand and guided her to the pastor. She wanted to ask Aldar what Locke meant, but Sledger spoke first.

"Sister Laird," he asked, "what could possibly make you look so concerned?" He gently took both her hands, dwarfing them in his.

"Nothing important, Brother Sledger," she replied, adding, "That was a stirring sermon."

He thanked her as other parishioners advanced behind her. Shiloh invited him to call, then left with Aldar.

On the walk home, Shiloh questioned Aldar. "What did Locke mean about changing your mind?"

"More than a year ago, he wanted me to give up the express business and work with him to get California admitted as a slave-holding state."

Shiloh stopped dead still and looked up at her husband. "You know how I feel about slavery! Surely you're not . . . "

"Of course not! But I'm in business, and I have to be careful what I say because I need Locke's account."

They walked on across the sand dunes. "In the short time we've been here," she said thoughtfully, "both Mr. Locke and Mr. Gladwin have talked to you about what's happening in California. I didn't think you had that much interest in the subject."

"My interest is in transportation, but I can't rule out the possibility of someday getting involved in politics. That's because it'll be necessary in my plans for expanding all over this state or territory, whichever it turns out to be."

"You mean you'd run for office?"

"I was thinking more of getting in the inner circles where I know everybody and everyone knows me. That way, when the business needs something, I'll know who's got the power to make it happen."

"What does Philander say about this?"

"He can't see beyond today, but I'm looking away down the road to five, ten, even twenty years from now. Whoever gets ahead in transportation is going to be rich. I intend to be one of them."

Aldar turned toward Fern Hill, rising steep and high above them. "Then I'll build you that fancy house up there so you can look out over San Francisco and all the rest of California."

They entered their home in companionable silence. Aldar said, "I made arrangements for Clay to bring a picnic lunch.

We can enjoy it on the beach, so would you watch for him while I change my clothes?"

Shiloh walked to the window facing the street. "Hmm," she said thoughtfully.

Aldar asked, "What do you see?"

"I almost never see anybody around here, but there's a man on a mule across the way. I thought he might have been watching our house, but I guess not. He's riding away."

"Forget him and come here." Aldar's voice had grown husky.

She approached where he stood with bare chest and hunger in his eyes.

He kissed her hard. Shiloh's doubts, fears, and concerns of the last few days slipped away before Aldar's ardor. Then she gently pushed him away.

"Not now. Clay will be here any minute."

Aldar groaned with mock despair.

"I'll be here afterward," she whispered, offering her lips again.

They were still clinging together when she heard the rattle of chains and creak of leather. "Clay's here," she said, pulling away. She straightened her clothes while Aldar went to the door.

Clay didn't stay. He handed Aldar a wicker basket of cold chicken, baked sweet potatoes, stewed prunes, and bread pudding. Shiloh noticed that Clay had the restaurant prepare one smaller portion neatly wrapped in a white cloth napkin. She picked it up and delivered it to Mara's quarters.

"Haven't seen you since this morning," Shiloh commented. "Are you all right?"

"I was visiting friends. I'm going back to meet them again this afternoon."

Shiloh nodded, thinking of Samuel and Joseph. "What happened earlier between you and Aldar?"

Mara shrugged, holding the food wrapped in the napkin

but showing no interest in it. "He accused me of spying, but I was just listening outside the door to see if you were awake before I knocked."

Shiloh was relieved. "Is that all?"

"Apparently it's enough for your husband where I'm concerned."

"I don't think that's true! Anyway, you're the two most important people in the world to me. I wish you would get along." When Mara didn't reply, Shiloh asked, "Why do you always refer to him as 'my husband,' and never by his name?"

Again, Mara didn't answer. Shiloh sensed it was time to end the conversation. She announced that she and Aldar were going picnicking while Mara visited her friends.

But when she stepped outside Mara's room, Shiloh saw that the fog was gathering at the bottom of the hill for its silent assault on the community. The wind had kicked up, whirling grains of sand into her face.

So much for a picnic, she told herself, and reentered the house. She saw that the fireplace blazed high, and that Aldar had removed the basin and pitcher from the marble-topped stand and dragged it in front of the fireplace. He used the second napkin as a tablecloth, set the food on that, and dragged the two heavy chairs up close, facing the fireplace.

"Changing weather can't stop our picnic," he announced.

Shiloh was touched. "Oh, Aldar!" she exclaimed, moving toward him. "What a thoughtful thing to do!"

"Thanks. You think Mara's going to stay in her room?"

"She's going out with friends."

"That's good. Now we won't be disturbed." His voice took on a husky edge.

"But it's not night yet!" she protested.

"Who said it had to be night?" His words, and the hunger in his eyes made Shiloh grow warm with anticipation.

By the time they had eaten, the room had grown dark as the sky became totally overcast with fog. They pushed the stand back to its place under the gilded mirror. They replaced the basin and pitcher. Aldar lit two candles and set them on the mantle. Then he took the pistol from his coat pocket and gently laid it on the smooth white marble.

Why don't you get rid of that thing? Shiloh thought, but didn't want to spoil the mood by speaking her thoughts.

Then Aldar went to their bedroom and pulled the mattress off the bed. He dragged it into the parlor and placed it in front of the fireplace.

"I've always wanted to do that," he explained, kissing Shiloh after completing his task. He held her close.

After a few moments, they stretched out on the mattress and stared silently into the flames.

At length, Aldar broke the silence. "I love you," he said, rolling over and taking her into his arms.

"And I love you. For the first time, I feel that I really belong to someone."

"Me too, so let's celebrate." His voice was low and thick with desire as he pulled her up and against his body. "Let's celebrate the real beginning of our life together, and the promise of tomorrow."

Their lips met. She heard his sudden sharp intake of breath and felt him tremble.

He whispered huskily, "I've waited a long time for us to have time alone like this."

She nodded, remembering how difficult it had been to really have privacy since they were married. The wedding had been in her adoptive parents' farmhouse.

Her strict mother had spoken to Shiloh about "wifely Christian duty," so she had come to her husband with trepidation. Yet he had proved to be a patient, gentle lover, yielding with understanding to her tenseness in the unfavorable conditions of making love for the first time as husband and wife in the bedroom adjoining her parents' room.

Later, there had been even less privacy on the crowded

sailing ship plowing its way southward on the Atlantic. Of course, crossing the isthmus in native dugout canoes and on muleback had provided no privacy at all. There was little more on the Pacific as the *Terrapin* beat her unsteady way northward.

In the occasional times they had been able to make love, Aldar had awakened in her something that she had never expected. She longed to share more of this experience with the man she loved.

"I'll be right back, my darling," she whispered as dusk gently bathed the room in soft darkness.

"But . . . "

She laid a forefinger gently across his lips, silencing him. "I want this to be special, so I won't be long."

In the privacy of the closet she let down her hair and shook it loose across her bare shoulders. She changed into a special white nightgown that she had secretly made the week before their wedding, but Aldar had never seen.

When she returned, she saw he had blown out the candles so the room was lighted only by the fireplace flames. He rose from the mattress and looked at her for a long time in silence.

Finally, he spoke in a husky whisper. "The firelight seems to catch in your hair, making the red and gold sparkle as I've never seen before."

Shiloh forced herself to stand just a moment longer with him drinking in the beauty of the gift she was bringing to him.

His voice was barely a hoarse whisper. "You are the most beautiful, most desirable woman in the world."

Wordlessly, she hurried into his arms, her head against his breast. She could feel his heart pounding.

He held her there for a long moment, then whispered, "There's nothing more beautiful than the God-given expression of love between a man and his wife."

She nodded and tilted her face up for his kiss. It lingered, then became a series of kisses, hard and hungry. He swept her up in his arms, the flames in the fireplace melding their shadows into one.

When she awoke the next morning, Aldar had dressed and gone. Shiloh lay still for several minutes, savoring the memory of the night before. Then, realizing it was late, she arose and started to dress.

At the nightstand, she started to pour water into the basin, then paused. He had taken the pistol again.

Mara knocked as Shiloh finished dressing.

"I made breakfast," Mara announced.

Shiloh was still thinking about the pistol when she entered the cookhouse. The smell of fresh biscuits and country gravy filled the room.

"You're the best cook ever," Shiloh exclaimed, inhaling deeply.

"You sure are happy this morning." Mara uncovered the hot dishes and motioned for Shiloh to seat herself.

"Does it show?"

"It shows."

As she had done since they were little girls, Shiloh spoke freely with Mara. "I talked to Aldar about starting our family, but he said we'd better wait."

"Sometimes nature decides and it doesn't make any difference what a man says."

Shiloh thought of the pistol and the disturbing things she'd heard since arriving in San Francisco. "Mara, you hear things from your friends, Samuel and Joseph, right?"

"Uh-huh. From some others I met since them too. What do you want to know?"

"Have you heard anything about Denby Gladwin and Jefferson Locke?"

"Not yet, but I'll find out." Mara took a bite of biscuit, chewed thoughtfully, then spoke again. "But if you want to know about that soldier, Rawlins, I already know something about him."

"How did you know I'd even met him?"

"What I plan to do in this town means I have to know everything. This Rawlins was married, but his wife divorced him."

Shiloh had never met a divorced person. "Really?"

"I heard she couldn't stand him being gone all across this country on soldier duty while she sat home alone."

Shiloh was quiet for a moment while her mind shifted back to her earlier conversation with Mara. Finally Shiloh asked, "Why don't you like Aldar?"

Mara looked Shiloh directly in the eyes and said bluntly, "We just don't think alike. And he keeps things from you."

"Nothing important," Shiloh exclaimed defensively.

"How do you know that?"

The question echoed through Shiloh's mind through the remainder of breakfast. After leaving Mara, Shiloh took a walk to sort out her thoughts.

Unconsciously, she made her way across the sand dunes toward where she and Aldar had walked before. She was so deep in thought she was only vaguely aware of the sea gulls screaming and diving, the waves exploding into white foam against the rocks at the end of the beach.

She remembered Philander's angry words to her husband. She recalled the question Denby Gladwin had asked Aldar, and the man's surprise when he learned that Aldar hadn't mentioned the subject to her. Then there was Jefferson Locke, who had asked if Aldar had changed his mind.

Shiloh admitted to herself, *I don't like not knowing what's going on with my husband. But Mara's wrong. He's not keeping secrets. He loves me, and is just trying to protect me, that's all. He'll tell me more when he's ready.*

She tried to believe that as she walked along the shore, just out of reach of the inrushing fingers of water that scoured the sand clean and then retreated.

Her eyes lifted, and her spirits rose too. *San Francisco is really a beautiful place. Oh, it's got some dirty spots, but overall, it's truly beautiful. Up there, on that hill, someday Aldar and I will run the wild goats off and build our home.*

Smiling to herself, Shiloh started to turn back, but something in the water caught her eye. *A log,* she thought. *Driftwood just beyond that boulder at the water's edge.*

Idly, she turned aside to take a better look. As she drew closer, she saw that it rolled in the water, but it wasn't a log.

Looks more like . . . someone . . . Dear God! Someone has drowned! Someone—

She never finished the thought. Her hands flew to her mouth, but they couldn't stop the scream torn from her heart.

CHAPTER VI

SHILOH LAY in bed staring at nothing through swollen, tear-filled eyes fixed on the ceiling. Mara sat silently beside her, alternately stroking her hair and lightly patting her on the shoulder.

Shiloh's throat ached from the series of screams that had torn their way through the damp morning air. That ache was nothing compared to the ache she felt in her heart and mind.

"I can't believe he's dead," she moaned over and over, as she had done when some passing men had run to her earlier that day in response to her heart-wrenching screams. Only yesterday, she and Aldar had made love and planned their future together. Now . . .

She groaned, throwing her head from side to side upon the tear-stained pillow.

As from a great distance, Shiloh was vaguely aware of someone knocking at the front door. Wordlessly, Mara rose and left the room.

Clay stood at the front door, tall and somber, hat in hand. "I just heard," he said. "Is it true?"

Mara nodded. "Yes. I'm expecting the constable."

"I came as fast as I could."

"You're the first, except for the doctor. He's been and gone."

Clay glanced toward the hallway where the bedroom was. "How is she?"

"She still doesn't believe it. The doctor gave her some laudanum to make her sleep, but she's fighting it."

"How did it happen?"

"She's too upset to talk sensibly, but apparently a knife was used. One stroke across the throat."

Clay closed his eyes and a pained look crossed his face. Mara remained silent until he opened his eyes again.

"Is there anything . . ." he began softly, but Mara interrupted.

"Yes. See if you can find out what's keeping the constable. Some of the men who brought her home went for him and others for the doctor, but maybe they couldn't find the officer."

"I know him; name's Logan. He probably went directly to the scene, and won't come until he's finished there." Clay hesitated, clearing his throat before continuing. "Do you know where it happened?"

Mara nodded and repeated what the men had told her. Clay replaced his hat. "I'll find the constable and be back as soon as I can learn anything."

All the old, hard memories flooded over Clay as he turned the team around. Painful images filled his mind. He saw the little cabin he and his wife had built on the desolate West Texas plains. He saw the broken door. Riding in that terrible afternoon, a bandanna over his mouth to protect against the blowing sand that had driven him from his work, that was the first thing he noticed—the door torn off its hinges.

Ground-hitching his mount, he yanked the neckerchief from his clean-shaven face and ran inside, calling, *Elizabeth? Mark?*

Fear had seized him well before he saw the bodies in the cabin's dim interior. Long blonde hair plastered with blood across her fair face. Their three-year-old son's tow head showing from under her stained apron. She had vainly tried to shield him with her own broken body.

Through his pain and grief, Clay had read the signs of what had happened in his absence. A single horseman had ridden up, his mount leaving familiar hoof prints in the dust. It was no ordinary print. By its unusual markings, Clay knew the mount used that day belonged to one of the Brakken boys. The Brakken boys took pride in making their own horseshoes with their brand seared into each.

Both Brakkens were equally mean and wild, but which one of the twins had come to terrorize and kill Clay's wife and son in their lonely, remote home?

Kneeling alone beside what remained of his family, Clay vowed to find out. He went first to the sheriff, an uncle to the Brakken boys, who refused to believe either had anything to do with Elizabeth's or Mark's deaths. He promised to investigate, but Clay knew it was only a gesture.

Clay began his own investigation, seeking proof of the killer's identity. While asking questions around the little community, he masked his rage under his usual quiet, taciturn manner, and thought about the long road he had traveled to this cruel moment.

That was seven years ago, Clay reflected, urging the mules at a fast clip over the sand dunes toward the bay in search of the constable. Clay's jaw muscles twitched, as he thought of Aldar's senseless death.

I tried to warn him to be careful, he told himself. *But I was really thinking of Shiloh. I didn't figure on anything happening to Aldar.*

They had met nearly two years ago and developed an instant friendship.

Clay shook his head to put the past behind him when he saw the constable on the beach at the crime scene. Clay was relieved that Aldar's body had been removed.

"What happened, Logan?" Clay asked without greeting.

The short, stocky officer scratched his bald head. "The way I figure it, somebody waited behind that big boulder. Tide's in now, so it's in the water. But one of the men who heard the woman screaming and came to her aid said the tide was just then coming in, bringing the body with it."

"And washed out all the tracks," Clay commented.

"Sure did, including the killer's. Or he may have just walked in the water up or down the shore and come out someplace far away. But it's so open around here that the only place a person could have lain in wait for his victim was behind that boulder. When he passed, the killer jumped out from behind."

"How do you know that?"

"Only way it could have been. Used a knife or razor. No stab wounds, just one swipe . . . "

"I know him," Clay interrupted quickly, not wanting to hear greater details. "His name was Aldar Laird. He's a partner in MacAdams and Laird Express Company. I work for them. And I was his friend."

"Sorry, Clay." The officer paused, cocking his head thoughtfully. "Laird? Ain't he the one that brought his wife here a few days ago?"

When Clay nodded, Logan sighed. "I heard about her. Pretty as a picture, they say. Newlyweds. Now she's a widow. She got any relatives or friends here?"

"None that I know of except a Negress companion." Clay hesitated, then asked, "When did it happen?"

"Looks like early this morning," Logan pointed. "The victim—uh—Laird's tracks show he came across the sand that way, then he walked along the beach just above the water line."

"Heading for work," Clay commented.

"That makes sense. Apparently the killer knew Laird took this way to work, and waited for him. He didn't see or hear the killer until it was too late."

"How do you figure that?"

"The attack had to come from behind and be very fast to deliver the kind of fatal stroke that killed your friend."

Clay swallowed hard before asking, "Robbery?"

"Apparently. Nothing on the body. I did find this half-buried in the sand." Logan held up a small pistol.

"Let me see that." Clay examined the weapon. "I gave this to him a few days ago."

"Oh? Then you had reason to think somebody was out to get him?"

"Not really, but this town's getting so lawless, I thought it was safer."

Logan flared, "Don't blame me! The town council hired two constables a couple of years ago, then let the other one go."

"I'm not blaming you. Everybody knows the town government's all tore up over the convention they're going to hold in Monterey."

Logan glanced around, then lowered his voice. "Don't say I told you, but Alcalde Leavenworth's power in this place is gone. And just when there's thousands and thousands of men flooding in here from all over the world, with just me to investigate things like this."

Clay nodded in agreement, thanked the officer, then hurried back to report to Mara. Clay couldn't understand a senseless murder just to rob a man. Aldar was well-liked and got along with everyone, except for an occasional disagreement with his partner, MacAdams.

Several men had gathered in a group some distance from

the Laird house. They stood in watchful silence like waiting buzzards, making Clay want to drive them away. But he didn't say anything, knowing that in their own way, they were standing with the new young widow grieving inside.

Mara opened the door to Clay's quiet knock. She motioned him inside and quickly closed the door.

"How is she?" Clay whispered.

"Sleeping, finally." Mara's tone was low. "What'd you find out?"

After Clay reported, Mara muttered, "One constable for this whole town!"

"He'll be over later to ask some questions."

"I suppose everybody will be over, soon as they hear." Mara glanced toward the bedroom. "I ache for her, but that's nothing compared to how she's hurting and will continue to hurt."

Clay took a slow, thoughtful breath and let it out. "What's going to happen to her now?"

"She will probably go back to Pennsylvania."

"I suppose that's logical. Aldar told me she's got family there. You going with her?"

"No. I came here to stay."

Mara's flat statement was so emphatic that Clay lifted his eyebrows in surprise. He started to comment, but Mara spoke first. "We'll need a preacher for the funeral."

"I'll find one."

"She and her husband went to hear one yesterday. Name was Sledger, I think she said. Held services in the tent-saloon called The Nugget, or something like that."

"I'll find it and the preacher. Or do you think we should wait until she can be asked?" He shifted his eyes toward the bedroom.

"She's not in any condition to make such decisions, so you just go ahead."

Shiloh called out and Mara replied, "I'm coming." She told Clay, "Thanks for finding the constable."

Clay let himself out and approached the team. Some of the men came over to ask about Shiloh. Clay answered briefly but politely, explained his mission, and climbed into the wagon. As the mules headed back down the sandy road, Clay shifted his thoughts back to a possible killer.

Was Aldar the victim of a stranger waiting for any passerby? Or, as with his wife and son, Clay wondered if Aldar's murderer was someone he knew who struck when Aldar was alone and without witnesses.

He had disregarded friends' advice not to build his home so far west. But Clay had been born on the frontier and pioneered as a three-year-old when his parents were among the first settlers led by Stephen Fuller Austin in 1821. Orphaned at twelve, Clay had become a self-sufficient tumbleweed. Barely eighteen, he fought with Sam Houston's troops in the victory of San Jacinto in 1836. Married two years later, he had scratched out a living during the days of Texas independence.

Clay shook the memories off when he finally got a solid lead from an old widow living alone in her small shack several miles closer to town than the Pattons.

"I know why you come," she began after exchanging greetings. "On the day of the killin's, I saw Alben Brakken riding by. What made me remember was that he wasn't takin' the main road. He was a riding the back way." She pointed behind her house.

"He was heading for your place, but rode down in that draw, sort of like he didn't want me to see him. A couple of hours later, I seen him coming back the same way, but his horse was lathered from being rode hard."

He had thanked her and started to remount his horse, but she called out in a thin voice. "Nobody asked me before, not that no-count sheriff nor nobody. But I figgered that soon or later, you'd come by. Now I ain't saying Alben done it, but I know you won't quit 'til you know the facts, 'cause yore wife and baby boy won't rest peaceable until justice is done for them."

The years had not softened the vivid mental images that Clay did his best to stave off. After learning from the old widow about Alben Brakken, knowing that the twins were as close as two brothers could be, Clay had watched for Alben to be alone. Clay trailed him outside of the little town toward the home of a young woman Alben had been romancing.

That night had been crisp and clear. There had been only the cold, distant stars, the desolate wagon ruts that passed for a road, and Clay's heavy old dragoon revolver in his right hand.

He squatted on his boot heels, making no silhouette. But Alben did, riding jauntily in the saddle along the dark road. The horse was almost even with Clay before Alben's horse smelled Clay's mount tethered a hundred yards away. Alben's horse whinnied, then shied as Clay rose silently to his feet.

"Alben!" Clay cocked his weapon. The sound was loud and ominous in the night.

Startled, the twin jerked his mount to a halt and twisted in the saddle. "Who's there?"

"You know who."

"Clay? I'm mighty sorry to hear about . . . "

"Shut up!" Clay didn't expect the other man to be armed since he was going courting. Still, Clay took no chances. He advanced slowly, aiming the gun at the rider. He was barely visible against the skyline, but Clay could see enough that he would not miss. He was sure that Alben could see starlight reflecting off the barrel.

"Stay in the saddle but put your hands behind your back."

"Now, look, Clay . . . "

"Do as I say!" Clay's quiet voice was so loaded with controlled fury that Alben instantly obeyed.

With Alben's hands bound, Clay led the horse to his own, mounted, and ordered the twin to ride in front of him.

"Where you taking me?" Alben tried to sound calm, but the fear showed in his voice.

"To my place."

"What for?"

Clay didn't answer. The only sound for a long moment was the steady plodding of the two horses in the night.

Alben twisted in the saddle to look back. "If anything happens to me, my brother will kill you. No matter where you go, he'll find you."

"I thought of that."

"You're a fool, Clay! Turn me loose and we'll forget the whole thing."

"I'll never forget. Never. But you'll be spared that kind of memory."

"Why?" Alben's voice showed that he already had surmised what the grim man with the pistol meant.

"Guess."

There was no pleasure, no satisfaction in what Clay did that night. None at all. They dismounted before the dark and silent house where Clay's family had lived, but Clay wouldn't let his prisoner enter. They hunkered down against the rough outside walls while the coyotes called in the distance and the wind moaned around the corners.

"What're you doing, Clay?" Alben finally asked.

"Waiting for daybreak."

"Why?"

"I want you to see the inside of this house before you hang."

"Hang?" Alben started to leap up, but Clay yanked on the ropes, forcing the other man back down.

"From the barn rafters over there."

The deadly earnestness in Clay's voice threw Alben into a panic. His threats turned to pitiful pleading and finally to a sobbing confession.

"I didn't mean to do it, honest, Clay! I just wanted to visit some, but she wouldn't let me in. I guess one thing led to another, so I broke in the door and grabbed her. We struggled and I hit her. That brat bit me . . . "

Clay backhanded Alben hard, breaking off his remarks and loosening a tooth.

At dawn, Clay took one last look at the isolated little home where he and Elizabeth had pioneered west, and where she and their son had died. Then Clay carried out his plan. After the house and barn burned to the ground, Clay mounted his horse and slowly rode away.

He had one lingering concern. The Brakken twins had been very close. It was possible that the surviving brother's rage would drive him to seek vengeance. Even after all these years, Clay suspected that somewhere on his back trail, a rider followed.

Clay could never really force the past aside, although he tried again as he neared The Nugget Saloon. He never stopped blaming himself for Elizabeth's and Mark's deaths. It had happened because he followed a dream, but he had followed it too far west. Now his family were long in their graves, so when Clay saw Aldar with Shiloh landing in San Francisco, Clay feared for them.

Now it was too late; Aldar had made the same mistake he had, except that now Aldar was dead and Shiloh was alone thousands of miles from family and friends.

Clay was roused from his brooding memories by the sound of a crowd. Ahead, a large group of men faced a street corner preacher. Clay had never seen John Sledger, but he was sure that's who stood on an upturned whiskey barrel facing the crowd, exhorting them from the Scriptures.

As Clay eased the mules past the listeners, a powerfully-built man in blue shirt, overalls, and dirty high boots stepped forward to stand directly in front of the preacher.

"Ah, shut up!" the man shouted. "I had enough of your

kind back home! So get down and let us through to the saloon."

Clay reined in the mules and watched as Sledger lowered his voice and smiled at the man who had interrupted.

"Brother," he said calmly, "it's plain enough that you've no interest in hearin' the Lord's Word. But some of them other men do. They're mighty far from home, an' surrounded by all kinds of wickedness."

"You going to shut up?"

The preacher didn't answer, but continued in a quiet tone. "I suspect these men 'member their mother's prayers, an' they like to be reminded that God is here, even in this most wicked city on the face of the . . . "

"You had your chance!" The belligerent miner interrupted, kicking the preacher's platform hard.

Sledger almost fell, but managed to regain his balance by waving his massive arms and teetering on booted feet.

"Brother," he said, his voice low but so powerful it carried clearly over the crowd. "The good Lord tells us we got to love everybody, even the likes of you. That won't be easy, but I'm gonna do it, right here an' now."

He jumped down from the barrel, arms outstretched.

The other man started to brace himself and throw a blow, but he was too slow.

For such a big man, Sledger was very fast. His great arms encircled the other man in a bear hug, pinning his arms before he could throw a single blow.

"Brother," Sledger exclaimed, his face turning red with the efforts of his straining, "I'm gonna love you 'til you either fall down an' repent, or the breath goes plumb out of your body—whichever comes first."

The crowd started cheering, choosing sides and encouraging their favorite.

Clay quietly watched as the two men swayed back and forth, grunting with their efforts. The belligerent man swore vehemently, struggling mightily but vainly to break the preacher's hold.

"Blasphemy," Sledger puffed, "is powerful sinful. Seems ye got more sin than I figgered. Reckon I'll jist have . . . to love you . . . harder."

Clay stepped back as the struggling men spun toward him. He thought he caught a joyful glint in Sledger's eyes as his powerful muscles continued to crush the other man, who was no longer cursing. He was not even speaking, but gasping for breath that he couldn't seem to get.

"Brother," Sledger panted, "you ready to repent?"

Perspiration rimmed the man's forehead. His eyes seemed to bulge. "Y . . . yes."

"I don't rightly . . . think . . . I kin hear you," Sledger puffed.

"Yes!" The word came out as a hoarse sound, then the man's head sagged forward against Sledger's.

He released his hold and gently lowered the man to the ground.

The crowd cheered. Some pushed forward to slap the victorious preacher on the back. He bent, spoke kindly to the fallen man, and helped him to his feet.

Clay shook his head in wonder, then pushed through the crowd to speak to the preacher. "You John Sledger?"

"Sure am, brother. Servant of the Lord, an' likewise servant of His people." Sledger was still panting. "What kin I do fer you, my brother?"

"Remember a young blond man and his wife from your service yesterday?"

"Do I?" The giant's eyes lit up and he rubbed perspiration from his forehead with a massive hand. "How could I ever . . . ? His words trailed off and his expression changed to concern at the somber look in Clay's face. "Something happen?"

"He's dead—murdered. She's . . . "

"Them yore mules?" Sledger interrupted. When Clay nodded, the preacher headed for them. "Take me to her and tell me on the way."

Shiloh awakened with a dull headache and a sick feeling. Then she remembered and thrashed about wildly in a fresh wave of grief. "Oh, Lord, no!" She cried aloud. "He can't be dead! Let this be a dream! It didn't happen!"

Mara entered the bedroom on silent feet. "Clay brought the preacher you heard yesterday."

"Send them away," Shiloh said with a moan.

"There's got to be a preacher for the funeral. I thought since you'd met this one, I sent for him."

Shiloh fought against her desire to curl up and die from grief and broken dreams. But in a corner of her mind, she knew that Mara was right. Still, she wanted to deny it. "Is Aldar really dead?" she whispered.

"Yes, he is." Mara's voice was tender but firm.

Shiloh closed her eyes hard while the tears squeezed through. "Help me straighten my hair, then send them in."

When hurried repairs had been made to her swollen eyes and her red-gold hair had been finger-brushed into some semblance of order, the two men were admitted.

Shiloh reached out to take Sledger's giant hand, but when she saw Clay's stricken face, she burst into fresh weeping.

The preacher offered condolences, but Shiloh didn't hear. She was more aware of his reassuring tone, than a quoted Scripture verse and a prayer.

Through it all, Shiloh kept her eyes closed, lost in her grief. At Sledger's "amen," she opened her eyes and saw that Clay still stood quietly beside the bed. His eyes showed a strange brightness in the semi-darkened room.

"Thank you both for coming," Shiloh managed say. "Mara will talk to you about . . . what needs to be done." She turned her face to the wall, struggling to stifle the wailing cry that welled up in her breast.

After awhile, Mara returned. "Everything's arranged," she announced quietly.

"I've been praying with all my heart," Shiloh said, looking at the other woman. "But nothing seems to help."

"Some things can't be hurried." Mara fussed with the bedding, straightening gently but expertly.

"What am I going to do without Aldar?" Shiloh asked with a soft moan. "All alone thousands of miles from everything that's familiar. Not a friend except you."

"You'll have friends, so don't worry. Aldar's friends are your friends. You'll see. But right now, you don't have to make any decisions. Try to sleep again."

The constable came while Shiloh was asleep. Mara briefly thought of turning him away, but realized there were things he had to know. Reluctantly, she aroused Shiloh, who didn't want to see the constable, but yielded when Mara insisted, explaining that time was essential in catching Aldar's killer.

The telling forced Shiloh to relive the morning's shocking discovery, and she frequently broke down and had to compose herself before continuing. But at last it was done, even to recalling how Aldar and she had walked there the day before. She finished with a sob, "He called it his Dream Rock," and could talk no more.

Mara moved from the cookhouse into the spare bedroom to be near Shiloh, who never knew how she got through the agonizing hours until the funeral. Clay came with a proper black carriage and a horse. Such an animal was rare in San Francisco because almost all the horses in town had been sold to miners headed for the gold streams.

The sky was clear, the air crisp and clean, with no trace of fog. The wind was sharp, but none of those things penetrated Shiloh's consciousness as she and Mara rode in somber silence toward Aldar's burial site.

The community's oldest cemetery was the Catholic one at the Mission Dolores founded in 1776 by Father Junipero Serra, but Aldar was to be buried on the southern slope of Telegraph Hill. Clay's route took the mourners past Fern Hill, but Shiloh could not look at it. Aldar's promise to build her a home there had died with him.

The pastor met Shiloh's carriage at the cemetery. It took all of her will power to walk toward the open grave site with Mara on her right and Sledger on the left. Clay followed close behind. Shiloh mechanically moved through the crowd that had gathered.

She was helped to one of the few chairs that had been placed before the plain, hurriedly made wooden coffin. Mara took the chair on the right. As Sledger stepped away, opening his Bible, Clay silently took the seat at Shiloh's left.

She was surprised to see how many people came. It seemed that everyone had turned out, a thousand or more.

Whether they knew Aldar or came out of curiosity, Shiloh didn't know or care. She was comforted that they were there, and that many of them were those she had met in the few days she'd been in San Francisco.

Through a mist of grief and tears, she dimly realized that Jessie Fremont was there, dressed in black, along with silver-haired William Gwin and that young military-looking man, Joseph Hooker. So was Thomas Butler King, President Taylor's personal representative in California.

Shiloh glimpsed MacAdams, her husband's partner, standing next to the youth who had offered a pouch of gold just for the privilege of shaking her hand.

Nearby stood a man of medium build with straw-colored hair and a two-inch scar on his right cheek. Shiloh couldn't remember ever seeing him, but neither had she seen most of the men in the crowd.

Mara whispered in her ear, "That's the Dutchman."

It took a moment for Shiloh to understand that Mara

meant Fritz Kroeber, the man who challenged Aldar to a duel. Shiloh didn't want that man to be present, but as she stiffened with the thought, Mara squeezed her hand in warning.

"Easy," she whispered. "Easy."

With an effort, Shiloh tore her eyes away from Kroeber and on to William Rawlins, the Presidio's commandant, whom she had met at the saloon-church. He stood by Denby Gladwin. Just beyond them, Shiloh spotted Jefferson Locke.

The preacher opened with a brief prayer, then led the mourners in a hymn. Shiloh didn't join in, but stared at the fresh piles of earth and the plain pine coffin. Sledger read from the Bible, but the familiar words she had heard at so many funerals back home barely penetrated the protective shell where Shiloh had retreated. There she vainly sought to deny the tragedy that had struck her life.

She was pleased that the preacher had taken the time to gather a few personal facts about Aldar. *Probably from Clay,* Shiloh thought, as Sledger gave a short eulogy, followed by familiar readings from the Scriptures.

"Jesus said, 'I am the resurrection, and the life: he that believeth in me, though he were dead, yet shall he live: and whosoever liveth and believeth in me shall never die.'"

Shiloh took comfort in those words, knowing that Aldar had believed them too. But he also believed there was a bright and happy future for himself and Shiloh in California, and all that it was to become.

Aldar had been so young and handsome and full of life, so full of dreams about the part transportation would play in the development of California, so convinced he would play a part in that. He had believed in all of that too, but now he was dead.

Shiloh sat in a daze, tears blurring the faces of all those who stood around the open grave. As the service neared an end, she retreated farther inside herself, trying to escape the reality of the moment. But there was no place to hide.

People moved somberly between her and the waiting grave, blotting out the sight as they murmured words of sympathy and comfort. Shiloh heard and saw them from a great distance, for now a new reality gripped her.

She turned and threw her arms around Mara. "I'm so sick and afraid!" she said with a groan. "Aldar and I didn't have any money, so there's no way to survive here, and no way I can secure passage back home."

"You'll make it," Mara said, patting her shoulder.

"I don't want to! I want to die and be with Aldar! All my hopes and dreams and love went with him!"

Over Mara's shoulder, through her tears, Shiloh saw Clay's somber face. Their eyes met.

"I lost somebody," he said softly so that for a moment Shiloh wasn't sure she had heard him. "My wife and son. But I lived, and you must too."

Shiloh stared at Aldar's friend, and she knew Clay was right. She had to survive. But how?

CHAPTER VII

THE DAY after the funeral, a monstrous wave of homesickness, loneliness, and anger engulfed Shiloh. *Why him?* she silently prayed. *Why? Why? He was so young, so alive. It's not fair!*

There was an intense stillness in the house. All the sympathetic people who had attended the services or come by afterward were gone. Only faithful Mara remained, moving about on cat-quiet feet so that Shiloh could sleep.

But there was no blessed escape in sleep from the crushing reality of her situation. She closed her eyes in the darkened room with the shades drawn. She forced her grief and anger and hurt aside to consider possible ways to implement her decision to find a way to survive.

Aldar had left her nothing. Earlier this morning, Shiloh had instructed Mara to search Aldar's trunk for a will. The search yielded nothing. Apparently Aldar hadn't felt the need for it.

"There's no will," Mara finally announced, "just some kind of handwritten document. Looks like it's just the partnership agreement between your husband and MacAdams."

Shiloh skimmed the first few legal-sounding words and put it aside. "I'll read it later," she said, handing the document back. "Put it back in Aldar's trunk."

Then Shiloh turned her face to the wall and again tried to fight off her anger and grief to focus on the desperate and immediate task of surviving.

She wept until she was drained and weary. Dry-eyed, sleepless, and emotionally and physically spent, she lay in the bed she had shared with Aldar and felt the sweet pain of their last romantic time together.

"Lord," her whisper was an agonized groan, "what am I going to do without him?"

When she married Aldar, she knew that—except for the passage funds to California—all the money he had was invested in the MacAdams and Laird Express Company. Shiloh had accepted that, just as she accepted her disapproving adoptive parents cutting her off without even a wedding gift. Lots of young people started married life together with little more than their love and hopes.

All of that changed suddenly for Shiloh.

"Dear Lord," she whispered, "Mara and I can't live here without money, and we can't go home for the same reason. So what shall I do?"

She fell silent while her mind leaped and tumbled. Not one thought promised a solution to her problem. Then she found herself recalling a fragment of verse. "Call upon Me in the day of trouble: I will deliver thee . . . "

Throwing back the covers, Shiloh swung a quilt over her shoulders and padded barefooted into the living room.

Mara looked up from where she sitting on the horsehair stuffed sofa and reading *The California Star,* San Francisco's second newspaper.

In some states, it was illegal for a slave to read, but Mara had become literate after being freed. She commented to Shiloh, "I thought you were asleep."

"Been praying and thinking. We've got to talk."

Mara patted the sofa seat beside her. "Fine."

"I'm thinking of us going back to Pennsylvania, but there's no money for that. So we've got to exist here until God provides a way. Any ideas?"

Mara deliberately folded the newspaper and laid it down before meeting Shiloh's eyes. "I'm not going back."

"What?"

"I mean it."

Shiloh leaped up, the quilt sliding unnoticed to the floor. "I've lost everything, Mara! I can't bear the thought of losing you too."

"I told you before we left Pennsylvania that I didn't ever plan to return."

"Yes, but I thought you were just talking about putting all your bad memories behind."

"It was much more than that, Shiloh. I knew that what I wanted could never be mine back there. But in a new land, thousands of miles away, it could happen. Now that I'm here, I know it will too."

Shiloh reeled emotionally from the unexpected development. She whirled about and rushed to the window. She looked out but saw nothing through her sudden tears. Mara followed, gently turned Shiloh around, and firmly gripped her shoulders. "We're grown up now, you and I. We've had a great friendship even better than sisters have. I will never ever forget you, or stop loving you, but if you return home, you'll go without me."

"But what will you do here?"

Mara smiled, looking into Shiloh's panic-filled eyes. "I have plans," she replied evasively.

"You always did, even when we were little, just as you were always a rebel, wanting to do things for yourself, and in your own way."

"Now you must learn to rely on yourself."

Shiloh declared, "With God's help, I'll get by."

"You got any ideas yet?"

Shiloh sighed and shook her head.

"You asked about my plans. In a general way, I've known for years what I wanted to do. But I didn't see how until last August when I heard gold had been discovered in California. That's when I got my answer, but that meant I had to come here and see for myself to be sure."

"And now you're sure?"

"Very sure."

"What're you going to do?"

"Take it step-by-step. When we came ashore, did you see that iron cookstove that had been dumped in the bay?" When Shiloh nodded, Mara continued, "I had Samuel check it out. It wasn't ruined by the salt water. Samuel and Joseph are cleaning it up and putting it in a little tent I talked a man into letting me use. That's the first step."

Shiloh frowned. "I don't understand."

"Come by tomorrow and you'll see."

"Where is this tent?"

"Just follow your nose."

Shiloh gave Mara a quizzical look, then excused herself and returned to her darkened room.

Mara watched her leave, but her thoughts had already jumped back ten years and thousands of miles.

At thirteen, she was more fully developed than Shiloh or any other girls of either race in their small community. Her light tan face clearly forecast the beauty she would become. None of that was lost on the neighborhood teenage males. Mara enjoyed all the attention, rewarding both black and white with a smile, but nothing more.

Once she and Shiloh accompanied Eldon and Martha Edgeworth into Virginia to visit an underground abolitionist friend. Mara saw some young female slaves hoeing in a field. She told Shiloh that she was going over to talk with them. Shiloh protested, but Mara, always the rebel, replied confidently. "I'll be back shortly, so don't you tell anybody."

On the way, Mara crossed a rural dirt road just as a group of three white *pattyrollers* spotted her. They were known to local slaves as poor country trash who patrolled between plantations seeking runaway slaves.

"Lookee yonder," the tallest one said with a grin that showed a front tooth missing. "Ain't that about the purtiest little yeller gal you ever laid eyes on?"

The second man made some remark that Mara didn't understand, but when he leered at her from a pock-marked face, she sensed danger.

"I have my freedom papers," she had said boldly, trusting in that fact to protect her. "I live in Pennsylvania. My family is visiting over there." She pointed.

"Well, now," the third man said, wiping tobacco juice from his week-old crop of black whiskers, "looks like we got us an ed'jacated nigger gal! Now, that ain't right, ain't right a-tall."

Mara's smile faded. An inner voice urged her to run.

"An' visiting old man Higgenbotham," the man with pock marks added. "I heard tell he's one of them dirty, no-good abolitionists."

Spitting tobacco, the whiskered man suggested, "Maybe we jist better take her off over yonder an' examine her papers, or whatever she's got."

She turned and ran, hearing vulgar laughter and coarse remarks along with the sound of feet pounding after her. But before she could scream, they caught her, and the nightmare began.

Later, she staggered into the Higgenbotham's backyard with swollen and cut lips. Her face and hair were full of dirt. Her tattered clothes were stained with reddish colored mud.

Entering the back porch, Mara found Shiloh.

She leaped up. "What happened?"

"Just help me, please."

"I'll call Mama."

"No! Don't tell anyone."

For privacy, they took refuge in the outhouse. Shiloh brought water from the well and a cloth from the clothesline. Gingerly, she helped Mara clean up. Then Shiloh ran to the house and brought a clean dress from her carpetbag. Only as Mara undressed did Shiloh's innocent mind finally grasp the horrible truth of what had happened.

Through it all, Mara said nothing. She did not cry out from pain or terror, but bore everything with a frightening, stoic silence.

"Say something!" Shiloh kept whispering fiercely. "Who did it?"

Mara did not reply. Later, the Edgeworths questioned why she was scratched and bruised. Mara lied, "I chased a little rabbit into a briar patch." The adults accepted the explanation, although Shiloh thought they must have been blind to have believed such injuries could have been produced by briars.

Mara swore Shiloh to secrecy, then told the whole sickening incident. She concluded, "Now we will never speak of this again."

"But those men should be punished!"

"I said," Mara replied firmly, "we will never speak of this again."

Neither mentioned it again over the next ten years, but

Shiloh, shocked by Mara's refusal to return to Pennsylvania, kept thinking back on Mara's rape.

She had been different from that day on. First, she stopped attending the little church pastored by a former slave. This brought unending reprimands from the Edgeworths, but Mara's iron will had always proved to be in sharp contrast to Shiloh's pliant obedience.

Shiloh wasn't too concerned about the change in Mara's behavior until about two months after the rape. Shiloh accidentally came upon three dolls behind some old boxes on a closet shelf the girls shared. They were crude dolls, but Shiloh noticed they were dressed to represent men. There was a long hat pin through each doll's heart.

As well as Shiloh knew Mara, she could not believe that she could be practicing something so frightening as this. Shiloh had learned about "dolls" like these from hearing her adoptive parents speak in horror of the primitive form of witchcraft that some West African slaves had brought with them to this country.

Shiloh couldn't believe that Mara, who had embraced Christianity when she was about nine, would slip into such forbidden pagan practices. Shiloh thought about questioning Mara, but the dolls disappeared. Shiloh would have forgotten about them if it hadn't been for a fatal accident.

The next time Papa visited the Higgenbothams by himself, he returned with a strange story. He told his wife, Shiloh, and Mara about three men, neighbors to the Higgenbothams, who had died when a wagon load of cotton overturned, smothering them.

Mara smiled a strange, satisfied smile that scared Shiloh, especially when she remembered the three doll figures. She tried to tell herself that there was no connection. After all, Mara hadn't even said how many men raped her. Still, Shiloh could not rid herself of the feeling that Mara believed her attackers had paid with their lives for assaulting her.

For a while afterward, Shiloh was uneasy, fighting doubts about how well she really knew Mara. But there were no more dolls, and Shiloh's concerns faded away.

"It was just coincidence," Shiloh said aloud to the silent bedroom. It was something she had convinced herself was true. Otherwise, she would never have been able to remain such strong friends with Mara.

Shiloh closed her eyes, desperately trying to ignore her grief in the driving necessity to find a solution to her present problem. *I've got to have funds for passage home,* she thought. *But what will I do when I get there? Nothing very exciting; it never was. But at least it's familiar, and I'll have a roof over my head and food to eat. I think Papa and Mama will let me stay there awhile.*

But there would be a price. Papa and Mama would say smugly, "I told you so!" She would have to listen to more radical abolitionist talk. Worst of all, Papa and Mama would probably again urge Shiloh to marry Seth, the neighboring farmer.

Her thoughts were interrupted by Mara coming to the bedroom door. "The constable is here again. He wants to ask you some questions."

Shiloh groaned. "I can't do that right now."

"He says you must."

Reluctantly, Shiloh arose, hastily dressed, and brushed her hair. Still, the mirror showed she looked terrible as she walked by on the way to the parlor.

Constable Logan was clearly ill at ease. "I'm sorry to bother you at this time, Mrs. Laird," he began "but I've got to do it."

"I understand." She sat on the sofa and motioned for him to take the chair facing her. "Have you learned who killed my husband?"

"No, Mrs. Laird. I'm working on it." A shaft of sunlight from the window reflected off his bald head as he sat. "But

I've been thinking about some things where you might help."

"Oh?"

"It appears to be a robbery turned violent, but I have to be sure. Can you think of anyone who would have wanted to kill your husband?"

"Nobody. Everybody loved Aldar. He was everybody's friend, always smiling and talking."

"He never quarreled with anyone?"

The question caught Shiloh off guard. She hesitated, then briefly told about the incident between Aldar and Philander MacAdams.

"But Aldar didn't sound angry," she concluded. "Besides, he said Philander was always blowing up, but it didn't mean anything."

"I see. Anybody else you can think of who might have wanted your husband dead?"

"Well, Fritz Kroeber certainly did at one time."

"The Dutchman who fought a duel with your husband?"

"Yes."

"I heard about that."

"Kroeber was at the funeral."

"Everyone in San Francisco was there, including me."

"I think he would have the decency to stay away. I wonder if he came there to . . . well . . . gloat. He could have killed my husband!"

"Please don't get upset, Mrs. Laird, but I don't think so. Any man who has fired his only shot but can still stand there, waiting for the opponent to shoot him dead, doesn't strike me as the type who would later kill in cold blood. It's a matter of honor."

Shiloh hadn't thought of that, so she flushed in embarrassment. To cover that, she demanded somewhat heatedly, "Then who killed my husband?"

"I can't say for sure at this stage of the investigation, but it looks like a case of being in the wrong place at the wrong time. A robber was waiting for a victim, and your husband happened along."

The officer stood. "Thanks for your time, Mrs. Laird. I'll continue to look for the killer so he can be brought to justice."

Shiloh walked Logan to the door. As she opened it, she heard the rattle of trace chains and looked out to see Clay coming. The constable stopped for a few brief words with Clay, who then came to the door. She admitted him although she didn't feel like talking to anyone else at the moment.

Clay stood with his hat in both hands, greeting both Shiloh and Mara who excused herself, leaving Shiloh and Clay alone.

"I just came by to see if you needed anything," he said, declining the chair she offered.

"Thanks, but I can't think of anything. There's still plenty of food that people brought after the funeral."

He nodded, slowly moving his fingers along the edge of his hat brim. "I hope Logan finds whoever did it real soon."

An awkward silence began to build. Hurriedly, Shiloh broke it. "From the way Aldar talked, you were probably the person he considered his best friend."

"Thank you, Ma'am." Clay shifted his hat to the left hand and reached toward his belt with the other. "I sold those pickax heads Aldar brought on the ship. Got top dollar for them. Here." He handed her a small pouch.

She was surprised how heavy it was. "What's this?"

"Gold dust, Ma'am. There's no real money in California these days, since there's no authority for making it. Some folks make their own slugs with what they say is its true value, and other men use Mexican coins and everything else, but most folks just prefer gold dust."

"Thank you, Clay." She breathed a silent prayer of thanks. *At least I won't starve,* she thought.

"I figured that you'd probably be wanting to go back where you came from."

"Yes, I'm planning on that."

"Well, there's not enough in that poke for passage back east, but it'll help." He reached to his belt and pulled out an even larger, heavier bag. "This should be enough to make up the difference, and give you enough to live on until you get settled back there."

Shiloh automatically started to reach for the second bag, then stopped, her fingers not quite touching it. She had been reared to believe that debt was sinful. "I appreciate your generosity, but I'm in no position to borrow money."

"It's not a loan. It's a gift to my friend's wife."

Shiloh didn't know what to say. Moments before, she had anguished over how she would survive until she returned home. But no matter what Clay called it, his kind offer was an obligation which she would be compelled to repay, and there was no way she could do that.

"Thank you anyway," she said. "But I just can't accept."

"Mrs. Laird, I don't think you understand. The pickax money isn't enough to get you passage back east, and there's no way to get the balance. So please take this." He again extended the larger bag.

She put her hands behind her back. "You are a very kind, generous man, but no, thanks. I can't accept."

He frowned. "Are you sure you understand the only alternative? If you don't have enough to return east, you'll have to stay here. But how can you do that?"

She thought of Mara, always able to do what she set out to accomplish. "I'll find a way, Mr. Patton."

His voice changed, taking on a flat, authoritative quality. "No offense, Ma'am, but this is no place for a woman alone."

"I'll have Mara."

"Even two women won't make a difference. You'd best leave before something else happens."

"Are you trying to get rid of me?"

"I wouldn't put it like that, exactly, but . . . "

Her emotions started boiling again. "I know you were Aldar's friend, but what right have you to . . ."

"Excuse me," he interrupted, his twitching jaw muscles making his black whiskers move erratically, "But I know what it's like to pioneer too far west. I made that mistake, and lost my wife and son. Now, as Aldar's friend, I'm trying to protect you the best way I know how, and that's to help you go back where you came from."

Shiloh spoke gently. "I'm sorry about your family. I appreciate your concern. Thanks for selling the ax heads, and now your generous offer. But I cannot accept such a gift."

His reply was low but with a hint of controlled anger. "I know you're hurting, Ma'am, and maybe you're not thinking real straight just now. But you can't get along without money, lots of it, especially in this town. Sure, you can survive here until the pickax money runs out. Then what?"

She replied without conviction, "I'll find a way."

"Doing what?"

"Well, I . . . " Shiloh faltered, thinking fast. Then an idea hit her. "I haven't had time to think it through, but Aldar was a partner with Philander MacAdams, so he should give me Aldar's share of the business."

"You don't know Philander very well. However, I didn't come here to discourage you. Sure you won't take this?" He held the bag out again.

"I'm sure."

He stood and replaced the poke in his belt. "I'll be going now." He turned toward the door.

"Thanks for coming."

He opened the door and stepped outside, replacing his hat. "Mrs. Laird, I don't want to frighten you, but did it occur to you that whoever killed your husband may not stop there?"

Shiloh stared in disbelief. "The constable says it was robbery." She paused, remembering his questions, and wondered if Logan had some doubts. She asked Clay, "Are you suggesting that my life might be in danger?"

"I'm not suggesting anything. It's just a thought, but anyway, you've got no reason to stay here and take a chance. Please go home."

"I will, as soon as I can pay my own way."

He nodded. "Call me if you need anything."

"Thank you." She closed the door after him and leaned against it as Mara reentered the room. Shiloh repeated what Clay had said.

Mara replied, "I hope he's wrong about it not being a chance robbery."

"But even if Clay is right, why should you or I be in danger?"

"I can't answer that. But I wish you had taken his money."

"You think I was wrong to turn him down, Mara?"

"I want you to stand on your own feet, so at least this was the first time I ever remember seeing you show any spunk."

"But was I wrong?"

"I guess you'll find out tomorrow, huh?"

"I guess so." Shiloh sank back into her chair while a cold tip of fearful doubt pushed like a knife point toward her heart.

CHAPTER VIII

DRIVEN BY the need to survive, Shiloh forced herself to dress the next morning and walk through San Francisco's thriving business section to meet with Philander MacAdams. Men along the way stopped their work to stand in respectful silence as she passed. Still, Shiloh was glad when she reached the express office building and left the gawking spectators behind.

Standing outside the second-floor office door, Shiloh had a momentary sense of panic. *What if he turns me down?* She shrugged off the doubts and knocked.

At MacAdams's gruff call, "Come in," Shiloh entered the small, cramped room.

MacAdams glanced up from beyond the counter. His broken nose and square jaw created an intimidating image until he recognized Shiloh. With a startled exclamation, he hoisted his big frame from a squeaking chair before his roll-top desk. "Mrs. Laird! What a surprise."

"Forgive me for intruding unannounced," she replied. "I felt the need to discuss some things with you."

"Of course." He motioned for her to come around the end of the counter. "Come in and have a seat."

She took the straight-backed chair he indicated. Like the rest of the office, it had no frills.

"I'm sorry about Aldar," he said, again lowering himself into his desk chair.

"Thank you. And thanks for being at the services."

He nodded and leaned back in the chair, making a steeple of his fingers.

In contrast to his relaxed, confident attitude, Shiloh felt frightened and a little desperate. The gold dust she received from the sale of the pickax heads would not long keep her from serious financial circumstances.

"I'll come straight to the point," she began. "I came to ask for Aldar's share of the business."

"His share of the business?" MacAdams repeated. When she nodded, he asked casually, "Did Aldar leave a will, or other legal documents?"

It was hard to keep from breaking down, but Shiloh kept her composure. "We had only been married a short time, and I'm sure he didn't expect to die so soon."

His eyes flickered. "I see. Well, that's certainly understandable. As I said, I'm sorry about Aldar, but under the circumstances, you surely don't really expect to receive anything from his part in this business?"

Shiloh's hopes plunged. "I thought his partnership in this business would be part of his estate. I mean, I'm only asking for what would logically belong to his survivor."

"That might be true back where you came from," MacAdams replied rather gruffly, leaning back in his squeaking chair, "but without a will or anything, you have no legal claim on Aldar's share of this business."

He leaned forward, adding, "Oh, don't look so stricken, Mrs. Laird. California isn't a state. It has a military governor, and has had since the war with Mexico ended. That means there are no civil laws, only military. They don't much concern themselves with business and estates."

Weak with disappointment, Shiloh stood. "I see," she said in a barely audible voice.

MacAdams also stood. "I'm sorry." He took her elbow and guided her around the counter's end. "Very sorry."

As she nearly stumbled through the door into the hallway, MacAdams added, "I'd like to at least give you something, but the truth is, Aldar nearly ruined this company."

"I don't believe that! Aldar told me that you two were both nearly destitute when you met. You were driving an ox team with loads of lumber around Tahoe. He was riding muleback, delivering packages and . . . "

"That's true," MacAdams interrupted. "But it was my idea to start the express company."

Shiloh's shock of failure in her mission began to turn to anger. "But it was Aldar's idea to go from merchant to merchant, asking for their business. Isn't that true? Isn't that what built up this company?"

"Well, yes, he was a salesman and . . . "

"Wasn't it that kind of vision that made MacAdams and Laird Express Company grow faster than the other companies just starting up?"

"Mrs. Laird," MacAdams said slowly, "that's true as far as it goes. But to put it bluntly, Aldar's ideas put the company in jeopardy. That's why I let him go to Washington to see if he could get some subsidy. . . ."

"You let him?" Shiloh exclaimed. "He was an equal partner! He had as much authority as you did!"

"Don't get upset! I wish I didn't have to say this, but you leave me no choice. While he was gone, I found some irregularities in the business."

"Irregularities?"

"Yes. Some money was . . . shall I say . . . misappropriated?"

Shiloh's voice turned cold. "Are you accusing my husband of stealing?"

"Call it what you want, the result was that now this company is in deep financial trouble. Besides that, lots of other competing express lines are springing up, causing the MacAdams and Laird Company to face bankruptcy."

"Mr. MacAdams," she said coldly, "I do not believe you! My husband had no money. I'm sure of that, which means I have none."

"There's no sense in quarreling," MacAdams said soothingly. "I tell you what I'll do: I'll give you enough money to return east. That's a generous offer, under the circumstances."

Shiloh wanted to cry, "No!", but her anger had cooled and her more practical side took over. She hesitated, her thoughts whirling. *It might be all I ever get,* she thought. *But I still think part of Aldar's share in the business should rightfully be mine.*

"I'd like to think it over," she said, and left.

Downstairs, Shiloh was somewhat annoyed to see Clay waiting for her with a carriage. She thought, *He's here to say, 'I told you so.' Well, let him, I guess I deserve that.*

"Morning, Mrs. Laird," he greeted her, stepping down from the rig. "Mara told me I'd find you here."

"Mara? Has something happened?"

"No, Ma'am. Well, nothing bad, anyway. Get in, and I'll take you to her."

Perplexed but still upset over the interview with MacAdams, Shiloh accepted Clay's hand up to take a seat in the carriage. He sat down beside her and lightly slapped the reins across the mule's back.

Shiloh expected Clay to comment about her talk with MacAdams. To avoid that, Shiloh asked, "Where is Mara?"

"I'm swinging downwind," he replied. "You ought to get a whiff pretty soon."

"A whiff of what?"

He smiled at her. "She said it was a surprise, so you'll just have to wait and see."

Shiloh noticed that several men in their high boots were hurrying along the board walks, heading the same direction as she and Clay. "What's going on?" she asked.

"They're following their noses." He tipped his head back slightly and sniffed loudly. "Smell it?"

When Shiloh also sniffed gently, her eyes widened in understanding. "Fresh baked pies!"

Clay's eyes lit up above the black whiskers. "Haven't smelled anything like that in years."

"So that's what Mara meant! She's going to make baked goods to sell!"

"Nothing like it around here," Clay assured her. "Some men make their own bread in Dutch ovens, and that's barely fit to eat. Most men get by on their own flapjacks that would kill a mule. So real woman-baked pies should be very popular."

As the rig rounded a corner, Shiloh saw that a crowd of men had gathered around the front of a large blue gambling tent with a smaller one beside it. Outside the second tent a monstrous black cookstove sat in the open, pouring wood smoke into the clear morning air. Samuel split firewood that Joseph stacked near the stove.

A railing of boards, wooden crates, and barrels had cordoned off a work area around the stove, Mara, and the two black men. A counter consisting of a plank supported by whiskey barrels faced the street.

Mara stood behind the counter, smiling and calling out cheerfully. "Fresh made this morning from dried apples and peaches and other good things like your mother used to make. One pie to a customer. I want everybody in town to have one of Mara's pies. Cost is only one pinch of gold dust, an ounce nugget, or an American gold coin. No other coins or slugs, just gold."

Shiloh smiled in spite of her own grief and disappointment. "That's Mara," she said admiringly to Clay as he tied the mule and helped her step down from the rig. They walked toward the open-air bake shop.

As each customer paid, he pointed to his chosen pie displayed with others on a makeshift table behind Mara. She slid the customer's pie from its pan onto a piece of newspaper and handed it to him. As he backed away, eagerly sniffing his pastry, other eager buyers crowded forward offering payment for their goods.

"There'll be biscuits hot out of the oven this afternoon," Mara announced. Still smiling, she took a hefty pinch of dust between right thumb and forefinger. "Fresh pies each morning and hot biscuits each afternoon. Bring your friends. And tell them to bring gold!"

This brought good-natured laughter from the waiting customers. Laughter also followed when she used her left hand to smartly smack the hand of a too-eager man who tried to shove in front of another customer. Even the chastised buyer laughed when Mara smiled at him.

The men stood respectfully aside as Clay took Shiloh's hand and led her to the counter to stop before Mara. Her forehead was perspiring lightly in spite of San Francisco's crisp air.

Shiloh had just suffered two great disappointments, but she was proud of Mara's enterprising spirit.

"Wonderful, Mara!" Shiloh said sincerely. "Great idea!"

"If you think it's so great, I could use some help."

Surprised, Shiloh considered, aware that the men now silently watching surely knew of her husband's murder, and that she was a young widow in mourning. She would rather have been at home, curled up in bed and trying to make the waves of pain and disappointment go away.

Mara added gently, "You'll be better off here than shutting yourself off alone someplace. Here. Please take this apron and wait on the customers. I've got to rescue some pies from the oven before they burn."

Shiloh started to protest just as four men off to the left suddenly shoved the barricade aside, pulled pistols, and leveled them at the two black woodcutters.

With hands perched defiantly on her hips, Mara hurried toward the intruders. "Why are you men pointing those guns like that?"

The burly leader kept his weapon on Samuel's big chest but spoke to Mara. "These niggers are runaway slaves, and we're here to return them to their owners. So you stay out of this or we'll ship you back with them."

"Don't you speak that way with me!" Mara snapped, moving over to place herself between the burly man's weapon and Samuel's chest. "I'm no slave!"

"How do we know that?" the leader replied sarcastically, placing the gun barrel under Mara's chin and tilting it slightly upward. "You got proof, you uppity yeller . . . ?"

Shiloh interrupted. "Yes, she has!" She hurried toward Mara, aware that Clay was right behind her. "Mara has her freedom papers. I'll vouch for that."

The leader took one look at Shiloh and whipped off his hat. "Beggin' your pardon, Miss, but . . . "

"Mrs.," she interrupted. "Mrs. Aldar Laird."

"Mrs. Laird," the man replied respectfully, lowering his weapon. "I didn't know this here yeller gal . . . "

"That's enough!" Shiloh spoke sharply, again surprising herself at the ability to do that. "You will speak respectfully of Mara. Do you understand me?"

"Yes'm. Now, not meaning no disrespect to you, but me'n my friends here been doin' some checkin', and we found out this big black buck here escaped from his owner in South Carolina some four years back. This other one lit out from down Mississippi way."

"So?" Shiloh challenged, aware that a few hundred men were taking in the whole scene in silence.

"So they both made their way up North where they sailed on a whaler bound for the Orient. There's a reward for runaway slaves, so we're taking them to claim it."

"By whose authority?" Shiloh asked, trying to sound firm.

"The Federal Government, that's who," the leader said, glancing at his three cohorts who nodded in agreement. "According to the Federal Act of 1793, slaves escaped from one state to another are to be returned to their owners. That's what we're doing."

Shiloh fell silent. From her abolitionist father, she had learned much about slaves and laws relating to them. She knew the slave catchers were right. "How much is the reward for these two men?" she asked.

"Why, three hundred dollars apiece."

"I'll pay you the reward, and you let them go."

Mara whispered, "Shiloh, no! You don't have . . . "

"I have the gold dust from sale of the ax heads."

"But that's . . . " Mara started to protest, but Clay cut her off.

Clay said in low, forceful tones, "Excuse me for butting in here, Ma'am, but you don't owe these slave catchers anything."

She turned to him in surprise, aware that everyone else had done the same. "What?"

"No, you don't," Clay assured her. "According to our friend here with the pistol, that law applies between states. Is that right, Mister?"

The burly man nodded. "Yes, but . . . "

"California's not a state," Clay interrupted. "At least, not yet. So the law doesn't apply. Now, why don't you gentlemen put your weapons away and let these men return to their work?"

"Now see here . . . " the leader blustered, but stopped as Clay raised both hands, palms outward.

"Wait," Clay suggested, raising his voice and turning to face the crowd. "What do you men say about this? Are you going to let them take away the helpers for the only good cook in this town?"

An angry chorus from the spectators left no doubt of their opinion.

The slave catchers started to put away their weapons just as Mara let out a shriek. "My pies! You made me let them burn!"

She ran to the oven which was pouring smoke. She reached in with a large cloth and pulled out a very black, very burned-smelling pie. In the same motion, she whirled and took a few quick steps toward the four slave catchers.

"Here!" she cried, throwing the pie at the leader. "Have some pie!"

The crowd exploded in laughter as the hot mixture of dried apples and burned crust landed on the leader's chest. He shrieked in pain and ran off, cursing loudly.

When the joviality had quieted down, Shiloh joined Mara to help sell the last of the earlier baked pies.

"Come back later," Mara called with a big smile to the disappointed men who had been unable to buy any baked goods. "I'll make some more as fast as possible. And tell your friends."

The prospective buyers pushed their way into the gambling tent, which was why Shiloh was sure the owner had let Mara set up her bakery business nearby.

Mara wagged a finger in Shiloh's face. "You took a mighty big risk, offering to buy Samuel and Joseph's freedom. If Clay hadn't come to your rescue, you'd be in worse shape for money than you are now."

"It just popped out."

"Well, you better think before you pop, or next time you may not have a cent to your name." Mara frowned, then added with a grin, "Of course, now that we've got the bakery business started, we won't starve."

"I can't take your money."

"And I can't let you go hungry. Sh! Here comes Clay."

He asked, "Would you two like a ride home?"

"Not me," Mara replied quickly. "I've got to finish my baking."

Shiloh added, "Thanks, but I'd better stay and help Mara. And I'm grateful for what you did to help Mara's friends."

"Anytime." He tipped his hat and walked toward the carriage.

Shiloh dreaded the night when she would again be alone in her bed. Mara seemed to know intuitively how much Shiloh hated bedtime. So she found ways to delay Shiloh's departure as long as possible, urging her to sit in the parlor and see how the first day's bakery receipts turned out.

"Nothing like gold," Mara commented, weighing nuggets on a small balance scale. She entered their weight on a sheet of paper, then gently placed the irregular-shaped pieces in a soda powder can.

Shiloh's thoughts were back on Aldar, so she merely nodded.

Mara finished with the nuggets, then reached for a buckskin pouch. She opened the draw strings and carefully weighed out the gold dust. After entering the results, she gently eased the dust into another poke and placed that inside a second soda powder can.

Shiloh watched, aware that Mara had found a way to survive. Shiloh had not.

Mara asked, "How did it go with your husband's partner today?"

"Not very well," Shiloh replied, and retold the whole incident with MacAdams. As she recalled finding Clay waiting downstairs, there was a knock at the door.

Both women exchanged surprised glances. Mara said crisply, "Throw something over this stuff, then I'll get the door."

Shiloh snatched a quilt from the end of the sofa and spread it over the gold. She finished and looked up to see Mara shoving a pistol into her apron.

"Where'd you get that?" Shiloh asked in surprise. She had never known Mara to own a weapon.

"Borrowed it from a friend." With one hand, Mara gripped the weapon in her apron pocket. With the other, she opened the door slightly.

A slender young man in military uniform stood there. "Begging your pardon," he said stiffly to Mara, "I am Lieutenant Harkins with a message for Mrs. Aldar Laird."

Shiloh moved toward him. "I'm Mrs. Laird."

"Thank you. Here." He handed her a sealed envelope. "Compliments of the commandant. He said I'm to wait for an answer."

Flustered and uncertain, Shiloh started to invite the lieutenant in, then remembered the gold under the quilt. "Please wait," she instructed him, then retreated to the nearest candle to read the note.

Mrs. Laird: It may seem inappropriate for me to address you so soon after your husband's untimely death, but I would like to call on you in the next few days to discuss ways that I might be able to be of assistance in your time of sorrow.

It was signed: *William Rawlins.*

Shiloh handed the note to Mara. She scanned it, smiled knowingly, and handed it back.

The officer asked, "Is there a reply, Mrs. Laird?"

Shiloh had understood Mara's smile. She told the soldier, "Please thank Mr. Rawlins, but I cannot accept."

The lieutenant replied, "There is a second note." He handed it to her, neatly folded.

Frowning, she opened it. *Mrs. Laird, I am reluctant to do this, but I've instructed the lieutenant to pass along this message only if it's necessary. You see, I would like to discuss the possibility that your husband's death may have had something to do with the political ambitions of certain parties in this community.*

Shiloh felt the color drain from her cheeks. "Political ambitions?" she asked, looking at the soldier.

"Sorry, Ma'am, but I know nothing of the contents in those messages."

"Of course." She quickly gathered her thoughts. "Lieutenant, would you mind asking Mr. Rawlins to give me a day or two to think this over?"

"Yes, Ma'am. Day after tomorrow?"

"Yes," she replied. "That would be fine."

When the officer left and the women were alone, Shiloh hurriedly reread the second note. Her mind reeled. Not robbery, but murder—over politics? Impossible! Or was it?

CHAPTER IX

MARA ASKED, "What about politics?"

Shiloh handed the note to Mara. She skimmed it, then handed it back. "I give Rawlins credit."

"What?" Shiloh's thoughts still whirled with the unexpected impact of the second note.

Mara uncovered the gold to continue counting her day's receipts. "As a divorced man, Rawlins is more experienced, so he's the first of the buzzards to start circling. But with such a shortage of women, that's to be expected."

"Are you saying this note is a ruse, and I'm too naive to see that?"

"Well, you certainly are naive. But Rawlins raises an interesting thought. Did your husband ever talk to you about being interested in political matters?"

"Not really, but he did introduce me to some men who are in that field: Denby Gladwin and Jefferson Locke."

"Oh, yes. Samuel and Joseph did some checking for me, but you were too upset to tell you about that before. Locke wants to have California admitted to the Union as a slave-holding state. Gladwin wants California to become a separate nation instead of a state."

"They both said something to Aldar about joining them, but that doesn't sound like a strong enough motive for murder."

"If it really was that."

"I'm just thinking out loud," Shiloh continued. "For instance, anybody plotting murder wouldn't talk about it except maybe to some accomplice. So how could Rawlins possibly know about somebody having Aldar killed for political reasons?"

"Maybe Rawlins himself is responsible."

"Don't be ridiculous! He has no reason."

"None that you know of, anyway."

When Shiloh shot a disapproving glance at her, Mara continued, "You're beginning to sound as if you believe it wasn't just a robbery gone wrong."

"I don't know what to think, but since Rawlins brought it up, I have to consider that possibility."

"If Rawlins isn't involved, then maybe he knows somebody with a motive. Rawlins wouldn't have sent those notes if he didn't have some suspicion, at least."

"How do you figure that?"

"Because if you meet with him and he doesn't have something to back up his remark, you'd be angry, and that's the last thing he wants to have happen. So who had a reason to want your husband dead?"

Faces flickered through her mind. "I've only met four men that I know were involved with Aldar: Kroeber, MacAdams, Gladwin, and Locke. But, except for Kroeber, I don't know why any of them would want Aldar dead."

"Your husband humiliated the Dutchman in the duel," Mara replied. "But that had nothing to do with politics. So what about the others?"

Shiloh recalled meeting Gladwin at the New York Hotel which he owned. "He certainly doesn't make a good appearance," Shiloh told Mara. "But there was a sense of power about him that I can't explain."

"How does that relate to the situation?"

"He told Aldar something like, 'If there's one thing that will give a man an edge in California politics, it's having a wife, especially if she's pretty.'"

"That sounds as if Gladwin and your husband had already talked about that subject."

"A minute after he said that, Gladwin yelled at Aldar that he was pigheaded, but that's hardly a motive for murder. Then Gladwin apologized and said that he hoped Aldar had changed his mind by now, and to come back later and they'd talk business. A strange man."

Shiloh repeated Aldar's and Locke's conversation at church. Shiloh concluded, "Later, Aldar told me that he wouldn't rule out the possibility of someday getting involved in politics to help shape the future of California. He didn't mean running for office, but getting into the inside circle. That way, when the business needed something, he'd know who had the power to make it happen."

Mara asked, "What does that mean?"

"I don't know, but that's when Aldar said that the person who got ahead in transportation was going to be rich. Then he talked again about building me a big house on that hill." She blinked back tears. "He said, 'that's where the giants will be.'"

"We'd better get ready for bed," Mara said, putting the lids on her soda powder cans and carefully replacing the gold scales in their small wooden box. "We'll talk again in the morning."

Shiloh lit a second candle from the one in the parlor and retired to her bedroom. There she lit still another candle and put them both on the stand next to the bed. As always, she read a chapter from her Bible and prayed on her knees before climbing into the high bed.

Sleep eluded her. Rawlins' note had been such a shock, and she didn't want to believe it, but her mind would not let go of the possibilities. If it was murder made to look like robbery, then who wanted Aldar dead? And for political purposes? Why?

MacAdams was certainly a rough-looking character, Shiloh acknowledged to herself. Clay had seemed to be warning Aldar when they first arrived about something wrong at work. What had Clay meant? If Aldar had found out, he hadn't told her. *I'll have to ask Clay what he meant,* Shiloh decided.

She had heard Aldar and MacAdams quarrelling, but that by itself didn't provide a motive for murder. Except for Aldar's trip to Washington to seek government mail subsidies, Shiloh could not see any connection with MacAdams and politics.

I'll not only have to talk with Clay, but I'm certainly curious about what Rawlins' note means.

Shiloh would not have thought of those things, but she had to. She also considered talking to Gladwin and Locke, but wasn't sure what she should say to them.

She closed her eyes and tried to sleep, but another thought jarred her awake again. Mara and Aldar hadn't liked each other. The morning he died, Shiloh had heard them quarreling outside her door. Of course, that had been explained away. Shiloh remembered the crude dolls she had seen once, and the three deaths that had happened so soon after that. Was there a horrible, evil side to Mara that not even Shiloh knew about? Shiloh couldn't bring herself to believe badly of her lifelong friend. She thought, *I know Mara would never do anything like that. I'm ashamed of even thinking of it.*

At dawn, Shiloh awakened with a slight headache from lack of sleep. She had too much on her mind to remain in bed, so she arose and walked woodenly outside to the cookhouse.

Shiloh entered through the door that opened into what had been Mara's bedroom before she moved into the spare bedroom in the main house following Aldar's death.

There was a small wood-frame single bed against the right wall. A candle stood on a small nightstand with an old rocking chair nearby. Shiloh walked to her left, entering an equally tiny room with a rough wooden table, four chairs, and a small wood heating stove.

Shiloh passed through this room to the kitchen which was dominated by a big, wood-burning range. It rested on red adobe bricks. Matching bricks had been used to make the firewall behind the range and stovepipe. Large pots and pans hung from sturdy wooden hooks in the walls. There were staple grocery items on the shelves and a small preparation table near the range.

Feeling guilty over her late-night suspicion about Mara, Shiloh gave her a quick kiss on the cheek. "Good morning. I want you to know how much I appreciate you."

"What brought that on?" Mara asked.

"I was just thinking how close we've been since we were little girls."

"What you really mean is that you want me to help you decide what to do about all the things facing you right now. Isn't that right?"

Shiloh smiled. "I meant what I said, but I could also use some suggestions. I'm still so numb that I don't trust myself to think straight."

"Have you decided about Rawlins' invitation?"

"I'll probably have to see him. But first, I want to walk down to the shore alone to think and pray."

"You need to be thinking about booking passage home. Maybe you need to pray about it too. With the money Clay got for selling the ax heads, and what we'll make selling baked goods, you'll soon have enough . . ."

Shiloh interrupted, "I told you that I can't take your money."

"I don't need it; you do. Besides, I'll soon have lots more. In fact, maybe someday I'll live up there with the goats on that hill your husband talked about."

Shiloh raised her eyebrows.

Mara explained, "Oh, not as somebody's wife. No white man's going to risk that. But nobody will say anything about some rich white man having the best colored housekeeper in San Francisco.

"Don't look at me that way! I gave up your provincial beliefs years ago. But this is not the time to talk about me. Right now, let's talk about your plans for today."

"I'll know those better after I get back from my walk."

"Just don't forget that your goal is to sail for home as fast as you can. It'd be easy to get sidetracked into trying to figure out if Rawlins is right and your husband's death had more to it than a robbery gone wrong. Leave that to the constable."

"I intend to, but I have been thinking about talking to a couple of those men."

"If you mean Locke and Gladwin, you'd better think again. They probably eat nice little girls like you for breakfast."

"It won't hurt for me to just talk to them."

"It might. Suppose that Rawlins is right, and somebody wanted your husband killed for political purposes. Gladwin and Locke are the only ones we know with ties like that. If you go nosing around, your life could be in danger too."

"Why on earth would anyone want to harm me?"

"We won't know that until and if we learn who killed your husband, and why. So be careful."

After Mara left for her bakery, Shiloh started walking north, seeking a quiet spot overlooking the bay.

Breathing hard with the exertion of climbing the hills that

blocked her way, she walked and silently prayed. She poured out her grief, pain, anger, and confusion.

She ended with a whispered plea, "Lord, please guide me. I'm so confused! I don't know what to do next."

She hadn't seen another person for fifteen minutes or so when she eventually found herself on a remote, scenic path. It ran along the side of a cliff above the bay with the Golden Gate to the northwest. The sight brought memories flooding back, and the tears came again, slipping unchecked down her cheeks.

Making sure she was alone, she sat down and gazed thoughtfully across at the Golden Gate while the past unrolled before her. Powerful memories stabbed her with bittersweet sorrow as she sat, face turned to the bay's faint horizon, remembering.

Shiloh and Aldar were side by side on the *Terrapin's* slanting deck as the ship's bow headed directly for that same gap in the headlands. Barely seven miles off shore, the two hundred forty-five passengers peered expectantly to the east. The only women aboard were Shiloh and Mara. Suddenly, through the morning mist, Aldar pointed and shouted, "There it is!"

A great shout went up from the weary passengers as the storm-battered vessel crept forward.

Aldar seized Shiloh and spun her around in his excitement. "We're almost home."

Home! There was such a bittersweet sound to the word, for to Shiloh that meant Pennsylvania and all that was familiar. To her new husband, it meant California, and especially San Francisco.

"Isn't it beautiful?" he asked, his voice husky.

Shiloh studied the barren hills, trying to garner the enthusiasm the sight brought to Aldar.

It took nearly an hour for the ship to enter the San Francisco Bay, already recognized as one of the world's truly great harbors. During that time, Aldar commented, "Who would ever have thought when we met that today we'd be sailing here to really start our life together?"

Shiloh smiled dreamily up at him. She had never seen anyone as handsome as this man with the curly golden hair of a child, but the chiseled male features of an ancient Greek statue. The weather had moderated, so the sky was clear and the latest snowfall crisp and firm the day he arrived in Parks Pond on a lathered horse.

He hailed the first person he saw. "Pardon me, Miss," he said to Shiloh, who was walking alone at the side of the rural road. She looked up, squinting into the sun behind him as he added, "I'm looking for Senator Abner Lorenzo. I understand he's in these parts?"

"Yes, he is, but he's preparing to leave for . . . "

"I expected that. Quickly, Miss, tell me how to find him before it's too late."

"He's at that farmhouse there." She pointed. "I'm going . . . " She didn't get to finish. The tall blond stranger kicked his booted heels into the horse's flanks and hurried away as fast as conditions allowed.

Shiloh stood staring after him, intrigued by his good looks but a little annoyed that he had twice interrupted her. *What an impatient man,* she thought, as she quickened her pace toward the house.

She arrived just as Senator Lorenzo turned away from the stranger who still stood by his lathered mount. Snow crunched under the senator's boots as he strode toward his waiting team and coach, black cape flowing behind him. Shiloh watched him with a certain fascination. He was a big man with a lion's mane of white hair, a prominent hook nose, and pale blue eyes that seemed to impale, and then bore right through anyone who dared meet his glance.

Shiloh was close enough for him to lift a hand in greeting to her as he neared his coach. He threw the cape over his shoulder with a flourish, then whirled abruptly to face the young stranger.

"What'd you say your name was again?" Lorenzo asked.

"Laird. Aldar Laird, sir."

"I like you, Aldar," the senator announced heartily. "You risked a lot on riding all the way from Washington on the chance that you could catch me. Of course, it was hard on your mount."

"I spared him as much as possible, Sir."

"No doubt. But somebody or something always has to pay for what the rest of us want."

"I'll rub him down and take good care of him, Sir. He'll be all right."

The senator nodded as Shiloh came even with the team. "I dare say so. And you will, too, young man."

Aldar Laird dropped the horse's reins and took a couple of quick steps toward the senator. "Does that mean you'll support my request?"

"It does."

As Aldar's face broke into a broad smile, Lorenzo spoke to his driver and the team sprang forward. The rear wheels threw snow which made Shiloh close her eyes and turn her head away. When she looked again, Aldar was smiling down at her.

"Sorry about that, Miss," he said. "But when you're as big and powerful as he is, what's a little snow?"

She started to make some reply, but Aldar suddenly cocked his head to look at her more closely. "Say! You're the young lady who directed me here! I appreciate that, because if I'd been another minute or so later, I'd have had a mighty long ride for nothing."

"I'm glad your trip was successful," she replied, then touched the horse's foam-flecked side. "You may rub him down in the barn if you'd like."

Aldar asked, "You sure the owner of this place wouldn't mind?"

"I'm sure. I live here."

"You . . . ?" Aldar halted his surprised comment. Instead, he said, "If I had known, I could have offered you a ride from the road to here."

"And killed your poor horse?" Shiloh asked with a smile. "Come on. Mara's in the barn. She and I will help you cool him down."

By the time they had reached the barn, Aldar had asked her name and learned that Senator Lorenzo, a staunch abolitionist, was an infrequent visitor with Eldon and Martha Eldridge, Shiloh's parents. Shiloh introduced Aldar and Mara, but Mara eyed the stranger with some suspicion, and didn't help with the horse.

Standing on the *Terrapin's* deck, Shiloh smiled to herself, thinking back on the instant mutual attraction she and Aldar had experienced.

He took his eyes off the approaching California shore and asked, "You smiling because we're almost home?"

"I was thinking about how we met."

He took her hand. "I'm glad we did."

"I guess someday we'll have to thank Senator Lorenzo."

"I'll have to do more than that if he works things out in Washington."

Shiloh looked up quizzically. "Works what out?"

"Next to old Senator Benton of Missouri, Lorenzo's the most powerful man in Congress. He can get things done that will help make our dreams come true here in California."

Shiloh knew about the dreams. She didn't know what Aldar had wanted with Lorenzo, and Aldar hadn't told her. She didn't mind. Her father had never told her much about his involvement in the abolitionist movement, either. That's the way things were.

Above the sound of the sails flapping and the swish of the water as the bow pushed through the bay, Aldar commented, "Lorenzo said a strange thing to me."

Shiloh was surprised that her husband was still thinking about Lorenzo. "What was that?"

"He said that only two things really count in life: money and power, and they go together to make everything else possible."

"Well, he's both rich and powerful."

"Yes, but I don't agree with him. The thing that really counts in life is to do something worthwhile. Like setting up a transportation system that will take people to and from places, bring them news, deliver their packages, take their gold to banks, and generally bind them together."

Shiloh reflected on that as Aldar raised his voice to explain what the passengers were seeing as the ship entered the Golden Gate. "That small fort up there on our right among the trees is the Presidio. It was started the year the United States became a nation."

Aldar pointed out San Francisco's other unique bay features shortly before the *Terrapin* turned slightly southward. Nearer shore, the island of Yerba Buena came into sight, with countless anchored ships showing flags of many nations. Across the bay, barely visible through the fog, Aldar pointed out the peak still bearing the Spanish name of Monte Diablo.

They followed the curved shore around to where Shiloh got her first glimpse of San Francisco. It was sheltered from the sea by a natural amphitheater marked by three steep hills.

Aldar pointed them out to Shiloh: Telegraph Hill closest to the water, Russian Hill beyond that, and almost straight back, Fern Hill. It rose massively farther to the south, behind the haphazard sprawling town of tents, shacks, adobe huts, and other temporary shelters.

Shiloh jumped as a naval ship offshore fired a shot to announce the latest ship's arrival, and the small boats put out from shore to take the *Terrapin's* passengers ashore.

Was it only nine days ago that Shiloh and Aldar had arrived in San Francisco? To Shiloh, it had been a lifetime. Slowly, she raised her head from where it had been supported on her knees. Through the mist of her tears, like the fog that partly obscured the great bay before her, she saw in her mind's eye what she must do.

She grimly reminded herself, *Aldar is dead, but I have to survive. That's my most pressing need. I'd like to see his killer brought to justice, but that's out of my hands, a job for professionals.*

William Rawlins' note suggests that Aldar's death might have been related to politics. I could accept Rawlins' invitation and learn whatever he might know. But if Mara was right, that might be the commandant's subtle way of being with me. That could cause unwarranted talk and embarrassment.

Shiloh sighed, thinking it through. There was a lot about Aldar she didn't know. She thought of two people who might be able to enlighten her.

Shiloh rose, brushed off her skirt, and headed back along the cliffside path the way she had come. She decided, *I'll just come right out and ask them. Now, which one shall I try first? Gladwin or Locke?*

By the time Shiloh had left the bay behind, she had made up her mind.

Denby Gladwin's office was a tiny corner in the back of his tent hotel and restaurant. The only privacy was a piece of canvas sail salvaged from one of the hundreds of ships rotting in the bay.

"What a nice surprise to see you, Mrs. Laird," he said, throwing his stub of a cigar into a brass spittoon. It shared the plank floor with a cluttered assortment of boxes, cans, and barrels.

Gladwin brushed off the only chair for Shiloh, then seated himself on an upturned wooden shipping box. He added, "I was hoping to see you again before you sailed back east."

"How did you know I was planning on that?" she asked in surprise.

"It's the only logical thing to do."

"Yes, I suppose it is," Shiloh replied, anxious to be finished with her unpleasant, self-appointed task.

She continued, "I won't take much of your time. Someone has suggested that my husband's death might somehow be linked to politics . . ."

Gladwin broke in angrily, "Do you think that because I called him pigheaded I had something to do with his death?"

"No, of course not," she protested, sorry she had triggered his quick temper. "But the more I think about it, the more I realize that Aldar had some connection with government. I just thought you might help me learn something that would bring his killer to justice before I leave San Francisco."

Her answer seemed to mollify Gladwin. He leaned back and spoke more gently. "I remember the look on your face Sunday when you realized he hadn't told you about my offer."

"He told me later. Please understand, we had only known each other a few weeks before we were married. There were more important things to talk about."

"Of course. I also know of Aldar's ability to be discreet. That was one of the reasons he would have been so successful if he had joined me in a noble movement to give California her true destiny."

Shiloh's eyebrows shot up at the thought.

Gladwin explained, "You see, Mrs. Laird, if the present unrest between North and South continues to grow back east, it will surely lead to a civil war between the states."

"I really can't believe that." The moment she said it, Shiloh remembered her father's rising anger at slave states and his determination to see the trade abolished.

"Most people don't believe it either, but there are some of us who can read the signs clearly. So some friends and I advocate California becoming a sovereign, independent nation. As such, when the war comes, California's gold and other resources will be sold to whichever side pays better."

He paused, then continued. "I can see by your face that you think I'm a cold-blooded person who'll sell to the highest bidder. But it's not that. I'm a businessman, and I see no sin in making a profit wherever possible."

Shiloh said nothing, but she could understand why her husband had not wanted to associate with this man.

"Besides," he added, "California is separated by thousands of miles from the rest of the Union, and logically should be a separate country."

"Aldar believed distance won't make that much difference when transportation is fully developed."

"Ah, yes, the golden-haired dreamer with his vision of first linking California together with transportation, and eventually, the whole country. His visionary skills in that way are like my own for a sovereign nation."

"Aldar didn't agree with you on that idea."

"He was wrong, just as most people are. Like all the fuss going on right now about electing delegates in August to meet the next month in a Constitutional Convention. If the wrong delegates are chosen, they'll vote for statehood. That will be bad for California."

Shiloh was intrigued by this man's reasoning. "How so?" she asked with genuine interest.

"If California becomes a state, regardless of whether free or slave-holding, we'll be drawn into war between the states. So why risk that?"

He crossed hairy forearms over his chest. "Doesn't that make sense?"

"I simply cannot believe that our country would ever get into a war over slavery."

"No? Let me give you some signs. Last year, the Whig Party won the election, making Zachary Taylor our new president. But some delegates left to form the Free-Soil Party. You know about them?"

"A little. My father is active in the abolitionist movement. I've heard him speak of the Free-Soil Party."

"Good. Then you know they were started because of rising opposition about extending slavery into those territories newly acquired from Mexico, including California. Last year, the Free-Soilers were joined by the Barnburners. You know that name?"

"I don't think so."

"They were a radical element of the Democratic party until last year. The name came from a story about a man who had rats in his barn, so he burned it down to get rid of them. The idea was that the Barnburners would do the same in order to do away with abuses in certain areas. But the important point is that this group was also opposed to extending slavery."

Shiloh struggled to keep up with Gladwin's explanation.

"Naturally," he continued, "the Barnburners were opposed by the Hunkers. That's the conservative faction of the Democratic party in New York. They pretty much controlled the party machinery. They also opposed the rising tide of agitation against slavery."

He hesitated, then added, "There's that word again: slavery. See the pattern?"

"I don't see what this has to do with what you wanted my husband to . . . "

"I'm coming to that. Everywhere back east, there are signs that this slavery issue is getting out of hand. Even the Whigs are fighting among themselves over antislavery and pro-slavery elements."

Gladwin's voice rose with his emotions. "As you know, the United States received thousands and thousands of acres of land from Mexico after they lost the war. There's a fight to have slavery extended into all this new country. That struggle is certain to get worse. In fact, the way I see it, politicians in Washington aren't going to be able to solve it anyway except by force of arms."

Gladwin leaned forward, his hard gray eyes bright with excitement. "If California becomes a separate nation, it can stay out of the fight and become enormously wealthy and powerful. Your husband is—was—a very well-spoken and likeable person. He could have been one of the top men in the new country, maybe even the king or emperor."

The thought amazed Shiloh. *King Aldar? Emperor Laird? Ridiculous! But why Aldar?*

She commented, "I would think you'd want that position."

Gladwin smiled knowingly. "Look at me. What do you see? A short, stout man with a belly and a quick temper. Voters don't elect the man; they elect his looks. I wouldn't have a chance. However, I was in eastern politics enough years to know how to get things done. I came here with a specific goal in mind: to help form a sovereign nation. Aldar would have been perfect to front the movement, especially with a pretty wife like you."

Gladwin took a slow, deep breath. "That's why I wanted him to come back so we could talk. I might have persuaded him to change his mind. Now, it's too late. Well, too late for him, but not for our movement."

"Our movement?"

"Certainly. No man can do this alone, but one man with the vision can gather others who will help make the Empire of Pacifica a reality. We're just not as vocal as those favoring California as a state, whether slave-holding or free."

Shiloh considered the idea totally improbable, but obviously there were others who thought it could come into being. Aldar used to say that all accomplishments began as ideas.

Shiloh left Denby Gladwin without any real answers, yet

she felt assured that he had not wanted her husband dead. But what about Locke? Shiloh had to find out.

CHAPTER X

FROM GLADWIN'S, Shiloh headed for a place where Mara's friend, Samuel, had said Jefferson Locke had his land office. As she moved along, she mentally reviewed what she planned to say to Locke. His interest in real property helped Shiloh recall what Aldar had told her about San Francisco's beginnings.

It had originally consisted of three settlements, with two dating back to 1776 when the cross and sword arrived. Established two months after the Declaration of Independence in the east, a fort was erected to strategically overlook the entrance to the west coast harbor. The San Francisco Presidio, as it was now known, had been occupied by Spanish and Mexican military personnel before the United States took command.

A month after the Presidio's beginnings, Father Junipero Serra founded the sixth of California's missions as Mission San Francisco De Asis. Located inland from the ocean and bay, it was commonly called Mission Dolores.

East of the fort and mission, a small village clung to the bay fronting inland. Originally called Yerba Buena, the community had recently been renamed to the much more pretentious San Francisco.

After the war with Mexico ended and gold was discovered, a rapid influx of miners and others had begun to fill in the areas between San Francisco's three original anchor points.

One of those areas was enhanced by scrub oak and brush, plus a spring. Sand hills, running inland with Market Street from the eastern bay side, sheltered the area of Happy Valley from the sharp seaborne winds. Shiloh guessed that upwards of a thousand tents had been haphazardly erected there.

Shiloh was relieved that her walk had not attracted as much attention as it had when she arrived. In the past few days, several other women had arrived, so she didn't feel as conspicuous as before.

However, she felt somewhat uncomfortable in talking to a pro-slavery man like Locke because her feelings were so strong the other way. *But,* she told herself, *he can vote, and I can't, so there's no use talking about abolition.*

She found Locke in a dusty shack with a sign outside proclaiming, "Lots for Sale."

When she pulled back the tent flap and peered in, she saw Locke standing by a younger, sallow-faced man who was seated before a table on which a map had been spread. Locke recognized Shiloh at once, greeted her, dismissed the other man, then invited her to take the vacated chair.

The short, balding Locke wore the same black suit he had worn in church. When he smiled at her, she again noticed the crooked teeth.

"I'm sorry about your husband," he said, pulling up another chair and sitting across the table from her.

"Thank you."

"I had hoped we would have had a little more time to talk after church, but Aldar hurried you off to meet the preacher. He's quite a character, that Sledger."

"Yes, he is unlike any pastor I've known."

"From what I hear, Mrs. Laird, you're also quite unlike any other woman I've seen in this town."

She smiled. "There aren't many women here by which to make comparisons, Mr. Locke."

"Well, I'm sure that even if there were thousands—and there soon will be—none would have done what you did with those neegras and the slave catchers."

Shiloh raised an eyebrow, surprised that Locke knew about that incident.

"It's all over town. But from the news brought by the latest ship, next year Congress is expected to introduce a more strict fugitive slave law. As I understand it, the law will penalize anyone aiding fugitive slaves. That would include *you.*"

Shiloh took that as a subtle warning. "Of course," she said a little tartly, "that same law will be fair and give slaves the right to a jury trial, won't it?"

"You know that's not possible. Why, they can't even give testimony involving a white man. If we gave neegras any such rights, the next thing you know, they'd want the vote."

"That would make women and them equal, since neither of us can vote." Now there was a sharp edge to her words.

Locke seemed not to catch her meaning. He added, "I hope the same law about coloreds is passed here in September when the Constitutional Convention meets in Monterey. I also hope the delegates will vote for slavery. We've got to keep these people in their place."

Shiloh tensed, but kept her voice calm. "And what is their place, Mr. Locke?"

"You know very well . . . " He hesitated. "Ah! I'd forgotten about your friendship with that yellow gal."

"Her name is Mara, and she's my friend. She has been ever since we were children!"

Responding to the chill in Shiloh's voice, Locke stood. "What can I do for you, Mrs. Laird? You want to buy a lot?"

"No, I . . . "

"Better think about it," Locke interrupted. "A hundred and fifty-foot-square lot over by Portsmouth Square brought $16.50 two years ago and $6,000 last year. It's now worth nearly $50,000. Better buy one now."

Shiloh ignored his remark. The coldness that had developed between Locke and herself forced her to speak quickly. "I wonder if you have any information about Aldar's possible involvement in politics that might have led to his death?"

"How would I know anything about that?"

Shiloh got to her feet. "When we met at church, you asked my husband if he had changed his mind."

"That's right, and when it was obvious that he didn't want to talk just then, Aldar suggested that he come by here the next day to talk. Unfortunately, he didn't live long enough to do that."

Shiloh remembered feeling the tension between the two men last Sunday, much as she now felt between herself and Locke.

"Later," she said, trying to keep her voice from betraying the discomfort she felt in Locke's presence, "my husband told me that you had urged him to give up the express business and work with you to get California admitted into the Union as a slave-holding state."

"That's true. If he had, maybe he could have been elected one of San Francisco's delegates to the Monterey convention. There he could have advocated California being admitted as a slave state. And, if California is admitted to the Union, as almost everyone expects, maybe Aldar could have become one of California's first two senators. Who knows how it might have been?"

"My father has been a lifelong abolitionist, Mr. Locke. My sympathies are with him and others in that movement. I'm pleased that my husband refused to participate with you in the slave-state issue."

"I should have guessed that, Mrs. Laird. Well, to answer your question briefly: I have no idea who would have wanted your husband killed, or why."

Shiloh thanked Locke a bit curtly and said goodbye. She walked out of the tent into the morning fog. It settled about her, as cold as she felt inside. She hurried across the sandy trails that served as sidewalks, frustrated and upset.

Locke, like Gladwin, had talked to Aldar about politics. Shiloh did not like Locke, but she could see no reason why he would have wanted Aldar killed.

Feeling the need to talk with Mara, Shiloh headed toward where she expected her friend to be baking. Instead, she found Mara supervising Samuel and Joseph in putting supplies into the smaller tent behind the big black cookstove.

"All sold out," Mara announced happily, brushing a lock of hair from her eyes with the back of her hand. "If this keeps up, I'll soon be able to open my own boarding house."

"Boarding house? That's the first time you've mentioned that."

"Baking out here in the open was just to make sure every man in town came by. By the time I've looked them all over, I'll have enough gold to start the boarding house. From there . . . ," she left the thought hanging tantalizingly in the air.

"Mara, you scare me sometimes," Shiloh said softly.

"I'm just someone who knows where she's going, and how she's going to get there. Now, tell me what you've been doing."

"I saw both Gladwin and Locke," she began, following Mara to where they could talk privately. Shiloh summarized the discussions. "I felt pretty good about Gladwin," she concluded, "but I can't say the same about Locke. I can't shake the feeling that under his calm, polite exterior, he seemed to feel very strongly about Aldar's refusal to join him. It doesn't make sense, unless maybe Locke is hiding something."

"Such as?"

"I don't know. Anyway, neither Gladwin nor Locke gave me any help in learning if Rawlins could be right about Aldar's death being tied to politics."

"Let the constable handle the investigation. You had better be thinking about boarding the next ship for home. With the money you got for the sale of those pickax heads, you can at least make reservations."

Shiloh slowly nodded. "Yes, I could do that. But I still don't have enough to get home and start life over again. So I've got to find a way to earn income."

"The only working women here are prostitutes."

"Mara!"

"Well, it's true."

"You're working."

"It's different because of my color. There's very little a decent white woman can do around here except get married."

"I won't even talk about that idea."

"Don't be proud, Shiloh. Take the money I offered. I can always earn more."

"Thanks, anyway." Shiloh turned away, ending the discussion. "There's one person I'd like to talk with, but I don't want to go alone. Would you . . . ?"

"You're talking about the Dutchman! The answer is, 'No, I won't.' And you stay away from him too."

"I didn't mention Kroeber."

"You don't have to." Mara frowned sternly. "I been hearing things about him. Samuel said a fellow who came over with him on the ship said this Kroeber left his homeland just ahead of the police."

Shiloh was startled to hear that. "Oh?"

"Seems he killed his wife. He might not mind doing the same for you if you go meddling. So you had better stay away from Kroeber and let the constable handle his job."

"There's only one officer to these thousands of townspeople. He doesn't have a chance unless he has some help, but you're right. I'll stay away from Kroeber."

"Good. Now, when are you going to see that soldier?"

Shiloh thoughtfully studied Mara. "How did you know I had decided to accept his invitation?"

"I know many things my white sister would never understand. I'm sure you realize that being seen in public with him, or any man, is going to cause gossip?"

"It's not as if he's courting me, Mara. He's just being considerate in helping find Aldar's killer."

"Uh-huh." Mara's voice was heavy with friendly sarcasm. "Well, there's no use trying to talk sense with you just now, I guess. Come on. Samuel and Joseph will walk us home and help protect the gold dust my baking earned today."

"You go ahead. I'd better head for the waterfront and see about reserving cabin space for the trip home. That is, if I can find one with a crew that hasn't deserted to the gold fields."

"You're in luck," Mara replied. "Samuel told me awhile ago that the last vessel to arrive had a smart master. He clapped his entire crew in irons after they dropped anchor. Look for the *Falcon.* It should be easy to spot."

Shiloh smiled at the thought of the angry and frustrated crew. "Well, at least there will be someone to man the sails when there's cargo and passengers aboard," she observed. "I'd better check on the cost of passage and sailing date."

Heading downhill toward the waterfront was easier which suited Shiloh. She had done enough walking for one day. She topped the last major sand dune and saw the dock area spread out before her.

Even from a distance, she could see the workmen were different from the miners who frequented the uptown area. The waterfront men spotted her and began raucous calls that made her stop and reconsider going on.

She would have to pass through those dozens of rough men to reach the building where she could inquire about passage home. Shiloh's nose wrinkled at the smell of garbage and other debris daily dumped into the bay. The sight and stench greatly distracted from what otherwise was a beautiful area. But the land was improving.

Even in the few days since she arrived, changes had taken place in the frantic building activity she had seen earlier. Two ships had been partially dismantled so that their bows stuck up on the shore to serve as a hotel and an office. All up and down the shoreline, buildings had been hastily erected. More were under construction.

In the cove, more ships had arrived and been abandoned. Only one showed any sign of life on deck. That had to be the *Falcon.*

Taking a deep breath and summing up her resolve, Shiloh prepared to head down toward the waterfront building where she expected to find a shipping office.

She heard hoofbeats behind her, and turned to see Clay Patton riding bareback toward her on a large brown mule. "'Morning, Ma'am," Clay greeted her, touching his hat brim. "Mara said you were headed this way."

"Good morning," she replied, and noticed that the jackass was blind in the right eye. She explained, "I was going down there to see when I could get a ship sailing for home, but . . . " she hesitated, shifting her gaze to the men below. They had returned to their work. Shiloh decided that was because of Clay's arrival.

"No need for that," he said with just a hint of the drawl she noticed from time to time. "I already checked. I'm sorry, but there's only one ship in the harbor with a crew, the *Falcon.* Her master told me that he would not take aboard a young woman traveling alone."

Shiloh was stunned. "But that's ridiculous!" she said with a bravado she didn't feel. "I traveled here with just my husband and Mara. I can certainly go back by myself."

Clay dismounted. "Not on that ship, it seems."

A wave of panic swept over Shiloh as she followed Clay's eyes across the forest of masts to where the *Falcon* lay at anchor. Shiloh had been very afraid to make the perilous return trip alone, yet she was also aware that her limited resources prohibited her staying here much longer. She certainly didn't know any other woman who might want to accompany her. Now she was really trapped, unable to stay or go without money.

Desperately, she wondered, "What will I do?"

Clay asked, "Do you ride?"

She patted the mule's neck. "I grew up on a farm, so I rode

horses. More recently, I rode muleback through the mountains of Panama. Why do you ask?"

"You probably noticed that horses and mules are rare around here. Owners get top dollar selling them to miners heading for the gold-mining areas. This jack is named Ulysses. He used to pull an express wagon for the company until he lost an eye. Nobody wanted him because he wouldn't be much good on a narrow mountain trail. So I got him cheap off of MacAdams."

"Poor thing," Shiloh said, patting the mule's neck.

"He gets along fine with one eye, and he's got a nice disposition for riding. I thought maybe you could ride him for awhile."

Shiloh was aware how tired her feet and legs were from walking over sandy dunes. "Thank you, but . . . "

"You won't have to ride bareback," Clay interrupted. "I know where I can get ahold of a sidesaddle. It belonged to a *Californio* senorita who left it behind when she and her family fled San Francisco after the war with Mexico ended. I'll bring it by first thing tomorrow."

"I'm very touched by your thoughtfulness," Shiloh replied as Clay dismounted, "but I have no way to care for an animal."

"No need to, Mrs. Laird. You've got room to picket him in back of your house, and I'll come by to water and feed him each day. Now, if you don't mind, I'll walk with you back to where it's a little nicer."

"That's very kind, but a lot of trouble."

"Not for Aldar's wife." Clay knew there was another reason too. He still blamed himself for having taken his wife and son into a dangerous frontier. By helping his friend's widow, Clay eased his sense of guilt for what he had failed to do for his family.

Shiloh fell into step with him as he led the mule behind them. "I appreciate what you're doing," she said sincerely, "but shouldn't you be making your rounds with the wagon so you won't get discharged?"

"Got a friend to spell me awhile."

"Everyone is so kind. William Rawlins sent a note saying he'd like to see me . . . "

"What?" Clay interrupted, stopping abruptly and looking down on her with a frown.

"It's not what you think," she said hastily. "He sent word that he thinks he may have some information that might help find Aldar's killer. Mr. Rawlins wants to talk to me about it; that's all."

Clay didn't say anything for a moment, but gazed at her so disapprovingly that she flushed and didn't know what to say.

"Sorry," he said curtly and started walking again. "I was just surprised. But it's none of my business."

The coolness in his voice rankled Shiloh. "That's what you said when Aldar and I first arrived, although you obviously knew something was going on at work." She paused, then asked, "Is it possible that you know more about Aldar's death than you're saying?"

"Do you think that I'd have kept quiet if I knew anything?" His voice hinted at restrained anger.

She took a deep breath and exhaled before answering. "I shouldn't have asked that, but naturally I'm very curious about what you meant as we arrived and you told Aldar that he hadn't returned a minute too soon."

"Makes no difference now that Aldar's dead," Clay replied stiffly.

"Even if it doesn't," she said, "you were Aldar's friend. Except for Mara, I don't have anyone, so let's at least try to get along."

"I want to be your friend."

"Then tell me honestly: what did you think when I told you about accepting an invitation from Rawlins?"

"It's none of my bus—"

"Please!" she interrupted, looking up him with imploring eyes. "I need to know."

He walked a few steps in silence before answering. "Well," he finally said, "it looks bad for a recently widowed young woman to be seen with any man."

She smiled in spite of herself. "What about you? People are seeing us together."

"That's different. I was Aldar's friend. Everybody knows that." Clay's tone hinted at the hurt he felt that Shiloh hadn't thought of the difference.

She defended herself. "I told you that I'm just seeing Rawlins to possibly learn something that might help find Aldar's killer."

"What could he possibly know about that?" Without waiting for an answer, he added, "It's not your motives I'm questioning."

"Then whose? Oh! I understand. You're just like Mara!" Shiloh's angry retort was out before she could stop herself. "There's nothing between Mr. Rawlins and me, and there won't be!"

Clay stopped and frowned down at her. "You're more blind than Ulysses if you believe that!" he snapped.

She was too startled at his tone to reply.

He continued to look down at her for a long moment, silently handed her Ulysses' reins, then turned and walked stiffly away.

Shiloh's own emotions were still high when she reached home. She tied the mule around in back as Mara came out the back door.

"Where'd you get him?" she asked, walking up to inspect the animal.

Shiloh explained about Clay. Then she added in an exasperated tone, "I don't think he likes me. I thought that when we first met, and I still do."

Mara drew a bucket from the well and emptied the water

into a pail. "Or maybe he didn't like what your husband did in bringing you out here, and he's just trying to protect his friend's widow."

Mara set the water where the mule could reach it before adding, "It sounds to me as if Clay suspects Rawlins has the same intentions I think he has."

"I'm surprised at you," Shiloh flared. "If I thought for one moment that you were right, I wouldn't even consider Mr. Rawlins' invitation. And if Clay thinks that—well, he's as wrong as you are!"

Shiloh regretted that she had allowed tensions to develop with Mara and Clay over Rawlins. Still, his note intrigued her.

After some agitated stewing, Shiloh decided that she had to know what Rawlins meant. When the lieutenant returned for her answer, she would hand him a sealed acceptance to meet with his commandant.

That evening, Shiloh wrestled with her dilemma. To survive, either here or by returning to her parents' home, Shiloh had to have some money. But how? Working women were very rare, and Shiloh had no marketable skills in this strange, faraway land.

She sat wearily on the edge of her bed, too drained physically and emotionally to think straight.

Lord, she silently prayed, *I see no choice but to accept money that I have no way to repay. Maybe I shouldn't be too proud to do that, but I am. Pride is about all I've got left, and I don't want to lose that. Is there something else I'm overlooking? Show me, please.*

Shiloh returned to the parlor where Mara was weighing the day's yellow receipts.

"I'm sorry, Mara," Shiloh said. "I didn't mean to snap at you awhile ago. I've got about all the troubles I can handle, but that's no reason to take out my frustrations on my best friend."

"I understand." Mara carefully set a nugget on the balance

scales. "Making decisions is easy, but making the right one is very hard. You'll work things out."

"I don't see how."

"You just have to know what you want, then figure out how to get it."

Shiloh's brow wrinkled. "I know what I want. It would be so easy if MacAdams would be fair and give me even some of Aldar's share of the business, I . . . "

Her voice faded off, causing Mara to look up. "What're you thinking?"

"About MacAdams."

"He's a hard, greedy man," Mara warned.

"And I'm a desperate woman. I'm going back to him tomorrow to try again."

Shiloh was awakened by Ulysses' loud braying. She looked out the window and saw the animal contentedly munching hay. A sidesaddle rested nearby, showing that Clay had already been and gone.

Shiloh silently chided herself for being rude to him yesterday. She thought, *I shouldn't have gotten angry. After all, I did ask his opinion about Mr. Rawlins. Now Clay will be even more upset because Rawlins' note has made me very curious. When that lieutenant calls for an answer, I'm going to accept. But first, I'll go see MacAdams again. This time, I can ride across town.*

Dressed and mounted in an hour, Shiloh turned Ulysses eastward. She mentally reviewed the new arguments she had thought of to convince MacAdams to change his mind.

The mule's hooves made little noise in the sand as Shiloh topped the first sandy ridge behind the house. Another jackass stood below with a man at his side. The rider's back was to Shiloh, who could see he was inspecting the animal's right front hoof. When he turned his head and brayed at the approaching Ulysses, the man jumped and whirled around. Shiloh gave him a quick smile before he spun away, his back toward her. But in that brief instant, Shiloh clearly saw that a reddish-purple birthmark covered the entire right side of his face.

"I didn't mean to startle you, sir," Shiloh apologized as Ulysses plodded up to the other jack and stopped. "Did your mule throw a shoe or get a stone in his hoof?"

"Stone." His voice was still muffled, facing away.

"Need any help? I grew up around livestock."

"No." He kept his back to her. "I can do it myself."

"Well," Shiloh said, uncomfortable at the man's strange behavior. "If you're sure?"

"I'm sure," he said over his shoulder.

Shiloh said goodbye and rode on. *Poor man! That terrible birthmark must cause him lots of grief.*

After reaching the bottom of the hill, she glanced back. The man had been watching her but turned away.

She hurried on, focusing her thoughts on what she would say to Philander MacAdams, yet she sensed that the man with the mule was now watching her.

He lowered the mule's hoof and silently cursed himself. *I shouldn't have let her see me. If this stupid jackass hadn't . . .* He broke off his thought to give the animal a kick.

"It's your fault!" he cried aloud, again kicking the mule. The agitated mule kicked at the air and moved away.

The man turned back to stare after the woman. He had watched her daily since she disembarked from the ship. He had been very careful, as always, and he was quite sure that neither she nor the Negress had noticed him.

No one came or went from the house without him being aware of it. The tall, bearded man's early arrival with hay and his departure without speaking to the two women in the house had intrigued The Watcher.

He had delayed, puzzling over that. But he would have

been safely away if the jack hadn't picked up a stone in his hoof.

Still watching Shiloh, the man subconsciously reached up and touched his facial disfigurement.

Then he hunched his shoulders, feeling for the hilt of the eight-inch knife he had sheathed beneath his jacket.

CHAPTER XI

At midmorning, Shiloh was prepared to knock on Philander MacAdams' office door when it opened. He hurried out wearing his hat and coat.

"Mr. MacAdams, do you have a minute?"

"I'm on my way to keep an appointment."

She thought, *This will only take a moment,* but as she studied the big man's once-broken nose and the square jaw, she was intimidated. "Oh, I see." She turned away.

"Hold on, Mrs. Laird. I can give you a few minutes." MacAdams removed his hat and motioned for Shiloh to come inside and sit. He continued, "I'm having a terrible time finding someone to solicit new accounts. In fact, things are so bad that I'm on my way to try pirating someone from the competition."

MacAdams sighed heavily. "Your husband was the best I ever met. When he called on a merchant in those hills, everyone liked him and bought from him. Now, all everybody wants to do is mine for gold, and nobody wants to sell anything, including this company's express services." His manner changed. "What's on your mind?"

"You offered to provide funds for my passage home."

"So you've decided to accept, huh? Well, let's get together some night soon to work out the details."

Shiloh involuntarily drew back.

"Look," MacAdams said, "I know you're still crying over your husband's death, but try to think of it in a more practical light. You're the first decent woman I've seen in three years or . . . "

Flushing with embarrassment at her naiveté, Shiloh rose and reached for the door handle.

In two quick steps, he caught her wrist and spun her around. "I'm sorry." It was the first time his voice had a gentle edge.

He released her, saying, "Forget what I said a moment ago, and let's start over. You want funds to go back east, and you'll have them. So if you'll have supper with me, I promise to be a gentleman and we can work out the details. What do you say?"

Shiloh's financial situation made her seek a safer alternative. "On one condition," she said, thinking quickly. "It's a business meeting, so no dinner. We'll meet at my house with my friend Mara present. Agreed?"

He hesitated, then nodded. "Tomorrow night?"

"Seven o'clock."

As she rode Ulysses toward Mara's bakery, Shiloh berated herself for having accepted MacAdams' invitation. Desperation, Shiloh was learning, made a person more willing to compromise. But it brought guilt too.

A dozen or so men were already lining up before Mara's plank counter although her pies wouldn't be ready for some time. She was still rolling out the dough.

Shiloh exchanged greetings with Samuel and Joseph, who were carrying supplies from the small tent to set near the stove.

Mara's discerning eyes narrowed as Shiloh approached. "Your face tells me you didn't get the passage money from MacAdams."

"No, but he promised it tomorrow night." Shiloh glanced at the crowd. "Looks as if you could use some help." She put on an apron and washed her hands in a metal basin while recounting her experience with MacAdams. "I shouldn't have committed you to be present without asking. Can you be there?"

"You know I will, but what makes you think he'll later give you the money since his obvious intention is to see you alone?"

"I—I don't know, but something will work out."

Mara shook her head. "Oh, Shiloh, my innocent little lamb! Anyway, if he won't give you the money, you can still have mine. With that and what you got for the pickax heads, you can get home. But then you'll only have one option: to remarry."

"What?" Shiloh exclaimed in surprise.

Mara brushed a loose strand of hair back from her eyes with a flour-covered hand. "There's nothing to do there but marry. Oh, don't look so stricken. Widows have to remarry, and usually as soon as possible. It's the only way they can survive. So that farmer, Seth Collins, may get you after all."

Shiloh's voice reflected her hurt. "How can you speak of my remarrying at a time like this?"

"It's called reality, Shiloh. Face it."

The cold, flat statement made Shiloh want to scream out a denial. *I loved my husband! He's only been dead a few days! How can you say anything about remarriage now?*

A man's voice called from beyond the crowd of waiting customers. "'Morning, Shiloh."

She turned to see John Sledger. Even in the open, his great bulk dominated the scene. Other men stepped back as he approached.

Shiloh smiled in greeting and motioned him to come around the counter. *He's a preacher,* she told herself with a sense of relief. *Maybe I can talk to him.*

Shiloh introduced Sledger to Mara, Samuel, and Joseph. Then Sledger asked if he could talk to Shiloh privately. They walked to where Ulysses was tied.

"I heard you might be here," Sledger explained, "so I come to see how you're gettin' along."

"I'm glad you came by. And I'm doing as well as can be expected, I suppose."

"It'll be hard, but you'll make it."

"I hope so."

Sledger slowly examined the mule in a manner suggesting he was experienced at judging animals. "He looks sound, except for that eye." The preacher turned to face Shiloh. "The Bible says God has a special heart for widders an' orphans."

"I couldn't even have come this far without the Lord's help," she replied sincerely.

"Anything I can do?"

She wanted to share her problems but wasn't quite comfortable discussing them yet. "Pray for me?"

"Been doing that right along," he assured her. "Will keep on too."

"Thank you."

"Well," Sledger said, his tone changing slightly. "if there's nothin' I can do for you, maybe you'd like to do something for me?"

"Of course. What can I do?"

"Lately, some boys and girls have moved here with their folks. Mostly speakin' foreign tongues, but they all belong to the Lord, regardless of their language, so they need spiritual guidance. I'd like to round 'em up and start teaching them from the Scriptures."

"Wonderful idea," she said, remembering the boys shoveling rats from under the sidewalk.

"Then you'll help?"

Shiloh's eyebrows shot up in surprise. "Help?"

"Yes. Boys an' girls will need a woman's touch, and you're just the one."

"But I can't, Brother Sledger. You see, I'm planning on returning east as soon as I can make arrangements."

"You're not serious?" When she nodded, he shook his head vigorously. "I never even thought o' that!"

"Now that my husband is dead, I have nothing here except Mara." She stopped at the disappointed look in Sledger's eyes.

"I was so sure that you were the right one," he said softly, still shaking his head. "I thought it the minute I laid eyes on you in church."

He turned and absently slapped the mule's neck with a great hand. Ulysses jerked his head up and swung it so his one eye could see the man. Sledger didn't seem to notice. He continued, his voice still showing disbelief, "Why, that first day I even said somethin' about you bein' the hope an' the future of this here place. I was plumb certain that you was God's sign . . . "

"I'm sorry, Brother Sledger," Shiloh broke in. "but I have no means of surviving here. Back home, I have my parents, and their farm, and friends."

"I reckon that's so, but this town needs you an' hundreds of good women—thousands really—like you." His voice low and heavy with disappointment. "They'll come in time, but you're here now, and the need is so great . . . "

He sighed heavily, leaving his sentence unfinished. "You dead certain that you won't change your mind?" he asked hopefully.

"I can't. I'm sorry."

"You've prayed about this, o' course?"

Shiloh frowned, thinking fast. She hadn't even considered that because returning east had seemed her only option. But she said firmly, "I have already made the final decision."

"Not if you ain't prayed about it and got the Lord's guidance."

"But I have no way of surviving here!"

"Maybe you don't, but if the Lord wants you to stay, He'll have a way. Will you promise to pray about it?"

She considered that a second, then nodded.

"Good enough. Let's have a word of prayer now, and then I'll be gittin' on."

She was a little embarrassed as Sledger lifted his huge hands and face to the sky. She had never seen anyone pray like that. She closed her eyes and bowed her head, hearing the preacher's voice rise with the intensity of his petitions. Feeling a little awkward, Shiloh opened her eyes and peeked out. All of Mara's waiting customers had removed their hats and stood in silence, heads bowed.

That afternoon, Shiloh stayed in her room, praying and thinking. *Am I wrong to go home, Lord? Is that why I can't seem to get the passage money I need? I'm lonely and afraid, and I don't feel comfortable here. Nothing's gone right since we arrived in San Francisco. And today Mr. Rawlins will want his answer. I want to know what his note meant, so I'll have to meet with him. Is that wrong?*

She read her Bible, seeking an answer in the familiar promises of the twenty-third Psalm. *Though I walk through the valley of the shadow of death. . . . Thou art with me.* She flipped the filmy pages, her eyes falling on words she had written down from a favorite passage in the Old Testament before leaving Pennsylvania: *Behold, I send an angel before thee, to keep thee in the way, and to bring thee into the place which I have prepared.*

Shiloh pondered that, waited, shrugged, then turned to the New Testament. *Lo, I am with you alway, even unto the end of the world.*

Shiloh closed the Bible and wondered, *Lord, are those promises for me? Help me to understand, please.*

Shiloh said very little that evening as she and Mara prepared dinner. Mara seemed to understand. When the meal was finished, Shiloh said she needed some time alone to think. She drew her cloak about her shoulders against the chill of dusk and started to open the door just as there was a knock.

The young lieutenant stood there. He greeted her formally and handed her a sealed note. Shiloh excused herself and carried the note to her bedroom.

Mrs. Laird, I trust that you will grant me the opportunity to see you in your home about seven on Monday evening to discuss the contents of my last note.

She wrote on the bottom of Rawlins' note: "That is agreeable with me." She signed it and took it back to the officer. When he was gone, she left on her walk.

A full moon was just rising across the eastern waters, and the western bank of fog had not yet rolled in from the sea. To the north, campfires burned outside the tents or makeshift cabins spread across San Francisco's hills. To the south, there were few lights in the unpopulated peninsula leading toward San Jose. The melancholy lights and shadows perfectly matched Shiloh's mood.

The pungent fragrance of wood smoke drifted to her nostrils as she thoughtfully made her way through the night. She reached the shore without seeing or hearing anyone.

Shiloh moodily watched the dancing bridge of moonlight on the bay until she came to a large boulder at the water's edge. She scrambled up and sat down, trying not to weep at memories of another great rock—Aldar's "dream rock."

She resumed her silent prayers. *Lord, it never occurred to me to stay here. Why should I? My husband is dead. His dream—our dreams—are gone with him. Mara is building her own life, as she should. I have no reason to stay in California that I can see, in spite of what Brother Sledger said. But on the other hand, what do I have to return to?*

She let her mind drift, visualizing the same old rigid Christianity that her adoptive parents practiced. There would surely be endless smug comments like "Aldar the dreamer," or "I told you so." Shiloh wondered if Seth Collins was still single. If so, she was sure her parents would again encourage her to consider him as a husband.

Shiloh continued silently, *Lord, I'd go back because it's familiar; my childhood home. I came here expecting to have my very own first home with Aldar. Instead . . .*

She let the thought drift away uncompleted. With a frown, she considered John Sledger's request. Her silent prayer continued. *I'm in no condition to help him start a school. I wouldn't be able to concentrate. I guess I never will until I know who killed Aldar and why. But even that takes a back seat to finding a way to survive. Oh, I'm so mixed up I don't know what to do!*

Her thoughts flickered to MacAdams, then Rawlins. Shiloh shook her head, remembering the disapproval in Clay's eyes over her plans to see Rawlins. She wondered what Clay would say if he knew that MacAdams was coming to her house. Exasperated, she wondered, *Why does everything have to get so complicated?*

She didn't know how long she sat there in the moonlight, lost in alternating thought and prayer. Gradually all the crushing problems engulfed her in fresh grief, and she began to cry softly.

After some time, she stopped her weeping. She was suddenly overwhelmed by a strange sensation that someone was watching her. Slowly, she turned her head, searching through the moonlight and shadows. She heard or saw nothing, yet the uneasy feeling persisted.

Not really frightened, and blaming her imagination, Shiloh nevertheless eased down from her rocky perch and headed for home. She kept glancing over her shoulder but reached the house safely. She stepped inside and momentarily leaned against the door.

Mara looked up from where she was making entries into her record book. "What's the matter?"

Shiloh felt a little foolish as she explained.

"Nothing strange about it," Mara assured her. "This town is full of men who would follow any woman they could find, especially a pretty young widow."

Shiloh hung up her cloak. "But I didn't see anybody. I just sort of sensed it. Oh, I'm sure it was silly."

After breakfast the next morning, Shiloh had finished dressing for church when she heard Clay's wagon arrive. Shiloh wanted to apologize for her remarks the day before, so she walked outside. Clay stood beside the wagon, working on her saddle.

"'Morning," he said, the hint of drawl noticeable. "I remembered that the cinch wasn't quite right on your sidesaddle, so I came to fix it."

"Thank you." She started to apologize, but without looking up, he spoke first.

"You own a gun, Mrs. Laird?"

The question startled her. "No. Why do you ask?"

He raised his eyes to meet her. "You went to the beach last night."

"Yes, but how did you know?"

He avoided a direct answer. "You know how to read sign?"

"You mean, tracks and things like that?" When he nodded, she said, "As a girl growing up on the farm, I could tell a rabbit track from a raccoon's, and . . . "

"I mean human footprints."

Shiloh tried to suppress the fear that arose instantly in her. "What're you saying?"

"Have you seen anybody hanging around here or following you?"

The question rocked her composure. "No." She frowned. She hesitated to mention her uneasy feeling of last night. "Why do you ask?"

"When I got here this morning, I noticed your footprints, and a man's. Yours started and returned to the house. I got curious and backtracked. He began following you about a hundred yards from here."

Shiloh felt goosebumps rise on her shoulders.

Clay continued, "He stopped about fifty yards from where

you went to a big rock. I don't want to alarm you, but whoever it was then followed you back here."

The ripples of gooseflesh erupted in a spasm down Shiloh's arms. "Are you sure?"

"I'm sure."

Before she thought, Shiloh blurted, "How do I know it wasn't you?"

Clay stiffened and got up very quickly, eyes blazing. Then, wordlessly, he turned and strode quickly to the wagon. He fairly leaped into the seat and released the brake. The mules took off rapidly with a rattle of chains and creaking of leather.

"Wait!" Shiloh called. "I didn't mean that!"

Clay didn't seem to hear but kept going.

Shiloh stared after him. *I've done it again,* she admitted with a sick feeling. *What's the matter with me?*

Shiloh dug around in her trunk and brought out a very simple dress for the planned talk in the parlor. That evening, Shiloh nervously answered the door to Philander MacAdams' knock. He wore a dark suit that didn't fit well.

She invited MacAdams in and introduced Mara.

MacAdams nodded briefly to the other woman, who returned the gesture but said nothing. He still stood, ignoring the upholstered chair where Shiloh indicated he should sit.

"There are some business matters we need to discuss privately, Mrs. Laird," he said with a disarming smile. "We're going out."

Shiloh shook her head. "I can't do that, Mr. MacAdams. We agreed to discuss everything here."

"I know," he said, still smiling. "But there are subjects that need to be addressed just between the two of us."

"I can't," Shiloh repeated. "You can say anything in front of Mara."

"I don't want to take that risk because this concerns Aldar. Besides, we won't be gone very long."

Panicky, Shiloh exclaimed, "Mara must come along."

"I'm sorry," MacAdams, said quickly, "but I have only a small carriage with room for two. I'm sure you'll both understand."

Shiloh understood that she had been duped. If she wanted the money to get home she'd have to go along with MacAdams. Her anger blended with embarrassment as Mara came into the room and handed Shiloh's cloak to her.

Mara whispered, "You'll be all right." She raised her voice to add, "I'll wait up for you."

Sitting stiffly in the carriage beside MacAdams, Shiloh berated herself for being a naive young fool. She wished she had been more firm in her refusal to leave the house. Instead, she stared silently at the sandy roadway and the moving shadows cast by the moon and the vehicle's faint tallow lights.

The horse turned his head to look back and whinnied. MacAdams removed the buggy whip from its socket and lightly flicked it over the horse.

"Fog hasn't come in yet," MacAdams commented.

Shiloh was too upset to reply. *He lied to me,* she stormed silently. *Well, it won't do him any good. I'm glad it's so dark that nobody will see us. What would they think if they saw me just days after Aldar's death?*

It was a mortifying thought, and each soft crunch of the horse's hooves in the sand made the mortification worse. She dredged deep inside herself to find some strength to say she had changed her mind and ask him to take her home.

She cleared her throat. "Mr. MacAdams . . . "

He interrupted. "Please call me Philander. And may I call you Shiloh?"

"Mr. MacAdams," she replied deliberately cool, "I would prefer to be called Mrs. Laird."

"Of course. My apologies." There was no contriteness in his

voice, only perfunctory politeness. "Mrs. Laird, do you have any idea of who might have wanted your husband dead?"

The question was unexpected, but she reacted with quick mental images. Fritz Kroeber's face flashed in her mind's eye, then was instantly replaced by memories of the angry words MacAdams himself had directed at Aldar the day she met his partner. Shiloh also remembered the strange questions Denby Gladwin and Jefferson Locke had asked her husband. But that didn't mean any of them had enough motivation to kill Aldar.

When Shiloh didn't replay, MacAdams prompted, "Well? Do you know of anyone?"

Shiloh slowly shook her head. "Except for the man Aldar fought in a duel, I can't think of any reason why someone would want him dead. Constable Logan feels Fritz Kroeber is an unlikely suspect."

"He couldn't have," MacAdams continued, "because several men swear he was playing cards at the time of the murder. He had been there all night."

Shiloh felt cheated that her prime suspect had such a firm alibi. *If it wasn't Kroeber,* she thought, *then I can't imagine who might have been responsible. Perhaps it was just a random robbery attempt after all.*

"Logan told me there was evidence the killer was expert with his knife, more than most ordinary men would have been."

Shiloh clamped her eyes tightly shut, trying to stop the gruesome memory of finding her husband's lifeless body rolling in the tidal waters, but the horrible picture was seared into her mind forever.

MacAdams continued, "You know, there could be more than one man involved."

Shiloh opened her eyes. "Why do you think that?"

"Well . . . " he began, but stopped when the horse whinnied and turned to look back. MacAdams reached out with the whip and lightly snapped it above the animal. When the horse was quiet again, MacAdams continued, "I would prefer to discuss that later."

"And I would prefer to discuss it now." Shiloh was startled at her own sharp retort.

"Very well," MacAdams replied. He hesitated and replaced the light buggy whip in its socket. "A few days before you and your husband arrived, I happened to be at the waterfront when a ship was putting passengers ashore. I recognized one of them."

MacAdams turned toward Shiloh, his face only faintly outlined by the reflected carriage lamps. "His name is Urbane Haddock. Ever hear of him?"

"No." She had no idea why that name had been introduced into the conversation.

"Well, I had, even before I came to California. He's a slimy character, like many who hang around Washington. He never moves in the light, but always in the shadows, making deals, planting rumors, quietly disrupting things or whatever else he was paid to do."

"I don't think I understand."

"As you know, greed, power, and money are the seamier parts of government which corrupt many men. That's what happened to Haddock."

A tingle of anticipation made Shiloh involuntarily draw her shawl closer about her shoulders. "What's that got to do with Aldar?"

"I'm coming to that. When I saw Haddock at the waterfront, I wondered who had sent him—rather—who had paid him, and what he was here to do. You can be sure it was nothing good."

"Are you suggesting that he killed Aldar?"

"Oh, no! Haddock's too smart to ever do anything himself. His technique is to find someone who will benefit from what he has in mind, make a deal with them, and leave the details to that person, whoever he is."

"Then you think he got someone to . . . ?"

"I don't know," MacAdams interrupted. "But he was only here a few days. Went on to Monterey, I heard. However, nothing has happened to anybody around here, except Aldar."

Shiloh said suspiciously, "Is that all you had to tell me, Mr. MacAdams?"

He seemed to sense her feeling. "No, there's more. I have learned that while he was here, Haddock talked to Jefferson Locke, Denby Gladwin, and William Rawlins."

Shiloh stirred uneasily in her seat, trying to understand what significance that might have.

MacAdams added, "I didn't say anything at first because I assumed that Clay Patton had told you or your husband. Clay knows Haddock, and saw him come ashore."

"He did?"

"Yes. But when I mentioned it to Clay a few days ago, he said he had not told Aldar or you. Clay said it was none of his business."

That's Clay all right, Shiloh thought. *Minding his own business. That must have been what he meant when he told Aldar he hadn't gotten back any too soon.*

"I appreciate your telling me this," she said sincerely, "but I've got to think about it when I get home. Please drive me back there now."

MacAdams reined in the horse and leaned toward her. "You are the best looking woman I've seen in years," he said in a husky whisper.

Shiloh quickly tried to draw back, but it was too late. His arm slipped around her shoulders and pulled her close, his breath hot against her cheek.

"Mr. MacAdams! Please! You promised to be a gentleman!" She struggled to pull back.

"Be nice to me," he said huskily, trying to kiss her, "and I'll be nice to you."

Suddenly a man's angry but wordless shout erupted out of the night.

"What the . . . ?" MacAdams exclaimed, releasing Shiloh and whirling toward the voice.

Shiloh saw a shadowy figure run across the roadway, his right hand upraised. Moonlight glinted on a long knife blade. Shiloh screamed as the attacker rushed the carriage, reached inside, and slashed down toward MacAdams.

MacAdams twisted away, raising his left arm to block the blow while his right arm reached for the whip.

Shiloh screamed again at the sound of clothing being ripped and the attacker's loud, furious breathing. Neither man spoke as the knife rose and fell again, but in his twisted mind The Watcher silently screamed, *Leave her alone! She's mine!*

CHAPTER XII

An hour later, Shiloh and Mara finished bandaging MacAdams' left arm and shoulder. None of the injuries was serious, although his coat was ruined.

"You were very fortunate," Mara said. "Those wounds could have been a whole lot worse, especially if he got you in the chest."

"Yes," Shiloh agreed, "it was a good thing you drove him off so quickly."

"He surprised me," MacAdams admitted.

After blocking all but the initial blows with his left forearm, MacAdams flicked the stinging leather-tipped end of the whip around the attacker's face and eyes. When he backed up, MacAdams reversed the whip, raining heavier blows upon the attacker with the handle. He fled into the night.

"It was the strangest thing, Mara," Shiloh said. "He never said a word."

"Obviously, whoever he was thought he was protecting you," MacAdams said. "But I'd guess there isn't a man in this whole town who wouldn't do that if he could."

Except you, Shiloh thought.

"It's my own fault," MacAdams continued. "I noticed my horse kept whinnying and looking back, so I should have been suspicious when another horse didn't pass us."

Mara picked up the white strips of cloth she had used for bandages. "If you had stayed here," she said pointedly, "it wouldn't have happened."

MacAdams shrugged. "I can't argue with that, but it was worth the risk."

"What bothers me most," Shiloh said, wondering if MacAdams meant that as a compliment, "is that whoever it was used a big knife, and . . . " She couldn't finish the thought as she saw again in memory what a knife like that had done to Aldar.

"It can't just be a coincidence," MacAdams said, using his right hand to pick up his coat. "I'll point that out to the constable when I report the attack."

"Better have the doctor look at that arm," Shiloh urged.

"I've been hurt worse." He headed for the door.

Shiloh followed him. "Mr. MacAdams, this probably isn't the time . . . "

He cut her off, "Be at my office tomorrow morning."

After he had gone, Shiloh sat down heavily on the sofa. "I think he's going to give me the money, so it will turn out all right, after all," she told Mara.

"You still trust him?"

Shiloh thought about that before answering. "Well, he did lie to me—twice, in fact. But I'm hoping that after what happened tonight he'll keep his word."

"Don't count on it," Mara warned. She turned to leave the

room, then added, "I hope you have better luck with that soldier when he comes calling."

"It's not the same. I'm sure he's a gentleman."

"Soldier or merchant, they're all alike."

Shiloh spent another restless night. She tried to imagine who had assaulted MacAdams, and why. There was no doubt in her mind that there was some connection between the knife attack tonight and Aldar's death, but she couldn't think what it was. Yet whoever it was had protected her. So could he also have killed Aldar?

With an effort, Shiloh turned her mind to Rawlins, and what he meant in his note. *I would like to discuss the possibility that your husband's death may have had something to do with politics.* He would explain tomorrow night, so all Shiloh could do was wait.

Her thoughts leaped again. *Clay is sure touchy. I wonder what he'll say about all this? Well, there's no use in telling him, so I guess I won't find out. But I must ask him about Urbane Haddock.*

Shiloh turned over, and again tried to sleep, but Mara's warning about not trusting MacAdams started running around in Shiloh's mind. *Well,* she assured herself, *that money rightfully belongs to me. It's not nearly worth what Aldar's share should be, but at least it's something. It will be enough to at least get home. But if Philander MacAdams breaks his word again, then what?*

She didn't have the answer to that question when she arrived at MacAdams' office shortly after nine o'clock the next morning. He did not rise from his chair when she entered, but she greeted him in a friendly fashion.

"How's your arm?" she asked.

"Hurts like blazes," he replied curtly.

"I'm sorry," she replied, sensing his foul mood. Fear about the success of her mission flitted through her head, so she plunged ahead quickly. "I appreciate the reason you invited me here this morning."

"It's a bad time for me," he answered, leaning forward in his squeaking chair. "I've been trying to hire someone to solicit clients as your husband did. The town is loaded with men, but they're all headed for the gold fields. Nobody wants to work at an ordinary job. I've just been turned down by my last real prospect."

"I'm sorry," she said, anxious to complete her business with him. "I hope you'll find someone soon."

"I'm running out of time. The next thirty days are crucial." He blew noisily through his mouth and leaned back. "But that's not your problem. You want money for passage back east."

"Yes. Your offer will make it possible for me to leave on the first available ship."

MacAdams shook his head. "I'm more sorry than I can say, Mrs. Laird, but I took a look at my books this morning, and I can't do it."

Shiloh knew she shouldn't be surprised, but she was hopeful and desperate. "Mr. MacAdams, you said . . . "

"I know, and I'm sorry, but business is so bad that I'm going to have to back out of my offer."

Shiloh rose in stunned silence.

MacAdams also stood. "If I could get a good man out there drumming up new business, I'd give you the funds. But I'll be lucky not to lose the whole business the way things are now."

Numbly, Shiloh started toward the door, then suddenly turned back. "Mr. MacAdams, I've *got* to have passage money home."

She forced herself to pause, afraid she was about to appear to be begging. But since the scare she had over someone following her, and remembering the attack last night, she was very anxious to leave San Francisco. Now, her only hope was slipping away.

MacAdam declared, "You'll have to look somewhere else." He followed her to the door but didn't offer to open it for her. "Uh . . . did you ever find out if Aldar left a will?"

She shook her head.

"Nothing? You never found a thing?"

"No. Well, some papers that I wasn't in the mood to read. Which reminds me, I'll have to find them again and read them, now that I can think a little better."

MacAdams studied her thoughtfully. His voice changed to brusqueness again. "You know, if you were a man . . . "

When he hesitated, she prompted, "Yes?"

"Forget it," he said.

Desperation made Shiloh grasp at any hope. "What difference would it make if I were a man?"

"I was just thinking that I need a man to call on merchants in Sacramento and the gold country. You know, drumming up business for this company. The pay is good, plus expenses and commissions. But there's not a man in this whole blasted town that would rather do that than try to strike it rich mining for gold. The fools! The real money's in goods and services."

Shiloh opened the door. "I have never wished to be a man," she assured him, "but right now, I almost wish I were. Well, I'd better go help Mara at her bakery. Goodbye, Mr. MacAdams."

She walked into the hallway and started down the stairs, fighting a sense of despair.

"Mrs. Laird, wait!"

She stopped and looked back at MacAdams. He had jerked the door open and stood in it, scowling.

"Yes?"

"I may be doing one of the most stupid things in my life," he said, "but come back inside a moment, please."

She reentered the office but didn't take the seat he indicated.

"Did your husband ever tell you what he said or did when he called on merchants for this company?"

"Many times. Why?"

"I am losing business hand over fist because there's nobody out in the field beating the bushes for new business, or calling on those accounts I already have. Now, nobody ever heard of a woman doing that, but this is California, and nothing's the same as back east, so I was thinking . . ."

MacAdams paused, shaking his head. "No, it won't work. It was just a thought."

"If you're suggesting that I might take my husband's place in calling on merchants—"

"Forget it, I said. I'm sorry I even mentioned it."

Shiloh reached for the door handle, then turned back to face MacAdams. "Are you willing to pay a man's wages for someone to call on merchants?"

"Plus expenses and commission. You want to try it?"

It was such a wild idea that Shiloh's natural inclination was to turn it down. But she was desperate. She also fleetingly recalled that Lydia in the Bible had been a seller of purple dyes and fabrics. Shiloh saw nothing wrong with a woman being in business, even though the concept was not widely accepted in the society of her day.

"For two weeks?" she asked. "That should be time enough to see if I can do it."

He bobbed his head in agreement. "Two weeks."

"Salary and expenses paid in advance." Shiloh was surprised to hear how quietly but firmly she said that.

He threw back his head as though he were going to laugh, then stopped. "You're desperate and so am I."

His eyes swept her pretty face and trim body. "It might just work, except . . . no, it wouldn't. A young widow alone in those rough mining camps. Unless your Negress would accompany you."

Shiloh didn't reply, but thought, *Mara's bakery business is thriving. She couldn't leave it.*

MacAdams shook his head, "Even if she would, that still wouldn't work. In fact, two women might even be worse. You'd need a capable man along with a gun."

Shiloh realized the hopelessness of what was being proposed. She thought, *If Brother Sledger was right about the Lord wanting me here, He's sure not making it easy.*

"Thanks, anyway," she said, starting out the door.

"Wait! Wait! I'm thinking. If I hired someone, that would raise my costs more, which I can't afford. But if I sent along someone who's already on the payroll."

Shiloh guessed who MacAdams meant and started to protest, but he plunged on.

"I've got an employee who was a good friend of your husband. Name is Clay Patton. I believe you've met him?"

"We've met," she said, thinking of her last thoughtless remark that had sent him angrily stalking away.

"I could reassign him to accompany you women."

"Oh, no! I don't think he . . . "

"He'll do it for two weeks if I order him to do so."

MacAdams turned to the desk, opened a drawer, and handed her a package. "Everything you'll need is in there: prices, the services we offer, contracts. I've had this ready for the man I planned to hire but couldn't find."

She took the package as he reached under the counter. "And here's two weeks' pay, plus expenses."

Shiloh looked at the locally made slugs which had a dollar value stamped on them. Shiloh remembered Mara's example and shook her head. "I'd prefer gold, Mr. MacAdams, if you please."

He stared at her, then chuckled. "Maybe you've got more business sense than I gave you credit for." He reached under the counter and removed the lid to a wooden barrel. "Here," he said, handing her a small buckskin poke. "If you want to weigh it, the scales are at the end of the counter."

"That's not necessary," she replied.

"Then we have a deal?"

Moments later on the street, the enormity of what she had agreed to do struck Shiloh. *What have I done?* she asked herself with a mental groan of anguish. Then she brightened. *Mara can't go, so the whole thing's off. But I sure hate to give back this money.*

Shiloh stopped by Mara's outdoor bakery to report on MacAdams' offer.

"You agreed to do what?" Mara exclaimed, putting the finishing touches on a pie before putting it in the oven.

"Keep your voice down, please," Shiloh urged, shooting a glance at the men crowding around the counter.

Mara almost hissed, "You're out of your mind!"

"I . . . I didn't know what else to do."

"Before you did anything involving me, you should have checked. I'm running a business here."

"Yes, I know. I figured that you couldn't do it, but with that money in my hands and the possibility of earning more through commissions—"

Mara interrupted, her tone softer. "Ordinarily, I'd be glad to go, but I can't leave my baking right now. Besides, things are changing, Shiloh. I'm going out on my own, and you're going on yours."

Shiloh hesitated, unwilling to accept the truth. However, when Mara continued her pie making as though the subject was closed, Shiloh slowly turned away. *I've got to return this money to MacAdams,* she thought. *Then I'm right back where I started.*

Mara called, "No hard feelings. Understand?"

"I understand. Now, what can I do to help?"

Shiloh stayed through the baking and selling of the pies, her mind spinning with the latest complication. When Mara started preparing to make biscuits to sell in the afternoon, Shiloh told Mara she had some things to do.

As she rode Ulysses toward home, she scolded herself for even considering MacAdams's offer. *I should return his money right now,* she thought. *But I'm not up to facing him again just yet. I've never sold anything in my life, so I'd probably have failed anyway. Then there's Clay. I'm sure he wouldn't be happy to go along after what I said to him. Well, I'll return the money tomorrow. Then what?*

At home, she unsaddled and picketed Ulysses, then walked to the back door. She was in the process of inserting her key into the lock when she noticed that the door had been forced open. She panicked. *Somebody's broken in! Maybe he's still inside!*

Her first thought was to get away, but she forced herself to stand still and listen. Hearing nothing, she gingerly pushed the door open and gasped.

"Oh, no!" she exclaimed. Everything was a shambles.

Alarmed, Shiloh whirled to leave, then stopped.

"My pickax money! Mara's gold!" Shiloh breathed the words aloud, then dashed across to the cookhouse. A quick peek through the windows showed that none of its three small rooms had been ransacked.

Retrieving the hidden key from a flowerpot hanging from a beam over the cookhouse door, Shiloh managed to make her shaking fingers work the lock. Fearfully, she stepped inside, eyes probing for a sign of any disturbance. There was none.

With rapidly beating heart, Shiloh knelt by the cold range and reached for a brick just in back of the right front metal leg. There was nothing to indicate that Mara had carefully removed a brick and replaced it. No one would have seen that it had been disturbed.

Please, Lord, let it still be there!

She removed the loose brick at the expense of two broken fingernails. A hole had been dug deep into the earth. There the hidden soda powder cans remained undisturbed. Still, to play it safe, Shiloh lifted each lid to check. The separate cans of dust, nuggets and gold coins were undisturbed. The pickax gold and Mara's bakery earnings were safe.

"Thank God," Shiloh whispered aloud.

Yet she felt violated because somebody had broken into her home during daylight hours. But whoever it was had not found the gold, for which Shiloh was very grateful.

She returned to the main house and quietly stepped inside. She strained to hear above the throbbing of her frightened heart. The house was silent. Carefully, tense and alert, Shiloh hurriedly searched every room. Every one had been thoroughly ransacked.

Drawers were pulled out, furniture knocked over, and anything loose scattered. Mara's bedroom had been searched, but Shiloh's was a total disaster.

Clothes were yanked out of the closet and thrown on the floor. Both hers and Aldar's trunks had been dumped and rifled through. Every dresser and highboy drawer had been pulled out and the contents spilled.

So far as she could tell from her quick search, nothing seemed to be missing. *But why would someone break in and not take anything?*

Saddling Ulysses, she hurried back to Mara's place.

Samuel was putting wood into the firebox on the big, black stove. Joseph was opening a barrel of flour. They greeted her, but she just nodded to them, going directly to Mara at the makeshift counter. The other side was lined with eager buyers of Mara's freshly baked biscuits.

"I've got to talk to you," Shiloh whispered.

"Not now." Mara gave a whiskered miner a big smile as she took his gold and handed biscuits across to him.

Shiloh leaned close to whisper into Mara's ear. "Somebody broke into our house!"

Mara's eyes showed fear. "Did they . . ?"

"No," Shiloh interrupted.

Mara relaxed. She spoke to the dozen or so male customers, each eager to be the next buyer. "Just a minute, please, gentlemen." Turning to Shiloh, Mara lowered her voice and asked, "Then what did they take?"

"Nothing I could think of. I'm frightened!"

"Samuel," Mara said, turning to the big black man. "Please find Constable Logan and have him come to the house after sunset. Then find Clay Patton and have him do the same."

The runaway slave put the flour barrel down, nodded, and left.

Shiloh stayed and helped Mara until the hot biscuits were sold. When everything was hurriedly put away, Mara gave Joseph a small bag of dust, telling him to split it with Samuel. Then the two women hurriedly walked home. Shiloh led the mule while speculating on who might have burglarized them, and whether he would return to search for the gold he had missed that morning.

The constable arrived shortly after the women finished inspecting the house. They led him through every room and the cookhouse. Neither woman mentioned the gold or where it was hidden.

Returning to the parlor, Shiloh asked anxiously, "Do you think he'll come back, Mr. Logan?"

"It's hard to say. Since you both say you can't find anything missing, it's possible that whatever he was after may be worth him trying again."

Shiloh licked dry lips, fearing the night. *What if he comes back and tries to force us to tell where the gold is?* Fighting off a shudder of fear, she asked the constable if MacAdams had reported last night's knife attack.

"Yes, he did. I was going to come ask you for your statement about what happened, but I was delayed because of working on your late husband's case."

"Are you making any progress?"

"Sorry to say I'm not. It's not from lack of trying, Mrs. Laird. Believe me, I'm trying."

"I'm sure you are."

He paused, hand on the doorknob. "I'll keep looking. But the truth is that it's not going to be easy to find your husband's killer. Fact is, even if we caught whoever that was, or the person who burglarized your home, this town doesn't even have a jail. However, there is talk of turning one of those abandoned ships in the harbor into a temporary jail."

He opened the door and started to step out, then paused. "I guess you don't have to be told that it's not a good idea to be on the streets at night. Sometimes even weekend afternoons are dangerous, what with the Hounds running loose."

"The Hounds?"

"Sometimes called the Regulators."

Mara said, "I heard about them. The alcalde . . . what's his name?"

"Thaddeus Leavenworth," Logan answered.

"He commissioned a bunch of former New Yorkers as a sort of unofficial police force. They work out of a tent they call Tammany Hall."

"Those are the ones," the constable agreed. "Anyway, it turns out they're among the worst kinds of men. Vulgar, unruly, and running in gangs, they've been going into restaurants and ordering food and drinks and then not paying. They form mobs and assault people. So far, they've mostly attacked minorities like Mexicans and Peruvians. But that doesn't mean anyone is safe."

"We'll be careful," Shiloh promised.

Logan nodded approval. "One more thing, Mrs. Laird. Is there some place where you two could get out of town for a while?"

Shiloh fought to keep her voice steady. "Are you saying that you think we're in danger here?"

"I'm just saying that you shouldn't take any chances. Do you know somebody away from here?"

Shiloh shook her head.

"Maybe you could go to Monterey with Mrs. Fremont," the officer said. "She's going down there in a few days to join her husband."

"I've met her, but I wouldn't presume to ask if I could join her."

"Too bad. Still, you might think about it and see if you can't find some way to get away from here until things quiet down. Maybe after the convention in Monterey we'll know if we're going to be a state or not. Then we'll get some government besides the military." He turned to leave. "Well, I hope you can work something out. Good night."

Shiloh and Mara began straightening up the house. Shiloh pondered the implied danger in the constable's warning to get out of town. She thought, *I wish I could.*

She heard the soft sound of hoofbeats in sand and the rattle of chains from a wagon. "Clay's here," she called to Mara.

Not that it matters anymore, she thought. *Mara won't go with me, so I'll have to find another way to get some money. Anyway, he's probably still angry over what I said to him yesterday. He'll probably be even more angry about what Mr. MacAdams wants him to do.*

She opened the door to his knock, but couldn't make herself look him in the eyes. She was relieved when she heard Mara reenter the room behind her.

Clay began, "Samuel said I was to come." He stopped, glancing beyond Shiloh. "What happened?"

"Somebody broke in this morning while Mara and I were away," Shiloh explained. "But so far as we can tell, nothing was taken." She added quickly, "Clay, I'm deeply ashamed of what I said to you yesterday. I spoke without thinking, and I ask your forgiveness."

He shrugged. "It's all right."

She was tempted to ask what he knew about Urbane Haddock, but knew this wasn't the time. Instead, she thanked him and broached the reason she had wanted to see him. "Have you talked to Mr. MacAdams in the last few hours?"

"Ran into him a few minutes ago." Clay's eyes kept moving around the room, taking in the mess.

Shiloh wondered momentarily how MacAdams had explained his bandaged arm. She was sure he had not told Clay the truth. Shiloh was very glad of that.

Clay continued, "He told me what you had in mind."

Because Mara couldn't go on the trip, Shiloh was sorry she hadn't been able to tell MacAdams so he wouldn't even mention the subject to Clay. Now it was too late.

Shiloh hurriedly explained, "It was his idea, not mine."

"Yes, he told me."

Shiloh was sure Clay wasn't a bit happy about any of this. "Anyway, it turns out that Mara can't go, so the whole trip is . . . "

"Hold on!" Mara interrupted, coming into the room. "That was before the constable said what he did about us getting out of town."

Shiloh drew back in surprise. "But I thought . . . ?"

"Changed my mind," Mara replied.

Clay asked, "What's this about getting out of town?"

Shiloh quickly explained what Logan had suggested. She concluded, "Well, now that Mara and I *can* go, what do you think about this trip?"

His thoughts flashed back to that terrible day when he had left his wife and young son alone. He closed his eyes against the memory of what he had found upon returning home.

Shiloh asked with concern, "Are you all right?"

He opened his eyes, but the sickening images remained. "Yes," he said huskily. Then, with an effort, he spoke in a normal voice. "I work for MacAdams, so I do what he says. Besides, I'll do anything I can to help Aldar's wife."

"Thank you," Shiloh said softly. "Mara and I will need to make plans for ourselves, but how long will it take you to get ready?"

"I thought about it a little after I left MacAdams. Probably a couple of days. Meanwhile, you two shouldn't stay here alone."

Mara said confidentially, "Nobody will bother us. I've let it be known that I have a dragoon revolver and I won't hesitate to shoot if necessary."

Shiloh wasn't too comfortable with that thought, but she assured Clay, "We'll be ready when you are."

After he left, the two women finished cleaning up so the living room was presentable once more. Shiloh had just enough time to dress before Rawlins arrived.

When he knocked promptly at seven o'clock, Shiloh was tense. *It's not just the day's unexpected events,* she told herself, *but what I'll find out about politics—and Aldar's death.*

CHAPTER XIII

SHILOH was surprised to see William Rawlins dressed in civilian clothes. It was the first time she had seen him without his uniform. Shiloh studied him thoughtfully, aware of the sense of command in his bearing. It wasn't just that he was well-built and nearly six feet tall. He was appealing, although at this time, Shiloh had no personal interest in any man.

She invited him in and introduced him to Mara, who promptly excused herself, saying she had some things to do in the cookhouse. This annoyed Shiloh, who suspected that Mara had deliberately left so Rawlins would feel free to make whatever move he planned. Shiloh forced a smile and invited Rawlins to sit down. She briefly explained about the break-in.

"Would you like some protection?" he asked.

"Oh, no. Mara and I will be fine. She's let it be known around town that she has a big dragoon pistol."

"I see. Well, if you change your mind, please call on me."

"I will," she replied and nervously cleared her throat. "Mr. Rawlins, your note—"

"Please call me Will."

"Thank you, but I prefer your surname."

"Very well, Mrs. Laird."

"About your note: you indicated that there might be some connection between Aldar's death and politics?"

"Yes." He leaned forward in his chair to fix her with his eyes. "The common belief is that your husband was killed in a robbery. That's logical, from what I've learned about the circumstances. However, as you may guess, my position in the community allows me to have access to some information which may be denied others."

Shiloh nodded, encouraging Rawlins to explain.

"Everyone who comes to California these days has plans, big plans, but all are motivated by the same thing: money. The miner wants to strike it rich, take his pile, and return home. The lawless person has come to change his name and ply his trade here, where presumably the pickings are greater."

"Yes?"

His voice changed. "Have you heard a song being sung locally, 'What was your name in the States?'"

She shook her head, so he continued. "Anyway, every day, men flock here with the idea of getting in on the beginning of great wealth and power."

Shiloh was impatient to know about her husband, but Rawlins seemed to be off on a tangent. He spoke of the power of politics, and of great military leaders like Caesar who had gone on to head up kingdoms.

"Power and money," Rawlins observed. "Men have always sought these, but only those who are willing to take great risks and pay the price will succeed. To do that, they must be supremely self-confident and take steps to be sure they are not suspected."

Power and money, Shiloh thought. *I keep hearing that. The whole of San Francisco seems interested in something that never interested me.*

She said, "That's interesting, Mr. Rawlins, but what does that have to do with my husband's death?"

"I'm coming to that. I believe you've met some of those power seekers."

"You mean Gladwin and Locke?"

"Those are the obvious ones. Gladwin's ambition to have California become a separate nation is well known. What perhaps is not as well known is that there is a covert movement of some strength behind his ambition."

"Is there, really? I thought . . . "

"Oh, yes," he broke in. "There is much underground support for the idea, unlike Locke's followers who favor California being admitted to the Union as a slave-holding state."

"As you may know, both these men wanted Aldar to become involved in their objectives," Shiloh commented.

"Yes, I heard." Rawlins added softly, "but that was not to be."

Shiloh's grief, which had been forcibly put aside in order to deal with the pressing necessity of surviving, threatened to surface. She struggled to control her emotions to ask, "How does all this involve my husband's death?"

"I was coming to that. A certain man who sells information recently arrived from Washington."

"Urbane Haddock?" she interrupted.

"Yes. How do you know that name?"

"It's not important. What about him?"

"I learned through my sources that he had secret inside information from Washington that he tried to sell. I don't know what that was, but I do know that it had something to do with your husband's recent trip to the nation's capital."

Shiloh was suddenly very interested in Haddock, and remembered what MacAdams had said about him. "I still don't see the connection."

"I have reason to believe that Haddock brought information which made it imperative that your husband be removed."

Shiloh felt her heart speed up. For the first time since Aldar's death, here was the possibility of startling information. She asked breathlessly, "Who would want to do that?"

"I have my suspicions, but no proof, so I would rather not say more about it."

"Mr. Rawlins!" she exclaimed in dismay. "You roused my curiosity with your note, and now you refuse to offer any evidence! I'm very disappointed."

"Please don't be. I have some more related information. When you've heard that, you may draw your own conclusions. I wouldn't be surprised if they coincided with mine."

Shiloh was not satisfied, but she nodded, indicating that he should explain.

"I have learned that Haddock talked to Locke and Gladwin, among others."

Shiloh recalled MacAdams saying that Haddock had also talked to Rawlins. She asked casually, "Did you meet this Haddock?"

"No, although he tried to see me. There is nothing I want to hear from a man of his reputation."

Shiloh frowned, deep in thought. "But what could this Haddock have possibly said that would cause someone to kill my husband? Why? Who would benefit? Or what other reason could there be?"

"I wish I knew, but there is too much of a corollary between Haddock's arrival and your husband's death. Someone had to have a strong motive."

Gladwin and Locke immediately came to Shiloh's mind. But what was it Rawlins had said? "Among others, you said. Like whom?"

Rawlins shook his head. "I don't have confirmation of those, only the ones I mentioned. But I thought you should know. It may be helpful in thinking who had the most to gain from your husband's death."

Who had the most to gain? The question made MacAdams leap to mind. He had reason, but there was no proof, Shiloh realized. Gladwin had everything to gain if Aldar had joined him. But what about Locke?

She was disappointed in Rawlins not having more specific information. She decided that she would have to ask Clay what he knew about Haddock. For now, she was satisfied that Rawlins had said all he was going to say about the subject. Shiloh let the conversation move to other topics. She tried to draw her guest out by asking questions about his interests, but he was noncommittal.

"The military is my only interest," he claimed, but he looked at her with such longing that she squirmed and looked away.

She wondered if he was going to prove Mara right and make some advances. However, he surprised her by abruptly standing.

"Well," he said, heading for the door, "I hope you will think about what I've said. Meanwhile if I can be of service to you in any way, please send word."

When Rawlins had gone, Mara came back into the parlor. "I heard most of what he said. He didn't have any real information, so I'm convinced he used that only as an excuse to see you."

"He was a perfect gentleman, Mara."

"It's part of his strategy. Disarm you. Make you trust him. Then he'll move because he has plans, and they have to include having a beautiful wife."

It was still early, so Shiloh thought about what Rawlins said as Mara took a candle and walked through the house making sure the doors were locked.

Satisfied, Mara returned, set the candle on the table, and laid the heavy revolver on the floor by her chair. She casually covered it with an apron, then brought out her soda powder cans from their hiding place. Removing the lids, she separated the cans into gold coins, nuggets, and dust before setting her gold scales on the table.

Shiloh puzzled over Rawlins' disappointing conversation, then shifted her focus to review the many details that needed to be worked out before leaving for the gold country.

She picked up the packet of material MacAdams had given her, painfully aware of how much she would have to learn before representing MacAdams and Laird Express Company.

She silently berated herself for the deal she had made with MacAdams. *I was foolish,* she scolded herself. *I don't know where I'm going or what I'm going to do when I get there. I wish I had Mara's confidence.*

Shiloh forced herself to remember what Aldar had always said he did when drumming up business. "Make them like you. Ask questions to uncover their needs. Meet those needs by showing benefits."

Making them like me shouldn't be hard, she assured herself. *I like people and they usually like me. But I know nothing of selling. I don't even have an idea of where to start.*

Her negative thoughts were interrupted by another. She sat up so suddenly that Mara glanced up.

"What is it?" she asked.

"I just remembered that Gladwin told Aldar he could have his account back! And Locke told Aldar to come see him and talk about getting his back! Why don't I call on them?"

"No reason."

"Clay said it'll be a couple of days before he's got the supplies. So tomorrow I could see Gladwin and Locke, but I've also got to talk to Clay about Haddock and get ready for the trip. It's going to be a full day."

The two women fell silent, but it was a companionable silence made possible by years of close friendship. Their serene surface hid Shiloh's many concerns. Shiloh kept alert to any strange sounds outside, and occasionally glanced with new appreciation to where Mara's gun lay under the innocent-looking apron.

Shiloh and Mara suddenly tensed at the distant sound of a clanging bell.

"Fire alarm," Mara said. "Sounds like it's close!" She hurriedly put the last of the gold dust into the can and closed the lid.

Shiloh set her express company materials on the sofa and stepped to the window.

"See anything?" Mara asked.

"Sky's lit up, but I can't see any flames. But it looks as if it's close, maybe just beyond that next hill."

Mara came to stand behind her. She pressed her hands against her forehead to cut out the glare from the candles in the room and put her face close to the windowpane. "Not more than a quarter mile away, but the wind's blowing away from us, so it won't spread this way." Mara turned quickly and picked up her scales, empty buckskin pouch, and soda powder can. "I'll put this stuff away, then go climb that hill for a better look. Want to come along?"

Shiloh started to decline, then changed her mind. "I don't want to be left here alone. I'll get my wrap."

Mara locked the door and the two women hurried through the foggy night, scrambled up the sand dunes and paused at the top of a hill. Below them, the fire had already nearly destroyed one shack and ignited the roof of its neighbor.

"Here come the volunteer firemen." Mara pointed to her left. "That little old handcart won't do much good against those flames."

Shiloh could see men running, pulling the hose cart, racing to stop the fire before it got out of hand.

Someone with a flaming pitch torch sprinted ahead of the cart, lighting the way in the town which had no lights.

"That's not much light to show those firemen where they're going," Shiloh remarked.

"That's not the purpose. Samuel told me that men often dig up the city streets and then don't cover or mark them at night. So the runner with the torch tries to spot the holes before the equipment falls into . . . oops!"

The torch bearer disappeared and the men following with the hose cart slowed and stopped.

Shiloh asked, "What happened?"

"I think the runner just fell into a hole."

"At least the firemen got the cart stopped before it fell in too. But it's too late." As Mara spoke, the roof fell in with a shower of sparks.

The women watched as the firemen with their small hose cart doused the remnants of the flames.

"That's no way to fight fires," Mara commented. "This whole town's a tinder box, but Samuel said the people can't agree what to do. Big fire engines will likely become runaways on San Francisco's hills."

Shiloh remembered the fallen draft horses she'd seen trying to climb one of the steep hills. "If they get bigger engines, and the fire is up a steep hill, the horses might not be able to pull the equipment."

"Fortunately, it's not our problem," Mara added.

The women turned and started down the hill, leaving the last of the fire behind. "I'll be glad to get out of this town," Shiloh commented. "Just a few more days and Clay will be back so we can start. Now, I'd better go think about meeting with Gladwin and Locke tomorrow."

Shiloh approached the New York Hotel with considerable trepidation the next morning. She dreaded having to walk alone through the many men who would be between her and Gladwin's office. She also did not relish the idea of talking with a hot-tempered man who favored California becoming a separate nation instead of a part of the United States.

Shiloh sighed with relief when she spotted him just leaving the front of his canvas business structure.

"What a way to start the day!" he greeted her, removing a dead cigar stub from his mouth. His gray eyes appreciatively swept Shiloh. "Like I told your husband, you're a mighty pretty woman. But here I am gushing like a schoolboy and not giving you a chance to talk. What brings you here today?"

She began, "Mr. Gladwin, when I met you, you told my husband that he could have your account back, and you would guarantee him some other big ones too."

"So I did. Too bad he got killed. He could have been somebody mighty important if he'd listened to me."

Shiloh again sensed the feeling of power that emanated from Gladwin. "I've come to ask you to sign up again with MacAdams and Laird Express Company."

"*You* have?" There was obvious surprise in his tone.

"Yes. I've agreed to work with Mr. MacAdams."

"I never heard of a woman working in that kind of business."

"Mr. Gladwin, I don't have a choice. Now, if you'll give me a few minutes of your time, I'd like to review the benefits you'll have by dealing with—"

He waved her to silence. "No need for that, Mrs. Laird. Just give me the contract."

Shiloh was so surprised she dropped her packet of papers. As Gladwin bent to retrieve them, Shiloh breathed a silent prayer. *Thank You, Lord! Maybe this is going to be easier than I thought.*

When Gladwin had recovered her papers from the boardwalk and led her into his office, Shiloh stilled her trembling hands enough to fill in the contract. He signed it with a flourish and handed it back to her.

"I liked your husband," Gladwin said softly, "and I like you. Is there anything I can do for you?"

"You mentioned helping get other accounts."

"So I did. Come back later and I'll have a letter of introduction for you with a list of men to call on. If they don't buy from you, I'll make them wish they had." He smiled, but Shiloh wasn't sure that he was joking.

Elated beyond words, Shiloh hurried to Locke's place of

business, but her good feelings ebbed as she remembered how abrasive he had been, and the tensions she had felt in their earlier meetings. But as she headed toward Locke's office, Clay came driving down the street from the other direction.

He reined in the team and smiled at her. "Sleep well last night?" he asked. "No more break-ins?"

"It was a quiet night, thanks."

"I'm glad I ran into you," Clay said. "I'm having a hard time finding a sidesaddle for Mara."

"Don't worry about her. We both rode astride crossing Panama on muleback. Of course, we shocked a number of the men traveling the same route, but Mara made us pantaloons, so we were fairly ladylike."

"This trip shouldn't be as hard as that."

"When do you think we'll leave?"

"Tomorrow, hopefully." He paused, then asked, "Where are you headed? Want a ride?"

"I'm going to see Jefferson Locke."

"He's not in. I made a delivery to his place a while ago, and his clerk told me."

Shiloh was disappointed because she had felt so much more confident after meeting with Gladwin. But now her thoughts shifted to Haddock.

"Do you have a minute?" she asked Clay. When he nodded, he stepped down from the wagon and they stood leaning against its side to talk.

"What do you know about Urbane Haddock?" she asked.

Clay's face clouded. "How do you know that name?"

"I've heard it mentioned." She didn't disclose her conversations with Rawlins and MacAdams.

"Then you probably know that I saw him get off a ship just a few days before you and Aldar arrived."

"Yes, I heard. But who is he?"

"I met him once before he sailed back east. He's not a person you'd like to meet."

"Were you referring to him when you told Aldar that he hadn't returned any too soon?"

Clay nodded. "I overheard him talking to MacAdams. I only caught enough to know that Haddock was selling information. Something about a big deal that Aldar had put together through some senator named Lorenzo."

That was all Clay could tell Shiloh, but it was enough to give her a clue. Rawlins said "among others," she thought, but he didn't mention MacAdams.

Shiloh thought about it on the way home and wondered whether that news could have cost Aldar his life. *No,* she decided, *MacAdams is a hard man to get along with, but would he kill somebody?*

She didn't want to believe that, but she couldn't shake the thought. *Just be careful,* she told herself. *I'll get my job done and leave.*

By late that afternoon, when she was at home again and had time to think, Shiloh's elation over her success in selling Gladwin was gradually replaced with concern that it had been too easy. She sensed that it wouldn't be like that in the gold country.

Someone pounded on a door.

"That's the back door," Shiloh said, frowning. "Who could it be?"

"Probably Samuel." Mara stood up. "I told him not to bother me here."

"Maybe it's something important," Shiloh cautioned, following Mara through the house.

"It'd better be, or I'll scald his ears and send him packing. He already asked me to jump over the broom with him, but I told him I don't intend to marry any runaway slave. Fact is, I'm not going to marry any—"

"Mara!" Samuel's voice came through the door. "Mrs. Laird, I got to talk to you real fast!"

"He sounds excited," Shiloh said as Mara opened the door.

The big black man's eyes were large with fright. "Dey done got Joseph!"

"The slave catchers?" Mara asked.

"No, not dem! Shanghai people! I seed dem a-carryin' ol' Joseph, limp as a daid rabbit, from dat saloon by de water! Put him in a boat and row for de ship! You an' Mrs. Laird de only ones I knows kin maybe he'p him befoh dat ship sails!"

Mara exploded, "I told both of you to stay away from those places! They can't drug you if you don't give them the chance!"

"I din't go, an' I done try to stop him, but he say he kin take keer o' hisse'f. Please, kin you all do somethin'?"

Mara shook her head. "The ship's master needs a crew so much he won't listen to Shiloh or me."

"We've got to try!" Shiloh exclaimed.

Mara's brow puckered in thought. "The only thing he might understand is gold." She called over her shoulder, "You stay right there, Samuel. I'll be back in a minute."

Shiloh followed Mara as she hurried to the cookhouse. "What're we going to do, Mara?"

"I'm going to try a bribe. You're going to stay here where it's safe."

"Safe? Alone in this house after it was broken into?"

"Maybe you're right. Better grab your cloak. It'll be cold before we can get back."

Shivering with excitement, Shiloh would rather have taken the one-eyed mule, but Mara and Samuel would still have to walk. So all three set out together on foot with the big black man setting a rapid pace through the gathering dusk. The runaway slave explained that the ship where Joseph had been taken was anchored in the cove off the north shore.

Mara observed, "That'll take us through the Chilean and Peruvian quarter. Those are good people who speak Spanish, but they live in far worse conditions than any of the white men do around here. Samuel and I probably won't get more than a passing glance, but your pretty white face is going to get a lot of attention. Just stay close to me."

As they puffed up one of the last of San Francisco's seemingly endless hills, Samuel suddenly stopped and held up his hand. "Listen!" he said sharply.

At first, Shiloh thought it was the sound of the sea, but almost instantly, she realized that it was angry people shouting loudly.

"What is it?" she asked in a low voice.

"Hounds," Samuel replied, "an' dey sound mad."

Cautiously, Shiloh followed the runaway slave and Mara to the top of the hill. Below them, a small mob of shouting white men with burning torches surged toward the Mexican and Peruvian quarter. The residents there were coming out of their tents and shacks to stare at the approaching horde.

The Hounds in front of the mob dashed toward the nearest tents and touched their torches to the canvas. Instantly, flames leaped up. Some residents snatched up boards or other possible weapons and prepared to defend themselves. But the mob rolled over them, beating, kicking, and burning. Some Hounds began chasing the women who fled screaming as the flames spread rapidly from tent to tent.

"Dear Lord!" Shiloh exclaimed, "We've got to help them!"

"Don't talk foolishness!" Mara snapped. "There's nothing we can do. Let's get out of here!"

"What about Joseph?" Shiloh asked.

"We can't get by that mob," Mara replied. "Come on! Let's get out of sight before those men turn on us."

Shiloh hesitated, then she saw the sails being raised on the shanghai ship. "Goodbye, Joseph," she whispered.

Shiloh couldn't sleep for a long time that night. The angry shouts and terrorized screams echoed in her mind. These were mixed with memories of the sickening sound of clubs on flesh, and the roar of wind-driven flames destroying the ramshackle community. Beyond the Spanish-speaking quarter, she could imagine Joseph on the ship, once again a slave headed for unknown ports.

The next morning, Clay arrived to feed Ulysses and to bring news to Shiloh and Mara that he was having trouble booking passage up the Sacramento River.

He explained, "There were so many prospectors already signed up that it may take another day or two before I can be sure there's room on board for three."

"I guess it can't be helped," Shiloh replied.

"I could use some extra time getting ready," Mara added.

Shiloh asked Clay, "Did you hear about last night's attack on the Mexican and Peruvian quarter?"

He nodded. "A friend of mine was close enough to watch. He said the Hounds burned, beat, and robbed."

"And raped the women," Mara said bitterly.

"Mara!" Shiloh whispered reprovingly at the word that generally was not spoken in mixed company.

Mara replied, "We all know that's what happened."

Clay added hastily, "We also know that at least two people are dead. There's a rumor that Leavenworth is going to hold a mass meeting tonight in the old Plaza. Portsmouth Square, it's now being called."

"What do they plan to do?" Shiloh asked.

"I don't know, but it'll be interesting because I hear Sam Brannan's going to speak. He's quite a fire-eater," Clay said.

Mara added, "He's the one who first ran down San Francisco's streets with flakes in a bottle shouting, 'Gold! Gold from the American River!'"

"That's right, and now it wouldn't surprise me if he called for the formation of a law-and-order party."

Later, as Shiloh dressed to call on Locke, she reflected on Clay's words. "A law-and-order party." San Francisco's lawless element was getting worse. She could hardly wait to leave in spite of her dread of what dangers and challenges she faced in gold country. *Still,* she told herself, *it can't be any worse than crossing the Isthmus of Panama. Or can it?*

CHAPTER XIV

LOCKE TURNED from his desk at the back of his tent-office and motioned for Shiloh to come in. Shiloh took a chair that had been hastily vacated by a sallow-faced clerk.

"We sort of made the sparks fly the other day when you were here," the short, balding Locke began, his crooked yellow teeth showing in a tight smile. "I'm a little bit surprised that you came back."

"I'm here because of an invitation you gave my husband at church the day we met," she began. "Remember, you suggested that Aldar come by the next day so you and he could talk?"

"Yes. So?" The brittleness in Locke's voice made her very uncomfortable.

"I came in his place. You had once been a client of my husband's express company, and I understood you to say that you might be agreeable to becoming so again."

Locke frowned. "Are you trying to sell me something, like some drummer?"

Squirming, Shiloh explained, "Mr. MacAdams asked me to call on some customers as my husband had . . . "

"Whoa, now!" Locke shook his head as though in disbelief. "Are you doing a man's job?"

His blunt manner unnerved her. "I know it's highly unusual, but so are the circumstances . . . "

"You're as stubborn as your husband!" Locke interrupted harshly. "Only in your case, it's worse! A woman should be at home taking care of womanly duties. A widow like you should find somebody . . . "

Shiloh heard no more. She leaped up and fled through the tent flap, her heart racing and her face burning. The man's incredible callousness made tears blur her vision as she untied Ulysses, hoisted herself into the saddle, and furiously drummed her heels against his ribs.

"I can't do it!" she exclaimed aloud, ignoring the men who turned to stare. "I just can't!"

She headed for Mara's outdoor bakery, where she and Samuel were telling a crowd of disappointed buyers that there would be no more pies or biscuits for a while.

Shiloh reined in the mule and tried to compose herself before the waiting customers could see her. That unusual action alerted Mara who hurried over.

"Are you crying?" she asked, reaching up to help Shiloh dismount. "Let's walk away from everybody while you tell me what happened."

Mara held Shiloh while she told through broken sobs what Locke had said. "There's no sense going on this trip," Shiloh concluded. "I just can't take it! It's too much!"

"He's a clod, but you're going to have to deal with such men."

"No, I'm not! I'm going to find Clay and tell him the whole thing's off! I'll give MacAdams' money back too! Then I'll get on a ship bound for home, even if I have to become a stowaway."

Mara sighed. "Wait here. We need to talk more privately. I'll tell Samuel that I'll be back after a while."

Shiloh looked through teary eyes at the big black slave. "He looks sad," she observed. "I guess he's missing Joseph."

"And thinking the next time he might be the one who's shanghaied." Mara started toward the baking area, adding, "Sometimes it doesn't pay to be an able-bodied man in this town."

While Mara shooed her toward the house, insisting that she would tie Ulysses for the night and be right in, Shiloh started for the back door. Then she saw the flowers. They were only three small blue blossoms neatly laid on the step in front of the door. But who placed them there?

Overcoming the fear that whoever had left the flowers might also have entered the house, Shiloh checked the lock. She was relieved to find it was undisturbed and there was no obvious sign of forced entry.

Shiloh called to Mara who was just approaching the house. "Look," Shiloh said, showing the wild flowers. "I found them there on the back step. But who left them, and why?"

"I have no idea who," Mara replied matter-of-factly, "but whoever he was, he's interested in you. That's what flowers mean when any man brings them to a woman."

"Maybe he left them for you."

"Maybe, but I don't think so. If a man wants something from me, he'll let me know."

"If they're for me, why didn't he just hand them to me?"

"Maybe he's shy."

"It's not amusing, Mara, especially after somebody broke in and scared us half to death!"

"Whoever left the flowers may not know that. Anyway, flowers on the doorstep are better than if they'd been left on your pillow, wouldn't you say?"

Shiloh had to admit that was true. "But," she added in an agitated tone, "Who is he? Why me? Why not you, or both of us?"

"In this womanless town, it could be any one of thousands of men. And I'd guess my skin doesn't appeal to him as much as yours."

Shiloh was apprehensive as they entered the house, but it was just as they had left it. Samuel had done a good job of reinforcing both front and back doors after the break-in, but there was something about finding flowers on the doorstep that made Shiloh uneasy once more.

"I think we should move," she declared.

"We're leaving for the gold country in a day or so."

"I know, but I'd feel better if we moved to a hotel until then."

"You wouldn't like a hotel here. They're mostly made of canvas, and the wooden floors are full of fleas. Samuel told me the tenants have to pour scalding water on the cracks every morning to keep the fleas under control."

"But I'm frightened. Somebody is obviously watching this place—watching us." She walked to the window and peered out. "Maybe he's out there right now." She turned to face Mara again. "What happens if he comes when I'm alone?"

"Judging from the flowers, I'd guess you could expect him to become amorous."

The thought of physical contact with some unknown intruder made Shiloh's stomach twist into a knot. "You know what I mean."

"You could get a gun."

"I can't do that. I couldn't shoot anyone."

"Maybe not, but a gun might scare him off."

"I suppose so, but I'm more afraid of a gun than of whoever he is."

"Then you've only got one other alternative: don't be here alone. Which reminds me: When we return from this trip, I'm going to start seeing someone in the evenings, so you had better . . ."

"You're going out?" Shiloh interrupted. "With Samuel?"

"No, of course not. I told you before that I have no intention of getting involved with that runaway slave. He's just a friend."

Shiloh's eyebrows lifted.

"Yes, I'm talking about a white man. I've already checked up on him. He's as rich as anyone in San Francisco, and he's going to be even richer."

Shiloh considered her next question carefully before asking, "Anybody I know?"

"No, and I'd prefer to keep it that way, at least for a while."

"Where will you go?" The possibilities were very limited, Shiloh knew. There were strict social taboos in California which the newcomers had brought with them from the eastern United States.

"We'll talk about it after our trip is over. If you don't want to be alone in the evenings, you'd better think where else you'd feel safer. But don't worry, I'll be home tonight."

Agitated because Mara didn't seem to take the flowers seriously, Shiloh hurried outside. She saddled Ulysses and rode toward the north shore to think. She wanted to be alone, but as she topped a sand hill, she met Clay. He was just returning to his wagon after making a delivery.

Clay approached her, asking, "What brings you over this way?"

Reining in the mule, Shiloh replied, "I was just going to look out over the bay." To cover the half-truth, she quickly asked, "Did you attend the meeting last night?"

"Sure did. Sam Brannan called for the formation of a law-and-order party, just as I expected. This morning, I heard that Alcalde Leavenworth resigned because of what his Hounds did to the Chileans and Mexicans. A grand jury will hear evidence against them."

Clay left on his rounds after briefly explaining that he expected preparations to leave for the gold country would be complete by Monday. Suddenly aware of the time, Shiloh thought of her own plans for the trip, and turned Ulysses toward home.

Rawlins in full dress uniform was waiting for her when she returned. "I was riding by," he said casually, indicating his saddle horse, "when I decided to stop and see if you needed anything."

"Thank you for being so thoughtful." She knew he would

never have just left flowers on the doorstep. He would want full credit for such a gesture. "Mara isn't home yet, so I can't invite you in."

"I understand perfectly. Let's talk out here."

They walked to the back steps between the house and the cookhouse.

"It was a pleasure to get to know you a little better last night," he said. He waited until she had gathered her long skirt around her ankles and sat before he seated himself beside her.

Not comfortable with the topic of conversation, Shiloh asked, "I've been curious about this man, Haddock."

Rawlins shrugged. "He's not worth thinking about."

"Weren't you the least bit curious about why he wanted to see you?"

"Not really. Oh, he tried hard. When he sent word that he wanted to see me and I replied that I was busy, he sent in a second request."

Shiloh said nothing, but looked expectantly at the commandant.

"This time, instead of a verbal request, he had scribbled a note."

Rawlins fell silent, but Shiloh's curiosity forced her to know more. "A note?" she prompted.

"It was ridiculous."

Shiloh felt that Rawlins didn't really want to say anymore, but she persisted. "How so?"

"He claimed that he had confidential information about a possible court-martial against some high ranking officers in this western area."

"Court-martial? Like the charges brought against John C. Fremont?"

"In Haddock's note, he claimed that some officers were suspected of favoring those men back east who seek to extend slavery to the West Coast."

"Is that serious?"

"It could be. As I'm sure you've heard, there are very strong sentiments for and against slavery."

"My father is a staunch abolitionist, but what does slavery have to do with a possible court-martial?"

"There are powerful men in Washington who claim they can look down the road and see a possible civil conflict between the states. If that happens, then all men in the entire United States military forces will have to face difficult decisions."

He was warming to his subject, the words coming more freely, but Shiloh was becoming increasingly aware of controlled emotions in the way Rawlins' voice rose.

"I don't understand," she said.

"American military officers come from every state representing both north and south. I suspect that the present high command is interested in trying to determine which officers would likely stand with the slavery states and which would be against if it comes to war. That would especially be true of officers with good disciplined forces under them."

Like you, Shiloh thought, but kept silent.

"But that's nothing new," he went on. "Throughout history, officers have had to choose. If they make the right choices, they become heroes, like George Washington. If they choose wrong, they're considered traitors."

Rawlins turned to look into Shiloh's eyes. "Do you realize that if Washington and his high command had lost the Revolutionary War, the British would have hanged him—and them—as traitors?"

"No!" Shiloh was genuinely shocked. "I never thought of such a thing!"

"Neither do most people, but it's true. If we had lost that war, this country might still be a British colony. And instead of being a hero and the father of our country, George Washington and his staff would have come down through history as men who betrayed their country, which was England when the war started."

"That is an absolutely fascinating thought," Shiloh exclaimed.

Rawlins smiled. "I'm glad you're interested. So many people don't even care."

She confessed, "I had never thought about it before."

He got to his feet. "Well, I'd better be getting back to the Presidio. Thanks for being such a good listener."

"I was intrigued," she said honestly as he helped her stand. Again, as with Clay's remarks, she was struck with the fact that she had somehow entered a world she hadn't known even existed.

Rawlins smiled warmly. "You are a delightful person."

Shiloh was pleased that he thought so, but she was also keenly aware that her husband had only been dead a few weeks. She didn't want to encourage Rawlins.

As she entered the house, she thought with satisfaction, *Mara is wrong. He's a real gentleman.*

Mara was not yet home when Clay arrived to feed the mule. Shiloh walked outside to talk with Clay.

From behind a sand dune a quarter mile away, the man with a facial birthmark and fresh whip marks across his face watched silently. His jackass was tied nearby at the bottom of the dune where he could not be seen.

The Watcher stared at the house where Shiloh was talking to the tall, full-bearded man who came daily to feed and care for her one-eyed jackass. The sight angered him, but daylight was no time to make a move. He lowered his head and savagely kicked at the sand beneath his feet.

All his life The Watcher had survived by his wits, stealing and learning to keep a low profile. His disfigurement had made him always a bystander, deprived of friendship and never sheltered from the pain by love.

He became a loner whose anger and resentment grew until

he found a way of striking back. That first blow against the world's cruelty came through his only companion, a long-bladed knife. He had stolen it from a hardware store and spent hours learning to use it well. He could throw it with deadly accuracy, or he could strike with it hidden in his hand so that he was confident no one else could be as fast.

He began imagining that he was invisible. He proved it to himself with a succession of victims. A ripple of fear went through the community.

Then one night he made a mistake. Standing over his victim, The Watcher didn't hear or see the stranger until he spoke from the darkness a few feet away.

"How much to do that for someone I'll name?"

The disembodied voice startled The Watcher. He crouched, reaching for the knife and trying to see more than the dark shadow of the man standing twenty feet away.

"How much?" the voice repeated. "In gold?"

So it began.

The last transaction had come about a month ago. The Watcher never saw the man who described Aldar Laird and told him to watch for his ship to arrive. The unexpected presence of the two women had only partially disrupted his plans, but not for long.

First the blond man, The Watcher told himself. *Then the women. The yellow one first. Save the other for last.*

Fantasizing proved so exciting that The Watcher kept watching, waiting for the right moment when the beautiful Negress would be alone. Later, when the time was right, he would return for the other woman with the reddish-gold hair.

Then one day she surprised him. He didn't hear her coming until it was too late. He had tried to turn away, but not before she smiled at him. She had not looked away, but had also spoken to him in a friendly manner, seemingly oblivious to his disfigured face. No girl or woman had ever smiled like that at him. That realization haunted The Watcher, and something changed.

His fantasies became different. He listened discreetly until he learned her name. *Shiloh.* He tasted the word, over and over. *Shiloh. Shiloh!* Day after day, he had new, strange dreams because she had smiled at him.

He wanted more than to see her from a distance, but his life had been spent in the shadows. He could kill a man in the night without regret, but he had not yet summoned the courage to approach Shiloh.

He followed her, imagining himself as her protector. She would like that when she found out. He was sure of that. She would appreciate him. So he followed her when it was safe. Then the men started coming. She had gone out with one at night. They drove away in a carriage, and he followed.

When the man tried to kiss Shiloh, The Watcher reacted. Blindly, unthinking, he silently charged out of the darkness and struck. He fled at Shiloh's screams before he could take the life of the man who had dared touch her.

While The Watcher still nursed the welts where the whip had cut into his face, a voice came to him out of the darkness at his rendezvous point.

A simple break-in. He didn't like the assignment, and almost refused. Daylight activities weren't The Watcher's style. The clink of many double eagles, first minted this year of 1849, had decided him. *Besides,* he thought, *it's an excuse to be inside her house, to be nearer to her, to where she slept, where . . .*

He interrupted his fantasy, remembering how angry the man had been when he reported being unable to find what he was hired to locate. The Watcher had not taken such a cursing in years, but he had not drawn his knife. That would end a source of gold.

Today, The Watcher had picked a handful of wild flowers and left them for her, mindful of his many rejections from other women. He noticed with satisfaction that Shiloh had picked up the flowers and carried them with her. *She's pleased,* he thought.

Then the soldier had come and talked with her this afternoon. That was the second man who had been alone with Shiloh. The Watcher felt jealousy—something he had never known before. Now she was alone with a third man, and more might come.

That's not right, he told himself. He stared over the sand dune at Shiloh and the tall man. *Maybe the time has come to fix it.*

CHAPTER XV

CLAY PITCHED a forkful of hay to the mule before turning to Shiloh. He asked, "Have you seen any signs of being followed since I mentioned those tracks?"

"No, I haven't."

"That's good. Did you ever figure out what he was looking for?"

She shook her head. "If anything's missing, Mara and I don't know what it is."

"I've been giving that some thought." Clay slowly looked in all directions. "Since it was a daylight break-in, whoever did it knew nobody was home. He also knew that this house is away out here at the end of a dirt road with no neighbors, so he wouldn't be seen."

Shiloh felt a tingle of fear, apprehensively glancing around, wondering if somebody was watching now.

Clay mused, "Whoever it was must have been after Mara's gold. Hundreds of men have stood around her bakery and seen her insist on gold coins, nuggets, or dust for payment. They must figure she had it all hidden here."

"It's still here," Shiloh replied. "It's safe."

"I mean that the burglar had to have been after Mara's gold

because nobody knows about what you got for the pickax heads, do they?"

"Nobody but Mara."

"Could she have told those friends of hers?"

"I doubt it. Besides, I plan to take my gold to the bank tomorrow, along with Mara's. She's afraid that if she walks in with her receipts from the bakery, they'll think she stole it."

"What puzzles me," Clay commented, "is why only the main house was searched. Why not the cookhouse?"

She turned to look toward him and shrugged. "Maybe," Clay said, "somebody knew that's where Mara slept, at least until . . . "

"What do Mara's quarters have to do with this?"

"Well, if whoever broke in was after the gold, he certainly would have searched the cookhouse, too."

"That sounds logical."

"So if he didn't, then he must have thought that whatever he was after was in the main house. That makes me wonder if there might be something else of value in there that you don't know about."

She smiled ruefully. "Believe me, there's nothing else. What Aldar had was invested in the business. He and I had nothing except the house, and Aldar told me that it wasn't paid for. There isn't even a will."

"I wondered about that. Too bad. I'm sure he didn't dream anything would happen to him at such an early age."

Shiloh did not answer while Clay turned to look into the distance. "Hmm? I was just thinking back. There were the tracks I told you about where someone followed you. Then the house was searched, especially your bedroom."

The words sent a shiver up Shiloh's spine. She thought she knew what he meant, but she had to be sure. "I told you, there's nothing of value . . . "

"There's you," he interrupted.

Frightened at the thought and flustered at Clay's words,

Shiloh glanced away, wondering whether she should tell Clay about the flowers. Mara refused to see anything in them to be concerned about. But Shiloh couldn't shake her uneasy feeling.

She decided to risk telling Clay. Without looking at him, she said, "Somebody left wildflowers on the step this afternoon."

Clay's eyes narrowed. "Were you home at the time?"

"No. Mara and I were both away. I came home a little while ago and found them. They frightened me somehow, but when I told Mara, she made light of it."

Clay didn't say anything, but she judged from the expression in his eyes that he was concerned.

He frowned. "Maybe we're overlooking something, Shiloh. Maybe there are two different men involved. One broke in looking for the gold, and another left the flowers outside."

Clay abruptly turned and again looked in all directions. "You stay here. Go on about your regular routine. I'll be back in a little while."

His words frightened Shiloh, and she wanted to ask him to stay, but he was striding away toward the road.

Shiloh went inside to her bedroom and tried to finish packing for the trip to the gold country, but couldn't concentrate. The knowledge that someone had violated her home and bedroom, and someone had left flowers, made her very concerned.

She flinched with alarm when she heard the back door open, but was relieved when she recognized Mara's footsteps. Shiloh hurried out to tell her Clay's theory about the break-in and the flowers.

Shiloh had just concluded her story when Clay returned. She met him at the door. "Where did you go so suddenly?" she asked.

"Took a look around." He avoided her eyes.

"You found some more signs?" she guessed.

"Yes. One man was right over there until a little while ago," Clay said, pointing to a sand dune. "Must have seen us talking and moved when I left. He's either very smart, or he's got a sixth sense."

Shiloh turned to Mara. "See? We can't stay here tonight!"

"It's all right," Clay assured them. "You'll be safe."

Shiloh guessed that he meant he would be on guard somewhere, and she was comforted. "Thank you, Clay."

"Well," he said, "now that you're both here, could we talk about our trip? We leave Monday."

When their final travel plans were completed Clay left, and Shiloh managed to sleep well in spite of troubling thoughts.

The next morning she went by Gladwin's office to pick up the letters of introduction he had written for her. She was in a hurry because there was much to do, but the separate-nation advocate was talkative. He invited her to sit down. She accepted, feeling obligated for what he had done with the letters. He talked of the weather, which was cool, with dense fog rolling in off the ocean at night.

Shiloh listened politely, trying to not show her impatience to be off to see MacAdams before meeting Clay and Mara to transport the hidden gold to the bank.

Gladwin abruptly shifted the subject to Aldar.

"Every time I think of what some lousy son . . . uh . . . man did to your husband, I get mad!" he exclaimed. "He was one incredible human being. Honest, close-mouthed, and smart, always thinking ahead."

Shiloh nodded, wishing this man with the strange ideas of a separate-nation had been in the express business instead. *If he had been Aldar's partner instead of MacAdams . . .*

Gladwin broke into her thoughts. "There are others interested in heading up the Pacifica movement, but Aldar was the ideal person. Pacifica, that's what California will be called one day, in spite of the opposition favoring statehood. But I couldn't convince him."

Shiloh wanted to ask who else was interested in the separate-nation idea, but decided that it would not be prudent. She kept listening.

Gladwin continued, "Some men, one in particular, would give anything for the chance I offered Aldar. In fact, one man with high qualifications really wants the job. But he's so power hungry that he would put his own selfish purpose ahead of the nation. Aldar wouldn't have done that."

"No," Shiloh replied. "I'm sure he wouldn't have."

"Blasted right he wouldn't."

Shiloh decided to risk a discreet question. "Is this other man still interested?"

"Of course! But I don't trust him. He loves power. He told me once that 'powerful people know how to get things done without getting their hands dirty.'"

Shiloh rolled the quote around in her mind. Everywhere she turned, she heard that word, *power.*

Gladwin continued, "With that kind of attitude, this man would always keep reaching higher. I'd probably wake up one day when Pacifica is a reality and find that I was out of the picture. Although I think I'm as smart as the average human being, this man is so clever that I probably wouldn't even know what had happened to me until it was too late. In fact, I might even be dead. Power makes people do strange things. Even murder, but made to look like something else."

Shiloh shot a questioning look at Gladwin, but before she could ask him anything more, he stood, indicating their time together was over. "I know you've got a lot to do," he said, "so I won't keep you."

Shiloh dwelt briefly on Gladwin's remarks while she rode Ulysses toward the express office. Then her thoughts shifted to guessing how MacAdams would react when she showed him her first year's contract.

She tried not to sound too pleased with herself when she

first mentioned Gladwin's letters of introduction, and then handed over his contract.

MacAdams silently examined it, then nodded. "Keep it up," he said without congratulating her, "but don't think they'll all be this easy."

"I know." She didn't want to mention how rude Locke had been. "But I'll do my best."

He stood, signalling her dismissal. "To be honest with you, Missus, I expected you to come crawling in here like a whipped dog, saying you'd thought it over and decided you couldn't do it."

Shiloh had to brace herself so she didn't show any indication that she had nearly done that.

He walked her around the counter to the door. "It was the money, wasn't it?" he asked. "You felt that advance gold payment in your hand, and you decided to keep it, even if you went up there in those hills and made a fool of yourself."

Shiloh felt her face flush. "You expect me to do just that, don't you?" she snapped. "Well, we'll see in two weeks!"

She was furious when she reached the bottom of the stairs, and also surprised at her outburst. She rushed into the street and untied Ulysses from the hitching post without being aware of the team and wagon standing there.

"Mrs. Laird, where're you going?" Clay's voice reached through her emotions and made her look up.

"Sorry," she said, "but that man made me so angry!"

Clay chuckled. "Aldar used to say the same thing."

"He did?"

"Many times. Well, if you're ready, let's go pick up Mara and head for your house."

Shiloh wondered if Clay had slept at all the night before. She was sure he had been on guard outside the house. But he showed no signs of fatigue as he tied Ulysses behind the wagon and helped Shiloh up to the seat. He sat beside her before asking, "You want to tell me what MacAdams said to upset you?"

After Shiloh had repeated MacAdams' remarks, Clay said, "It's too bad, but that's the way he is, so you may as well accept it."

Shiloh's thoughts shifted to the letters of introduction. "Clay, do you know any other men involved in Gladwin's movement?"

"About all I know about him is that he often caught up with Aldar as he moved around town. The Pacifica movement isn't nearly as popular as statehood."

"Do you think Pacifica even has a chance?"

"No, I don't. First, it doesn't have the mass appeal that statehood does. That's understandable because most of the people in California came from other states, so that's what we think is normal. And if you don't have the popular support, then you've got to have money or muscle. That's what Aldar told me one time."

Shiloh looked up with a puzzled look. "He said that?"

"Yes, but he was quoting somebody. He didn't talk like that himself, you know."

Mara had disbanded her outdoor bakery by the time Shiloh and Clay arrived. Samuel's great strength, augmented by helpful customers, had even managed to wrestle the huge black stove into the smaller tent with the other supplies.

"Aren't you afraid to leave things like that in a tent that anyone can enter?" Shiloh asked as they walked to where Clay was waiting to give her a hand up to the wagon seat.

"Nobody will touch a thing," she replied firmly. "They all know there won't be any more pies or biscuits in two weeks if anything happens to those things."

"That's a very good reason," Shiloh conceded as she approached the wagon.

Mara rode Ulysses and kept an even pace alongside the wagon as they headed toward the house. "There's one little thing that troubles me," Mara confessed. "Samuel told me that those slave catchers were hanging around again the last couple of days."

"Are you afraid for him?" Shiloh asked with concern. "Would he be safer if we asked him to come along with us?"

"He's a big man, and thinks he can take care of himself. Besides, it's totally impractical to even consider him coming along."

Shiloh glanced at her friend with mixed feelings. *Mara sounds so hard,* she thought, *yet she was willing to use her own gold to buy Joseph's freedom from the crimps.*

The wagon was quickly loaded. "I guess we're about ready to head for the bank," Clay said. He pulled a revolver from under a sack beneath the front seat and shoved the weapon into his waistband. Then he retrieved a shotgun, carefully dusting it off with his hands.

"You know how to use this?" he asked, handing it to Shiloh.

"I grew up on a farm, so I've fired a few guns."

"Could you hit a man with it?"

Shiloh drew back in surprise. "What?"

"I can," Mara said, reaching over and taking the gun. She quickly checked the load. "I brought all the gold out and set it just inside the back door. You load and I'll keep my eyes open so we're not disturbed."

Shiloh glanced around apprehensively as Clay carried the cans and pokes to the wagon. He covered them casually with an old horse blanket while Mara locked the cookhouse door and Shiloh did the same with the main house. Both keys were handed to Clay.

Mara said, "This time, I think I'll ride back here behind you two." She laid the shotgun on the wagon bed and climbed nimbly after it in spite of her long skirts. She used them to cover the weapon while Clay helped Shiloh up to the seat. Then they drove off with Ulysses trailing along behind the wagon.

The Watcher observed everything from his hidden spot behind a sand dune. He began cursing fervently but quietly. *I shouldn't have waited!*

They were nearing the bank before Mara raised her voice. "Don't look now, but I think we're being followed."

Shiloh tensed and resisted the temptation to turn around.

Clay asked, "Mara, is he riding a mule?"

"How'd you know?"

"I've seen his sign. I think he followed us from the ship the day you arrived."

"You do?" Shiloh asked in alarm.

"Yes," Clay replied. "He's the one who's been watching the house, and almost surely broke in."

"I remember somebody saying that when we neared the house that first day," Shiloh exclaimed. "And then there was the time I saw a man and his mule near the house. I thought he must live nearby although I've never seen him since. Unless he was the same man I surprised when his mule had picked up a stone in his hoof behind the house. I smiled and spoke to him, but he kept his face turned away from me."

Clay asked sharply, "Did you get a good look at him?"

"Enough to see that he had a big birthmark that covered the entire side of his face."

Clay slapped the reins across the mule's rumps. "Let's get to the bank, but keep an eye out for Logan. He'll be interested in what you can tell him about all this, Shiloh. Then we'll take Ulysses to the barn before heading for the boat."

Arriving safely at the bank, Shiloh and Clay made the deposits while Mara remained in the wagon, to all appearances a servant or slave waiting patiently, as was commonly expected. Her hand rested on the covered shotgun although she had lost sight of the mule rider. Mara still had not seen him when Shiloh and Clay returned.

They drove to Logan's office, but he wasn't there, and nobody seemed to know exactly where he was. There was not much chance of finding him by driving around, Clay explained. He reluctantly headed for the express company's mule barn near the north bay.

The hostler tied Ulysses, then climbed in the wagon to drive it back from the dock after unloading.

There the passengers boarded the steamer *Senator* which soon cast off for its fourteen-hour run. It headed north across the bay while Shiloh stood at the stern with Mara and Clay. Shiloh's heart wrenched as she recalled how San Francisco looked when she landed there with Aldar. Shiloh focused on watching the water. There was something soothing about it, and that feeling improved as they passed Alcatraz Island and continued north. By the time they turned east into the Carquinez Straits, Shiloh felt quite relaxed. She had to work at pushing back the memories of Aldar though.

As the stern wheeler churned along, the captain blew his whistle at passing vessels while Sandwich Island crewmen tossed cordwood into the furnace to keep the steam pressure up.

Clay pointed to the left bank. "That's Benicia," he explained. "The arsenal is there. If this business over slavery ever erupts into war, you can bet your life that's going to be a prime target."

"For whom?" Shiloh wanted to know.

"For whoever doesn't control it. At this time, the federal government does. Right now, the government is trying to build a navy yard at Benicia. However, that's proving to be nearly impossible because all the sailors get gold fever and take off for the diggings. The thought of getting rich makes them forget their oath of allegiance."

Getting rich. Money. Power. Shiloh shook her head. Was nobody immune to what California seemed to offer even ordinary sailors?

The steamer passed into Suisun Bay and continued to where the Sacramento and San Joaquin Rivers merged. The *Senator* turned northeast into the Sacramento.

Shiloh noticed the dramatic change in the weather. She had become used to San Francisco's cool climate, blowing sand,

and the great masses of fog banks. Now, heading inland, this balmy weather was replaced by heat that drove Shiloh and the others out of the merciless sun and into the *Senator's* elegant salon for shade. The heat was dry, and there was no humidity, which pleased Shiloh. She didn't like the mugginess of her eastern summers.

At dusk, with the air rapidly cooling, Shiloh stood outside at the rail, sandwiched between Mara and Clay. He pointed out a herd of elk grazing on the shore. Beyond those, a small band of wild horses galloped across low, rolling hills already turning from green to brown.

"Mustangs," he said. "That's what they call them."

The word clanged in Shiloh's memory. Mustangs, Aldar had said, would be used to pull the great stagecoaches he envisioned owning. Mustangs, small, wiry animals with great strength and lots of heart. But Aldar was now buried, and the horses roamed wild and free.

Thinking of Aldar made Shiloh's tears start. There had been no proper time for grieving. Immediately after the first shock and disbelief, there had been the crushing necessity of surviving, of trying to get home to Pennsylvania. Then there had been all the strange events that kept her from having time to do what she most desperately wanted: to loosen her restraints and let the pain of loss pour out in endless tears.

Clay cleared his throat. "Would you like to be alone?" he asked quietly.

She started to nod, feeling her lower lip start to quiver. Then she realized there were too many men around who would not understand.

"No," she said, a catch in her voice, "I'd like to talk."

"All right. Anything in particular?" Clay inquired.

She thought a moment before answering. "At the funeral," she began, then had to stop to gain control of her voice, "at the funeral, you said something about losing someone too. I was so upset at the time I didn't really understand what you meant."

She looked up at him through misty eyes. His brow slid down and a darkness came over his face.

"If it's too painful . . . " she said hastily, but he shook his head, stopping her.

"I never even told Aldar," Clay began, turning to look out over the wide river.

"I don't have to know either," Shiloh assured him.

Mara said, "I think I'll walk around a little," and moved away.

Clay turned toward her. "You don't have to go, Mara."

"I think it might be easier if I do," she replied, and kept walking.

"I can't quite decide what she's thinking, or even what she's like," Clay commented to Shiloh, "but I'm sure she has a good heart. Like the way she defended her two friends when the slave catchers tried to take them."

"Yes," Shiloh agreed, "and like her being willing to give her own money to free Joseph from the shanghaiers."

Strange, she thought, *Aldar didn't like Mara, and she certainly didn't like him. They argued just before Aldar died. Strange how people think so differently about one another.*

"Aldar told me that you and Mara were raised together," Clay commented.

"Yes. It's a long story. Maybe one night around the campfire we'll tell you about it. Right now, if you don't mind, I'd like to hear about what happened in your life."

He sighed noisily before answering. "I was married. We had a little boy. Then I pioneered too far west, away out where we were pretty much alone."

He hesitated, and Shiloh waited.

Finally he said huskily, "It's hard to talk about it even after all these years."

"I'm sure it is." When he didn't reply, Shiloh asked, "did that have anything to do with the way you acted when we first met?"

"I didn't think my feelings showed."

"They showed. I thought you didn't like me."

He turned to face her. "I never would want you to think that. I was happy that Aldar had found a good woman. I was happy for him, but . . . "

"You remembered something painful?" Shiloh guessed.

He nodded. "I remember coming home one day and finding them both—" He broke off abruptly.

Shiloh waited, feeling his pain as she was sure he felt hers. "Was it an accident?" she asked softly.

"No." He paused a long time before saying, "Murdered."

She sucked her breath in sharply. "Your wife and little boy?"

Clay didn't answer for several seconds. "Both," he said at length. Taking a long, shuddering breath, he added, "I found the man who did it."

Again, she waited, wanting to know, and yet dreading the torture that the memories brought to him.

When he spoke again, his voice was so low Shiloh barely heard him. "I killed him."

She tried to keep from showing any reaction.

"I killed him," he repeated, his voice thick with emotion, "just as surely as I killed Elizabeth and Mark by exposing them to unnecessary danger."

"Oh, you mustn't say that! What you did isn't anything like what he did. Not at all."

"It was my fault. I think about that every day. When I saw that Aldar had brought you away out here, thousands of miles from your home . . . "

He gave his head a quick shake. "I guess I wanted to put you on that ship again and send you right back where it was safe. But it wasn't my place to say anything."

She thought carefully before asking, "Are you feeling some guilt because of me?"

He raised his eyebrows as though thinking about that. "Maybe. I didn't think of it quite that way, but I guess that's part of it."

"And as Aldar's friend, you want to do what you can to protect me. Is that what you're doing?"

"Is that wrong?"

"No, Clay. It's very sweet of you. But, as Mara is fond of telling me, I've got to learn to stand on my own two feet. Oh, it's not easy. I tell myself that's what I should do, and then every time something happens, like the break-in yesterday, and even the flowers, I run to her like a little girl to her mother."

"We all run from something." He turned again to gaze across the water. "From memories, from other people, lots of things."

"From other people?" she repeated.

"The man who killed my wife and son was a twin. They were both mean and wild. After I avenged Elizabeth and Mark's deaths, I left those parts in a hurry. I expected that the other twin would come looking for me. He was that kind of person."

"You don't still think . . . "

"I wouldn't be surprised. I've been to a lot of places since then: New York, across the country with the army, and yet, well, I still find myself looking over my shoulder from time to time."

Clay never meant to, but he began to open up to Shiloh. Before long, the two slipped into a companionable exchange that made Clay comfortable enough to confide details about his life that he had never disclosed to anyone. As Shiloh listened intently, Clay explained that right after avenging his family's death—before the U.S. annexed Texas in 1845 and brought on the war with Mexico—he drifted to New York. "It's like the life just went out of me," he told her. "I didn't care about anything. I just . . . existed."

He related how he joined General Stephen Kearny's dragoons and headed west with them to carry out President Polk's orders to establish an American government in California.

Shiloh found Clay's experiences to be quite riveting. It seemed to her that Clay's life had already been filled with more adventure—even danger—than anyone she knew.

Now that he had begun speaking so candidly, the details about this lost, painful part of his life just kept flowing. In December 1846, Clay was wounded along with Kearny and several others. Another twenty-two Americans died when the *Californios* attacked at the Battle of San Pasqual near San Diego. The *Californios,* all superb horsemen led by Andres Pico, triumphed in the bloodiest of California's battles with little more than lances and lariats. Kearny, who lost an arm, led Clay and other survivors to a hill. In the darkness, the famous scout Kit Carson, with Lieutenant Edward F. Beale, slipped away to bring back reinforcements from San Diego. "While we waited, we avoided starvation by eating mule meat," Clay admitted.

"Mule meat!" Shiloh shuddered, thinking suddenly about poor old Ulysses.

"After I was discharged, I joined in the first rush to find gold. But after a week of backbreaking labor in icy streams with only a little 'color' to show for it, I switched to the express business. That's how I met Aldar."

Now she understood. Strange, how just as she was beginning to get to know the real Clay, she was preparing to leave San Francisco forever. With any success at all in the gold fields, she would have enough funds to sail home, once she found a female traveling companion.

The preacher might be able to help her find someone. Then they would be off on the first available vessel, leaving behind all the troubles and fears that San Francisco had brought her. Was she going home to Pennsylvania, or running away from something—like Clay? *No matter!* She brushed such ideas from her mind.

There would be no more watching man stalking her. There would be more break-ins, not even any flowers mysteriously left on her doorstep.

She could forget the man who stalked her. She would remember only Aldar, and his dream which was gone like her own. *But,* Shiloh warned herself, *if I fail. . . .*

She didn't want to think about that. Still, as she stood on the deck heading up the Sacramento, she found herself looking back over her shoulder.

CHAPTER XVI

THE TEMPERATURE was in the high eighties in late afternoon when the *Senator* slowed prior to docking. The steamer was greeted by the firing of a cannon and Sacramento City's cheering inhabitants.

The community, located immediately south of the river, largely resembled San Francisco with haphazard wooden business structures that started on the riverbank and spread inward. Some of the wooden buildings seemed to perch precariously on timbers that raised them so high above the dusty street that steep wooden steps had to be climbed to reach the door.

These were mixed in with tents where gamblers or merchants plied their trade. Without doubt, Clay explained, the principal business here as in San Francisco was conducted at the saloons and gambling tents. Men who never touched liquor at home often stopped on their way back from the hills, had a celebration drink, and ended up losing all their "pile" to the gamblers.

Shiloh and Clay joined the male passengers lining the rail. Mara had moved away from the others shortly after the trip upriver began.

Shiloh had talked to a few passengers on the trip. A few expressed their good fortune in having been able to obtain such fast passage as the steamer offered. Fare was only twenty-five dollars and meals were two dollars. The *Senator* made it a lot easier for folks to get upriver now that she was running three times weekly during daylight hours.

Almost without exception, the passengers were prospective gold miners eager to be ashore and head toward the foothills. There, Shiloh had been told by a couple of young men from Boston, they expected to find gold lying right out in the open, waiting for them to just come pick it up.

Clay had later assured her that the miners were in for a rude surprise. The gold was there, all right, as it had been for thousands of years, but it was hidden under rocks, in cracks and crevices. Most of that was submerged in icy mountain streams, although some were in "dry diggings" without water.

No matter where it was sought, there was a price to pay for mining the precious flakes and nuggets. Often the cost in sickness, accident, and death was higher than the actual value of the recovered gold.

Shiloh didn't want to think about death. She quickly brushed away all thoughts of Aldar's body floating eerily in the tide. "Why are those buildings on stilts?" she asked Clay.

"Floods. In the winter, this river joins with the American which is just east of here, and they spread out over all this flat country. When the winter rains come, they overflow the banks and wash everything away, leaving terrible mud behind. San Francisco's hills keep it from flooding, but the sandy streets all turn to mud anyway."

"It rains in San Francisco?" Shiloh asked. "I've only seen fog."

"Rains real hard in the winter. In fact, there's a story told about a fellow who saw a hat in the middle of the street after a couple months of rain. The man reached down to pick up the hat and found that another man was wearing it."

Shiloh laughed. "I guess that's one of the tall tales you tell out here."

"That's not all," Clay assured her solemnly, "The man wearing the hat was also riding a mule."

Shiloh smiled, seeing a lighter side of Clay that was entirely new to her.

Clay lowered his voice. "Don't look now, but when you get a chance, take a look at that nice looking young man standing over there. I think he's got eyes for you."

A few seconds later, Shiloh casually turned to look at the passenger. She was already aware that he had been stealing glances at her during much of the trip, but so had most of the other men on board. His high boots, red shirt, and wide brimmed hat were all obviously new, marking him as a prospective miner.

Clearing his throat and looking at Clay, the stranger said, "Excuse me, but you sound as though you've lived in California for a while."

"For a while," Clay agreed.

"I'm from Illinois and going to get rich mining gold. Name's Jesse Brown." He extended his right hand.

Clay took it and introduced himself, then Shiloh. She hid a smile behind her hand as Brown apologized for intruding on their privacy. Shiloh knew that he had been trying to think up a subtle way to meet her during the last hour. With the boat soon to dock, he was about to lose his last opportunity.

"You must know a lot about this country, Mr. Patton," Brown said. He had stopped looking at Shiloh since she was introduced as a married woman.

"Some," Clay replied.

Shiloh sensed that he was trying to discourage Brown from becoming too friendly. That was fine with her.

"I'd appreciate any helpful hints you can give me, Mr. Patton."

"I know just enough about mining gold to be in another line of work, so I can't be of any help."

"I see." With a final glance at Shiloh, Brown said, "Well, thanks anyway. Nice meeting all of you."

When Brown was out of hearing, Shiloh commented, "Friendly man."

"Curious is more like it," Clay replied. "He wanted to know if a pretty woman like you was available."

Shiloh glanced up at Clay, aware for the first time that he had noticed her as a woman. She was pleased with the compliment, but she was also instantly uncomfortable. They were going to be together for a couple of weeks when she would welcome Clay's presence as a friend and protector, but nothing more.

"Excuse me," she said, "I'd better go see how Mara's doing."

Clay watched her go, silently castigating himself for her sudden departure. *I shouldn't have said that,* he told himself. *It just slipped out.*

For the first time since Elizabeth, Clay had really noticed another woman. There had been brief encounters with others over the past few years, but none who really touched him. Until now. And that wouldn't do.

She was Aldar's wife, he sternly reminded himself. *He was your friend. Now you're looking at her like Brown did. At least he had the decency to walk away. You can't do that, but you can keep from making any more slips.*

His eyes roamed over the flat countryside that stretched out for miles in every direction except east. In that direction, some forty miles away, the foothills showed brown with tall, dry grass. Beyond them, the Sierra Nevada Mountains rose grandly into the sky. He could still see a few white patches of snow on the higher peaks.

Shiloh approached Mara who stood alone at the stern. "I can't believe how hot it is," Mara commented, fanning herself with her open hand. "Is it always like this?"

"I asked Clay awhile ago. He says it gets much hotter; above a hundred degrees in the summer."

"At least it's dry heat. I hated the mugginess and stickiness back east." She tried to hide a smile. "I noticed that brazen young man trying to get acquainted with you."

Shiloh's mind was elsewhere. "He called me pretty," she said softly.

"He had his nerve! Perfect stranger like that."

Shiloh shook her head. "Not him, Clay."

Mara's eyebrows arched. "Clay?"

"Yes." Shiloh repeated the sentence Clay had used.

"Good for him," Mara exclaimed.

"You approve?" When her friend nodded, Shiloh reminded her, "A moment ago you were condemning that other man just for introducing himself."

"This is different."

"Is it? Do you realize what that means?"

"Of course. You're a woman, and Clay's a man, and he finally noticed the difference."

"Don't be flippant! Over the next couple of weeks, we're going to be together an awful lot, and in close quarters too. I want him as a friend, Aldar's friend. That's all."

"Maybe that's what he wants too. But that doesn't mean he can't find you appealing. Would you feel any better if he thought you were as ugly as a mud fence in a rain storm?"

"There's no use talking to you," Shiloh snapped, turning away. "They're lowering the gangplank. I'm going to be glad to be ashore."

Mara stood for a moment, shaking her head.

There was a strained silence between Shiloh and Clay as they stood on the wharf with the smell of the river and the cottonwoods and willows in the air. Clay said he would go find out about obtaining an express wagon and a team from the MacAdams and Laird station while the women waited for their meager supplies to be unloaded.

"Look, Shiloh," Mara said as Clay walked off through the crowd of disembarked passengers, hotel and restaurant runners, "you're going to have a difficult enough time with your work, so let's not you and me get cross with each other."

"I'm not cross. Well, maybe I sounded a little that way. But I didn't dream what Clay was thinking."

"Oh, stop it! It isn't as though he asked you to marry him! He just paid you a compliment, which you should accept for what it is."

"I suppose you're right, but I've got to be careful just the same."

They had their belongings together when Clay returned with the borrowed team and wagon. He was quiet while loading the tent, their small baggage, food staples, and necessary hardware like shovel and ax.

Shiloh tried to make casual conversation as she sat beside Clay on the wagon's single narrow seat. "I have one regret about leaving San Francisco," she said. "I didn't get to speak to Brother Sledger."

"Didn't you know?" Clay asked, turning to look at her as the team plodded down a street that seemed almost ankle deep in dust. "He's in Sacramento City."

"He is?"

"He left a message at the office for an express man to pick up his supplies, so I took it and him to the boat yesterday. He's staying at the same hotel where I hope we can get rooms."

Shiloh was cheered by the prospect of seeing the unorthodox preacher, but puzzled about why he had come to Sacramento City.

The Parkinson House was more than Shiloh expected. This was no tent, but a real frame structure on a side street where it was quieter than downtown. Clay approached the desk in the small lobby that smelled of dust and tobacco.

"Yes," the thin, balding clerk replied in answer to Clay's question. "You're in luck. I've got room for you, Mister, if you don't mind sharing it with several other men. That's the way it is here these days." He glanced curiously at Shiloh and Clay.

"I've done it before," Clay replied, "so it's no problem now. But the ladies require separate quarters."

"Well," the clerk said, lowering his voice and leaning across the desk toward Clay. "I can manage that for her," he jerked his head slightly in Shiloh's direction, "but we can't accommodate the slave."

The words were not intended for Shiloh's ears, but she heard, as she was sure Mara had. Shiloh whirled toward the clerk. "She is my friend, not a slave, and she can sleep in my room."

The clerk licked his lips nervously. "I—I don't think you understand, Missus."

"Oh, I understand," she replied crisply. "Sometimes people's prejudices follow them, even to this faroff place. If Mara can't stay here, then neither will I."

The clerk coughed nervously. "Please try to understand. It's not my idea, but the management . . . "

"Hang the management!" a voice boomed from behind Shiloh.

She turned with Clay and Mara as John Sledger strode across the small lobby and leaned across the desk without speaking to anyone.

"Mister," the preacher said, lowering his massive head to where his eyes were only inches from the little clerk's, "did you ever hear about anybody rassling a grizzly bear and living to tell the tale?"

The strange question obviously surprised the clerk, as it did Shiloh. When he shook his head, Sledger laid both immense hands, palms down, on the counter.

"Well, if I told you that I had, would you believe me?" Sledger said loudly.

"Uh . . . yes, sir. I . . . I would."

"Why would you believe such a thing?" Sledger demanded, still ignoring Shiloh and the others, which now included several curious men who had stopped to watch.

"I . . . uh . . . I'd believe it because you're alive."

"You're a real smart man," Sledger said, smiling and straightening up. "In fact, I think you're smart enough to find a room for this here nice lady." He turned to extend a huge arm toward Mara.

"Uh, yes. Yes, I believe I can work something out," the clerk exclaimed in obvious relief.

"We'll share a room," Shiloh told the clerk before reaching out to shake hands with Sledger. "I'm so glad to see you," she exclaimed with a bright smile. "I was just telling Clay that I regretted not having had an opportunity to speak to you before leaving San Francisco."

"The Lord's good timing," Sledger said, taking her and Mara by their elbows and steering them toward a sofa. It was the only piece of furniture in the lobby. Clay followed. "Introduce me to this fair lady," Sledger said, looking directly at Mara, "and then all we'll go somewhere and have a nice, long talk."

A short time later all four people were seated under a two-hundred-year-old white oak, which Sledger said was locally called a valley oak. It was cool under its great spreading branches.

Shiloh commented, "Brother Sledger, I'm surprised to see you here in Sacramento City."

"I'm trying to buy enough lumber to build a church."

"That's wonderful news!"

"We've outgrown that gambling and saloon tent where we been meeting. More women are coming every week, it seems."

"They are?"

"They sure are. Unfortunately, a couple of them are widows. One lost her husband on the way, and the other woman's man died after they got here. Neither has children, but the others do, and that's going to help us grow. That's where you'd fit in right nicely, Shiloh."

"I'm sorry, Brother Sledger, but I'm still planning on returning home."

"I see." Disappointment sounded in the preacher's voice. Then he brightened. "So what brings all of you this way?"

Shiloh explained, concluding, "I think everyone back east has heard about Captain John Sutter, and how he owns thousands and thousands of acres around here. I thought I'd call on him before leaving for the gold camps. If I could sign him up, then anything else on this trip would be extra."

"Don't count on him," Sledger warned. "His employee, James Marshall, discovered the gold not far from here at Sutter's Mill a year ago January. Sutter thought he was going to be wealthy beyond words, but he was wrong. Men are overrunning his property, butchering his cattle, and ignoring him like he didn't even exist."

Clay commented, "I had heard he was having a hard time of it."

"The worst is yet to come," Sledger assured him. "You can be sure there will be court fights over miles and miles of land Sutter claims. The lawyers will get what the varmints don't."

The preacher turned to Shiloh, "I don't think you better count on landing Sutter as a customer."

She leaned back against the trunk's rough bark while Clay took up the conversation.

"John," he began with a faint smile, "I thought you preachers believed it was a sin to tell a lie."

"Lie? What lie?"

"Back there with the clerk when you told him you had wrestled a grizzly."

"Whoa, there! I didn't do no such thing! You think back. What I did was ask him if he believed I ever wrestled a grizzly. He said he did, and I got what I wanted in asking him the question in the first place."

"I don't know, John," Clay said, giving Shiloh a sideways glance as if to let her know he was teasing the big man, "if it wasn't a lie, it sure was misleading."

"Well, now, let's just think about the Scriptures and see if I done wrong. You remember when Samuel the prophet was afraid of old King Saul who wouldn't have hesitated to kill him?"

"It's been awhile, but I remember most of it."

"Then you'll remember Samuel told God he was afraid of Saul, and the Lord told him to take some animals and say he was going to a sacrifice. It worked too. Now, is that an example I could follow with ease of mind?"

Clay made an exaggerated pretense of considering that carefully. "I'm not sure I could do that, John, but if you're satisfied, I'm satisfied. After all, you don't ever have to answer to me."

"That's why people are different, Clay. Like you an' me; well, we got different personalities. Did you ever notice that God often changed men, gave them new hearts and like that, but He never once changed their personalities?"

"I'd never thought of that."

"I have. Take Paul the apostle. When he was still Saul, breathing out threatenings against the church, he was always speaking his mind and doing what he thought was right.

"Then he met the Lord, and Saul became Paul. Why, he turned the world upside down! He still always spoke out, always got in big trouble, but he never stopped doing what he felt was right. See, he never changed, but his heart and purpose did."

Clay grudgingly nodded. "I see what you mean, John."

"Same with me, Clay. God changed me after what I done back then, but I still like to rassle a grizzly bear now and then, even if it's not the real thing. Safer this way, you see."

Shiloh smiled with delight. "Brother Sledger, you have a most unusual way of seeing things."

"Sometimes I don't always see things right, though," he confessed, looking somberly at her. "I was so sure you belonged in San Francisco, but you're still bound and determined to sail away soon."

"When I get back from this trip, I should have the money," she replied. "Then I'm off on the first ship that will take me."

"You did pray about this like I asked you?"

"Yes, I did."

"And you're still going?"

"I'm still going."

The big preacher cocked his head and looked her over very carefully. "You're not gone yet."

The simple flat statement was somehow disturbing to Shiloh. She started to protest that she had nothing to keep her here, but Sledger spoke first.

"And I'm not through praying about it."

Those words bothered Shiloh, even late the next morning when Clay had returned the borrowed team and wagon. Explaining that jackasses would be more practical in the gold country, Clay bought four sturdy mules, loaded one with their equipment, and led the way through the deep, powdery streets of Sacramento City.

He wore his brimmed hat and the women wore sunbonnets because Clay had warned about the dangers of riding for hours under the blazing sun. Shiloh and Mara rode astride in the loose-fitting trousers they had so appreciated when they rode muleback across Panama's mountains. There the pantaloons had been a practical necessity that the men accepted. But in Sacramento City, attractive women were about as scarce as in San Francisco, and women riding astride was so novel that it brought crowds of men to gape in open-mouthed amazement.

Shiloh tried to ignore the stares as Clay led the way from the river area inland.

"I'll take you by Sutter's Fort," he explained, "so you can see for yourself what everybody talks about whenever there's a mention of California's gold. Then we'll swing east and pick up the American River just above where it joins up with the Sacramento. We'll take the American up past where gold was discovered, then follow it all the way to the foothill gold camps."

The main gate at Sutter's Fort was open with a small cannon standing guard. Shiloh, recalling the preacher's remarks about the pioneer Sutter, thought of the cannon as an empty symbol of something rapidly passing.

It was still pleasantly cool, as it had been last night, and there was nothing to do except stay in the saddle, so Shiloh let her thoughts drift.

Sledger's words echoed in her mind. *You're not gone yet,* and *I'm not through praying about it.*

Mara moved her mule closer to Shiloh's so they were riding side by side. "I've been thinking about your preacher friend's words," Mara began. "While I don't hold with his or your beliefs anymore, I think maybe he's right. It wouldn't surprise me if you ended up staying in California."

"That's not possible!" Shiloh spoke with some emotion. "I'm homesick, I've lost my husband and the plans we had . . . "

"I've heard all that before," Mara interrupted. "I'm just giving you my thoughts, so don't get upset."

"I'm not! But I've already had enough bad experiences in California to last a lifetime. As fast as I can earn the money, I'm going home, and nothing or nobody's going to stop me."

Mara didn't reply, but moved her jackass away a few feet so Shiloh was able to be alone with her thoughts.

She closed her eyes, letting the mule pick his way behind the lead animal. *Lord,* Shiloh prayed silently, *I'm trying to do the right thing, but it's not easy. Show me what to do, please.*

Clay called back. "You asleep, Shiloh?"

She opened her eyes and straightened up. "No."

"Wouldn't want you to fall out of the saddle," he said with a hint of a grin. "So maybe you'd like to ride up here with me so we can talk. I'll try to not bore you so you'll stay awake."

She understood that he was trying to ease the tension that his remark on the boat had caused. "That's the best offer I've had all day," she replied, trying to add a light touch to her tone.

They rode on together, their mounts a few feet apart on the

flat, seemingly endless valley floor. He started pointing out the meager sights. They consisted primarily of scattered clumps of oak trees growing out of soil that Clay said would likely not feel rain again until autumn.

There were occasional herds of scrawny, wild cattle which silently watched them as they passed.

"You don't ever want to get down from your mount with those cattle around," Clay warned. "They've been chased by the *Californio vaqueros* who used to ride all this country when it was mostly Spanish land grants.

"But if you're afoot, those cattle might mistake you for some kind of dangerous animal, and they'd charge you. While their horns aren't as long as those down in Texas, these can hurt you plenty."

Shiloh was pleased there seemed to be none of the tension which had erupted yesterday. She encouraged the sense of easy companionship.

The miles of flat open valley had been spoiled by a few newly built fences. Their posts stuck out of the ground that held nothing else except the oaks. In the distance, a few rolling hills showed, now brown with sun-scorched grass.

"Smell the river?" Clay asked after a while. "It's right over there by that crooked line of trees. We'll stop there and let the mules drink and we can stretch our legs."

After resting, they forded the American River and followed the road to the gold country. The road led along the river which was marked by countless men following the stream toward the hills. Some men were fortunate enough to have mounts and a pack mule for their mining equipment, cooking utensils, and personal items. Most walked, trudging along with picks and pans banging against their legs.

"There's something to remember, Shiloh," Clay remarked as they passed along a line of foot-weary men. "They've come from back east and many countries, over thousands of miles of ocean or land, all with one hope: to find gold. Most will probably never make much more than day wages of six or seven dollars.

"They've faced a thousand dangers and they'll face another thousand. Some will die of disease and accidents and other things, but the survivors will keep going. That's what hope does for a man."

Shiloh commented, "When I first met you, I thought you didn't ever say much."

"Didn't have much to say." He grinned at her. "But now that I've got you where you can't get away, I'll show you my true self: a man who can talk, even if what I have to say might be better left unsaid."

"You sounded sort of, well, philosophical a moment ago," she replied.

"When a man spends years alone, or pretty much so, he has time to think."

"I don't like to be alone very much. Too many sad or frightening thoughts seem to come at times like that."

He rode without speaking for a minute, then said, "As long as you're not alone, are there some thoughts that you could talk about with me?"

She considered that. "I think of Aldar and the happy times we had together."

"I'd like to hear about them," Clay said.

She hesitated, letting her memory run free, seeing things again as they had been just a few short months ago back home.

Home! It sprang full blown into her mind so that it was almost as if she were standing in front of the Pennsylvania farmhome where she had grown up. It was big and square, solid and respectful in appearance. *Like Mama and Papa,* Shiloh recalled.

They were a quiet couple, and the house reflected that except when abolitionists gathered to discuss strategy. At such times, Shiloh and Mara had always been barred from the meetings.

That is, until she turned seventeen and a twenty-year-old neighbor started attending the meetings. Seth Collins owned some prosperous acreage down the lane a couple of miles. He was big boned, sunburned, and strong, but all he ever talked about was farming. Crops. Prices. Animals. Farm equipment.

"Well?" Clay broke into Shiloh's thoughts.

"Oh, I'm sorry," she said, "my mind was going so fast I forgot to talk."

He waited, riding in silence, until Shiloh was comfortable sharing her memories.

"There was this neighbor," she began, "named Seth Collins. He wasn't very interesting. Well, to tell the truth, I found him downright dull. Dull!" She repeated the word, thinking back on the times he had courted her, but without imagination.

Clay suggested, "You mean, no buggy rides to church, to pie suppers and other social events. No hay rides in the autumn, no sleigh rides in the snow?"

"How'd you know?"

"Just a lucky guess. Go on with your story."

"Well, there wasn't a whole lot of choice in Parks Pond where we lived. It's a farming community. Anyway, it was generally accepted by everyone that Seth and I would someday get married. But Seth never mentioned marriage to me.

"One moonlit night he surprised me. Instead of coming by in his spring wagon, he drove up with a horse and buggy. We started to church for the evening services, and he surprised me again."

She paused long enough for Clay to prompt, "How so?"

"He turned down a side road and entered a small covered wooden bridge over Skillet Fork. That's a very small river outside of town. Well, I'm almost ashamed to say this, but I had the feeling he was going to try to kiss me. The old folks all called it the Skillet Fork Bridge, but us younger ones called it the Kissing Bridge. It seemed like everyone who got married in Parks Pond had their first kiss on that bridge."

Clay looked at Shiloh with a faint smile.

"Oh, don't misunderstand me!" she exclaimed. "I wouldn't have allowed it. I was brought up to believe that a woman only kissed when she got engaged, and even then, only one kiss."

She hesitated, studying him. "I'm serious," she assured him. "One kiss to seal the engagement, and then no more until the wedding. Are you laughing at me?"

"No," he protested although he was chuckling. "I was thinking about Elizabeth. She was exactly that way, too."

"Really?"

He held up his right hand. "Only one."

She studied Clay thoughtfully before deciding he was telling the truth. "Well," she said, "to get on with the story, it wasn't that girls didn't expect neighboring farm boys to try kissing them. So when Seth drove onto the bridge that night, I was ready to explain my beliefs to him."

She dropped her eyes. "I shouldn't be telling you this. I've never even thought of such a thing."

"It's a long ride, and your story will go no farther," he assured her.

"I suppose. Anyway, Seth drove straight through the Kissing Bridge without even slowing down. I guess I was a little surprised and maybe a little hurt. So after we got to church, I made the mistake of telling the other girls. Since you can't expect anyone to keep a secret that you couldn't keep yourself, pretty soon everybody for miles around knew about my kissless buggy ride through the Kissing Bridge. I probably got as much teasing as Seth did."

Clay looked at her expectantly. "Is that all?" he asked.

"No, I was just leading up to how Aldar proposed to me." She turned away. "Oh, I can't tell you that! It's too personal."

"I understand, but I admit I'd like to know."

"Maybe later," she replied, unable to share with Aldar's friend that very special moment in Shiloh's life.

"How much farther do we have to go?"

"A long way . . . " Clay interrupted himself, gazing at a clump of willows they were approaching.

"What's the matter?" Shiloh asked, trying to follow Clay's gaze.

"I thought I saw somebody move behind those willows."

"We've passed hundreds of men this morning, so why should . . . "

Clay started to reach for his revolver as two men stepped out into the open with pistols leveled.

"That's far enough, Mister. We'll take over from here!"

CHAPTER XVII

THE HIGHWAYMEN moved away from the clump of willows. Both were young, of medium height and weight, dressed as typical miners with red shirts, felt slouch hats, and knee-length boots. The face of the man on the right had been scarred by smallpox. The other man had a long, narrow face. Shiloh took that in with a frightened glance that included the pistols pointed toward Clay.

The pockmarked man made a threatening motion with his revolver. "Drop your gun, Mister, nice and slow."

Shiloh's eyes flickered to Clay who was between her and the gunmen. She saw his right hand move slowly toward his gun butt as if in obedience to the outlaw's command. However, Shiloh sensed that he was not going to hand over his weapon. "Don't!" she whispered urgently.

Clay gave no indication that he had heard her.

The long-faced highwayman called, "You heard him!" He took

a couple of quick steps forward, then suddenly looked down, leaped wildly backward, and fired into the dead grass. "Snake!"

Shiloh heard the warning rattle just before the shot, but her mule started bucking, spinning her away so that she couldn't see what happened next.

"Whoa!" she cried, pulling back hard on the reins and trying to stay in the saddle.

She heard a second shot and but couldn't look back until her mount stopped bucking. Then she saw that Clay had drawn his big revolver and aimed it at the pockmarked man. He had obviously been distracted by his partner's shot. Dust drifted away from where Clay's ball had struck inches from the gunman's feet. He still held his gun, but the barrel had wandered off target.

"Drop it!" Clay commanded, "Do it now!"

The way he held the heavy revolver emphasized his threat. "Both of you get your hands up!"

"You heard him!" Mara shouted, wagging the barrel of her revolver.

The pockmarked man dropped his weapon and raised his hands. His companion did the same as some miners came running up from the river to investigate the shooting.

After Clay explained to them what had happened, the miners seized the gunmen and retired to the shade of a cottonwood tree. Shiloh, Mara, and Clay followed.

Shiloh asked Clay, "What're they going to do?"

"Hold a miner's court."

"You mean, just a bunch of men are going to try these two who tried to hold us up?" When Clay nodded, she asked, "Is that legal?"

"Maybe it doesn't have any precedents in law books back east, but that's the way it's done out here. Just remember that most men are decent and believe in fairness. So they'll appoint a judge from among themselves, and then other men to act as lawyers for those two men."

The impromptu court was held under a large cottonwood tree with the sound of the river in the background. The miners squatted on their boot heels in the manner of outdoorsmen who rarely saw a chair.

A balding man about forty named Osborne was appointed by his fellow miners to act as judge. Two other miners were chosen to be lawyers for the defendants.

These proceedings took less than fifteen minutes, while Shiloh noticed that all the miners kept looking at her and Mara.

Clay leaned down and whispered to Shiloh, "I asked them to call me as the only witness. Mara might have her feelings hurt if they call you, but out here Negroes can't give testimony against a white man."

Shiloh understood that it was the way things were, just as women could not vote.

Judge Osborne picked up a river stone, rapped on the cottonwood's trunk, and announced that court was now in session. Clay was called to testify. He took only a couple of minutes to tell what happened.

When Clay had finished, Osborne said, "Mr. Patton and his fair companions must get on their way, so the court will dispense with asking for other witnesses. Will the lawyer for the defendants state their case?"

A tall, thin man stepped forward and pleaded for leniency on the grounds that no harm had been done by his clients.

The judge, glancing appreciatively at Shiloh and Mara, decided otherwise. He ordered the defendants to stand before him.

"But for the grace of God," Osborne began sternly, "these fair women might have suffered a cruel fate, and their protector would likely be dead."

There was a murmur of agreement from the assembled miners.

"Up to now," Osborne continued, his voice rising with indignation that Shiloh suspected was for her and Mara's benefit, "there's been no crime in this area."

Again, there was murmuring approval before the judge resumed his summation prior to passing sentence. "Why, we could leave our picks and crowbars anywhere, and they'd be safe. We even left our gold poke sitting around, and not one was ever touched."

"That's right," one of the younger miners said, jumping to his feet. "We don't aim to let nothing get started now!"

The judge said sternly, "Owen, I'm the judge here."

Owen nodded a bit sheepishly and sat down.

Osborne turned his attention back to the defendants.

"Having had a fair trial, it is the finding of this court that you both be whipped on your bare backs, have your ears notched, and . . ."

Shiloh sucked in her breath. "No! Oh, please!" she cried, taking a few quick steps to stand before Osborne.

The judge raised his eyebrows. "I'm not surprised that a good woman like you would plead mercy for the likes of these two, even though they would have done you great harm. Swift and sure punishment is an example to discourage others who might stray from the straight and narrow path of righteousness. But this court would be interested in hearing your alternative suggestion."

Shiloh had no answer. She glanced at Clay and Mara, but they said nothing.

The judge explained, "We're the Illinois Company. Been together since we left home. Back then, we drew up a contract which we all agreed to honor. That includes a list of crimes and proper punishment. We haven't had to use them up to now, but in this case, this court's judgment is letting them off easy. They could be hung."

"That's right," Owen cried, getting to his feet again, "let's hang 'em! That'll learn them not to bother any woman around here."

"Owen," Osborne yelled, "one more word out of you and I'll hold you in contempt of court."

The miner again squatted on his boot heels and the judge turned his attention to Shiloh. "What would you like to see happen to these men?"

She considered that, and wondered what she would say if they were Aldar's killers. "I would rather leave that decision in your hands, only please don't mutilate them."

"Your plea for mercy is granted," Osborne assured her. He turned to the defendants. "You are banished from this river forever. If either of you is ever seen again, you'll hang from the nearest limb. Court dismissed."

As they journeyed on toward the foothills, Shiloh flanked Clay on the right. Mara rode to his left.

Mara marveled, "Justice was sure quick back there."

Unlike San Francisco, Shiloh thought.

Aloud, she said to Clay, "Mara and I can never thank you enough for what you did today."

"No thanks necessary. The rattlesnake was just the distraction we needed."

"Thank God for that snake," Shiloh said fervently. She added, "But you still took an awful chance by drawing your weapon."

"Had to be done." Clay turned to Mara. "Thanks for backing me up."

Mara smiled at him. "You're welcome."

They rode on, but Shiloh noticed that Clay was more wary, his eyes probing for more likely ambush sites ahead.

Late in the afternoon, Clay began looking around for a place to camp for the night. He said they would reach Starvation Flat tomorrow. Shiloh would make her first call on a banker named Thayer. Gladwin had given her a letter of introduction. Shiloh, tired from being in the saddle for hours, welcomed the prospect of a restful camp.

Half an hour later, they made camp in a canyon fringed

with live oak and ponderosa pine. Monstrous boulders, smoothed by eons of melted snow rushing downstream, waded serenely in the river. It was so clear that Shiloh could see large rainbow trout.

"It's so peaceful and beautiful," Shiloh commented to Mara while dinner was cooking over the open fire and after their tent was pitched. Clay announced that he preferred spreading his blankets under the stars.

So much depended on whether Shiloh succeeded or failed in her first day of trying to sell the services of MacAdams and Laird Express Company. She had read the material MacAdams had given her. She would use that information when she presented Gladwin's letter of introduction to the banker. If he signed a contract, Shiloh would gain confidence, but if he refused, then she was afraid her trip would be disastrous.

But after the meal, with the soft wind playing a soothing symphony in the pine needles overhead and the steady, rhythmic melody of the river, Shiloh sat with Clay and Mara while all stared silently into the dying flames.

There is some strange fascination with campfires, Shiloh thought. She had noticed that on the torturous trail across Panama, but there danger from a thousand sources lurked on every side. Here, there seemed to be only a spirit of peace. Yet she was worried.

"Tomorrow," she whispered.

Clay sat across the fire from her. "What about tomorrow?"

"Oh, I guess I spoke out loud," Shiloh replied. "I was just thinking about how important it is that I succeed."

"You'll do just fine." Clay's voice held a strong, confident note. It gave her courage.

"I hope so, but I'm frightened more than I can say."

He didn't reply, but looked across the fire at her. She felt compelled to explain.

"Everything depends on what happens tomorrow because it

will either give me confidence or concern me even more. If I have to go back to San Francisco without earning passage money, I'll have to stay there."

She reached out and moved a stick of wood deeper into the fire. "But I can't stay in that house any longer," she continued, watching the stick catch fire.

Clay said, "You don't need to worry."

There was such quiet assurance in his words that Shiloh believed him. "Thank you," she said, not wanting to ask how he planned to see that she need not worry.

Clay stared at the stars for a long time after Shiloh said goodnight and entered the tent. He stared upward, but saw only Shiloh. Her red-gold hair and hauntingly beautiful eyes seemed to fill the night sky, replacing the starry canvas above him. His heart pounded as he found himself filled with strange, strong emotions.

Had he ever seen her smile? Perhaps she was smiling the day she arrived in San Francisco. Clay couldn't recall. All he knew was that hearing her soft, muffled sobs at night when she thought he was asleep made his heart turn awkwardly in his chest. Her pain knifed through him as if it were his own. He wanted to console her, comfort her, stroke her hair, soothe her sorrow. But he knew he could not—*dare not!*

So he listened in silence to her soft crying until he could almost bear no more of it. When the sobbing finally subsided, Clay breathed a quiet sigh of his own, turned on his side, and drifted off to sleep.

They broke camp shortly after dawn the next morning for the final hour's ride toward Starvation Flat. They topped the final ridge and the mules followed a dusty wagon trail down the mountain side. Black and live oak could be seen among the virgin stands of graceful ponderosa pines and occasional cedars.

The sun had not yet risen high enough to penetrate the canyon where Starvation Flat nestled on a shelf above the south fork of the Yuba River. Through the trees, Shiloh saw that the community was larger than she had thought. She caught glimpses of hundreds of small tents, one large one made by joining two together, a few rag shanties, and a short row of wooden buildings that marked the business district.

The bank building was the only structure with any indication of permanence. It was barely twenty feet wide and sixty feet long, but it was imposing because it was made of adobe brick.

Stopping a quarter mile away from the town, the tent was hastily erected so Shiloh could change from her men's attire to proper women's garments. Then, dressed in her Sunday best, she pushed through the tent flap, carrying her favorite bonnet.

Mara walked over and took it from her. "Here, let me tie that so it shows off your pretty face."

Shiloh glanced over at Clay. He looked up from where he was checking the hoof on one of the mules. An image of the man with the facial birthmark flashed into her mind.

Mara commented, "You got a little sunburn yesterday in spite of your bonnet. There. It shows off your face very well."

Shiloh thanked Mara, then took a deep breath. "Well, we'll soon know if we've come a long way for nothing."

"You know what you want, so go get it," Mara replied. "Knowing and doing, that's the secret."

Shiloh had to pass Clay on her way into town. He set the mule's foot down and smiled at her.

"I believe in you," he said softly.

"Thanks. I wish I could believe in myself."

"Until then, I've got enough faith for both of us."

She was moved, but simply nodded before starting off again. She stopped impulsively and looked back. "Would you pray for me?"

"Already have. I'll keep doing it too. When you come back with that contract, we'll celebrate."

The sun was up, showing fine particles of dust in the air as Shiloh walked down the street. Panic began seeping through Shiloh's thoughts as she neared the downtown area. A few men stared openly and then nodded politely to Shiloh. Most of the five thousand or so miners were already working the river and tributaries.

At the brick building, Shiloh took a deep breath, said a brief silent prayer and pushed open the heavy oak door.

The stench of tobacco smoke made her wrinkle her nose while her eyes adjusted to the difference between the bright sunlight outside and the bank's darker interior.

Three patrons were already lined up before the cashier's grill. The first one in line set down two leather bags of gold dust on the counter. They made a loud, solid thump.

The men all turned to look at Shiloh. They were a scroungy looking lot in jack boots and unwashed blue or red shirts. Their untidy hair was long, and their beards wild and unkempt, but each man quickly and politely removed his weathered felt hat.

The cashier behind the brass grill cage had pale white skin that contrasted sharply with the deep tans of the miners. Beyond the cashier's grillwork, two other bank employees looked up at Shiloh. One man's hand suddenly froze in midair, remaining suspended above the balance scales where he had been weighing gold. Across from him, a heavyset man dropped a large leather bag into a sturdy wooden box in preparation for shipping. That sight gave hope to Shiloh.

Shiloh's throat suddenly constricted. She smiled at the cashier and announced, "I'd like to see Mr. Thayer, please."

The gold weigher knocked on a door at the back of the bank and spoke through it. "Walter, there's a lady to see you."

"Send her in."

The bank employee opened the door for Shiloh. She

stepped inside a small but neat office. It was simply furnished with two massive chairs that undoubtedly had been brought around the Horn, the same as the banker's heavy desk and leather chair.

"Excuse me," he exclaimed, leaping up from behind the desk. He was so thin as to be almost cadaverous. "I was expecting Mrs. Randall. She's the only woman around here. Runs the boarding house." His words had come in a rush, but he regained his banker's demeanor. "I'm Walter Thayer, founder of this institution."

"I'm Mrs. Laird, Mrs. Aldar Laird."

"Of MacAdams and Laird Express Company?" When Shiloh nodded, Thayer continued. "I used to know him in Sacramento. A most personable and likeable fellow. But I didn't remember him being marri—" He broke off and began coughing.

He reached for a handkerchief to cover his mouth, alerting Shiloh that he probably had lung consumption.

When Thayer excused himself and replaced his handkerchief, Shiloh explained, "We were married a few months ago when he was back east."

"That's wonderful! Best wishes to you, Mrs. Laird. When can I see Aldar and congratulate him?"

Although she had anticipated questions about Aldar's whereabouts, Shiloh had to hesitate a moment before replying. She had earlier chosen to not say he was murdered because that would lead to explanations and certainly distract from her mission.

She said simply, "He died a few weeks ago in San Francisco." After Thayer's words of condolence, Shiloh headed off further questions by saying, "I'm sure you'll understand that it is distressing to dwell on the details."

"Of course, Mrs. Laird. We see so much of tragedy here, just as in crossing the plains. Cholera, smallpox, accidents . . . I'm sorry. What brings you here?"

In those final four words, his manner changed. He was suddenly brisk and businesslike.

She forgot all about Denby Gladwin's letter of introduction. She did remember some things that Aldar had told her in the long, monotonous days of first sailing down the Atlantic coast, then up the Pacific coast following the Panama crossing. *Ask questions to uncover hidden needs.*

"What is your greatest business need, Mr. Thayer?"

"I hadn't expected that question," he admitted with a wry smile.

She didn't answer, remembering Aldar telling her to say nothing until the prospect was forced to think it through. Through the door she heard voices and the thump of gold pouches.

"Well," Thayer said, "I suppose it's to find a qualified man to open another branch bank for me. Why do you ask?"

She didn't answer his question, but posed her next one. "What is your second most pressing need?"

"I'd have to think about that."

"Could it be a way to get your gold shipments safely to San Francisco?"

Thayer's gray eyes showed interest. "I can't possibly imagine why a young woman like you would want to know, but yes, that is a problem."

"How are you doing that now?"

He stirred uneasily. "May I ask where you're going with these questions, Mrs. Laird?"

"Of course. How would you like to have your gold shipments taken safely and regularly to San Francisco by the fastest, most honest and reliable means possible?"

Thayer tilted his head back in understanding. "I see now. You want me to let your husband's express line convey my shipments to and from Sacramento. Is that it?"

"I want you to do what is best for your bank," she replied, relying on Aldar's words and the presentation material in the packet MacAdams had given her.

"Do you know how many express businesses there are now? How many more seem to start up each day? They're more numerous than mushrooms after a spring rain."

"I'm sure a man who's as obviously capable as you are knows that it's not numbers that count, but service and dependability. I believe that MacAdams and Laird is the very best, and has everything you need to help your business make more profit."

The banker smiled broadly. "You're good, Mrs. Laird. I'll give you that. Did you learn that from your husband?"

"Some of it," she admitted, "but I believe what I'm saying. This is the best express service in this area because my husband has . . . had . . . the vision to make it that way, and then to plan to make it the best in all of California."

Thayer's face sobered. "That's undoubtedly true, Mrs. Laird, but I'm a practical man. Your husband is gone. How do I know that his surviving partner will continue to have that philosophy and degree of service?"

Shiloh's heart seemed to skip a beat. She hadn't thought of that. She searched wildly in her mind for an answer, but none came.

Thayer stood. "I'm sorry, Mrs. Laird. From a personal viewpoint, I am deeply sorry that I cannot grant your request. But as your husband undoubtedly told you, business is business. I must do what I think is best for this bank."

Shiloh rose, fighting a sudden feeling of light-headedness. Everything she had hoped for was evaporating like morning mists on San Francisco Bay. She started through the door he opened for her. All the men in the bank looked at her, and she was crushed, humiliated at her total failure. She wanted to run to Mara for consolation and comfort.

No! Shiloh told herself, straightening her back and fighting back the tears that threatened to flow. Her despair was replaced by anger.

"Mr. Thayer," she said, turning to look him squarely in the

eyes, "I have told you the truth. At this time, there isn't a better express service available. It may not always be that way, but for the present, it is the very best."

Her voice rose. She was aware that she was being rude, and that everyone in the bank was listening, but she plunged on.

"I assume that is what you want for your bank. I have given you that opportunity. I respect your right to decide. I am truly sorry that I failed to convince you. Thank you for your time."

It was all she could do to control her desire to let herself go, releasing the sobs that sought to escape from inside. It was even harder to keep from breaking into a run that would carry her away from her failure. With great determination, she held her head high and walked dry-eyed back toward camp.

She reached the shelter of some live oak trees with branches that touched the ground. Then she remembered the letter of introduction and groaned. After a quick glance back to make sure nobody in town could see her, she broke down and cried hard.

Finally, she raised her head. *Oh, well,* she thought bitterly, *it probably wouldn't have made any difference.*

She dried her eyes and scolded herself. *I can't let Clay or Mara see me like this. And I can't always run to Mara like a little child.*

Shiloh looked around for a place where she could rest until she felt sure that her eyes wouldn't be too red and puffy to face Mara and Clay.

She stepped around the tree to sweep her eyes across the town. The nearest business on the short street was housed in the joined tents she had noticed earlier. A crude sign on the front read, "Mrs. Randall's Boarding House." Shiloh headed that way.

She stopped outside the tent and listened, but heard no voices. The fragrance of coffee greeted Shiloh when she entered. There were a few log benches at plank tables and a high counter in back separating the kitchen from the eating area. Shiloh was relieved that there were no customers. She started to sit down at the nearest table when a large, matronly woman looked over the counter. She picked up a coffeepot and a cup and came toward Shiloh.

"Well, now," the woman said in a loud voice, "I seen my share of pretty flowers growin' on these hillsides, but I swan! I never seen anything as purty as you away out here! I hope you like your coffee black, 'cause that's the only way it's served."

"Black will be fine."

"I'm Mrs. Randall," the woman said, pouring for Shiloh.

"I'm Mrs. Laird, Shiloh Laird." She noticed the woman's eyes narrow and realized the red eyes had been noticed. But the woman said nothing and headed back to the kitchen with the coffeepot.

Shiloh relaxed, glad to not be questioned. She judged that Mrs. Randall couldn't have been more than forty, but her face was lined like a spring-washed ravine and her hair, parted in the middle and tied behind, was quite gray. It was obvious that she had led a hard life.

She picked up another cup and filled it. "Where'd you come from, Honey? And why're you away out here?"

Shiloh started to reply, but the other woman didn't wait for an answer. "Me, I come from just about everywhere at one time or another."

She didn't wait for an invitation to join Shiloh, but eased her considerable bulk onto the bench across the table from her. "You was gonna tell me where you hail from."

Shiloh didn't want to answer that and get into a long discussion. She decided to prevent that by making one last try to sell something before retreating in disgrace. "Mrs. Randall, before I answer that, what's your greatest need?"

"That's right easy! I need a helper in here who can cook a decent meal and bake a pan of biscuits, especially tonight and tomorrow night. Not quite a year ago, this town wasn't anything more than a scab on the side of a mountain. It was rightly named back then, but after some miners struck it rich, the word spread and everybody come a'runnin' to see if they could do that, too.

"Now we got maybe five thousand men livin' hereabouts. They get mighty tired of their own cookin', believe you me, and like what I do, but I can't do it alone. Why, Honey, I'd be rich if I had some good woman to help. But there's nary a one hereabouts except me."

Shiloh forced a smile. "I didn't mean that kind of need."

"Tonight and tomorrow night," the woman continued as if she hadn't heard Shiloh, "the miners are having themselves a little get-together. I'll have two, three hundred men in here, and not even a little child to help me. Life ain't always easy, is it, honey?"

"It certainly isn't." Shiloh glanced around and realized this boarding house operator probably had nothing that would require express service. The woman rambled on about something, but Shiloh wasn't listening.

There goes my last hope, she thought. *I tried, but I'm just not cut out for this. I've lost.*

Her head dropped in despair.

Mrs. Randall asked, "You sick?" She reached across and tipped Shiloh's head up. "I noticed you been crying. Lemme see that purty face again."

"I'm all right," Shiloh replied, sliding off the bench. "I must be going."

"Coffee's on the house. I'm just so glad to have another woman to talk to I could just die. You sure you can't stay a spell? Here, sit back down."

"I really must go. Thanks for— " Shiloh left her sentence unfinished. "I just thought of something. I'll be right back." She hurried toward camp.

CHAPTER XVIII

ENTERING CAMP, Shiloh hurried to Mara who was mending a rip in her dress. "Where's Clay?" She didn't want him to see her red, puffy eyes.

"He went to the river. Have you been crying?"

"Never mind that. Would you like to help bake some biscuits for the woman who runs the boarding house?"

"I don't know. Why?"

"It's a chance to make up for the money you're losing by not being in San Francisco."

"I'm more concerned about those tears."

"You said I've got to quit always running to you with my problems. I'll work this out myself."

"Suit yourself." A hint of a smile showed on Mara's face. "I think I will go down and talk to that woman."

While Mara was gone, Shiloh sat on a stump and considered her feelings. She wanted to run away, to never call on another person or face rejection such as she had from the banker. Yet she had no choice if she was to earn the passage money home.

She remembered something Aldar had said: "First meet the customer's needs and he'll meet yours. Everybody needs what I have. My job is to prove that to them, and that takes persistence."

Slowly, Shiloh rose. *I've got to at least try again, and this time I won't quit so easily.*

She washed her face and went back down into town.

The general mercantile store owner seemed her most likely prospect. She found him standing in the middle of a small frame building displaying everything from mining equipment to groceries.

After introducing herself and inquiring how business was, Shiloh asked her question.

The owner wiped his hands on the burlap sack tied as an apron around his protruding middle and scratched his head. "My greatest need, huh? Well, I'd guess it's for better freight service from Sacramento."

He swept his hands around the room. "Last year things were so bad I nearly starved, so supplies didn't matter much. But since the big strike, I can't get enough of anything. Why do you ask?"

"Would you be interested to know of a dependable delivery service for most items except heavy freight?"

"I guess so. Why?"

Shiloh took a quick breath and began her presentation. Following the guidelines in the material MacAdams had given her, she took the merchant step by step through the services MacAdams and Laird Express offered. As she did, she realized that Aldar had surely been the one to create the sales package.

After making her points and asking questions to uncover other hidden needs, Shiloh asked, "Would you like to make your deposit in American coins or gold dust?"

Shiloh left a few minutes later with her first signed agreement and a poke of dust. Elated, she made three more calls, but without success. Discouragement again nagged her thoughts. She walked along the short street, fighting the desire to give up and return to camp. Then she saw a dry-goods store.

Lord, she prayed silently, *I don't believe in asking for signs, but I don't know what else to do. So I'll try this store. If I fail, I'll give up. If I succeed, then I'll keep trying the rest of the week, no matter what.*

Half an hour later she walked out with her second contract. Feeling much better, she called on all the remaining businesses, but without success.

She returned to camp with a lopsided record, assured that she could do this for a week, but wouldn't want to do it longer.

But if I don't succeed . . . No! Don't think of that.

Clay looked up from where he was mending a saddle strap in camp. "How did it go?"

"Got two contracts." She held them up.

"Congratulations. I knew you could do it."

"Thank you. And thanks for believing in me."

"You're welcome."

"I got more rejections than sales."

"Aldar used to say that selling is an average."

"I remember."

"Did he ever tell you that the reason he called on so many people was because each time he got turned down, he was that much closer to the one who would sign up?"

"I seem to remember something like that."

"I'm sure he would be proud of you because you're off to a great start, Mrs. Laird."

She studied him for a moment. "I think it's time you started calling me Shiloh." She didn't wait for his response, but excused herself and went to Mara.

"Did you bake for Mrs. Randall?"

"Yes, thanks. She gave me a ten-dollar gold piece just for helping this morning. She said there'll be another this afternoon, and more tomorrow. But I told her we'll be moving on. How did you do?"

Shiloh showed the contracts before an idea came to her. "It's only a few miles from here to Dutch Hill. I could ride over there this afternoon and again tomorrow so you could work for Mrs. Randall again."

Mara laughed. "You couldn't ride a mule in that outfit, and you sure can't show up in our men's attire."

"That's true, but if I can rent a wagon from someone around here, it would work for both of us."

After the midday meal, they asked Mrs. Randall, who loaned her old horse and spring wagon. Clay drove Shiloh to Dutch Hill. It was the first time she and Clay had been alone.

There wasn't the tension between them as in the past. Their conversation was relaxed and easy.

"This trip has been a whole lot different from crossing the Isthmus," Shiloh said. "We haven't even seen a grizzly bear, or almost drowned after falling out of a dugout canoe. In Panama, I had a terrible fear of tumbling into the river with the alligators."

"That's what Americans call them, but they're actually crocodiles. Alligators only live in the southern United States."

"Really? How did you learn that?"

Clay shrugged. "I just picked it up here and there."

That was a side of Clay that Shiloh hadn't known about. She wanted to ask more, but he asked what else she remembered about Panama. The question caused mental images that still made her uncomfortable. The memory of naked native men paddling dugout canoes faded, replaced by the terror of seeing a giant snake hanging from a branch over her head as the paddlers slid under it.

There was the time when they dined with a native official who served baked monkey. The local delicacy so resembled a human child that Shiloh could not touch it, although she was certain her host was offended.

"That's an experience I'd rather forget about," she replied, trying to shove the Panama horrors aside. She did not plan to return that way, but would risk sailing completely around the Horn even though it had other dangers, and the trip was much longer.

They reached the small community of Dutch Hill which was populated mostly by German placer miners. Shiloh called on every prospect, but got only one contract.

"You'll do better tomorrow at Bedbug Bar," Clay said confidently as they drove back to Starvation Flat. "It's a lot bigger than either of these towns."

Shiloh wasn't so sure, but at the end of the second day, she had three more contracts. Clay congratulated her and turned the borrowed horse toward camp.

Shiloh suddenly exclaimed, "Oh, my! Yesterday morning I completely forgot to show Mr. Thayer the letter of introduction that Gladwin gave me. That might have made a difference so he would have signed up with me."

"Yes, or maybe he doesn't agree with Gladwin's idea about California being a separate nation, and you might have lost the sale."

"That's possible, of course. But he's a banker, and probably wouldn't let his personal beliefs influence his decision on what was good for business."

"It's too late to see him today, but you could go back tomorrow morning before we break camp."

"I just don't want to risk being turned down twice. No, I think we'd just better move."

Clay dropped Shiloh off at camp, saying he would return Mrs. Randall's rig. Shiloh started the campfire in preparation for dinner.

The fire was getting hot enough to start cooking when Shiloh heard voices. Clay and Mara were walking up the hill with the banker. Shiloh watched apprehensively, trying to guess why Thayer was paying them a visit.

After exchanging greetings, he said, "Mrs. Laird, I've been thinking about what you said yesterday, and you're right."

She wasn't quite sure what he meant. "Oh?"

"There's not a business anywhere that can guarantee that the same owners are going to be there tomorrow. I can't even do that, although I've got plans to have branch banks all over. I came to apologize, and to give you an opportunity to convince me that I should give my business to your express company."

When he left half an hour later, Shiloh had her signed contract. She wanted to shout with joy as she accepted Clay's and Mara's congratulations.

The next morning they left Starvation Flat. Mara was a little richer from gold pieces and dust, and Shiloh was more confident of her mission's success.

Throughout the remainder of the week, most of the merchants on whom she called treated her well, even if they didn't buy. She usually left a community with one or two contracts. MacAdams and Laird Express employees manning distant stations were very glad to see her, with each one having some story or personal remembrance of her husband.

On the next-to-last night, Shiloh was still short one major year's contract. With it, she would have enough to assure passage money home for herself and a companion.

She rose at dawn on the final day in their camp just outside of Dry Diggings. Its name was less colorful that many of the other mining communities. They boasted names like Red Dog, Whiskeytown, and Rough and Ready.

Clay asked at breakfast, "How do you feel?"

"A little frightened," Shiloh admitted.

"You'll get that last big one," he assured her.

She thought about that while she walked down the hill to begin her day. Over the week, Shiloh's successes and failures were still lopsided against her, but she was beginning to feel differently. She wasn't as discouraged anymore when someone turned her down. She had confidence that sooner or later, someone would sign up. Maybe it would be the big one.

Late that afternoon she returned to camp. Mara wasn't in sight, but Clay was splitting wood for the evening fire. Another man on the hill above the tent was cutting firewood limbs off a downed ponderosa log.

The sharp ring of axes, the raucous squawk of scrub jays, and the faint sighing of a breeze in the pines were familiar sounds in what often was a splendid solitude.

Shiloh greeted Clay with a radiant smile. "You were right," she said cheerfully, holding up the contract.

He smiled broadly and lightly embedded his ax into an old stump. "Congratulations, Shiloh. I'm pleased."

It was the first time he had used her name. She looked at him and started to return his smile, but added quickly, "Don't misunderstand. I'm heading for home as quickly as I can secure passage and find a female traveling companion. Now I've got the money for both of us, and there should be some left over."

His eyes clouded. "Yes, you're right."

Shiloh glanced around. "These mountains are beautiful, in spite of how wild and untamed they are."

"Yes, but these are only foothills maybe fifteen hundred to twenty-five hundred feet high. That's where most of the gold has been found so far. But the real mountains, the Sierra Nevadas, are just a few miles further east."

Shiloh followed the direction of his arm as he continued to point out interesting aspects of the incredibly beautiful vista that stretched before them. "The nearest pass through them is something over seven thousand feet. That high country is more beautiful than I can say. It's certainly a whole lot different from where I came from down in Texas."

"What was it like?" She hoped he would reveal more about himself, but he turned the topic back to the present. "I'm glad you like these hills," he said. "They soothe the soul."

That's true, Shiloh realized. *But it's not home.* She excused herself and walked back to the tent. She could hear the woodcutter on the hillside above still chopping away.

It was warm inside the tent although it had been pitched under twin ponderosas. Shiloh changed out of her good dress, listening as the steady rhythm of two axes mixed with the gentle wind whispering in the treetops.

She thought, *It's like a lullaby or a wordless hymn.*

She had not felt like singing since Aldar's death, but now she started humming "Amazing Grace." She decided to go ask Mara what she could do to help prepare dinner. She stepped out of the tent, still singing the lyrics.

Clay's back was to her. He put down his ax and was piling

firewood onto his forearm. She walked toward Mara who was removing dried clothes from a burgundy-limbed manzanita shrub.

A rumbling sound stopped Shiloh. It sounded like thunder, but when she glanced up, the sky was clear.

Puzzled, she glanced uphill and gasped.

The woodcutter was wildly waving his hands above his head while a forty-foot-long ponderosa log, sheared of the limbs which had held it in place, rolled down the hill. "Look out!" he shouted. "Get out of the way!"

Shiloh stood transfixed as the speeding log came crashing down the slope, directly toward her. She watched speechlessly as it crushed a few evergreen saplings and smashed a young manzanita shrub.

The juggernaut continued to plunge downhill, faster and faster, gouging a neat path through the low, smelly undergrowth that miners called "mountain misery."

"Shiloh!" Clay's frightened shout spun her around. He was out of sight behind the tent when the runaway log smashed into it. The canvas instantly collapsed as the log shot through it and continued its wild roll.

"Shiloh! Shiloh!" Clay shouted, running frantically toward the tangled pile of tent canvas. He bent and frantically began pulling the loose canvas aside.

She roused herself and ran toward him, hearing the fear in his muffled voice as he continued to call her name from under the tent's remains.

"I'm here," she said. "I started to find Mara . . . "

Clay's head popped out from under the canvas. "Oh, thank God!" He threw his arms around her. "I thought you were under there!"

She felt him tremble, and realized the depths of his emotions. Her own were mixed, but it felt so good to have someone care about her, to have strong arms around her again.

Clay abruptly released her and stepped back. "I'm sorry—I

shouldn't have done that," he said huskily, turned, and walked rapidly into the forest.

On the long ride back to Sacramento, Clay was as quiet and distant as when Shiloh had first met him. By day, he rode in silence. At night after dinner, he stared into the campfire and did not join in conversation.

Shiloh had anticipated opportunities around the campfire to learn more about Clay, but he had shared little of his personal background. However, there had been an easy, relaxed atmosphere which was now changed.

The muleback return trip to Sacramento was uneventful. The fast steamer was not available, so they had to take a slow launch, dangerously overloaded with cargo and a few passengers who were either heading home with their "pile" or in discouragement. During the monotonous five-day journey, Shiloh reflected on what she had accomplished.

I feel good about it, she admitted. *I made a very difficult decision and acted on it. It was hard, but it turned out fine. I can hardly wait to see MacAdams' face when I show him those contracts.*

San Francisco had changed in the short time they were away. As the launch eased alongside one of the newly built wharves, Shiloh saw that more permanent buildings were going up, testifying to the community's continued rapid growth.

During the two-plus weeks they had been gone, Shiloh managed to forget about the break-in of her home, the attack on MacAdams, and the man who stalked her. As she stepped ashore, her fears returned. She tried to take comfort in Clay's earlier assurance that she need not worry. But after he hired a carriage to drive Shiloh and Mara home, she could not shake off her uneasiness.

She handed him the key, but as he started to unlock the door, he exclaimed softly under his breath. "It's already open!"

Shiloh saw the broken lock and pushed the door open.

"He's done it again!" she exclaimed.

Clay took his revolver and quickly checked the rooms, stepping over toppled furniture, scattered papers, and tumbled clothing. Shiloh followed Clay while Mara carried her gun out to the cookhouse to check it out.

Shiloh examined each room in the house, trying to determine what had been taken. "This time he really searched thoroughly," she announced, returning to the broken door lock. "He tore the bed apart, opened all the drawers, and threw all the pots and pans on the floor. But so far as I can tell, nothing's missing."

Mara returned from the cookhouse saying, "This time, everything's been ransacked out there. But he still didn't find my hiding place for the gold. Not that it would matter because it's all in the bank now."

Clay said, "Either he was very angry, or he was desperate to find something."

"Find what?" Shiloh asked. "He must have known we wouldn't leave the gold or other valuables here while we were away."

"I wish I knew," Clay replied.

Shiloh recalled his remarks after finding the flowers. "I wasn't here," she said pointedly.

If he understood her reference, he gave no indication. Instead, he commented, "I'd guess the reason he made such a mess was because he knew nobody was home and he could take his time. Whatever he's looking for had to be something specific. If he was just a burglar, he would have carried off everything of value."

"That makes sense," Shiloh agreed, "but regardless of who he is or why he's broken in again, I don't want to stay here tonight."

"You'll be safe," Clay replied.

"But he won't be," Mara said grimly, "if I get a chance to use my revolver."

Shiloh would have preferred to go to a hotel, regardless of the fleas, but Clay started to leave with the only transportation available.

"I'll notify the constable," he said. "Tomorrow morning I'll bring Ulysses back so you can ride him to MacAdams. I sure would like to see the look on his face when he sees how well you succeeded."

Shiloh slept fitfully even though she knew Clay was close by under the stars, alert to any danger.

The next morning, Shiloh was awakened by Ulysses' loud braying. Leaping out of bed, Shiloh pulled the curtains aside and peeked out. Clay had already been and gone, she realized with disappointment.

She hurried to dress, relieved that the night had passed without incident, and eager to see MacAdams. She would try not to act too triumphant in presenting the stack of contracts.

She rode Ulysses downtown, tied him to a hitching post outside the express office, and climbed the stairs. Before MacAdams could ask about the trip, she proudly handed him the sheaf of contracts.

He silently examined them before commenting. "I guess you earned your money."

Shiloh waited, expecting him to congratulate her or at least say something more. When he didn't, she felt like exclaiming, *Look, I got the new business you wanted! I got more than you expected, and you know it. So why can't you say so?*

Instead, she said nothing, realizing that he had expected her to fail. That gave her such a good feeling that she smiled at him.

He didn't seem to notice. "I'll get the additional money I owe you."

Minutes later, she walked down the stairs with gold coins and pokes of gold dust. She told herself, *That's just the way he is. Frankly, I don't see how Aldar put up with him at all. Well, now I've got to do is find a traveling companion and then I'll be on my way home. Maybe Brother Sledger can help me find someone.*

She didn't know where to find the preacher, so she rode Ulysses over to where Samuel was helping Mara set up her bakery once more. If anyone knew, he would. Her thoughts shifted to Clay. He had offered to book passage for her when she was ready. That would avoid having to endure the rude dock workers who had discouraged her first attempt.

As Shiloh approached Mara's bakery, there was the usual crowd of men, but there was something different about them. They weren't lined up against the counter waiting to buy. Instead, they had circled the bakery area like spectators watching something. Suddenly alarmed for Mara's safety, Shiloh pushed her way through.

"Oh, my!" she exclaimed.

Mara stood rigidly looking at what little remained of her business. The big black stovepipe had been crushed and the rest battered into large chunks. The little tent where the ingredients and baking utensils had been stored lay in a heap. The sacks of flour and other ingredients had been dumped out and sand poured over them.

Those responsible had left a barrel stave sticking up in the middle of the mess. Shiloh turned her head sideways to read the crude message scrawled there.

Go home nigger

That night at the house, Shiloh continued straightening up after the second ransacking, but Mara sat stiffly on the parlor sofa. There was a coldness that frightened Shiloh.

"Say something, Mara!" she said for perhaps the tenth time.

"What is there to say?" she replied. "My bakery business was ruined by those pattyrollers who wanted to grab Samuel and Joseph that time. But it's all right. I'll just open the boarding house sooner than I had originally expected."

She paused, then added with a smile, "Of course, I'll have to raise my prices."

"They'll pay it," Shiloh assured her.

Someone knocked at the front. "Who is it?" Shiloh called while Mara reached for her pistol.

"William Rawlins."

Mara furtively hid her pistol under a corner of her dress. When she nodded, Shiloh opened the door partway.

"Please forgive my manners," he said, smiling at her, "I was riding by and saw the light, so I thought I'd stop and see how you've been."

Shiloh hesitated to invite him in. "Mara and I have been away."

"I wish you had let me know before leaving." His voice held a hint of reproof. "Several times during the past weeks I sent the lieutenant with a message. I was concerned . . . " He glanced beyond her, leaving his thought dangling. "What happened?"

"There was another break-in while we were gone. We haven't had time to finish straightening up."

"Is there anything I can do?"

"No, thanks. The constable should be here soon."

Rawlins stood awkwardly in the doorway before saying, "Did you have a good trip?"

He's fishing for details, Shiloh thought. "Yes," she replied, "very good."

"I'm pleased," he said, but sounded disappointed that she had not volunteered more information. "Well, I guess I'd better be going. Please forgive me for just dropping by."

She blurted, "I'm getting ready to sail for home."

"What?" He shook his head. "You can't *do* that."

Shiloh stiffened at the tone of command. "Mr. Rawlins, I don't believe you meant to say that."

"I'm sorry! Look, you just can't go off without letting us have an opportunity to get better acquainted. I had thought that in due time you might like to accompany me to a social function. I would be honored to introduce you to some of San Francisco's most influential citizens."

"That's very thoughtful of you."

He stood uncertainly for a moment, his eyes darting to Mara and then back to Shiloh. "Under the circumstances," he began, "I'm going to risk asking you now. There's a concert this Friday night. Would you do me the honor of accompanying me?"

Before Shiloh could answer, a rig stopped outside. John Sledger cried joyfully. "Shiloh! Welcome back!"

"The preacher's come to call," Rawlins said, waving to the new arrival. "I'll leave you to talk, but I would really enjoy your company Friday night. So say yes, won't you?"

CHAPTER XIX

IN A SUDDEN defiant impulse Shiloh exclaimed, "Very well. I'll go."

"Wonderful! See you then!" Rawlins turned away and shook hands with the big preacher. They talked for a moment while Shiloh stood in the doorway, chiding herself for having accepted the concert invitation.

The men parted, Rawlins going to his rig and Sledger entering the parlor at Shiloh's invitation. She explained about the break-in while he seated himself.

"Glad you're back," he said. "How was the trip?"

"Successful," she replied, and explained.

When she had finished, Sledger said, "That means you now have enough money to sail away and leave us. Well, if that's the

Lord's will for you, I'm glad. Personally, I wish you'd stay. San Francisco needs you."

"I'm sorry, Brother Sledger, but I've prayed about it, and He has provided the means, so I'm going."

"Then you'll be interested to know that two recently widowed ladies in our congregation are returning on the first available ship, so . . . "

"We can go together! Oh, Brother Sledger, I've needed a traveling companion! Now, I'll have two!"

"Will you be at church?" When she nodded, he said, "I'll introduce you to them there."

As Shiloh closed the door behind him, Mara entered the room. "You're learning to make decisions. That's good, but be careful that they're the right ones."

"You think I'm wrong about going home?"

"I'm not saying that. I was just thinking about you going courting with that soldier."

"I didn't plan to accept," Shiloh explained. "I just panicked when the preacher showed up unexpectedly. And it's certainly not courting."

"You don't have to defend yourself. As I told you before, he's got a reputation of getting what he wants."

"Well, he's not going to get me! I'll soon be ready to leave for home. I had not planned on being seen in public with any man."

"You won't be invisible at that concert."

"That's what worries me. There will be talk, and I don't want that." Shiloh took a couple of quick, agitated turns across the floor. "I returned from this trip feeling more confident than I ever had in my life. But that second break-in unnerved me, and now this."

"What difference does it make? You're leaving."

Shiloh stopped and faced Mara. "You're right. I should at least have a look at San Francisco's cultural side before then."

Shiloh planned to ask Clay if he would check on sailing

schedules so she wouldn't have to risk passing through the rough crowd of men on the waterfront. She was waiting for him when he came by to feed Ulysses the next morning.

He listened to her request with an expressionless face. "All right, if that's what you want," he said.

"It is." Her voice held more conviction than she felt, but she thought it was the right thing to do.

"I have a couple bits of news," he said, turning away to start pitching hay. "I saw the constable having breakfast at the hotel. Kroeber has returned to Germany."

"That's a relief." Now she would never have to meet the man her husband had faced in a duel.

"Second bit of news from Logan," Clay continued, "is that the man who's been watching you has been arrested and jailed on the prison ship out there in the harbor."

"Thank God!" She could sleep peacefully again.

"His name is Otis Tynan, and he had a big knife on him. Logan thinks it might have been used to . . . to take Aldar's life, but Tynan denies it. He'd risk hanging if he's guilty."

It was the first indication that anything had been accomplished toward finding Aldar's killer. "I hope the constable can prove it," Shiloh said. "I'd feel a lot better knowing that justice is finally done. But if he did it, why not just rob Aldar instead of killing him?"

"Logan and I discussed the possibility that perhaps it was a planned murder made to look like robbery."

"That's what Mr. Rawlins said. He thinks politics might have been involved."

Clay frowned so briefly that Shiloh wasn't quite sure she had noticed it.

Clay said, "Tynan is a Barbary Coast character who obviously has no interest in politics. If he did kill Aldar, then somebody must have paid him. That would have to be a person with a strong motive."

MacAdams has that kind of motive, Shiloh thought.

Clay continued, "Although Tynan denies killing Aldar, he did admit breaking into the house two times."

"But he didn't take anything, so why break-in?"

"Tynan won't say, although Logan said Tynan got very angry when he talked about men hanging around you."

Shiloh sensed something unsaid in Clay's tone. "Why should he be concerned about that?"

"My guess is that Tynan can't stand the thought of any other man being near you."

Shiloh remembered the knife attack on MacAdams when he tried to kiss her. "But I don't even know this Tynan. Why should he feel that way?"

"That facial birthmark has made him a loner. He's a strange man. No one seems to know much about him. But Logan said Tynan did leave the flowers on your doorstep."

"Oh, so he's the one?"

"Yes. There's more. Tynan told Logan that the day we left on our trip he had seen you with Rawlins and then me, and planned to do something about it."

The meaning horrified Shiloh. "Oh, my! It's a good thing we left when we did."

"Looks that way. Logan said Tynan admitted attacking MacAdams." Clay's eyes had a hurt expression. "I didn't know you had gone riding at night with him."

"It wasn't like that! Let me explain— "

"No explanation necessary," Clay interrupted, turning to drive the pitchfork into the hay.

"Oh, please! I wouldn't go out with any man so soon— "

"Wouldn't you?" Clay interrupted, his tone sharp. "At breakfast, some young lieutenant was telling everybody in there that you were going to the concert this Friday night with Rawlins."

"It's not what you think, Clay!"

"It's what everyone will think."

She snapped, "You mean that you don't believe me?"

"Up to now, I've always felt that what you did was none of my business. But I can't stay out of it any more."

Shiloh drew back at the controlled anger in his voice.

"Aldar was my friend," Clay said in a clipped tone. "He's not here to care for you, but I am. I don't want you to go to the concert with Rawlins."

"Are you forbidding me?" she demanded, voice rising.

"Call it what you want."

The pent-up tensions of the past several weeks unexpectedly erupted. "Look here, Mr. Patton," she flared, "I'm a grown woman, and I'm going to leave here soon, so nobody is going to tell me what to do!"

He raised his voice. "Is that your final answer?"

"Yes!"

He opened his mouth so wide she thought he was going to shout at her, but he hesitated, then wordlessly stalked to his wagon. He slapped the lines sharply across the mules' backs and rode away yelling at them. She had never heard him do that before.

She stormed into the kitchen where Mara was preparing breakfast. Blurting out what had happened, Shiloh complained, "From the minute we met, we didn't get along! I thought that had changed on the trip, but I was wrong."

"Sit down and I'll pour you a cup of coffee."

"I don't want to sit down!" Shiloh reached up to the pots and pans hanging from wooden pegs and knocked them clattering onto the stove and then the floor. "But do you know what I do want? I'll tell you! I want to be my own woman for a change."

"Feel better?" Mara asked, looking at the fallen cooking utensils.

"Sorry." Shiloh started picking them up and replacing them on their pegs. "All my life, I tried in every way I know to be good, and do what others wanted. I did what Papa and Mama wanted, then Aldar. But what did it get me? Absolutely nothing! Instead, I've lost everything."

"Not quite everything. You think about that."

"You know what I'm going to do, Mara? I'm going to start going out with other men, not just Rawlins! After all, I don't know what kind of life is waiting for me in Pennsylvania, but I suspect it won't be very exciting. So while I'm still here, I'm going to do what I want!"

"That's something I would do, but not you."

"No matter what I do," Shiloh continued, "nobody will approve. It's like Papa and Mama and Seth Collins. They didn't approve of Aldar, but he was the best thing that ever happened to me. And now when Rawlins invites me to a concert, Clay gets on his high horse. Oh, he makes me so mad!"

Friday night, Shiloh and Rawlins arrived just before the concert was to begin. She wore the French blue watered silk gown Mara made for her from a real Paris pattern. Its portrait neckline revealed her creamy shoulders, framing them with several layers of delicate lace. The pale gown created the perfect foil for Shiloh's prize possession—her radiant red-gold hair. She wore it piled high and spilling down the nape of her slender neck, which was encircled with a delicate gold necklace given to her by Aldar. She briefly touched her fingers to the cold metal, remembering. Then she walked down the aisle, pushing away the shard of pain that threatened to overtake her lovely evening. She found, to her surprise, that she actually *enjoyed* the fact that every man in the place was staring.

She tilted her chin higher, aware that she looked her best, and that the handsome commandant in full-dress uniform was proud to guide her by the elbow.

They had barely been seated when Gladwin and Locke left their seats and came to greet them. Shiloh did not remember what they said, but she smiled and tried to look interested. Other men who knew Rawlins hurried over to speak to him, but their eyes were on her. That continued until the conductor took the podium.

As the last sounds of the instrumental practices faded, Rawlins leaned over and whispered. "How does it feel to be the most beautiful woman in San Francisco?"

Wonderful! Shiloh wanted to reply, but she merely smiled and turned to face the orchestra. Yet she was aware that eyes from all over the auditorium were on her and not the musicians.

Rawlins' breath was warm on her ear. "Some of the most powerful men in San Francisco are here tonight. They're going to help run this country someday, but right now, they'd give anything to be sitting here with you."

Shiloh started to correct him: *state, not country,* but the music started before she could speak. She tried to listen, but instead reveled in the strange new sense of her own power as a young, beautiful widow in a land that still virtually belonged to men.

At the intermission, other men came, all ostensibly to speak to Rawlins, whom they knew, but really to be introduced to Shiloh.

Returning to their seats, Shiloh felt a continuing rush of excitement previously unknown. She tried to listen to the music and the singers, but her thoughts soared. *I never knew it could be like this,* she told herself. *I love it!*

On the way out after the concert, as others surrounded her and Rawlins, she noticed two good-looking young men whispering together. One came over, spoke to Rawlins, then drew him aside. The other man pushed through the admirers and flashed a great smile.

"While my friend distracts your escort, allow me to introduce myself," he said, taking her elbow. Ignoring the other men, he guided her a couple of steps away. "I'm Lemuel

Damron, lately of Boston. Forgive my forwardness, but I would like the honor of calling upon you."

"Hold on, Damron!" a dark-haired man interrupted. "Observe the proprieties, please!"

Damron bristled, but Shiloh smiled at both men. "Gentlemen, I must return to my escort." She gave them all a coy smile and rejoined Rawlins.

On the ride home, Rawlins chuckled. "I thought if you got a taste of what life can be like in the upper circles, you would like it."

"It was wonderful. Thank you for taking me, Mr. Rawlins."

"I'd still prefer that you call me Will."

"Very well, Will. You may call me Shiloh."

"It's a beautiful name, and so are you."

"Thank you."

"I want to see more of you, Shiloh. Much more. How about tomorrow night?"

She hadn't expected anything so soon. She fumbled for an excuse. "I would love to, Will, but I must start packing. When you saw Brother Sledger the other night, he had come to tell me that two widows in the congregation are sailing for the east coast on the next available ship. I'm going with them."

"No! You can't!" He reined in the horse and turned to look at her in the semidarkness.

Shiloh was instantly annoyed. "Please don't use that tone with me."

"I'm sorry, but you surprised me. I just can't imagine this place without you."

"I have nothing to keep me here, Will," she explained in a gentler voice. "Now I have the means to return east, and I am going back to what I left."

"Please reconsider! If you stay, I'll make you the most famous woman in the west, with more money than you ever dreamed about. I'll show you glorious sights that you would never imagine. I'll—"

She interrupted. "What are you saying?"

He hesitated, then leaned close and slid his arm around her shoulder. "I knew the moment I saw you that you would be perfect for me. At the time, of course, that didn't seem possible, but now it is."

"Please, Will! It's only been a few weeks—"

He broke in. "I know what I want, and I want *you.* But it is not a selfish desire, for I will give you greater honor and more riches than you ever dreamed." He leaned forward quickly and sought her lips. "I want you so much . . . so very, very much."

She turned her face aside so his lips brushed her cheek. She drew back, yet found herself intrigued by this handsome man who offered so much. "I think you'd better take me home," she said.

"Very well, but let's not end this evening with tension between us. Please?"

She was aware that in this brief exchange, she had influenced a strong man with her own newly discovered form of power. "Well," she said, softening her tone to let him know she agreed.

"Let me make it up to you, Shiloh. Even if you're packing, you have to eat tomorrow night. Why not have dinner with me? I'll bring you home early if you want."

She thought, *Why not? People are going to talk anyway!* Still, she hesitated, "Will you wait until tomorrow noon for my answer? If you'll send someone over for a message, I'll give him my decision."

"I would rather have you say yes now, but if that's the way you want it, I'll do that."

"Fine. One thing more: If I accept, after dinner, you'll bring me straight home. Agreed?"

"Word of honor," he said, smiling triumphantly.

Shiloh was glad Mara was still up so they could talk. "He

was a gentleman, even though what he said made me think he didn't want to be. Even so, I don't really want to even have dinner with him, yet I'm curious. What do you suppose he meant about riches and honor? Military officers don't make much, do they?"

"High ranking officials do, I suppose."

"I'll just have dinner with him tomorrow night, and then no more. I don't want to encourage him."

"I don't think that soldier is easily discouraged."

"I suppose. Anyway, I liked being wanted. And I found it exciting for all those men to flock around me. Oh, sure, the boys back home hung around me as they did all the girls, but these are men who are bright and good-looking and are going to be important to the future of California, not just farmers raising stock and crops."

"You are in a different world now, Shiloh. This place is something unique, and you are a far rarer commodity than the gold which brought them there."

"You make me sound like something to be bought, like an animal or a sack of flour," Shiloh said reprovingly.

"Your presence tonight told those men that you are available. They're only responding to your signal."

"I'm not available! I loved my husband, and he's only been dead a few weeks! How can you say such thing?"

"Because I have always been honest with you."

"And I've been honest with you. Why shouldn't I go out with Rawlins or some of those other men? I've got the money to sail home, but I don't know when a ship will be available. I miss Aldar; I miss him terribly. But I'm alive and he's dead, so while I'm waiting, why shouldn't I do something besides sit here hurting and alone?"

"I didn't tell you what to do, Shiloh. You made the choices. I simply pointed out what you can expect from what you did tonight. It seems to me I've had a few lectures from you about sowing and reaping."

Shiloh went to bed feeling confused. She awoke in the morning to Ulysses' braying. She thought of Clay, and rankled at the memory of his actions. Still, she decided to dress quickly and go speak to him.

She pulled back a corner of the curtains to peek out. Clay wasn't there. The mule was contentedly munching hay. Clay had come and gone quietly, avoiding her.

I guess he's really angry this time, she thought, and started to get dressed. She had just finished touching up her hair when there was a knock at the door.

She opened it to see the brash young man from last night's concert smiling at her. "Remember me? Lemuel Damron? Forgive me for showing up so early."

"I remember." She stood in the doorway, deliberately not encouraging him. "From Boston, I believe."

"Right! You didn't have an opportunity to reply to my invitation last night. But I've made dinner reservations—"

"Mr. Damron!" Her tone was sharp. "You are assuming a great deal."

His smiled flickered uncertainly off and on. "I just thought that since you were starting to . . . "

"Good day, Mr. Damron!" She stepped inside and slammed the door. She stood there shaking with indignation and humiliation. *I'm not ready!* she silently cried. *I will never be ready! Oh, why can't they see that I just don't want to sit home crying?*

San Francisco's weather had turned cold and foggy, as always in late spring and summer, totally unlike the hot inland valleys. That night, Shiloh dressed warmly and Rawlins put a lap robe over her knees before turning his horse and rig toward the bay.

They drove through the fog that made its nightly assault on the peninsula. The mists were not dense like she had heard about in London, but still she was glad that Otis Tynan was a prisoner and not able to attack Rawlins as he had MacAdams. It would be frightening to have him stalking her in such weather. She remembered that Logan suspected Tynan had planned to kill Rawlins and Clay.

"Will," she said as the horse's hooves crunched along the sandy streets, "what do you know about the ship where they keep prisoners?"

"Not much, except that San Francisco doesn't really have a jail, so they take prisoners out to one of those abandoned ships in the bay. There are no bars or things like that, but the ship works well enough."

"Could someone escape?"

"Not unless he had a boat. The currents are too treacherous to try swimming. Why do you want to know?"

She explained about Tynan and his reported threats.

"I wouldn't worry about him," Rawlins commented, turning onto Montgomery Street. His tone changed, "Did I tell you they're talking about filling part of the bay so that someday Monterey Street will be inland?"

Shiloh wasn't going to be sidetracked. "You once said that you thought Aldar was killed for political purposes. I've thought a lot about that, and I can't think of who would benefit politically by Aldar's death."

"Have you considered MacAdams? Your husband got that mail franchise through a politician, Senator Lorenzo."

Shiloh protested, "But that was to benefit MacAdams and Laird Express Company."

"That's certainly not what your husband got, is it?"

Shiloh took a slow breath. *No,* she admitted to herself, *he certainly did not.* Aloud, she asked, "Are you suggesting that MacAdams wanted Aldar dead?"

"I'm not suggesting anything, my dear."

The sounds of loud music and a cacophony of noisy, strident voices sifted through the fog ahead. Shiloh asked, "What's that?"

Rawlins turned the horse into a side street before answering. "Sydney Town. Some people are starting to call it the Barbary

Coast. British prisoners chose to be exiled here rather than Australia. They have a bunch of rat warrens and cribs at the corner of Pacific Avenue and Montgomery Street. We'll go around."

"Cribs?" Shiloh asked innocently.

Rawlins didn't answer, but she sensed his chagrin. Shiloh had never heard about the tiny places where prostitutes from many countries worked, but she knew that San Francisco had many women who practiced the ancient trade. "Oh," she said, suddenly understanding.

Rawlins covered her embarrassment quickly by saying, "The crimps have their saloons in Sydney Town, too. They get paid by ships' masters to drug their men customers' drinks, or club a man on the street. At night, they're rowed out to the ship and end up in China or someplace."

"Shanghaied," Shiloh said, remembering Joseph.

"Let's talk about something more pleasant," Rawlins suggested. "I hope you enjoy the restaurant."

She did. It was a delight to walk through a newly erected fine hotel made of wood instead of canvas, and admire the beautifully carved furniture and real gilt mirrors that had come around the Horn. The fog was illuminated by many candles set in brass reflectors that shone out over the water.

She was intrigued by the waiters' deferential treatment of her escort and herself. The fresh fish was excellent, although she declined the wine which Rawlins drank in moderation. Shiloh wore a high-necked dress of emerald green damask. Its small, turn-down collar was accented with a painted brooch Mara had once given her. The dress was simple but elegant in its understatement. She wore her hair twisted into a demure chignon at the back of her neck. She was most conscious of the customers, some of whom stared so boldly that it made her uncomfortable. Yet, before the meal was over, she had begun to rather enjoy the silent attention.

Back at the house, Rawlins reined in the horse and turned

to her. "You are the most beautiful, desirable woman I have ever met," he said, his voice husky.

She wondered if he had said that to his wife before their divorce. "Thank you. I've had a lovely evening."

"Let's have another one tomorrow night."

Shiloh said firmly, "Thank you again, but there is so much to do before I can leave for the east."

"Then I'll see you at church," he said, getting out and coming to help her down.

He saw her to the door, thanked her for coming, and walked back into the fog.

The next morning, he was true to his word, waiting outside the saloon tent which had been cleared of customers for the morning services. He pushed his way through the men waiting to enter. Shiloh was happy to see four women. She started toward them, but Rawlins intercepted her with a welcoming smile.

"If there were seats," he said, possessively taking her elbow, "I would find some for us. But I'll help you through this crowd and make sure you have as comfortable a place to stand as possible."

She stepped away from his hand, not wanting to appear to be with him in church, of all places. There was already enough loose talk, and there would probably be more from the men who had seen her at dinner last night.

"Thank you," she said, her voice cool with control. "I have to meet with Brother Sledger." She turned around and hurried toward the preacher. He greeted people at the tent entrance.

She eased her way through the crowd. "Excuse me, please. Excuse—" She broke off when a tall, clean-shaven man with dark hair just ahead of her turned and looked down at her.

She stared, then blurted. "Clay? I hardly recognized you without your beard."

"You've changed more than me," he replied tersely. He turned his back on her abruptly and strode into the tent.

Shiloh stood in humiliated shock, aware that the preacher and all the men near her had seen and heard the brief exchange. Sledger started toward her, but Shiloh whirled around and rushed out of the tent, away from everyone.

CHAPTER XX

SHILOH HEARD both the preacher and Rawlins call her name, but she fled without turning around. Clay's harsh words burned into her mind, driving her into the chill San Francisco night. Finally, Rawlins caught up with her.

"What's the matter?" he asked, taking her arm.

She drew back. "Please leave me alone!"

He didn't reply, but stood where he was while Shiloh started angrily stalking off toward home. She stopped after a short distance. *I've got to meet those women,* she reminded herself. *I've got to wait.*

A glance toward the saloon tent now serving as a church showed that several people were staring at her. The preacher and a couple of other men spoke to Rawlins, but he simply shrugged and disappeared into the tent.

Shiloh kept walking away until she passed a nearby brick building which housed a men's clothing store. This blocked anyone's view of her, so she stopped, trying to fight back hot tears.

Clay is so wrong! she silently stormed. *And it's no concern of his anyway. What I do is nobody's business. They're all a bunch of hypocrites! No matter what I do, they're going to talk, or act like that Boston man did yesterday!*

She kept mentally reviewing Clay's stinging accusations, and at the same time curiously marveling at how different he looked. He had a clean, strong chin. *Why, Clay is handsome!* she realized.

She sternly rebuked herself. *Why should I even notice? I don't care if he's clean shaven or lets his beard grow until he trips on it.*

The opening lyrics to a hymn indicated the service had started. She checked to make sure that nobody was still outside. Then she sought a place where she could listen.

A worshipper had tied his horse in the shade of the men's store, so she climbed into the carriage, leaned back in the seat, and tried to reach a worshipful mood.

The preacher's powerful voice came clearly to her through the tent's canvas sides. "The Lord be praised that we have an even dozen women and seven children with their husbands and fathers among us today. Most of them arrived overland or by ship since the last Lord's day, and more are coming."

He told about the new wooden sanctuary the men were helping build, and announced that services would be held there in a month or so.

Shiloh thought, *I won't be here to see it.*

Sledger introduced his sermon with the observation, "It's been said today, San Francisco is the wickedest city in the world. You've seen that yourselves, for wickedness is all around you. Men who never tasted spirits in their lives now spend all their time in saloons."

The preacher's voice began to build in power and tempo. "Men who never even thought about a game of chance are gamblin' away all they got. They're swept up in sin, and it abounds on every side. They're lonely and confused, and huntin' for a way out of their troubles. They have changed. They ignore the still small voice of God they knew when they left home."

Shiloh squirmed uneasily on the carriage seat while Clay's words echoed in her mind. "You've changed."

Sledger continued, "Let's compare our present state with the story about Ahab and Jezebel, and that great prophet, Elijah. You'll remember that Elijah, through God, had just done two great miracles. Elijah should have felt wonderful. But when Jezebel threatened his life, he ran like a scared rabbit. He even prayed for God to take his life, saying everybody else had forsaken God and His covenants, and only Elijah was left. I suspect that's how some of you feel here today.

"If you brought your Bibles, turn with me to the book of First Kings, the nineteenth chapter, in the eleventh and twelfth verses."

Shiloh tried to remember the reference, but it eluded her until Sledger began to read. 'The LORD passed by, and a great and strong wind rent the mountains, and brake in pieces the rocks before the LORD; but the LORD was not in the wind: and after the wind an earthquake; but the LORD was not in the earthquake: and after the earthquake a fire; but the LORD was not in the fire. So how did Elijah finally know where the LORD was? Verse twelve . . . "

Shiloh remembered and said the words aloud with the preacher. "'And after the fire a still small voice.'"

The words echoed in Shiloh's mind: *a still small voice.*

After the service ended and the people filed out of the tent, Shiloh left the carriage and walked around in back of the tent until the crowd drifted away. She wanted to speak to her potential traveling companions before they left and became alarmed when two women started to leave. Shiloh hurriedly made her way around the back side of the tent to where she expected to find the preacher. He was talking to Gladwin and two women.

"Oh, there you are, Shiloh!" Sledger exclaimed, moving to meet her. "I called to you when you were about to enter the church awhile ago, but I guess you didn't hear me. Are you all right?"

"I just needed to be alone for a while," she replied.

Gladwin said, "When I saw you leave, I thought maybe one of those young bachelors had spirited you away."

"Nothing like that," Shiloh assured him, shifting her gaze to the women. They were only slightly older than she, with the same style hair parted in the middle and pulled straight back over their ears.

Sledger presented them. "Mrs. Hanks, Mrs. Bradshaw, this is Shiloh Laird, the young woman I told you about. I thought you three might like to travel east together."

"What?" Gladwin exclaimed. "Shiloh, you're not leaving us, are you?"

"I plan to leave on the first available ship if these ladies and I can work out traveling arrangements."

"But you can't!" Gladwin protested before the other women could even acknowledge the preacher's introduction.

"That's what I tried to tell her," Sledger said.

Gladwin studied her with serious eyes. "I hope you'll change your mind, but if you won't, then I would appreciate a few moments of your time. I think you would find it to your advantage to consider my request."

Shiloh's curiosity started to rise. "I could come by your office tomorrow," she said.

"I'll be in all day." Gladwin excused himself and left.

Shiloh turned her attention to the older widows and began discussing their common desire to get back home. The three women quickly agreed they would like to travel east together, but it was too difficult for them to take the Panama crossing. They decided to book passage on the first available ship sailing around the Horn.

After the women left, the preacher asked, "Is there something you want to talk to me about?"

Shiloh hesitated. At home, she could talk comfortably with old Brother Wilmot who had farmed during the week and pastored part-time for more than half a century. But Sledger was much younger, and Shiloh wasn't sure she could tell him all her concerns.

He seemed to understand her reticence. "Shiloh," he said, "I can imagine some of the struggles you're going through. I saw what happened this morning with both those men, and from the way you left, I knew you were upset."

"I was hurt and angry at the same time," she admitted.

"I preached your husband's funeral services less than two months ago, so I know how lonely and confused and scared you must be. But for your own sake, I'm sure you know how important it is to not do anything that will cause talk—and people *will* talk."

"Oh, I know that!" she exclaimed bitterly.

"I'm sure you do. These are not normal times, and San Francisco is not a normal city. But God never changes. What He said to Elijah thousands of years ago is what He tells you today. When you feel like running, as Elijah did —"

"Running?" she interrupted. "Do you think I'm running?"

"I'm just sayin' that you should do as Elijah did—stop and listen to that small voice. Then you'll be guided in what to do."

She thought about that on the way home, but when she got there, Rawlins was waiting.

"Forgive me," he began, "but I was so concerned about your abrupt departure from church this morning that I had to come by and make sure that you're all right."

"I'm fine," she assured him.

"Are you up to a ride along the coast and lunch?"

Shiloh recalled the preacher's words of caution, then Clay's harsh remark in church. *He says I'm changing. It's not true, but he wouldn't believe me anyway.* She smiled at Rawlins. "That sounds lovely."

The next morning she saddled Ulysses, aware that he always had food and water, proving that Clay kept his commitment. However, he always came when she was asleep or away, so he became an invisible phantom, avoiding her.

At Gladwin's hotel, he greeted her pleasantly and suggested they take a walk because conversations could be overheard in his tiny canvas-walled office.

They walked down the street which had some planks and barrel staves laid over the loose sand. She felt increasingly rebellious at Clay's recent remarks, and rather immune to the comments she was sure were being made about her around town.

"I'm genuinely sorry that you're leaving us," Gladwin began. "I thought your husband was a very remarkable man, and I'm of the opinion that you are cut from the same cloth."

"Thank you."

"You two would have made a great combination. Pacifica will come into being, but it will be the loser because Aldar and you will not be there."

"How about your anxious candidate? Does he still want the position?"

"Of course, but his ego is so big he's convinced he will still become emperor. He might, if it weren't for me. But I have moved to block him."

"Oh?"

Gladwin nodded but shifted the conversation slightly. "I don't think you realize what an important time this is in California's history."

"I know that delegates are being elected in a couple of weeks for the Monterey Convention, and that the talk seems to be more in favor of statehood than a separate nation."

"The struggle is not over, Shiloh. Even if there is a predominance of statehood advocates, whether slave-holding or not, the separate nation movement will not die. If the United States continues to drift toward civil war, the possibility of California becoming the Pacifica Empire will have another chance of success."

"And if it doesn't?"

Gladwin shook his head. "Then my idea may become only a small footnote to history that most people in years to come will not even remember. But this idea will not die, even if California becomes a state for a while."

There was something almost ominous in his words that Gladwin refused to clarify. Shiloh kept thinking about that all week. She was disappointed to learn that no ships would be available for several days, so she accepted invitations from three men who called on her, as well as Rawlins. Everywhere she went, she was the center of attention. She found herself enjoying the experiences and tried to ignore what wagging tongues were undoubtedly whispering behind her back.

One night she accompanied Rawlins to a forum where San Francisco's prospective candidates were to discuss how they proposed to vote on the issue of statehood if they were elected and sent to Monterey.

She had almost declined because she had not felt well lately, but she decided to go because her father's strong abolitionist stand had deeply influenced her thinking. She couldn't vote, but she could listen to how the men might vote.

As usual, upon her entering the hall, conversations ceased and all eyes turned to her.

"Please," she said when Rawlins had introduced those closest to them, "go on with your conversations."

"You wouldn't enjoy it," a short, stout man replied. "We were talking about a number of us working together to raise capital for a stageline. Hardly woman talk."

"On the contrary," she replied. "My husband's dream was to build a transportation system that would link all of California, and eventually the nation."

Most of the men had known Aldar and referred to conversations they had with him on the subject, and how great a loss his death had been.

When the men filed in to take their seats, Shiloh's thoughts returned to Aldar's dream. Now, if he had lived, these men were ready to financially back such a venture. However, Shiloh knew that MacAdams would never have risked moving away from the profitable and expanding express line.

As the speakers took their places at a table in front, Shiloh's eyes roamed over the audience and stopped abruptly on Clay. At the same moment, his eyes met hers.

She still wasn't used to his new appearance, but his clean-shaven face seemed to emphasize his eyes. They were more penetrating now, she thought, breaking eye contact. She faced the front as the program started.

In their first statements every candidate made it clear that he favored a free state where slavery was prohibited. The highly partisan crowd, obviously mostly from northern states, applauded vigorously and often.

Rawlins did not participate in the demonstrations. She leaned over and whispered, "Don't you agree with them?"

"A man in my position has no public politics, but carries out the policy of others," he assured her. "I only came to listen and learn."

Shiloh nodded and returned to listening, although occasionally glancing at Clay. Once again their eyes met, but he looked quickly away.

About halfway through the debate, Shiloh began to feel unwell. Yielding to a sudden urge, she hurriedly excused herself and left, aware that many eyes followed her as she moved rapidly toward the back. She exited the building and went around in back, aided by flaming torches placed in barrels.

Feeling better, she returned to the front of the building. As she stepped inside, she was aware of a man standing over to one side. He moved toward her, and she thought Rawlins had come to see if she was all right.

But it was Clay who stepped out of the shadows and into the light of the candles placed in polished wall reflectors.

"I need to talk to you," he said, his face stern.

"I've got to get back to—" she protested, but Clay interrupted.

His voice was hard. "We must talk *now.*"

"If you insist," she replied stiffly, "but please be brief."

"I've been thinking a lot about whether to say anything to you or not," he began. "Sometimes I think I should just keep my mouth shut and pretend it's none of my business. Other times, I think of how Aldar was my friend, and the woman he married needs help."

"So you've decided that I need help?"

"Something like that."

"And you're doing this for Aldar?" Her voice had a hint of doubt.

He hesitated for several seconds before answering, and for the first time, his clean-shaven appearance gave her an opportunity to see the emotion in his face.

"That's not the issue," he finally replied. "The important thing is that you've changed from the honest, unsophisticated woman I first met to a totally different person."

"Is that so?" *Who does he think he is, judging me?*

"It is. You're becoming more and more like the men in this town who are seeking position, power, and money, but in your case, it's plain to me that you're using your womanly charms to get what you suddenly seem to want."

Her voice rose angrily. "It's none of your business what I do or with whom. But the truth is you're jealous because I've been meeting important people and I've achieved a social status that you haven't attained."

This remark obviously infuriated Clay. His face turned dark and his voice quivered with controlled emotions. "Not very long ago, that would have been of little importance to you. Now I have far more significant matters that concern me. While you've been seen with that Rawlins and other men all over town, I've been quietly developing capital to form a transportation company that will have a tremendous impact on California's future."

"You're capitalizing on Aldar's idea!" she snapped.

"That's not true!" He turned abruptly away, then swung back, his voice harsh. "Obviously, Aldar never told you that he planned to sell out his share of the business to MacAdams, who always hated Aldar and frustrated his plans to expand."

"Aldar was going to sell out?" The surprise showed in her tone.

"We were going to form a new partnership. He'd run the business end; I'd handle the field work."

"MacAdams wouldn't have let him do that."

"He would have been glad to get rid of Aldar because we weren't going to compete in the express business. We would start with stagecoaches and build from there."

Clay sounded sincere, but Shiloh still found it hard to believe. She recalled Mara saying Aldar kept secrets.

She asked, "Why didn't you tell me this before?"

"Two reasons. First, I could tell that Aldar hadn't yet told you, and after he was dead, there was no point in saying anything."

Shiloh was convinced that Clay was telling the truth.

He continued, his tone cold and hard. "On your selling trip I saw you developing into a strong, confident young woman. I was proud of what you accomplished. But you've wielded that confidence in a manner I wouldn't have expected of you. Well, now you know, and I hope you have a safe voyage home."

He paused, then added softly, "Goodbye, Shiloh."

She stood staring after him as he walked out the door and into the night. There had been such a finality about his goodbye that it drove a chill through her. She wasn't even aware Rawlins had approached her until he spoke.

"Where have you been?" he asked, studying her face. "What's the matter?"

"I . . . uh . . . I'm all right. I'm sorry to have had to leave like that, but I didn't feel well."

"You all right now?"

"Yes, I'm fine. We can go back in now."

Rawlins studied her carefully. "I think perhaps we should get you home." He took her arm and led her toward the door.

They said little on the carriage ride. At her door, Rawlins

said, "Thank you for coming. I'll check up on you tomorrow to make sure you're feeling better."

Mara was waiting up for her.

"What happened?" Mara asked, getting up from where she had been sitting.

"What do you mean?" Shiloh answered crossly. "Do I look as if something happened?"

"Did you quarrel with the soldier or Clay?"

"Why do you even mention Clay?" Shiloh retorted, removing her cloak.

"Just a feeling, that's all."

"I don't want to talk about it."

"That's a switch," Mara replied with a smile. "Well, then, I've got some news for you."

Shiloh hung up her cloak and waited expectantly.

"I'm opening my boarding house."

Shiloh tried to sound happy. "I'm glad for you. I know you'll be very successful."

Mara got up and crossed to the table where two tall candles burned. "Guess what I found?" she asked, picking up some papers.

Shiloh was in no mood for guessing. "What?" she asked without interest.

"Read these." She handed the papers to Shiloh.

Puzzled, she approached the candles and by their weak, flickering light, glanced at the top page.

"These look like the papers you found when we were looking for Aldar's will."

"They're the same ones. You didn't feel like reading them at the time, and asked me to put them away. When I was packing I remembered I'd hidden them at the bottom of the hole where I keep my gold."

Shiloh skimmed the words, then looked up in surprise.

"This is just the contract between Aldar and MacAdams. If I read it right—"

"You're reading it right. That's a legal document, duly signed and witnessed. It also shows that you are entitled to half the business."

Shiloh's mind whirled. She sat down on the couch, clutching the papers. "You sure, Mara?"

"I've read them very carefully. It says that the two signers, both bachelors, agree that if either marries and then dies, the surviving partner has to pay the other partner's widow half of the current value of the business."

Shiloh had not yet grasped the full significance of the documents. "I think I see. A woman can't own a business, but as a businessman's widow, she can receive half of the estate's value as her own?"

"You've got it. But if MacAdams can't pay you, then he'll have to sell half of the business to pay you off under terms of the agreement."

Shiloh leaped up and embraced her friend. "Oh, I can't believe this! It means that—" She broke off as the truth hit her.

"Yes," Mara said softly, "it means that when MacAdams asked you if you found a will, he was really wondering if you found these papers. It also means he had this place broken into in hopes of finding these."

"It could also give MacAdams a strong motive for my husband's murder," Shiloh said in a voice that showed the sudden weakness sweeping over her.

"Looks that way," Mara agreed.

"He's responsible for Aldar's death." Shiloh said the words slowly and thoughtfully, unable to believe it.

"First thing in the morning, we'll tell the constable. He'll know what to do."

Shiloh didn't sleep much that night. The significance of the contract kept spinning her thoughts off in different directions. She found it hard to believe that MacAdams could be so greedy, but now she knew why. Haddock had left Washington with word that Senator Lorenzo had helped get the mail franchise for Aldar. While he stayed and courted her, Haddock had brought the news about the mail franchise. MacAdams didn't know Aldar was married. With him dead, MacAdams stood to become sole owner of the thriving express business.

Suddenly, Shiloh sat up in bed, wondering. Would MacAdams have killed Aldar himself? She couldn't imagine it. But he could have hired somebody: *Tynan!*

What would happen now? Shiloh tried to think through the long sleepless night. In between her thoughts on this new turn of events, she remembered her quarrel with Clay and the terrible finality of his goodbye.

Shiloh didn't know how late it was when she finally fell asleep, but she woke nauseated. She barely had time to pull the chamber pot from under her bed before she began vomiting.

Mara came in, wet a cloth in the wash basin, and handed it to Shiloh.

She wiped her mouth and said wryly, "Must have been something I ate. I awoke feeling queasy yesterday morning, but today it was worse. I'm trying to remember what I've been eating."

Mara sat down on the edge of the bed. "It wasn't something you ate; it was something you did."

Shiloh thought back on yesterday's emotional encounters. "I guess so," she replied. "Nothing went right last night."

"It's more likely caused by something that happened weeks ago."

Shiloh frowned. "Several— oh!" She stood up suddenly, panic-stricken.

Mara nodded. "I'm pretty sure you're pregnant."

Groaning in anguish at this unexpected blow, Shiloh sank weakly onto the bed. She remembered the last wonderful moments with Aldar the night before his death. After some quick calculations, Shiloh realized that Mara was probably right.

Shiloh wanted to scream and run away from the latest complication in her life.

"I always dreamed of someday having a family. Aldar and I discussed that, of course, but I never imagined he wouldn't be here." She stood, agitatedly pacing the floor. "I've barely been able to support myself these past few weeks. How can I take care of a baby?"

"You don't have to have it," Mara said.

Shiloh didn't understand for a moment, then she shook her head. "No! I can't do that! I won't take the life of my unborn child."

"At this stage it's hardly a child."

"You're wrong, Mara! God gives life, and all life is sacred, even the unborn. It's a gift. I thought I had lost everything, but now I'll have a part of Aldar forever. I won't let anyone take that from me."

Mara replied, "Then think about this: Suppose the ship's master won't take a pregnant woman aboard?"

"Why shouldn't he? I'll pay my passage."

"You're going to be on that ship about three months, if you don't hit bad weather. If you're now about six weeks to a couple of months along, you'll be around your sixth month before you dock in New York."

"I'm sure I'm not the first pregnant woman to ever sail the world's oceans."

"True, but suppose there are complications at sea? There probably won't be a doctor on board. What if you lose the baby, or your own life?"

"Nothing like that will happen."

"You can't be sure of that. But let's say you do get back to Pennsylvania without incident. You knew how your folks felt about Aldar, yet you married him against their will. Do you think they'll welcome you or his child?"

Shiloh hadn't thought about that.

"How will you support yourself?" Mara continued in a

practical tone. "That farmer down the road wanted you when you were single, but will he want you now with another man's child?"

Shiloh weakly admitted, "I hadn't thought of that."

"Your only logical choice is to stay here and marry somebody right away. Marry either that soldier or Clay before they know your condition."

"Mara!" Shiloh was genuinely shocked.

"It's a reasonable and practical solution, Shiloh. So far as I know, Clay has no money. Now that we know about those papers, MacAdams may soon be out of business and Clay may not have a job. That leaves the soldier. He has position and a career. Sleep with him, then in six weeks or so, tell him that you're carrying his child."

Shiloh looked at Mara as if she were a stranger. "We have been best friends since we were little girls, but I can't believe what you're saying."

"You can't afford to fight with me, Shiloh. You may not like what I'm saying, but I'm still your best friend. You're not thinking clearly, but I am, so give some thought to what I said."

Someone knocked hard on the back door. Mara went to answer it while Shiloh sat in stunned silence, mulling over the terrible new complication of her pregnancy. She heard Mara open the door and Clay's anxious voice. "I just saw the constable. Tynan's escaped, and Logan thinks he'll come after Shiloh!"

CHAPTER XXI

"HOW COULD Tynan escape?" Shiloh called, hurriedly pulling a blanket across her shoulders. She started to leave the room, but a fresh wave of nausea hit her. She sat back down on the bed.

"Logan said the jailer told him that a small boat pulled up alongside the prison ship just about dusk last night. Tynan jumped overboard and the man in the boat picked him up. The jailer fired at them, but they both pulled on the oars and escaped as darkness fell."

"So he's been free since last night?"

"Yes," Clay called, "but I checked for signs, and he's not been around here. Not yet, anyway."

The words sent a cold chill over Shiloh as she tried to ignore her queasiness. "I'm not dressed, so I can't come out," she explained. "But how could Tynan have made arrangements for somebody to send a boat for him?"

"He couldn't, not while he was a prisoner on that ship. Logan said somebody on the shore had to have made those arrangements."

MacAdams! Shiloh thought.

Clay called, "Logan says Tynan may come looking for you, so he suggests you go someplace safe."

"Didn't Tynan also threaten you?"

"Yes, along with your friend Rawlins." Clay sounded a little sharp. "Do you have someplace where you can go until they recapture Tynan?"

Shiloh couldn't think of any, but she said nothing while more nausea threatened to overcome her.

"There's a ship in the harbor bound for New York in a couple of days." Clay's voice had lost the sharpness. "If you could book passage, maybe the master would let you come aboard early. You should be safe there."

"What about you?"

"I can take care of myself. But you'd better warn your friend Rawlins."

There was a silence, and Shiloh thought Clay had gone. Then he called, "Shiloh?"

"Yes?"

"If you'd like, I can see about getting you on board that ship."

"Thank you, but I'm going to travel with two ladies from the church. We've got to be sure we're on the same vessel."

"I'll go find the preacher and see if we can't work something out. That is, if it's all right with you."

"That would be wonderful."

He's being very kind after the terrible disagreement we had, she thought.

"I'll let you know," Clay called.

Shiloh heard the back door close. She realized that he hadn't said goodbye this time.

Mara came into the room with a smile. "What a nice change. You two didn't sound angry."

"It's not a time to be angry. But when I see him again, I'd better apologize for what I said earlier."

"Keep your choices open," Mara advised. "You're going to need them with that baby."

"I'm not doing it for that reason! Besides, I'm sailing for home as soon as possible, so forget your idea about marriage."

Mara shrugged. "What're you going to do about Tynan?"

"Get away from here as fast as I can, of course."

"The way I figure it, Tynan probably thinks he's in love with you, but you haven't been faithful to him."

"Faithful? I don't even know the man!"

"Probably makes no difference to the way he thinks. As I remember, Logan said Tynan didn't like other men hanging around you. That's why he's threatened Clay and the soldier. Fortunately, they can both take care of themselves. But the next time Tynan comes around here, he might do more than leave flowers on your doorstep."

Shiloh's heart leaped at the implied danger. She said, "We'd both be safer on that ship."

"Us? He's not after me."

"How do we know that? Tynan obviously doesn't think straight, so you might be in as much danger as I am."

"I don't see why. I'm not going anywhere. If he comes around me, he'll find out I carry a gun."

"Aldar carried a gun, but didn't get to use it."

Mara took a slow breath. "I see what you mean. All right, I'll go with you temporarily in hopes they catch Tynan quickly. In the meantime I'll get us packed in case Clay comes back with the captain's permission. But meanwhile, what about the soldier? He may not know that Tynan's escaped."

"Could you send Samuel to the Presidio with a message? I'd go, but I'm not feeling up to it."

Mara agreed to do that and soon left.

By the time Shiloh was dressed, her morning sickness had passed, but her mind was in a turmoil. She felt the need to visit Aldar's grave where she had often found peace and comfort. It was also where she did most of her grieving. She saddled Ulysses and rode through the cold, damp fog which blotted out the sun.

She stood by the wooden marker and gently brushed sand particles from the carved lettering. *Before I sail home,* she thought, *I'll give Brother Sledger some money to have a proper marble headstone made.*

She knelt by the mound and closed her eyes. *Lord,* she silently prayed, *I know that Aldar is with You. I don't know if what I'm about to ask is proper, but if it isn't, please forgive me. I would like Aldar to know I love him, and I'm carrying his child.*

Both our lives are in danger and I don't know what to do. I'm so tired of all the complications in my life. I want to run away, as Elijah did. Lord, I need to hear that still, small voice. I need to hear a word behind me saying 'this is the way.' There was a time when I just prayed but depended on others. Lately, I've tried to take responsibility for myself. I'm willing to do my part for my baby and me, but I can't do it alone. Help me to know what to do!

She waited expectantly, but nothing happened. There was no voice, no word, nothing except the sound of the wind whipping sand against the wooden marker.

Shiloh rose and glanced around nervously, aware that she had not kept a proper watch for Tynan. She mounted Ulysses and rode off in deep thought.

There were so many unanswered questions: How should she let MacAdams know that she had found the partnership papers, and that she wanted what was rightfully hers? She dared not go near him, fearing that if he was the one who had taken Aldar's life, she could be in danger. Telling Logan would be the best course, Shiloh decided. Let him handle it. But could she get her share before the ship sailed?

Glancing around to make sure she wasn't being followed, Shiloh asked herself more questions.

What about the house? Well, I guess Brother Sledger could help sell it and send me whatever equity Aldar had in it. Or should I forget sailing home and stay here? Even what I might receive from Aldar's share of the business, combined with what I have from sale of the pickax heads and the trip, won't last forever. I'd have to have some ongoing form of support.

Mara's marriage suggestions taunted her. *From what Rawlins said, I think he'd marry me. But Clay? No, we don't get along too well. Besides, he's never given any sign that he's interested in me. If I stay, I'd have to marry Rawlins. But is that what I really want?*

Somewhat fearful that Tynan might be watching the house, Shiloh approached cautiously. Then she saw Clay's rig parked outside, so she dug her heels into Ulysses's sides and hurried forward.

Clay's smile told her he had good news. "The master of the *Raven* said it's highly unusual, but he has a daughter your age back home, so you're welcome to come aboard tomorrow. You'll be safe until time to sail away."

"Tomorrow?" The thought of spending another night in the house frightened Shiloh.

"The ship is taking on cargo and isn't ready to have passengers. But don't concern yourself. You'll be safe tonight."

Shiloh was moved by the meaning behind his words, and was ashamed of the way she had last treated him.

"Thank you. What about my traveling companions?"

"Sledger took me to talk to them. They're agreeable to

going back on the *Raven* too. I asked about Mara, just in case, and the captain said she's welcome to stay aboard until sailing. So neither of you will have to stay in this house after tonight."

"That's a great relief to me, Clay! I can't thank you enough for all you've done for me."

"I want to be sure you're safe."

"I'll ride Ulysses over to Mara's new place and tell— Oh! I forgot about Ulysses."

"I'll take him back."

"Clay, I'm sorry for what I said to you the other day."

"I was out of line in saying what I did."

A silence began to grow between them until Clay turned toward his team. "I have a small delivery to make but I don't want to leave you here alone."

"I expect Mara shortly, so I'll be fine." Shiloh wasn't as sure as she sounded, but she knew Clay had other things to do.

He hesitated as though about to say something, but instead, he started to step up on the wagon spoke to reach the high seat.

"Wait," she said impulsively, reaching out to lightly touch his arm.

He turned back to face her, then glanced down at her hand. She hastily withdrew it.

"You've been a good friend," she said softly. "You've helped make it possible for me to return home."

"I'm glad because it's the right thing for you. You'll be safe there."

He took a deep breath and continued, "But I have to be honest with you, Shiloh. I can barely stand the thought of you leaving."

He almost leaped into the wagon and drove off, calling loudly to the team.

Shiloh stood staring after him, a strange emptiness in the pit of her stomach.

She spent another sleepless night, mentally wrestling with many hard questions. She awoke to hear Ulysses braying his morning welcome to Clay. Shiloh started to get out of bed to peek at him through the window when nausea engulfed her. She reached under the bed and pulled out the chamber pot. When she felt better, she arose and looked out. Clay was gone.

Mara came in. "You'll have this morning sickness for a while," she warned. "I hope it's not combined with seasickness on the way home."

Shiloh moaned, recalling how ill she had been sailing both down the Atlantic and up the Pacific. "I don't need to hear that," she said.

"I'm just reminding you what you might be in for."

"I'd rather be reminded of what it'll be like at home, among all the old familiar places."

"I don't think it'll be the same. You've seen too many new and exciting things here."

"There's nothing here I want."

"Isn't there?" Mara asked the question and left the room before Shiloh could reply.

When she felt better, she had her morning devotions, reading her Bible and praying. She sat for a while with her eyes closed, vainly trying to quiet the two opposing thoughts that battered her mentally.

Now that I can go home, why don't I feel happy? Why do I even think about staying?

She didn't feel like having breakfast, but sat with Mara while she had hers. All the while, Shiloh's queasiness made her miserable.

Shiloh suddenly jerked in alarm at the sound of a man's footsteps outside the window. She started to leap up, then relaxed upon seeing the constable.

"I'm so glad you came," Shiloh assured him. "I have some important matters to discuss with you." While Mara poured a cup of coffee for him, Logan apologized for being so late in getting around to talking with them about Tynan's escape.

"There's no way on this earth that I can even begin to take care of the reports pouring in," he complained. "I'll be glad when this statehood problem is decided and we can have some kind of government with money to hire more constables."

Shiloh was anxious about Tynan's escape, but she waited while the officer finished sipping his coffee.

"Tynan's still on the loose," he began, "but I saw Clay at breakfast and he told me you two are going aboard a ship until it sails."

"That's right."

"I think it's wise that both of you are leaving the house," he said, looking at Mara. "I've been giving Tynan a lot of thought, and I think he's dangerous to anyone connected with Aldar."

"You think Tynan is the one who killed him?" Shiloh asked.

"No doubt in my mind. But I don't think it was robbery. He just wanted it to look that way. My theory is that he's a paid assassin."

"It's a horrible thought but I think you may be right," Shiloh agreed. "And I have information now that shows someone with a strong motive who might have hired him."

"Who?" Logan asked, looking over his cup.

Shiloh told about finding the papers which she offered to let Logan examine.

After he had done so, Logan said he would talk to MacAdams. "I'll try to report back before you leave for the ship."

As the women left the cookhouse and started toward the back door of the house, they heard fire bells sounding.

Mara took a few steps to the corner of the house to look. "They'll never put this one out with their little hose cart. It's too big."

Shiloh joined Mara. "Looks like that entire end of town is on fire."

"It's a bad one, all right. But fortunately for us it's far away."

They entered the house to pack toilet articles and a few last-minute items.

A knock on the door made Shiloh jump.

Mara said, "Relax! It's just your soldier, not Tynan. But he's knocking forcefully, so he's either very impatient to see you again, or he's got news."

Spurred by the urgency of the knocking, Shiloh followed Mara as she opened the door.

Rawlins stood there, his horse ground-hitched behind him. "Hello, Mara," Rawlins said. "Where's Shiloh?"

"Right here," she replied, stepping to where he could see her.

"I just saw that Negro you call Samuel. He was running this way on foot with a message, so I told him I'd ride on ahead and tell you."

Shiloh's anxiety rose. "What kind of message?"

"Your friend, Clay Patton, has been shanghaied."

"What?" Shiloh exclaimed, stepping past Mara. "That's impossible! He wouldn't go into one of those crimp's places."

"He didn't. Apparently, he was jumped by several of them right on the street. Samuel saw it, he said."

"How do you know it was crimps?" Shiloh asked, wanting to deny that it had happened.

"It seems Samuel knows everybody and everything. I don't doubt him."

Shiloh's heart speeded up. "Where did it happen?"

"In the Barbary Coast area. That's where the fire is burning." Rawlins turned to look at the black smoke billowing into the sky. "A crimp named Shanghai Kelly runs a place down there at Pacific and Montgomery."

"We've got to help Clay!" Shiloh exclaimed. "Can you take me there, Will?"

His face hardened as he studied her before answering. "I'd like to, Shiloh, but I've got troubles of my own." He paused before saying, "I wasn't going to tell you this just yet, but, well, I've been ordered back to Washington to face court-martial charges."

"What for?" Shiloh exclaimed.

"It seems somebody is trying to discredit me with my superiors. I'm being brought up on charges of suspected treasonous remarks and sympathies."

"That's impossible!"

"Improbable, yes, but not impossible. The charges are very real, but not factual. I'm as loyal as any soldier. Personally, I suspect that somebody is trying to separate me from you, just as they are in having your friend Clay shanghaied."

"Why?" Shiloh cried.

"It looks as if someone wants to separate you from anyone who is trying to protect you. All I know is that I'm on my way to Washington, and Clay is on his way to some foreign ports, unless—"

"Unless what?" Shiloh prompted.

"I was just thinking," Rawlins said thoughtfully. "Those unfortunates that the crimps drug or knock out physically are usually held until after nightfall. Then they're rowed out to the ship where the master has paid to have a crew shanghaied. Maybe . . . no, forget it."

"No!" Shiloh exclaimed. "What are you thinking?"

"Well, sometimes the crimps can be bribed by someone offering them more to release a man than the ship's master is paying for another hand."

Shiloh turned to Mara. "Will you saddle Ulysses for me while I get some gold?"

Mara protested, "You can't do that! You need the money to sail home!"

"You would have saved Joseph if you could. Now, will you help?"

Rawlins said, "Excuse me, Shiloh, but you're overlooking something. The fire is burning that direction, and the way the wind's kicking up, the flames could overrun the Barbary Coast."

"All the more reason to act quickly!" she replied. "Will, I am more grateful than I can say for bringing me word."

"I thought you might be," he said. "Sorry I can't help. My advice would be to not place yourself in danger." He turned and walked rapidly toward his horse.

Mara was just cinching up the saddle when Shiloh ran out carrying a large leather pouch of gold dust.

Mara cried indignantly, "Have you lost your mind? That looks like everything you own!"

"It is. I may need it. Here, hold it while I get mounted."

"You realize what you're doing?" Mara asked. "You can't leave here if you give all that gold to free Clay."

"Never mind!" Shiloh settled into the sidesaddle and took Ulysses' reins. "Hand that up to me, please."

"You're taking an awful chance! That's the worst area in town, not to mention that fire. Wait a minute and I'll give you my gun."

"There's no time." Shiloh kicked her heels into Ulysses' sides and forced him to a rare gallop.

She leaned low over the mule's neck and urged him on with voice and heels. *Please, Lord,* she prayed, *let me be in time!*

The closer she got, the worse the fire seemed. A stiff sea breeze fanned the flames, sending them leaping over the horizon, destroying hundreds of wooden shacks and canvas tents. Black smoke boiled into the sky and spread out across the bay. It was an awesome, scary sight.

The mule wasn't made for speed, but Shiloh urged him to his best efforts while her mind raced off in many directions. She tried not to think about what would happen to Clay if she weren't successful in her mission. *These last few weeks have taught me that I can do what has to be done. And now, somehow I have to find Clay.*

Her bravery faltered when she caught the first whiff of

smoke. Ulysses slowed to a walk. She tried vainly to urge him on, but he sniffed the wind and rolled his eyes.

"Don't be like that!" she cried in exasperation, driving her heels harder into Ulysses' flanks. "Git up!"

The mule reluctantly obeyed, but it was obvious that he wasn't going to get much closer to the fire. Shiloh desperately looked around for another way to go on.

She spotted the driver of a hotel carriage parked alongside the street watching the fire. Shiloh forced the frightened Ulysses up alongside the carriage.

"Can you take me to Pacific and Montgomery?" she asked, her tone desperate.

"Lady, that's right in the path of that fire!"

"I know! Will you take me? Please?"

"It'll cost you plenty."

"That's all right." She slid off Ulysses' back and handed the pouch of gold to the driver. Then Shiloh dropped the reins over the mule's neck. He whirled to go kicking back the way he had come, away from the fire.

Shiloh stepped up into the carriage and took back the gold. She saw the driver's eyes light up as she hurriedly seated herself in one of the six seats. She realized that he had guessed what was in the pouch. "Please hurry," she cried.

"Hold on to your hat, lady," the driver cried, cracking his whip above the team of horses.

The horses leaned into the traces, but started throwing their heads from side to side.

"That team's too scared to take you all the way there, lady," the driver called, turning to look back over his shoulder. "They got good sense. You sure you want to keep going?"

"I'm sure."

"Then I'll take you as close as possible, but I'm not going to guarantee anything."

"Then take me as far as you can, please. And hurry!"

She leaned forward as if her body would somehow help

speed the team toward her destination. The smell of smoke was stronger, and bits of flaming embers drifted high overhead like giant fireflies back in Pennsylvania.

Clay, she thought. *Oh, Clay. This is all MacAdams' fault! I know he hated Aldar, but why Clay? Unless MacAdams somehow found out that Aldar and Clay were planning to go into the stagecoach business? Why didn't MacAdams have Aldar shanghaied instead of having him killed? That way, I'd at least have some hope that someday he might return.*

The horses began whinnying and trying to turn away from the smell of smoke. Shiloh had to grab the seat to keep from being thrown out.

"Lady, this is as far as I go." He hauled back on the reins. "You sure you don't want to ride back with me while you've got a chance?"

"I'm sure." She thrust a fair-sized nugget into his hand and stepped down to the sandy street.

As the driver turned around, Shiloh wanted to call for him to stop so she could change her mind. Then about a block ahead she saw the rude hand-lettered sign: *Shanghai Kelly's*

That's it, she told herself, taking renewed hope. *But how do I find where they've got Clay?*

The foolishness of her mission struck her hard. The patrons had all gathered outside the saloon to watch the rapidly-advancing fire. They weren't even aware of her, she realized. If she just knew where to look, she might be able to slip inside unseen and free Clay.

She started forward, carrying the gold and beginning to choke on the thickening smoke.

The whinnying of a frightened horse caused her to look around. Up the slight hill above her, she saw a drayman cutting his draft horses loose from a loaded beer wagon. In his haste, he didn't cut the wagon's wheels sharply to prevent a runaway. He leaped onto the back of the nearest horse and drove them away from the fire.

The wagon started rolling, very slowly at first, then faster and faster. Shiloh was directly in its path. She leaped to the nearest building and pressed herself against the wall. The wagon careened wildly past her, rolling toward the bay.

She was so panicked, she could hardly breathe.

She turned back toward Shanghai Kelly's in time to see all the spectators begin to scatter. Shiloh stared at the fire.

It has shifted directions! It's coming right this way!

Her pace slowed as highly flammable dwellings and businesses in the rats' warrens seemed to explode the moment the fire got near. Thousands of large glowing embers sailed through the air like fiery snowflakes. Some landed on the crimp's roof.

"No!" she screamed, running toward the flimsy wooden structure. "No!"

An orange tongue of flame leaped up on the rooftop, devouring the surrounding tinder-dry shingles, and then seemed to explode along the entire length of the building.

Running, panting, and sobbing, Shiloh fell headlong. She automatically dropped her gold poke to break her fall, then quickly scrambled to her feet.

"Shiloh!" The shout behind her made her whirl about, unaware that anybody else was near. A horse and carriage raced toward her, the animal fighting the bit with every step.

"Will!" She picked up her gold and ran to meet him. "Clay's in there! Hurry! We've got to save him before the whole roof falls in!"

Rawlins reached down and grabbed her arm. With a strong pull, he helped her into the seat beside him.

"Thank God!" she cried, her voice high and thin with fright. "I don't think I could have made it by—"

She broke off as the horse shied violently and fought the bit. Rawlins fought for control, then pulled hard on the right rein.

"It's no use! He's too frightened to go on!" The horse swung wide to the right, crossing the middle of the street.

"What're you doing?" Shiloh exclaimed.

"Turning back! Hold on! This horse is so terrified he's trying to run away with us."

"Stop and let me out!" She glanced over her shoulder, then groaned in anguish.

The entire building was a mass of flames and smoke.

CHAPTER XXII

SHILOH COULDN'T look any longer. She turned away, covering her face with her hands to blot out the sight of the crimp's burning building.

Above the roar of the advancing fire, the sound of the carriage wheels, and the horse's frightened whinnying, Shiloh heard Rawlins' voice.

"So I was right." There was something about his tone that made Shiloh turn to look at him.

His face was grim while he struggled to keep a tight rein on the spooked horse.

"Right about what?" Shiloh asked.

Rawlins managed to slow the animal. "About your feelings for Clay."

Shiloh was totally confused. In the midst of a major fire, Rawlins' remark seemed completely out of place. But she was too concerned with Clay's danger in the burning building to care much about Rawlins' comment.

"Hurry, we have to help Clay," she exclaimed.

Rawlins looked back. The near wall of Shanghai Kelly's saloon was flaming high, sending up dense black smoke to mix with dark columns of smoke and ash twisting upward from the roof.

"Too late," Rawlins replied.

Shiloh sagged in the seat with a groan. *Why?* she asked herself in silent anguish. *First Aldar and now Clay. Why did I ever come to this terrible place?* She looked at Rawlins. "You told me back at the house that you couldn't help me. I'm so grateful you changed your mind. I could have died here if you hadn't come along."

She felt the slowed carriage turn a corner, revealing the burning section of the city directly ahead. Alarmed, she asked, "What are you doing?"

"Correcting a mistake I made."

His answer made no sense to Shiloh. She pointed. "The fire's coming straight toward us!"

"I know." He pulled back on the reins. "Whoa."

"Why're we stopping? We'll die—"

"Whoa!" Rawlins repeated his command while the horse moved nervously, fighting the bit in an effort to turn around and escape the flames and smoke.

"I rarely make mistakes," Rawlins announced with a touch of pride. He turned his eyes on her and added, "But my feelings for you impaired my judgment. Now it seems that I have to correct the situation. I have my ways of getting things done, but you've put me in a position where I have to get my own hands dirty."

The words sounded familiar, but Shiloh was more concerned with his strange behavior. Then she remembered.

Gladwin had said something similar to her, but he was quoting somebody, Shiloh recalled. Something about men of power never getting their own hands dirty. He hadn't named the person, but identified him as someone with a great ego who wanted—

"Oh!" Shiloh blurted as realization struck her. "It was you who wanted to be emperor of the Pacifica Empire!"

The instant she said it, Shiloh knew it was a mistake. She drew back from the look in Rawlins' eyes.

"Get out," he said coldly.

"What?" She raised her gaze to the advancing fire.

"Out, I said." He reached over and gave her shoulder a hard shove. "Leave the gold. You won't need it."

Abject terror seized Shiloh as the full impact of his meaning struck her. She looked around desperately for someone to help, but everyone had fled the area.

"You can't mean that!" she cried. "Please take me—" She left her sentence incomplete as he pulled his sidearm from the holster.

"You wouldn't!" she whispered fearfully.

"Nobody will ever notice anything except what the fire did to you." He shoved her again, harder. "Out!"

"Why?" she asked in a frightened tone. "What did I ever do to you?"

"You failed my test. I had to be sure you were everything I wanted, but Clay was a personal threat to me, as your husband was to my plans for this country."

Country. He had used that word at the public meeting and she had wanted to correct him: state, not country. But Rawlins had meant what he said.

"You didn't have to kill Aldar! He didn't want to be emperor! He just wanted to build a transportation system!"

"I couldn't take the chance that Gladwin might persuade Aldar to change his mind. Too bad, but it had to be done. Same with Clay. I had to be sure how you felt about him, so I told you that he had been shanghaied to see what you would do."

She glanced back as Shanghai Kelly's saloon roof fell in with a shower of sparks and embers.

"No, Shiloh," Rawlins said, "Clay isn't in there."

She breathed a fervent, "Thank God!"

"He never was, but you thought he was. When you set out to try rescuing him, you failed my test. It's a shame. You would have made a lovely wife for the emperor. Now, are you going to get out by yourself?"

You're mad! Shiloh thought, reaching with trembling hands to hold on to the carriage so she could step down.

She frantically tried to think of a way to save herself and her unborn child. She couldn't outrun a shot. "I'm going to have a baby!"

Rawlins expression did not change. "His?"

"Yes, Aldar's, of course!"

"That's one more reason why you wouldn't have been right. For the last time, get out!"

Her trembling lips moved in prayer as her feet touched the ground. She glanced at the nearest building. It stood on a corner. Maybe if she made a dash for it.

She heard rapid hoofbeats crunching behind her in the sandy street. She glanced around in time to see Otis Tynan spurring his mule from around the other corner and straight toward the carriage.

As when he attacked MacAdams, Tynan said nothing.

Rawlins swore and dropped the reins. "You fool!" he shouted, "What's the matter with you?" He swung his pistol away from Shiloh toward Tynan.

Tynan didn't say a word, but struck with his knife.

Rawlins cried out in pain and dropped the gun. It fell into the street. Profanity streamed from Rawlins' mouth as he jerked his wounded arm back and tried to stand to defend himself. Tynan leaped from the saddle. His momentum knocked Rawlins off balance just as the horse, feeling the reins go slack, leaped ahead, throwing both men out of the carriage. The turning front wheel caught Shiloh's long skirt. She was violently jerked off her feet and dragged feet first through the sand.

"Whoa!" she yelled frantically. "Whoa!"

The panicky animal paid no heed, but turned so rapidly the rig tipped over, raising the right front wheel and freeing Shiloh's garment. She lay stunned in the center of the deserted street while the horse dragged the carriage on its side away from the fire.

Shaken, Shiloh unsteadily got to her feet, wincing from a sharp pain in her right knee. She wanted to run after the horse but at the first step, her knee buckled and she collapsed.

Out of the corner of her eyes, she glimpsed the two men struggling in the sand. Tynan was many pounds lighter than Rawlins, but Tynan had landed on top of his adversary. Rawlins used his uninjured hand to grip Tynan's right wrist above the knife, preventing it from completing a downward stroke.

Rawlins kept up a steady torrent of shouted curses, but Tynan still had not said a word. Shiloh heard only his labored breathing behind her as she forced herself to stand. She started hobbling away from the two men who had planned to kill her.

The fire, driven by a strong sea breeze, was now less than a hundred yards away, sending thick black smoke and flying embers down the street. Shiloh choked and coughed, but kept moving.

She looked back in time to see the bigger man throw Tynan off. In the same motion, Rawlins rolled over and reached for his nearby pistol.

Shiloh stopped in fascinated horror. Her hand flew to her mouth as Rawlins brought up the weapon and pulled the trigger. There was a click as the gun misfired.

Tynan was also on his feet, rushing Rawlins with his knife at the ready. Rawlins swung his pistol like a club, trying to strike Tynan's hand, but missed.

Dropping the useless weapon, Rawlins started backing up toward the fire, his eyes darting about in search of anything he could use to defend himself. "You crazy fool, Tynan!" he shouted. "Stop her! She's getting away!"

Tynan spoke for the first time. "I won't do your dirty work anymore. I told you to leave her alone! She's mine!"

The words sent goosebumps rippling over Shiloh's shoulders. She started half-running, half-staggering, down the street while the flames raced closer.

She whirled when a scream unlike any she had ever heard before cut through the night. Through the swirling dark smoke, Shiloh saw that both men had advanced through a corridor of burning wooden buildings. Rawlins lay facedown in the street. Tynan stood several feet in front of him. Shiloh didn't see the knife anymore, and shuddered with the realization of what had happened.

She watched in horrified fascination as Tynan turned from his victim and started toward her. "Shiloh, wait," he called above the crackling flames.

"Oh, Lord, no!" she whispered, pivoting around to continue a limping run for her life. Tynan kept calling, his voice sounding closer as he gained on her. She stumbled on, panting hard and trying not to not break into terrorized sobs.

Suddenly, ahead of her, a two-story frame building exploded with such force that Shiloh was knocked to the ground by the concussion. She had never heard a black powder keg explode, but she thought that's what it must have been as she scrambled to her feet.

She cried out in dismay. The explosion had scattered burning pieces of wood in all directions. Fires were already starting in nearby buildings that had survived the blast. At the same time, the wind shifted direction and a solid wall of flame erupted before her with an ominous "whoosh."

Shiloh stood uncertainly for a moment, watching her planned avenue of escape erupt into a fiery corridor. She was cut off. Spinning around, she saw Tynan still coming toward her through the rolling smoke.

I'm going to die, she thought. *My baby and I are going to die!*

"No!" she shrieked aloud as acrid smoke burned her eyes and made her cough. "Lord, help me!"

Casting about for a way of escape, she saw an alley between two new brick buildings. She limped toward them.

"Wait," Tynan called. "I won't hurt you!" His words were lost in a crashing sound that stopped Shiloh in her tracks.

One of the burning buildings had collapsed, knocking over another structure which had twisted out into the street where she had last seen Tynan.

For a moment, Shiloh couldn't see him, but as the smoke cleared momentarily, she saw that he lay facedown. A large wooden beam lay across Tynan's shoulders. He tried to reach it, but couldn't.

Shiloh's mind screamed a warning. *He'll be burned alive! But he killed my husband, and I'll die here if I don't get away.*

She thought of her unborn child and started again toward the alley between the two brick buildings.

Against her better judgment, she turned and limped as fast as she could toward Tynan. *I can't leave him!*

"No!" he forced the word out. "Go away!"

"I'll have you free in a minute," she replied, seizing the timber with both hands. Ignoring the splinters, she tried to lift it.

"No, please!" Tynan cried hoarsely. "Leave me!"

Tears streamed down Shiloh's face from the stinging smoke, and she began to cough. "Got to . . . move it!" she puffed, straining mightily at the timber.

"Go on!" Tynan urged, his eyes wide with fright. "The fire's coming real fas—"

He interrupted himself and glanced behind Shiloh. She looked over her shoulder as an express wagon shot out of the alley drawn by a large mule.

"Clay!" Shiloh leaped up. "Oh, thank God you're safe!"

"Whoa!" he called to the jackass, pulling back hard on the lines. As the animal stopped, Clay called to Shiloh, "Grab the mule's halter. Don't let him run away." Coughing and choking from the smoke, but with sudden new hope, she obeyed. It took all her strength to control the mule while Clay leaped from the wagon. He used another piece of stout wood to pry the heavy timber off of Tynan. Clay scooped him up in his arms and quickly laid him down in the wagon bed. Clay vaulted in behind him, climbed over the high seat, and picked up the reins.

"Shiloh, let go and get in!" he shouted, pulling back hard on the reins to keep the mule from bolting.

The instant she let go of the halter, the mule started forward. She reached up to Clay. He swung her into the air and deposited her on the wagon bed behind his seat. Clay called to the mule and slapped the lines smartly across his back. He needed no urging. He swung the wagon around in a tight circle and raced down the alley between the two brick buildings.

Shiloh crawled the few feet along the bouncing wagon bed to where Tynan lay. "Are you all right?" she asked.

"Feels like a mountain fell on my chest." He coughed blood before looking up at her. "You tried to save me. Nobody ever did anything for me before," he said weakly.

"I just couldn't leave you there like that."

"You would if you knew that I killed your husband."

"I already knew, but I didn't know that it was Rawlins who paid you. In fact, I thought it was someone named Philander MacAdams."

"He only paid me to find some papers in your house, but I didn't find them either time I broke in."

"Mara had hidden them very well. Now it's going to cost MacAdams for trying to cheat me. But when I came to the Barbary Coast today, I was sure that MacAdams was the one who paid you to kill my husband. That mistake almost cost my life."

"Rawlins sent word that he'd get me off the prison ship so I could do another killing for him. But when he told me it was you, I told him I wouldn't do it."

Tynan's face contorted in pain before he continued, "I felt betrayed because Rawlins was taking you out. I know now that I was dreaming, but for a while, I thought maybe you really were going to be mine."

Tynan was seized by a coughing spell that produced frothy blood around his mouth. Shiloh could only hold his hand until the spasm passed.

"Anyway," he continued weakly, "I didn't trust Rawlins. That's why I followed him today."

"You saved my life," she said softly.

"And you saved mine. With his help." Tynan jerked his head toward Clay.

Tynan sounded weaker when he continued. "Earlier, I was going to kill him and Rawlins for hanging around you. Before that, when I saw you get off the ship, I had other plans for you and that friend of yours."

"What changed your mind?"

"You're the only woman who was ever kind to me, the only one who ever smiled at me—and didn't look away. Then I just wanted to be near you. Like now." His voice grew soft until it was barely audible.

Shiloh remembered his shouted words to Rawlins a few minutes ago. "Leave her alone. She's mine!"

Tynan closed his eyes with a sigh. When he spoke again, his words were almost a whisper. "I didn't mean to frighten you, Shiloh."

When Clay had put the fire and smoke behind them, he stopped, jumped to the ground, and walked around the wagon bed to where Shiloh sat beside Tynan.

"He's dead," she reported quietly.

"When I pulled him out from under that timber, I didn't figure he could make it." Clay reached up both arms to Shiloh. "Let me help you down."

He picked her up from her sitting position and lifted her free of the wagon bed. His arms closed tightly about her. He pulled her close and they clung to each other. She lifted her face and he bent to kiss her, then stopped, breathing hard.

"Not yet," he said in a hoarse whisper. "Aldar was my good friend, and it's too soon to say anything to you, but if you stay in San Francisco, I want you to know that I'll be here for you. When it's time, I'll tell you what's on my mind and heart. Will you please sta—?"

She quickly placed her fingers across his mouth. "There's something you should know."

He gently removed her fingers and lightly brushed them with his lips. "You mean about the baby?"

"How did you know?"

"When I saw Mara, she said you were headed for the Barbary Coast to try bribing the shanghaiers to release me. She told me to be careful because you were expecting."

Clay slowly released her. "Of course, I can never thank you enough for what you did. And I certainly can't replace Aldar as a father, but I'd treat his child as if he were my own. That is, if you'll stay?"

She smiled up at him and nodded. "I'll stay."

A few days later everyone gathered at Shiloh's home to discuss all that had happened since the fire. It had burned itself out, and residents were already rebuilding. This time they were putting up more substantial homes and businesses, reflecting San Francisco's sense of permanency and growth.

John Sledger opened with prayer, then turned to Shiloh. She stood, looking around the room, her gaze drifting from the preacher, to Clay, then Mara.

"Each of you has been very special to me lately," Shiloh began. "God has blessed me with such wonderful friends." She looked back at the preacher. "Brother Sledger, when will the final papers be signed transferring all of MacAdams and Laird Express Company?"

The big man cleared his throat. "Next week, the lawyers said. I wish you could have seen MacAdams' face when I told him you'd found the surviving partnership papers he and Aldar had signed. Then he got mad and said that if a woman was going to be part owner, he'd sell his half and leave town. So he sold his share to Clay, with payments to MacAdams to come out of future earnings."

Shiloh said, "I'm grateful for your explaining to those two women why I couldn't sail home with them."

The preacher smiled broadly. "They understood, and wished you God's blessings. And now that you've accepted my invitation to help with the kids at church, Shiloh, I expect our congregation will grow even faster."

"I'll try to help them grow up to listen for that still, small voice," she said fervently. "I wasn't really aware that's what it was at the time, but when I thought my baby and I were going to die in that fire, well, that's when I remembered another verse that helped me have faith to come through it."

Mara said, "You didn't tell me about that."

Shiloh turned to her. "It says in Deuteronomy 30:19, 'I have set before you life and death, blessing and cursing: therefore choose life, that both thou and thy seed may live.'

"I wanted that more than anything, and I realized that all the attention and money and power were nothing compared to life. That was the voice I heard behind me saying, 'This is the way, Shiloh, walk ye in it.'"

"It's still a choice," Sledger said. "Which reminds me of something I heard: 'Some people find strength through adversity; others find only despair, but each person has a choice.'"

A few days later, Shiloh set out to do something she felt had to be accomplished before her condition made it impossible. She became the first woman to climb Fern Hill. Alone, but with Aldar very much on her mind, she slowly and carefully worked her way up that great mass of ancient mountain.

Her thoughts leaped like the wild goats that bounded away at her approach. Five San Francisco delegates to the Monterey Convention had just been elected, including William Gwin whom she had met. It was generally believed that all the California delegates would vote for admission to the Union as a free state. Jefferson Locke's slave-holding ideas seemed certain to be defeated.

Denby Gladwin had told Shiloh that statehood would only

delay his plans for a separate nation. If civil war broke out, that would be a good time to secede from the United States and form the Pacifica Empire. This time, it might be necessary to use force of arms.

Of course, Gladwin would now have to find a new man to front that quiet movement. At least, Gladwin had told her with satisfaction, William Rawlins would never have had that honor. Gladwin had submitted secret documents to Washington that would have had Rawlins court-martialed on charges of treason if he had lived.

Shiloh sensed that she and Mara were drifting apart because their ideas were no longer compatible. That was sad, Shiloh thought, but it was Mara's choice.

Shiloh put these thoughts aside when she at least reached Fern Hill's summit. She gasped at the indescribable panoramic beauty spread before her in all directions.

Slowly, she turned, her eyes taking in the peninsula to the south toward San Jose, Monte Diablo in the distance beyond the eastern bay shore, Alcatraz Island and the Marin headlands to the north, and the unending expanse of Pacific Ocean to the west.

Oh, Aldar, she thought, *this is breathtaking! I wish you could be here to share this moment that we had talked about. But you are very much here in my heart and memory.*

The dark, lonely days of fear and doubt that followed your death are behind me. Whatever lies ahead, I can now face with confidence because I won't be alone in this land where you saw so much opportunity. Your child—our child—will be with me, and your friend Clay will take good care of us.

I won't forget your dream, Aldar. I expect to have a house up here on the hill with the giants you said will someday live here. I just thought you would like to know.

She stood a moment, again surveying all that lay before her. Then, with the wind caressing her vibrant red-gold hair and the sea gulls' raucous cries overhead, she started down the hill to take the next step into her future.